STILL SEE YOU EVERYWHERE

LISA GARDNER

STILL SEE YOU EVERYWHERE

GRAND
CENTRAL

New York Boston

Grand Central Publishing
Hachette Book Group
1290 Avenue of the Americas, New York, NY 10104
grandcentralpublishing.com
@grandcentralpub

First Edition: March 2024

Grand Central Publishing is a division of Hachette Book Group, Inc. The Grand Central Publishing name and logo is a registered trademark of Hachette Book Group, Inc.

The publisher is not responsible for websites (or their content) that are not owned by the publisher.

The Hachette Speakers Bureau provides a wide range of authors for speaking events. To find out more, go to hachettespeakersbureau.com or email HachetteSpeakers@hbgusa.com.

Grand Central Publishing books may be purchased in bulk for business, educational, or promotional use. For information, please contact your local bookseller or the Hachette Book Group Special Markets Department at special.markets@hbgusa.com.

Library of Congress Cataloging-in-Publication Data

Names: Gardner, Lisa, author.
Title: Still see you everywhere / Lisa Gardner.
Description: First edition. | New York : Grand Central, 2024. | Series: A Frankie Elkin novel ; 3
Identifiers: LCCN 2023046023 | ISBN 9781538765067 (hardcover) | ISBN 9781538766606 | ISBN 9781538768365 | ISBN 9781538768372 | ISBN 9781538765098 (ebook)
Subjects: LCGFT: Thrillers (Fiction) | Novels.
Classification: LCC PS3557.A7132 S75 2024 | DDC 813/.54--dc23/eng/20231003
LC record available at https://lccn.loc.gov/2023046023

ISBNs: 9781538765067 (hardcover), 9781538766606 (large print), 9781538768051 (Canadian edition), 9781538768365 (signed edition), 9781538768372 (B&N signed edition), 9781538765098 (ebook)

Printed in the United States of America

LSC-C

Printing 1, 2023

For friends old and new and those we've lost along the way.

In loving memory of:

Pamela "Pam" Jezukawicz

Born teacher and dedicated coach who taught me everything I know about hiking, and quite a few more things about life. I feel your spirit guiding me up each mountain.

Virgie Chadwick Lorenz

Beloved aunt and favorite pinochle partner whose huge smile and booming laugh lit up every holiday. I hear your joy brightening my darkest day.

James Daniel Farias

Dear friend and gifted stylist whose passion for food, friends, and family made the world a more beautiful place. I picture your smile reminding me to breathe.

I still see you everywhere.

STILL SEE YOU EVERYWHERE

PROLOGUE

I STILL SEE YOU EVERYWHERE.

I roam the gray-washed corridors of our old house, peering into shadowed rooms now populated by ghosts. I pass drywall still bearing the impact of Daddy's fist. The dingy bathroom where he'd go fill the tub with that look in his eyes, and I knew to run, though I was never fast enough. Here's the entryway where he cracked Mama's prized koa-framed mirror. Here's the dining room where he'd bend me over the chair while snapping out his leather belt.

And here's the tiny bedroom where you and I slept together each night, our twin beds so close your outstretched fingertips could brush against mine. I remember your big brown eyes, peering at me solemnly in the dark. Then the sound of your hushed breath as you slowly drifted off, your hand slipping away.

I watched you sleep so many nights, your body a still lump under the covers, so unbelievably small. My throat would grow thick, my chest tight. And I'd murmur all sorts of nonsense, that

I'd keep you safe, that I'd never let him touch you, that I'd always take care of you.

My love for you was an ache in my bones, a buzzing in my head, a terrible, immense sense of wonder that swelled my body and electrified my limbs.

No one has ever understood that. They judge me. Call me cold-hearted, evil incarnate. All while they gasp over every scintillating detail of my crimes, feigning horror at the body count, then cheering at the verdict: death sentence for the Beautiful Butcher.

And still, I see you everywhere.

Now I chase your shadow around a corner. I call out your name and beg you to come back to me. I follow your racing feet into our little room, where I collapse on your bed and fist the corners of your quilt, searching for some sign, some scent, to tell me you're still here. That you haven't left me totally.

That I didn't fail you completely.

Mama's gone. I didn't cry a drop when I stood next to her grave. Didn't have any tears left in me. Do you know? Are you with her? The two of you huddled together in some heavenly kitchen, where she's braiding your hair and whispering all the secrets she'd never tell me. Have you discovered peace?

Because I awake each morning boiling over with pain and rage. Some days I add to Daddy's holes in the walls. Others I clutch your old pajamas and shamelessly beg for your forgiveness. I cry and wail. Then I rock back and forth, crying and wailing some more. I'm not whole. I'm not sane.

I live with a hole in my chest and hate in my heart, and come nightfall...

It's no wonder what I did most nights.

———

Right after Daddy's passing, I stood in that same horrible bathroom and filled up bucket after bucket with hot water and Pine-Sol. I attacked the entire house. Room by room, mopping the floors, scouring the countertops, scrubbing the walls. Dining room chairs? Threw them into the front yard where I made my own little bonfire that scattered the chickens and made the goats bleat in protest. Daddy's favorite recliner, where he'd lounge every night popping open beers and belching out his opinions? I took an ax to it—nothing like cheap furniture to burn, burn, burn. More skittering chickens and fussing goats.

But cleaning wasn't enough. So I went room by room tearing down the heavy drapes and piling them in the corner. Let the light flood in. Let it burn every fucking awful memory from this fucking awful place in this fucking awful town I swore I'd never see again.

Later, I changed my mind on that subject. I rehung the musty curtains, added blackout blinds. I came to crave the dark and the secrets it helped me protect.

I threw myself into daily life. Brew coffee, eat breakfast, gather eggs. Feed pigs, milk goats, muck stalls. Plant, weed, harvest. Cook, clean, repeat. Pay this bill, pay part of that bill. Buy more pigs, add to the chickens. Work, work, work.

Repeat, repeat, repeat.

Till sundown comes and there you are, peering at me from down the hall. And no matter how many times I run after you, how many times I try to grab your hand, hold you close…

You're gone. Disappeared from this earth. And the love I feel for you, the terrible, immense sense of wonder, it shudders through my body, nowhere to go. That's the true emptiness of being alone. Not no one to love me, but no one for me to love. No dark eyes regarding me solemnly in the night. No tiny fingertips brushing against mine. No sound of hushed breathing filling the space beside me.

And so I head out on Friday nights, driven by loneliness, fueled by hate, light and dark scissoring through me in equal measure. I sit at the bar. A man offers to buy me a drink. Handsome, ugly, kind, nasty, single, married. Doesn't matter. I touch his arm, smile as he talks, nod my encouragement. I let him think it's his idea to take me home. I pretend to be shy as I lead him to our parents' bedroom and, piece by piece, remove my clothes.

And for an hour, I'm no longer alone. There is the touch of fingertips, the sound of breathing in the space around me.

But of course, it's not what I really want, and afterward, I cry as the yawning hole once again rips open in my chest. Everyone who has gone. Everyone who never stayed. The true barrenness of my home, my heart, my soul.

Now I beg my lover not to leave me. I plead for him to stay. Come back, come back, come back, as he snatches up his clothes and flees for the door.

After that, it's easy. No man truly fears a woman.

Not even one who is her father's daughter.

Once it's done, I drag their bodies to the shed. Daddy taught me to butcher my first chicken there. This isn't much different. And the pigs certainly love the addition to their diet.

I learn as time passes. To venture farther afield, so as not to draw too much attention. How to identify strangers just passing through, which provides even more cover. I also learn about my pigs. How they can gnaw right through human bone, but won't touch hair and teeth. They prefer the long bones already broken up. Same with the skull.

Soon, people come from all over to buy my pork. Best ribs and bacon around.

Your eyes in the dark. Fingertips brushing against my hand. The hushed sound of your breathing. I chase you down the hall. I beg you to come back. I choke on the sourness of my pathetic passion for the person I already failed. Are you with Mama now? Does she hold you close, braid your hair? Do you know peace?

I get up each morning, tend to chores, pay the bills. Then, come Friday night, hey there, good-looking, of course you can buy me a drink. Wanna come home with me? I don't mind driving.

Saturday morning, I rinse my knives and hose down the stainless steel tables and burn the clothes of men who never should have pretended to care. Another week done, another week begins.

I still see you everywhere.

When they finally come for me, I don't protest. I watch the long line of police cruisers churn up the dusty road as they snake their way to our farm. I walk out onto the front porch and silently hold out my wrists. Daddy always said I was good for nothing. Turns out, I'm a bit more dangerous than that.

Later, I hear that people all over the county vomited upon hearing what was in their locally sourced pork. The media published photos of rows of baby food jars, each filled with a complete set of teeth. Made identifying the victims easier, not that it mattered to me. I confessed from the very beginning. Waived all appeals. I am death. You won't get any apologies from me.

When all is said and done, they credit me with eighteen kills.

They're off by one, but that's between me and my daddy. I offer no protest when the great state of Texas sentences me to join the other six women on death row. I get to live in the Mountain View Unit with my own special number. It all sounds rather grand if you think about it.

Of course, I don't.

I loved you from the very first.

I will grieve for you to the very last.

They will come for me in a matter of weeks. Transfer me to the Walls, where strangers I've never met will protest my execution. Some because of my gender. Some because of my race. Some because of principle. Doesn't matter.

I know what's going to happen next. My brief stay in the death-watch cell before I journey to the execution chamber, already strapped to the gurney as a willing sacrifice.

I'm not afraid. I'm in that dingy bathroom, filling up the first bucket of water to clean the mess I made. I'm running through the yard, your giggle echoing behind me. I'm grabbing Daddy's hand before he slaps you. I'm seething with rage as Mama once more turns away.

I'm tucked in the bedroom, feeling your fingertips resting atop mine.

They can tie me down and fill my veins with poison. The witnesses can watch my twitching limbs and gasp in horror or cheer in celebration.

I will keep my eyes open. I will stare straight ahead.

And I will see you everywhere.

CHAPTER 1

IN MY LINE OF WORK, I have seen people die, but I've never seen one put to death. My first thought as I stare at the redbrick entrance of the Mountain View Unit in Gatesville, Texas, is that I don't want to start now.

The Mountain View Unit is infamous for housing female death row inmates. No one is executed here, however. For that, the prisoner will be transferred the afternoon of their date with death to the Huntsville Unit, which is even more infamous for being the most active execution chamber in the United States.

These are disquieting facts for a woman who's been up all night on a Greyhound bus. I look terrible and I smell like it, too, which I'm trying very hard to ignore as I'm anxious and unsettled enough already.

In my line of work—which isn't exactly a real job if you consider I have no training and receive no pay—I normally choose my cases. I can't always explain why this missing person cold case versus that one. Given there are hundreds of thousands of missing people at any given time, and even more grieving loved ones desperate for answers, I'm always contemplating a tragically long list. I gravitate mostly to underserved minorities, the kind of people who were overlooked in life and garner little to no consideration after they vanish.

None of that completely explains why I'm here now, with bruised eyes and lanky hair, answering an urgent summons by some lawyer who clearly has excellent investigative skills, because I'm not the kind of woman who's easy to track down. I have no mailing address, no property or utilities in my name, and don't even own a real phone. I do, from time to time, use an internet café to post on a message board that focuses on missing persons. That's where I got the note. Short. Desperate. Mysterious.

I've never been good at ignoring mysteries.

I'd left my entire life's possessions—a single roll-aboard suitcase—in a locker at the bus station in Waco. Given that visiting hours in any kind of penitentiary are subject to change, I called the lawyer upon arrival to confirm my appointment. Victoria Twanow sounded almost as tight and anxious as I felt, which didn't help my nerves. She notified me that I was allowed to bring in a single clear bag with up to twenty dollars in change for the vending machines. Why twenty dollars? Can you even spend twenty dollars in a vending machine? Given how much my stomach was growling, I figured I might come close, but then I wondered if the vending machine money was meant for me or for my death row hostess.

It was all too much for my sleep-deprived brain, so I gave up on clear plastic bags filled with loose change and settled for buying a Snickers and a bottle of water while waiting for yet another bus, this one to take me from Waco to Gatesville.

And now, here I am. A fortyish woman in worn jeans, dusty sneakers, and a frayed olive-green army jacket.

My name is Frankie Elkin, and finding missing people is what I do. When the police have given up, when the public no longer remembers, when the media has never bothered to care, I start looking. For no money, no recognition, and, most of the time, with no help.

But I still have no idea what a condemned murderer would want with me.

THE LAWYER, VICTORIA Twanow, meets me at the front entrance. She guides me through the various security gates till I arrive on the other side, blinking under the yellowish glare of fluorescent lights.

"I've arranged for a room," she starts without preamble, already striding forward.

I'd gotten this from her messages. Victoria Twanow doesn't mess around. She's a woman on a mission, with a client scheduled for lethal injection in a matter of weeks. In person, she's younger than I would've expected. Mid-thirties, with long, dark hair she has clipped into a low ponytail. She's wearing a crisp gray skirt and blazer with the requisite white collared shirt. Her concession to fashion seems to be a chunky silver necklace, etched with exotic symbols. Mayan would be my guess. A tribute to her Belize heritage (I've Google-stalked her just as much as she's apparently Google-stalked me), or just a piece that caught her eye? There's no time to ask as she sweeps us down a corridor, heading straight for a stern-faced corrections officer.

His expression immediately softens as she approaches. "Victoria." He nods warmly.

My lawyer escort flashes him a bright smile. They are friends of a sort, I realize. It makes sense. Twanow probably visits this place on a regular basis. Of course she's come to know the guards, form some relationships.

It leaves me feeling even more awkward, like the new kid at school. My shoulders round self-consciously. I don't like this place, with the glaring lights and overly antiseptic smell. The sounds are too loud and all at once, doors buzzing open, chains clanking, and so many people talking, talking, talking with a nearly rhythmic punctuation of sharp, angry exclamation. I've worked bars in rough neighborhoods filled with loud, drunken patrons one sip away from exploding into a brawl, and it still felt less stimulating than this.

Twanow touches my arm, offers a bolstering smile. "It's okay. Focus on the people, not the place. Believe me, it helps."

Given I'm about to meet a woman nicknamed the Beautiful Butcher for dismembering eighteen men and feeding them to her pigs, I'm not sure how.

The corrections officer holds open the door. Twanow breezes through. I follow much more hesitantly.

The room is small and barren. A single table, three molded plastic chairs. I was expecting more of the classic visitor setup: you know, a nice piece of solid glass between me and the convicted killer. This looks more like the basic interrogation room from every police station I've ever visited. Given I haven't always been sitting on the law enforcement side of the table, I shudder slightly.

"This room is for attorney visits," Twanow explains, setting down her briefcase. "If anyone asks, you're now part of Keahi's legal team."

"Kayahee? I thought her name was Kaylee—"

"Focus. Here she is."

A door to the right opens, and a woman with her wrists shackled at her waist appears. Having studied her picture before coming, I thought I was prepared, but I'm not. Even in shapeless prison whites, Kaylee Pierson is stunning. Rich black hair. High, sculpted cheekbones. Dark eyes set in lightly bronzed skin that speak to her Hawaiian heritage. She moves with a catlike grace as she enters the room, powered by a sinewy, muscular presence she makes no effort to diminish. I can absolutely see this gorgeous woman leading men home from bars. And I can also imagine her bulging arms wielding a saw over their dead bodies hours later. A beautiful butcher, indeed.

She pauses just inside the door, studies me from head to toe, then breaks into a grin.

There's no warmth in her expression. It's all cold calculation. If I wasn't spooked before, I am now.

"Hello, Frankie," she says in a low, throaty voice. "Welcome to my world."

"DO YOU MIND?" Kaylee turns toward her accompanying guard. She raises her wrists slightly, and he unlocks her shackles. She winks. He steps back, his expression wary. Based on his response, I'm guessing that prisoners aren't usually shackled for movement around the prison—which makes me wonder what Kaylee Pierson has done to receive such an honor.

"We're all set," Twanow addresses the corrections officer crisply, clearly eager to get to work.

The CO retreats out the door. I take a deep breath and have a seat. In for a penny, in for a pound.

"Did you really ride the bus here?" Kaylee is asking. "We'd have been happy to provide airfare."

"Miss Pierson—"

"Call me Keahi. It's the name my mother wanted to give me, but my father refused. He had no use for her people or culture. Keahi means fire. A strong name for a baby girl my mother already knew would need to be tough to survive. I went through life with my father's name. I will go to death with mine."

I'm not sure how to respond to such sweeping statements, so I go with the highly obvious: "Your mother was Hawaiian."

"She met my father when he was stationed in Honolulu. Married herself a fine sailor boy and returned with him to Texas. Stupid woman."

"Your father was abusive."

"My father was a monster. But I think we can all agree, I'm the bigger monster now." She grins again, a movement of her lips that doesn't match the darkness in her eyes. According to everything I read, Kaylee, or Keahi, Pierson has never apologized for her crimes. Nor has she sought reprieve from the death penalty. Others, like her determined lawyer, Victoria Twanow, have filed appeals on her behalf. But Keahi has made no bones about her willingness to be put to death. She killed, and now she will be killed.

I'm so far out of my league here. "What do you want?" I strive to keep my tone as flat as hers and am pleasantly surprised when my question ends with only the tiniest quiver.

"Victoria says you find missing people." Beside me, Twanow nods. She has a legal pad out and looks like she's taking notes. Keahi continues. "People no one else is looking for."

"I specialize in working missing persons cold cases."

"But you're not a private investigator?"

"No."

"Are you a computer hacker, someone who can discover a speck of sand in the desert just by following its purchase patterns on the internet?"

"Don't even own a smart phone."

Keahi frowns. "Then what are you?"

"A person with a really obsessive hobby."

Her frown deepens. "Victoria says you've found everyone you've ever searched for. How?"

"I ask questions. Lots of questions. Sometimes, it's as simple as people being willing to talk so many years later. And sometimes, it's that I'm not the police, making neighbours in certain communities more willing to disclose the truth." I shrug. "Once someone starts to talk, I make sure I listen. Not enough people do that anymore."

"How many cases have you solved?"

"Nearly twenty."

"You brought people home to their families?"

"I brought closure to their families."

Keahi's lips quirk. She isn't fooled by my answer. Neither am I.

"You don't take money."

"No."

"Why not?"

"It's not about the money."

"What's it about?"

"What do you care?"

She grins at my burst of temper. I make my first realization about my new serial killer friend. She likes anger, feels comfortable with rage. Kindness, on the other hand, is probably incredibly threatening to her. And someone like me, who helps people for no other reason than I want to, must seem like a foreign species.

Finally, we're on equal footing—both of us are alien to each other.

"They will kill me in three weeks," she says now, clearly seeking another reaction.

"Do the crime, serve the time."

Keahi actually laughs. Beside me, however, Twanow has stiffened in distress. Apparently, she cares more about her client's upcoming execution than her client does.

"We still have options," Twanow starts now.

Keahi is already waving away her lawyer's words. "I'm not looking to delay the inevitable. I don't repent killing those men. Let me out of here tomorrow and I'll start right back up again. I'm an animal. Animals get put down."

Twanow blinks her eyes rapidly, her gaze now locked on her yellow legal pad covered in scrawled notes. She's young and idealistic, I think. Maybe that committed to a client she's had years to come to know, or maybe just that determined about defeating the death penalty. There's one more element, however, that no one is mentioning: earnest lawyer Victoria and her stone-cold killer client are roughly the same age. In fact, Keahi is probably the younger, scheduled to be executed at the ripe old age of thirty-two. She doesn't look fresh-faced and dewy-eyed, though. Her beauty comes with a hard edge, lips that might be full but never happy, eyes that are deep, dark pools, but mostly of homicidal intent.

"Why?" I speak up now. I can't help myself; I'm genuinely curious. "Why did you kill those men?"

"They lied to me. I asked them to never leave, and they did. After that..."

"You picked up strange men in bars and expected them to stay?"

"Bad strategy?"

"Big lie. You knew they'd leave. That's an excuse for what you did, but not your motive. You wanted something, needed something way more personal than that to butcher eighteen strangers."

Keahi stills. She tilts her head to the side, studies me all over again. And for just a moment, her beautifully sculpted face loses its cold veneer. Her eyes remain dark pools, but they're no longer sheened in ice. Her mask slips, and behind it...

I have to look away. Her pain is less an emotion than a primal scream. It slices to the bone, too awful to behold. I have seen grief in many forms, but I've never encountered anguish as terrible as this.

"I am empty," she states softly. "When I am standing behind them, holding my knife, knowing their lives now belong to me, I feel less empty. The pulse on a man's neck, racing beneath my fingertips. The feel of his blood, pouring hot and thick down my arms. The last choking sound he makes before crumpling at my feet...I need it. Without it, I would have nothing at all."

Twanow's pen punches through the legal pad.

I decide never to ask a serial killer about her motivation ever again.

"You've lost someone." I've heard enough to fill in the pieces. "You want me to find them."

"My baby sister. You must locate her. I need to know that she's safe and sound. This is my dying wish. You have three weeks to get it done."

She smiles again, triumphant and arrogant, and filled with quiet menace.

I go with the obvious answer. "No." Then I sit back with some triumph and arrogance of my own.

CHAPTER 2

Y OU WOULD DENY A DYING woman—" Keahi leans forward, features already darkening. I wonder how fast the guards can move. "How dare—"

"Stop it!" Twanow slaps the table, startling both of us. Keahi and I both blink in surprise. We'd already dismissed Ms. Idealistic from our conversation. Our mistake.

"You came." Twanow turns her attention to me first. "You responded to my note by spending nearly twelve hours on a Greyhound bus. That must mean you have some interest."

"Curiosity, yes. Interest, TBD."

Keahi's turn. Twanow pins her client with the same gaze she just used on me. "You are a woman about to be put to death due to your own horrible actions. You don't get to make demands of others now."

"Feisty, aren't you?"

"Stop. Just stop it. With the exhausting displays and endless manipulations. Three weeks, Keahi. That's it. Three weeks left here on earth. You really want to find your sister, gain some sense of closure? Then cease with the drama and get down to business."

I take it all back. I'm incredibly impressed by young gun Victoria Twanow after all.

Since I hadn't lied about my curiosity, it's easy enough to play along. "Tell me about your sister. Her name?"

"We called her Lea, but her secret Hawaiian name from our mother was Leilani, or heavenly child. She was a miracle baby, born fourteen years after me. There'd been other pregnancies in between, but none of them…" Keahi rolls a white-garbed shoulder. "From the very beginning, Lea was different. Happy. Sweet. Almost…sparkly. She laughed all the time. Offered up hugs and kisses just because. Would break into this huge smile every time she saw me even if it had been only five minutes before. My mother loved her best. She would spend hours in the kitchen brushing out her hair and plaiting it into elaborate braids. I understood. I loved Lea best, too. And the kitchen was the safest place for her; Daddy rarely ventured there."

Keahi regards me seriously. "I am my father's daughter. But Lea was my mother's child."

I get the picture. "What happened?"

"In the beginning, it was easy to keep Lea away from my daddy. He had no interest in a baby. But as she grew older, could toddle about, of course she came to his attention more and more. Daddy had no patience for sweet and kind. The sound of laughter would throw him into a rage. It was his nature. Anything light and pure must be beaten into something dark and twisted."

"He beat her, too," I fill in. "Like you, like your mother."

"Not if I was around." Keahi raises her chin. "If I saw him lift a hand, I got there first. He wanted to beat the shit out of me, what did I care? Nothing that hadn't happened before. By seventeen,

I met my father hate for hate. The more he beat me, the more I defied him. The more I bled, the more I promised to make him bleed. The nights I lay awake, picturing every horrible, sadistic thing I would do to him..."

"You murdered all those other men in lieu of killing your father?" I ask drolly.

That curl of her lips again. "How do you know I didn't?"

"Keahi," Twanow warns, but she doesn't need to continue. I'm already making a note to never ask questions I don't want the answers to.

"My mother was no match for him," Keahi states flatly. "Weak. Small. A tiny little mouse that spent her days scurrying about to fulfill his every demand, while keeping her head down and lips sealed. Sometimes, when he was away, I would hear her sing softly in Hawaiian. When I was young, I wanted more. When I grew older, I wished she would just shut up already. But then Lea came, and not only did Lea like her singing, Lea would sing along; I'd come upon them in the kitchen, humming these little duets. It was...painful." Not the word I was expecting. Keahi clarifies: "The sound of hope in a house where no such thing exists."

Unfortunately, I know from experience there's only one direction this story can go. "I assume something terrible happened."

"No." Keahi shakes her head, sounding surprised even after all these years. "Something *good* happened. The morning of my eighteenth birthday, my mother crept into the bedroom Lea and I shared and announced we were leaving. Not her, she didn't have enough money for that. But she had purchased two tickets to Hawaii for Lea and me. We were to go, find her family, and never come back. And...it worked. She filled my father with whiskey and beer till he passed out cold. I took Lea's hand and ran all the way down our driveway to the main road, where a neighbor drove us to the airport. I told everyone Lea was my daughter, and just like that, we were on a plane. We were free."

Keahi's voice breaks slightly on the last word. I give her a moment to recover. There's a softness to her features when she speaks of her sister, a wistful look in her eyes. She's either an incredible actress, or she truly loved Lea. I don't know why Keahi would lie on the subject, though. Reconnecting with a long-lost sibling would hardly change her sentence at this point. Especially as she seems not just resigned but resolved to die.

"You and your sister made it to Hawaii. Did you find your mother's family?"

"They were kind. Especially to me. I might've looked like them, but I knew nothing of their culture. More haole than Hawaiian. Lea, of course, took to everyone and everything immediately. We shared a tiny room in my auntie's house. She had a small farm, not so different from my parents', though no pigs." Keahi flashes a quick smile. I refuse to take the bait.

She continues. "I got up early each morning and rushed out to do chores, working twice as hard as any of my cousins because I had to. I was terrified my auntie would change her mind, send us back. Or worse, Daddy would show up one day and burn it all to the ground. I already knew I'd kill him first. He was never going to touch my sister. I promised it to her. I swore it to myself."

"Keahi." The lawyer's warning tone again.

Keahi dismisses her with another wave of her hand. "What are they going to do, give me a second lethal injection?"

"But your father never appeared," I hastily interject, trying to get us back on topic. "You and Lea were safe in Hawaii?"

"For two whole years."

"What happened?"

Her lips compressed into a tight line. "I proved to be my mother's daughter after all. I met a man."

"I STARTED WORKING a little farm stand, selling eggs, vegetables, and cut flowers from my auntie's garden. One day, this man pulled up in a baby-blue convertible. I'd never seen anything like it, certainly not in Texas. The guy who got out was as flashy as his car—expensive Hawaiian shirt, linen trousers, fancy loafers. Handsome, too, but I wasn't that stupid. He asked about the eggs, teased me about how many boys bought the flowers just to give them to me. I did my best to ignore him, but he kept chatting away. Wanted to know my recommendation for places to go on the island. Seemed interested in my answers. He smiled. All the time. Often. Easily. I thought to myself, *He isn't anything like my father.*" On the table, Keahi's hands clench and unclench. "So maybe I was a little stupid after all."

"You fell in love?"

"What is love?" The Beautiful Butcher rolls one shoulder dramatically.

I'm now as impatient as the lawyer. "You ended up with this guy. You and your sister?"

"Of course. I'm dependent on my aunt for every bite of food, and I'd never seen much outside of a Texas pig farm. And this man, he's handsome, charming, and rich. Like crazy rich. In a matter of months, Lea and I had left my auntie's tiny house for Mac's oceanside villa.

"My auntie didn't like him. She said I was too young, and he was too pretty. She didn't trust a man who didn't have calluses on his hands. But he was good to Lea. Bought her dresses, dolls, even got her a kitten. I saw how he treated her, and I thought, *There is a good man. I'm the luckiest girl around.*

"Have I mentioned yet my stupidity?"

I stay quiet, watching her strong fingers twitch in agitation.

"Mac had an entire household staff—chef, housekeeper, grounds crew—so no more chores for me. My sole obligation became to look gorgeous every evening when he came home. And Lea, she was ecstatic, running though this huge mansion, splashing around in the pool, playing games with her kitten. The staff adored her. They were more reserved with me, however. From the beginning, I recognized some of their looks were pitying."

"When did he first hit you?" I ask softly. Again, there is only one direction this story can go.

"I asked him one too many questions when he came home from work one evening. He slapped me, then immediately apologized."

"You accepted his excuse."

"I slapped him back."

This grabs my attention.

"He liked it." Keahi regards me intently, her dark eyes nearly glowing. "He liked it very much. We were late to dinner that night, he liked it so much." She pauses, as if this should shock me. I keep my features neutral. I would like to say this is the first time I've heard of such things, but it isn't. Finally, Keahi continues in a more casual tone. "Lea was too young to understand. But the moment she saw us, she stopped chattering away with the cook, grew subdued. I got it then. She didn't have to know what had happened to know that we were back home again. We'd come all the way to Hawaii to live like Texas. I'd failed. I just didn't know how badly yet."

"It grew worse."

"Gloves were off. Mac would strike me for no reason, just to see what I'd do. And I'd explode on him. It felt great." Keahi's voice is nearly feral with satisfaction. "He hit me; I punched back harder. He knocked me to the ground; I kicked the legs out from underneath him. I didn't care how much I hurt, as long as I could make him hurt worse.

"I wanted to believe I gave as good as I got. Except, of course, I didn't. He was bigger and stronger. I bruised his jaw; he knocked me out. I blackened his torso; he had me spitting up blood. And soon enough, he was reminding me it was his home I lived in, his clothes on my back, his charity keeping my sister safe. I learned to wear a lot of makeup and ignore the staff's concerned glances. I'm sure you can fill in the rest."

"He hurt your sister."

"Huge, climactic brawl." Keahi's tone is once again flippant, which is how I know this part of the story matters. "I was on the floor, Mac kicking and punching the shit out of me. Lea came running into the room. She tried to grab his arm to stop him. And he threw her across the room so hard I could hear the thud of her body hitting the wall. That was it. My jaw was fractured, my ribs broken, but I didn't care. I went after him with everything I had while screaming at Lea to run. I heard her get up. I thought I saw her flee from the room. Then Mac was on his feet and I was on my back and I don't remember much after that. When I regained consciousness, I was in the hospital, most of my body covered in bandages and my auntie holding my hand."

Keahi's breathing has grown ragged. She seems to realize it, draws in a deep lungful, then slowly lets it out. Anyone else, I would feel compelled to touch their arm, offer comfort. In this case, I don't want to lose the hand I'm pretty sure she'd snap off at the wrist.

"I asked about Lea," Keahi continues now. "I begged my aunt

to find her. She went straight to Mac's house and demanded to see her niece. Mac denied it all. Claimed he hadn't seen Lea since the night I physically attacked him. Most likely she'd run away, terrified of her violent older sister, and instead of harassing him, my auntie should be thanking him for not pressing charges against me. Given the damage to his face . . . My auntie waited outside the gates, catching the grounds crew as they were leaving. They swore they hadn't seen Lea. As they were locals, she believed them, even though she couldn't believe Mac.

"After that, my cousins scoured the city, searching for Lea. But Honolulu is big, and there's only so much ground they could cover."

"Did they go to the police?"

"The police." Keahi already sounds disgusted. "Do you know how many native Hawaiian girls disappear each year? Versus how many they bother to look for, let alone find?"

"No one knows," Twanow murmurs, glancing over at me. "Federal studies gather data on Native Americans and Alaska Natives, but not Indigenous Hawaiians, as they don't have tribal lands that fall under federal jurisdiction. What we know from the populations that are tracked—one report found that of the fifty-seven hundred missing and murdered Indigenous girls, only a little over a hundred show up in the Justice Department database. And in Hawaii, which is a major hub for sex trafficking, those numbers are probably even worse."

I'd like to say I'm surprised, but I'm not. All the cases I've worked these past dozen years have been filled with statistics just as depressing as these.

"You never found your sister." I look at Keahi.

"Once I was out of the hospital, I tried everything. Days and nights, nights and days, flashing her photo to anyone who would look, pleading for information. I even broke into Mac's villa. Her room was empty. Like she'd never been there. Like she'd never existed at all."

Keahi looks away, a muscle twitching in her jaw. "I spent two years on the island, living off my auntie's generosity while I searched for my sister. In the end, even my auntie told me it was time to let go. Lea was most likely dead. I had to accept that."

"How long ago was this?"

"Lea disappeared almost a dozen years ago. She was five years old. Only five years old."

I understand. "After you gave up the search, you returned to Texas? Your father?"

"What choice did I have? I couldn't stay in Hawaii forever. My auntie had done enough, and what had I given her in return? I had no job, no skills, no formal education. So that was that. I came home. Whatever my daddy did now, at least I deserved it."

I take a deep breath, my mind whirring through the story of Keahi's life, trying to make the pieces fit. "All right. Your sister had disappeared, you return home and spend, what, the next three years taking out your rage on other men? Which may or may not have included your father?"

Twanow glares at me.

"He happened to die shortly after I returned to the homestead," Keahi retorts blithely.

Ahh, here is the murderess I've come to know and not love. "You never returned to Hawaii, followed up with your auntie, cousins, whomever?"

"No."

"But now, three weeks before your execution, you're suddenly overcome with the need to locate your baby sister?"

"I've always been overcome with the need to save Lea. I just assumed it was no longer possible."

Finally, I get it. "Something changed. You have a lead on her, a reason to believe she's still alive?"

"I received a letter, handwritten by her, telling me she still loves me."

"How do you know it's her handwriting? You last saw her when she was five."

"I know."

I sigh heavily. I've not had enough sleep for such dramatics. "Have you given this letter to the police, notified Hawaiian authorities?"

"They won't help."

"Because she's Native Hawaiian? I think an actual note from a missing girl would get their attention."

Keahi shakes her head.

"Because of who you are, then?" I press. "You think they'll ignore her plight because she's the sister of a convicted killer?"

"No. This isn't about me. It's because of who *he* is."

"Who?" I'm truly bewildered.

"Mac. He has her. All these years later, she's with him. Except no law enforcement agency is going to challenge him. Not a man like Sanders MacManus."

I stare at her. Blink. Stare again. "Mac is Sanders MacManus? The tech mogul? The guy who has a net worth greater than most developed countries?"

"And who's buying up most of Hawaii," Twanow fills in. "One island at a time."

I'm honestly not sure what to do with this. I've spent the past twelve years of my life living in mostly marginalized communities searching for people who don't even rate mention in their local papers. I have no illusions that life is very different for the haves versus the have-nots. Meaning trying to take on a man of Mac-Manus's wealth and privilege...I struggle to think of options.

"Your sister is how old now? Seventeen, eighteen?"

"Seventeen and nine months. Still a minor," Twanow provides. It's a salient fact.

"Investigating Sanders MacManus would certainly require some finesse," I venture, "but that doesn't mean it couldn't be done. Especially if he's holding an underage girl."

"He'll cover his tracks, buy them off, whatever it takes." Keahi's already dismissive. "A man with that much money and power? The police will never gain access to even look for her."

"But I can?" I shake my head furiously. "This is way out of my league—"

"We can get you to Hawaii," Twanow interrupts.

"First class if you want," Keahi adds. "I have plenty of money."

"You have money?" I feel like I'm caught in some surreal play.

"Death row men don't get to have all the fun. We ladies have our fans as well." That smirk again. I'm really starting to hate it.

"We can get you to Hawaii," Twanow repeats. "MacManus bought a small atoll an hour's flight from Honolulu. He's developing it to be an ecolodge and needs workers. You're an experienced bartender, yes?"

"Sure, but—"

"I have a contact in the company that's handling staff recruitment. The crew is bare bones right now, an advance team studying the site for development, but they still need people to manage the kitchen, handle housekeeping, etc. That'll be your in. The rest is easy—MacManus visits the atoll regularly to appraise the situation.

You can meet him in person, determine if Lea is with him, then make contact."

"So now I'm an undercover operator? Hell no. I don't have the experience. Hire a private investigator."

"Never work," Keahi states immediately. "Do you know how many people have tried to get to him over the years? He'll spot a professional a mile away You're not a professional."

"Exactly!"

"Better, you don't need to be undercover," Twanow pushes. "Just be yourself, a wandering nomad who picks up work along the way. You have hardly any internet footprint, records in your name, anything. Even if he grows suspicious and has someone look you up, it'll take weeks for them to make headway. Certainly it took me that long."

"I work missing persons cold cases," I begin.

"That's exactly what this is," Keahi assures me.

"No! If what you're saying is true, your sister is a kidnapping victim. You need someone experienced in extraction, not to mention self-defense, gunslinging, and other random acts of saving the day." I hold up arms that are stick thin compared to the rippling muscles on the woman before me. "Do I look like someone who can win a fight if the going gets tough? I talk my way through investigations. Absolutely, positively no physical confrontations. I'm not that kind of gal."

"Then you'll have to choose your words carefully." Keahi's stare remains fixed. "It has to be you. There's no one else who can do it. And someone must save her. You can't sentence her to spend the rest of her life with that abusive, entitled fuck!"

"Just see if she's there," Twanow offers placatingly. "Make contact, then let me know. I'll assist with the rest."

"Call in the cavalry? A platoon of Navy SEALs?"

"Whatever's needed. If you can confirm Lea is being held against her will, then the authorities will have to take action. This will work. I wouldn't have spent so much time and energy hunting you down if I thought otherwise."

I have a sick feeling in my stomach. This is not my area of expertise. I don't like violence or blood; there's a reason I work missing persons and not murder cases.

But at the same time, if what Keahi says is true, if her sister really is being held against her will by a vicious and powerful man...how do I walk away from that?

"You'll do this," Keahi states.

"Oh, shut up." I am so done with requests from serial killers.

"You'll do this," she repeats firmly. "You help people who are forgotten. My sister is forgotten. But even more importantly, she's alive. I have proof she's alive. And when was the last time your search ended with finding the living? Forget about me, *you* need this win."

"I fucking hate you right now."

Keahi grins again, that slow, feral smile that was probably the same one she wore right before slitting the throats of each of her victims. She's got my number and she knows it.

"Excellent. Then it's all set. Victoria will get your ticket to Hawaii. You will save Lea. And three weeks from now, when I finally arrive in hell, I'll dance in the flames knowing my baby sister is safe and sound."

CHAPTER 3

I WANT TO SEE THIS LETTER." I'm walking so fast, Twanow can barely keep up. I don't care. I need out of this prison, right now.

"Of course. I have a copy."

"You really think her sister is alive?" I pause just long enough to peer intently at the lawyer, then have to get moving again. Honest to God, the walls are closing in.

We arrive at the front, what, reception area? I don't know the correct penitentiary lingo and don't want to learn now.

Twanow grabs my arm long enough to get me to sign out, then I'm off again. The first wave of fresh air against my face feels like a celebration. I stop just to savor it. Of course, there's still heavy fencing, coiled razor wire, and watchtowers marring the horizon. Fuck it, I'm back to moving.

"I have to think about this," I inform Twanow as I bustle along. I also need to shower, sleep, and eat something other than a candy bar. I feel simultaneously exhausted and wired.

"I stay at a local hotel when I'm in the area." Twanow scrambles to catch up. "It's nothing fancy, but it's quiet and clean. I took the liberty of reserving a second room for you."

I halt abruptly. "What is she to you? Why are you doing all this on behalf of a woman who didn't just murder eighteen men but genuinely enjoyed it?"

"I have no illusions about who Keahi Pierson truly is," Twanow says quietly. "She's a cold-blooded killer."

"But?"

"She still shouldn't be put to death. Study after study has shown pervasive racial bias when it comes to the death penalty. Just look at Keahi, who's half Native Hawaiian. Most death row inmates spend decades awaiting execution, while her sentence will be carried out in a matter of years. Have you ever heard of such a thing—"

"Because she pled guilty, waived all appeals."

"Because she believes she is a monster. And why is that? Would you like me to quote you more statistics on the cycle of violence and lack of social services for marginalized populations? Keahi blames her father for who she is, but I blame society. We failed her, her mother, her sister, and countless others. They were born into a perfect storm of abuse, alcoholism, and poverty. And even knowing what the results of such a childhood will most likely be—another generation mired in abuse, alcoholism, and poverty—we did nothing. Now the state cares about Keahi Pierson. Now the state wants to step in to protect future victims. I say, where was the state thirty years ago, when she needed that same kind of attention herself?"

"Fine." I resume my beeline toward the parking lot.

"It's not fine! None of this is fine. It's tragic. It's awful. It's not fine!"

"It's fucking tragic. Better?"

"Can you just slow down for a minute?"

"No! I need out. And that hotel room you offered. Because I don't disagree with you. This whole thing...it's fucking awful." I feel like I should have something more profound to offer than that, but my mind is too fried for intelligent responses. "Food. Is there a drive-thru near here? I need a cheeseburger. And a milkshake. Chocolate. No, strawberry. No, definitely chocolate. Yeah, take me for food, and maybe I'll survive long enough for you and your death row client to kill me."

"I can do that. My car is just over there. You're going to do this, then? Right? Because it's going to take most of the day to get to Hawaii, and we don't have much time left."

"What kind of name is Sanders MacManus?" I mutter. "Anyone with the first name Sanders has gotta be a douche."

The lawyer simply nods, leads me across the packed parking lot.

"Did Lea write that letter? Is she still alive? I guess that's the key question." I'm rambling, my thoughts ping-ponging around in my overtired brain. "Except, what would be the upside for pretending such a thing? Not like the appearance of a long-lost sister makes a difference for Keahi's upcoming execution, right? There's no sudden-appearance-of-a-missing-relative clause that makes one exempt from lethal injection?"

"Definitely not."

"Is it about money? Keahi implied she had plenty. Could this be an imposter heiress sort of play?"

"Not that kind of money," Twanow assures me. "More like if you only have a month left to live and want to go wild at the prison commissary kind of wealth."

"She offered a first-class ticket to Hawaii."

"She has benefactors—"

"Future husbands? Or would that be more like future widowers?"

Twanow rolls her eyes. We've arrived at a sensible silver compact with a rental company sticker on the top corner of the windshield. She unlocks the doors, gestures for me to get in.

"Getting the money for a plane ticket to assist with Keahi's dying wish won't be a problem," she provides. "But that's not to say these gentlemen have a ton of resources, or would magically hand them over to a long-lost sibling."

"Then why the letter now? I don't like that timing. God, I have a headache." I slide into the front seat, scrubbing my temples furiously.

"Food," Twanow states firmly, already putting the car in reverse. "I'm starving, too, so it'll help both of us. As for the timing, Keahi's case has been all over the news as the date approaches for her execution."

"Her face was all over the news seven years ago when she was arrested for eighteen murders," I retort dryly.

"Seven years ago, Lea would've been ten. Young for taking action, let alone did she have access to news and TV coverage? If she was under MacManus's control, he'd have reason to keep her in the dark."

"But she found out now."

"Older, wiser. And being a teenager, probably plenty tech savvy."

"So she sent a handwritten letter? Not an email, message board post, something quicker and easier for a computer-age teen?"

"Too traceable. Anything she did on an electronic device would leave digital footprints for someone like MacManus to find. Sneak out and slip a note in a mailbox, however, and she leaves no evidence behind. Doesn't have to worry about someone going through her phone, laptop, etc."

"Assuming she has access to electronics. Or, for that matter, assuming she has access to a mailbox."

"She could give it to a sympathetic party to mail. Early in my career, I worked a few human trafficking cases where that's how they got out a message for help."

"Isn't it still early in your career?"

"I can only hope." Twanow flashes me a quick smile, then pulls into the promised fast-food heaven.

Last time I was this hungry, I'd barely survived several days in the wilds of Wyoming with a psychopath picking off the members of our search party one by one. I made it out. But not everyone did. Those long weeks of recovery afterward...I don't like to think about that case, though maybe I should. I survived. I healed. I carried on.

Compared to that, just how frightening could investigating some tech billionaire on a tropical island be?

The rich, greasy smell of hamburger hits my nose. I forget about the past, place a highly enthusiastic order for the present, and get down to the serious business of eating. Twanow not only inhales an entire cheeseburger but also dips her fries in her chocolate shake. I respect her on those grounds alone.

That lasts all the way to Waco, where we liberate my suitcase from the bus station, then check into the as-promised, no-frills motel, and finally get down to the business of finding a billionaire.

———

"ARE YOU FAMILIAR with Marlon Brando and the remote island he bought back in nineteen sixty-seven, after filming *Mutiny on the Bounty*?"

"Haven't a clue."

We'd each taken a sixty-minute break—Twanow claiming she needed time for a run. Me, who never ran unless someone was chasing me, using that time to wash the prison out of my hair. Now we're sitting in her room. I'm barefoot and cross-legged on the bed. She's in the lone chair in front of the window, looking even younger and fresher in a pair of black leggings and a dark green tunic top. She's wearing socks, which probably says something about her opinion of the cleanliness of the carpet. On the other hand, given some of the places I've lived, I consider this room the height of luxury.

"Marlon first visited Tetiaroa, an atoll in the French Polynesians, while filming the movie," she explains now. "Legend is he fell in love with the island and bought it, determined to protect its natural beauty and cultural legacy. Eventually, he hired Richard Bailey, an American hotelier in Tahiti, to develop the first ever eco-friendly, completely sustainable, incredibly luxe resort. Challenging premise from the start, as luxury generally implies waste—elaborate lighting, frigid air-conditioning, and excessive amounts of everything."

"Okay." No idea where this is going.

"Long story short, it worked. The Brando on Tetiaroa is now one of those places movie stars fly into from all over the world to enjoy remote sandy beaches while experiencing deep seawater air-conditioning, solar-powered lighting, and buildings created entirely from locally sourced materials. And that is what Sanders MacManus now wants to do on his own personal atoll, Pomaikai."

"This is the place one hour outside of Hawaii?"

"You will fly into Honolulu. Then catch one of the MacManus Group charter flights to Pomaikai."

"Just like that?"

"The charter flights depart once a week to bring supplies, including food and staff. Guess which one you are?"

"I'm already hired as staff? Again, just like that?"

"There's been a lot of turnover lately. Apparently, while everyone thinks they want to work in paradise, few have what it takes to survive such a *remote* paradise."

"How remote?"

"You won't be watching TV, checking emails, or phoning home anytime soon. For that matter, best not to spike a fever, develop an infection, or sprain an ankle. Are you allergic to bee stings? Because if so, I'm going to need you to lie about that."

"*What?*"

Twanow is already moving right along. "We just need to get you to Hawaii in the next thirty-six hours to catch the private charter."

I'm so flummoxed I don't know where to begin. "You planned all this before even meeting with me." I can't decide if I'm outraged or impressed.

"You agreed to take a bus all the way to Gatesville to see Keahi. That was good enough for me."

I grimace, irritated on principle. Apparently, having a curious mind and self-destructive personality is predictable after all.

"You're an alcoholic," Twanow states, as if reading my mind. Her tone is curious, feeling me out.

"Yes. Born and raised by generations of alcoholics. Got any booze on you, I can prove it."

She ignores my sarcasm. "But you work as a bartender."

"Being around booze isn't a trigger for me." I shrug. "Breathing is."

Twanow studies me for a long moment. "There's alcohol on the island. Wine, beer, hard liquor. There are rules about drinking, given that everyone must be able to muster on a moment's notice. In other words, all alcohol in the camp is controlled and monitored. Which will be one of your jobs."

I'm running out of shocked *what*s, so I go with startled blinking instead.

"MacManus is still in the early stages of development—there's no luxury hotel, just a collection of rustic cabins and a couple of larger common buildings to shelter the forward crew. The staffing includes engineers, naturalists, an archaeologist, the architect, the project manager, two cooks, and now you—dishwasher, laundress, and supply tech. You're in charge of overseeing provisions, including alcohol."

"If that's not irony . . ." I roll my eyes, then force myself to focus on the relevant matters at hand. "Do I have a long and sordid relationship with alcohol? Sure. Do thoughts of drinking and the siren song of cheap booze still haunt my dreams? Absolutely. But that's the life of a recovering alcoholic. There's temptation wherever I go." I shrug for a second time, as eloquent as I get on this subject. "I've continued to work as a bartender as it's my only employable skill, and a girl's gotta eat. As part of that job, I inventory, order, and pour endless amounts of booze on any given night. Sounds to me like this gig isn't that different."

"You can handle it?"

"Some of my fellow friends of Bill would tell you no way. But being around other people drinking doesn't get to me. I have my own set of issues." Remembering my first real love, Paul, dying in my arms; pouring myself into a case to save someone who can no longer be saved; watching other people, total strangers, going about the business of life while I remain on the outside, looking in.

At this stage of my life, I've chosen to lean into my fatalism. As long as I belong to no one and nowhere, use it. Commit myself to others and their problems. Which has the added benefit of allowing me to avoid my own.

Paul: "Why are you doing this? Why can't I be enough for you?"

Me, standing there, unable to answer.

"You're an addict." He answered his own question bitterly. "That's why. There will always be something you need more, some high you have to chase. Jesus, Frankie. I love you."

Me, still standing there, unable to answer.

Paul turning away. Paul walking away.

Me, not following.

Now Twanow digs a manila folder out of her computer case. She places it on the empty space in front of my curled legs and starts pulling out individually clipped reports, each one topped by a photograph. *The galley of rogues*, I think, otherwise known as the forward crew.

"Here's the deal," she states crisply. "A development project like the one MacManus wants to undertake requires a lot of dotting i's and crossing t's. I don't care how much money the man has; ecological impact matters at both the state and federal level, not to mention he can't risk tainting his future luxury resort with bad PR. To that end, there's roughly a dozen people stationed on Pomaikai to conduct the necessary studies while also ensuring everything proceeds according to plan. Needless to say, it's not the happiest job for many of them."

"Needless to say," I echo, already getting it. MacManus equals rock. Fragile ecosystem, hard place. I'm suddenly very happy to be the person simply required to tidy things up while doling out booze. Go me.

"Sanders MacManus." Twanow taps his photo with her finger. I obediently pick up the report, studying his picture.

"Keahi was right, he's a good-looking guy if you're into the preppy type. Is it just me, or does he dress like the business casual version of Thurston Howell? He come from money?"

"Not at all. Grew up in Southern California. His mother was a real estate agent; his father taught math at the local high school. MacManus's claim to fame is befriending the right kid— Shawn Eastman, class nerd—and then defending him from bullies. Shawn developed the code that would become their business's claim to fame, a rolling algorithm that aids in corporate security software. MacManus was the CEO and face of the operation, Eastman the brains. They took the company public ten years later and both became overnight millionaires. Then Shawn died in a plane accident. Within a year, MacManus sold the company, saying he couldn't continue on without his partner. Being the sole shareholder, he made half a billion overnight. Been investing it in real estate ever since."

"His partner's death made him the sole shareholder? Sounds awfully suspicious to me."

"There have been rumors circulating for years, but nothing concrete. The thing to remember about MacManus: he's no tech genius. He's a salesman, in his own words, or a con man, according to others. He's plenty smart, but he's also arrogant, self-absorbed, and condescending. You are exactly the kind of person he won't bother to notice."

"Yeah me!" But I get her point. His dismissiveness will make my job easier.

"MacManus is due to visit the site next week. You should have a few days to settle in before his arrival. Which brings us to the next important person, MacManus's right-hand man and project manager, Vaughn Winslow Austin. He's running the show, and he will be studying your every move."

"Seriously? Vaughn Winslow Austin? Sure he and MacManus didn't meet at some prep school in their tennis whites?" I pick up the next clipped report. Vaughn looks different than I expected—wavy brown hair, crinkled blue eyes, a hint of a smile set in weathered features. Handsome, but only in a Matthew McConaughey sort of way.

"Austin has developed two other major resorts for MacManus. He knows what he's doing and runs a tight ship. My advice: be yourself, a wandering soul picking up work as you go. Most of these jobs are contract employees. You won't be the only one who doesn't have a mailing address."

"Good to know."

"I'll give you these reports to study overnight; just don't take them with you. You don't want someone to discover something this incriminating if they go through your luggage."

"I'm inexperienced, but not stupid," I assure her.

"Third person to know for now, Aolani Akamai, MacManus's architect, who's working with the archaeologist and naturalists on the environmental impact statement. This project is a big deal for her. MacManus hired her as a concession to the locals—look at how much he wants to honor Hawaiian culture and heritage; he's even hired a local architect. She's no puppet, however. She's gifted, ambitious, and razor sharp. She's also still getting to know Mac-Manus, which is to say, if you have reason to immediately fear for Lea or yourself, Aolani might be your best bet for assistance."

"Okay." I pick up her bio, study the photo. She's tall and slender, with the kind of willowy build I associate with models and women I want to hate. But there's a determined set to her jaw I find redeeming. Clearly, someone who doesn't mind a fight.

I gesture to the collection of reports. "You've done your homework."

Twanow settles into a stubborn expression. "I'm very good at my job."

"But this isn't your job. Getting Keahi off death row is. This is more like a favor for a friend. You like her that much, your homicidal client who would be happy to get out of prison and butcher even more men?"

"I already told you, I have no illusions about who she is."

"Then why this? All of this? Because I'm pretty sure this is the walking definition of going above and beyond."

"You've agreed to help. Why are you doing it?"

I give her a look. "Because this *is* my job. Finding people no one else is looking for. I'm in it for Lea, just like I'm always working for the missing."

"Then we're in agreement. This is for Lea—"

"No. Because you did all this before you knew for sure if there was a Lea or a way to make contact. You..." I get it then; it hits me like a proverbial whack over the head. "This is your guilt." I point at each packet of information. "You know you can't save your client. Keahi will be executed three weeks from now."

Twanow's jaw tightens, but for once, she doesn't prevaricate. "At this point, it would take a miracle for it to be otherwise. In case you didn't realize, Texas isn't known for its last-minute stay-of-execution orders."

"This is your amends. You can't save Keahi, so you'll save her sister."

"Does it matter?"

"Only because I've never flown on a plane before."

"What?"

"I've never flown on a plane before. I've never gone to Hawaii, let alone a remote tropical island where at least one of the very few people present is most likely a psychopath with a taste for sex-trafficked victims. So, yeah, to me, your motives matter very much."

Twanow exhales, her shoulders dropping from their defensive stance. "All right, then here it is. I can't save Keahi, so I would like to save her sister. Keahi said you would take this case because you need the win. Well, I need the win, too. Otherwise, these past four years of representing Keahi, getting to know everything about her, the death penalty, the injustice of the justice system...I need to know it wasn't all in vain."

"Okay."

"Okay?"

"I needed to know where you were coming from. Now I do. So, yes, let's get me on a plane. How bad can it be compared to twelve hours on a bus?"

Twanow finally smiles. "Thank you. I'd like to say I'm only a phone call away, but of course..."

"No cell reception in paradise," I repeat from her earlier comment.

"Technically, there's some sat reception so staff is afforded short windows of opportunity to connect with the larger world. There's also limited internet access, though I understand it's reserved for the professionals. If you get desperate, Aolani and Vaughn should have authorization given their responsibilities. You'll just have figure out a way to gain their permission."

"Yippee. Can't wait." But inside, my stomach is already clenching, memories of Wyoming once again flashing through my mind. Bullets and blood, running and falling, last stands and terrible screams, some of them my own.

I used to think the universe owed me something. Now I know better.

I gather up the papers, climb off the bed. "Time for my nap."

"I'll book your ticket and prepare a list of essential supplies. We can grab them on our way to the airport."

"Essential supplies?"

"Sunscreen, swimsuit, wide-brimmed hat, flip-flops. You know, clothing suitable for a tropical climate." She gestures at my worn jeans and frayed flannel shirt, which basically match the rest of the items in my suitcase, with the exception of three short-sleeved shirts.

"I'm so not ready for this," I allow.

"Don't worry, I am." Then Twanow is powering up her laptop, back to her full-efficiency mode.

I'm so exhausted, I can't handle even watching. I return to my room and go straight to bed.

I dream of things I don't want to dream. I remember things I don't want to remember.

I wake up to the sound of insistent knocking.

And all these years later, my first thought is, *Good God, I could use a drink.*

CHAPTER 4

I'M USED TO WORKING MY cases my own way at my own pace. This is not that.

Twanow ruthlessly tosses the contents of my small suitcase in search of appropriate clothing. Ironically enough, the few items that pass muster—two pairs of lightweight cargo pants and one thin, long-sleeved hiking top—are from my last shopping binge, which took place in Wyoming after I'd lost most of my worldly possessions.

"Get ready," she informs me now. "We need to hit the road if we're going to get all our shopping done before catching your flight out of Austin."

Which brings us to a mall—the kind of place I abhor and avoid at all costs—where we're now moving blithely from store A to B to C. At least Twanow is. I mostly trail behind, praying for death.

Swimwear makes a certain kind of sense, as well as rash guards to protect my nearly vampire-white skin from the sun's abusive rays. Add to that coral-reef-safe sunscreen and a wide-brimmed hat (for the record, I don't have the kind of head/face that looks good in a hat), and my minimalist self would like to be done. If only I were that lucky.

I need to "blend in" with my surroundings, which apparently involves a fresh round of outdoorsy activewear, not to mention something I've never owned before, a pair of Crocs.

"Yes," Twanow informs me when I eye the rows of chunky slip-ons dubiously. "They will protect your feet from the prickly beach—"

"There's such a thing as a prickly beach?"

"Atolls are formed from a ring of coral creating a barrier reef on top of a sinking volcanic island. In other words, the white sandy beaches will be peppered with washed-up coral, volcanic rock, and seashells. Not to mention all the crabs underfoot. Flip-flops are too flimsy, while sneakers will never dry out in the humidity. Hence, Crocs. Trust me on this."

I have no choice but to trust her, though it doesn't make me feel great about things.

T-shirt purchase I can handle. Same with sports bras and new and improved lightweight pajamas—basically men's boxers with a tank top. For nearly a decade, I slept in one of Paul's T-shirts. Maybe some of this will be good for me, after all.

Twanow is all hustle and bustle, credit card at the ready. Again, not something I love—a key piece of my job is to remain independent. But as a woman whose only paying gig is part-time bartending, I can't afford to argue.

Especially once she spies my flip phone. "What the hell is that?"

"My phone."

"That's not a phone; that's a historic relic. No wonder you're so hard to find. You truly are a Luddite."

I take immediate offense. "I'm not a Luddite. I'm of limited means. There's a difference."

"You mean to tell me when you're living in housing projects, everyone else has a flip phone like you?"

Her look is pointed. I don't take the bait. No matter where I live or what I do, *everyone's* phones are better than mine. Possibly I'm a Luddite after all, though I swear I know how to Google just fine. The limited times I'm at an internet café.

"Prepaid, correct?" She stares at me.

"Yes."

"Fine, but you need a better model than that. This will be your only link to the outside world, got it?"

After Wyoming, I get it completely, so I don't say a word as she upgrades my TracFone with a smart phone model I'd never buy on my own. She also adds a monster data plan, like an entire year's worth of activity in my cost-conscious world. I enter in my entire contacts list—about eight names, including one for a Boston detective I keep meaning to delete, but never do. To test out my new and improved appendage, Twanow forwards me my digital airline ticket. Opening it on my screen feels pretty slick, like I'm finally seated at the adults' table.

When we're done, I'm the proud owner of flip-flops, Crocs, and my old sneaks. Not to mention two bathing suits, two rash guards, one wide-brimmed hat, and a modest assortment of shirts and tops. Everything is some kind of microfiber that declares itself breathable and quick drying. At least my clothing will be able to handle the upcoming situation.

Of course, this leaves me with a pile of old clothes that no longer fit in my suitcase.

"Burn them," is Twanow's advice.

I stare at her till she agrees to store the clothing items. I stare at her harder, till she agrees not to burn them herself.

Then I'm as prepared as one can be prepared. An entire carry-on suitcase filled with tropical possibilities.

We climb back into her rental car. I fire up my new prepaid smart phone and start Googling "first time you fly." As with so many things these days, there's a YouTube video on how to navigate an airport, pass through security, and board a plane.

I watch it intensely four times through. Then we're at the Austin airport and this is it. Two planes. One layover in LA. Then, roughly twelve hours from now, Honolulu. I feel slightly nauseated.

"This is a virtual number," Twanow says, taking my brand-new phone, programming it in. "Call or text this, and it'll find its way to me. Can't risk dialing direct, in case they're listening."

I nod.

"Daily check-ins would be ideal, say four p.m. Hawaiian time, so I can determine what progress you're making. But—"

"I won't have that kind of reception."

"Do what you can. Would be good to know you're okay."

I nod again, even though the final part of her statement is clearly an afterthought.

"Just be you," she reiterates for the umpteenth time, "while keeping an eye out for Lea. That's your goal. See her in person, establish basic contact, that's it. In, out, gone."

I don't believe her for a second, and neither does she.

"Take care of yourself," Twanow exhales, her tone more tired, more honest. "If Sanders MacManus really has Lea . . . she deserves to come home; she deserves to be safe."

I don't bother to question what that's going to look like. Lea's family farm is long gone, not to mention an infamous crime scene. As for her sister...nothing Lea can do about Keahi's fate.

To a certain extent, however, these are all esoteric issues. A young girl, forced into sex trafficking...Lea doesn't care about the details. Lea deserves to be free.

These are my marching orders.

For her I get out of the car, square my shoulders, and grab my sole piece of luggage. I have no idea what I'm doing or where I'm going. I'm totally, completely a stranger in a strange land.

Which is to say, I'm exactly in the sweet spot of my comfort zone.

Watch YouTube video. Have a valid driver's license as well as a plane ticket. I go forth and find my flight.

MY TICKET IS first class, which I should probably feel guilty about, but I am too terrified to care. Turns out that has its own security line, so I basically stand in the wrong line for thirty minutes to have some cranky TSA agent inform me I could have been in the shorter queue all along. The "dumbass" part of his statement was implied.

Twanow had set up my toiletries in a clear plastic bag, so at least I have that part right. Electronics boils down to my brand-new fancy phone, so I survive that test as well. I must've looked terrified passing through the body scanner, however, because on the other side some sweet old lady pats my arm in reassurance.

"First time flying, dear?"

"Maybe. I'm not on the plane yet."

"Where are you headed?"

"Hawaii."

"Oh, that's wonderful. Red-eye flight? Just close your eyes and next thing you know, you'll have arrived in paradise. Tip from a frequent flier, never hurts to have a couple of drinks before boarding. I'm partial to whiskey myself. Then, nighty night."

I nod obediently, not having the heart to tell her I don't want a shot of whiskey. I want the entire bottle. Or tequila with a twist of lime, vodka with a splash of cranberry. I was never partial to one kind of booze; in my heyday, I'd drink them all, my only concession being to go light on the mixers. Didn't want to risk filling up on fruit juice or tonic water. Heaven forbid.

My father loved Jack Daniel's. Early on, I swiped a half-filled bottle and snuck it into my room, where I drizzled the potent brew across my fingers, inhaling its heady fragrance while trying to understand the mysterious power this elixir had over him. For the longest time, I thought Jack tasted like love. But really, it tasted of loss, of the father I missed so much, who was never a bad man, and in fact could be quite a silly man, in the rare moments he wasn't passed out on the sofa.

I grab my suitcase by the handle and roll it behind me toward the gate. I'm shaking. Weirdly enough, the airport reminds me of Keahi's prison. Too loud and overstimulating. I have to force myself to breathe in deeply, then exhale.

The tinkle of ice cubes hitting the bottom of a glass. A long pour from some bartender, showing off to his captive audience. The scent of hops as I pass a table topped with a pitcher of foamy beer.

I keep my gaze straight ahead, trying not to notice all the lounges, bars, and restaurants intent on medicating anxious airline travelers with booze, booze, and more booze.

Even a sweet old lady is having a whiskey right now, I think resentfully. But for all my inner cravings, at this moment I'm all right. I know this world isn't meant for me; I can't handle it. I have two decades of my life I barely remember, thanks to my disease. Hooking up with strange men in order to score free drinks. Waking up in pools of vomit. Listening to my aunt's phone call notifying me that both my parents had been killed in an auto accident, then hanging up and heading back into the bar.

The person I was then isn't the person I want to be. That person couldn't save anyone. That woman couldn't even save herself It took Paul's intervention and determination to pull me back from the abyss. And then, after all that...

I'm going to board this plane. I'm gonna freak out a little, and some kind flight attendant will calm me down. Then I will close my eyes and sleep till the plane lands at LAX, after which I'll find my new plane, sleep some more, and voilà, paradise.

I can do this. The guy in the YouTube video said so.

Now I arrive at my designated gate, which, at first glance, looks like a refugee camp. People huddled everywhere, many sporting ripped jeans and well-worn pajamas, all of them staring at the ground—or their cell phones, as the case might be. I claim twelve inches of available wall space, grateful to be small as I wedge myself in and lower myself to the floor.

I have an hour till boarding begins. I use the time to dig through my messenger bag until I locate Twanow's research folder.

My final orders are to burn the documents upon arrival in Honolulu, then check in with the employment company, which will have paperwork for me to do.

(*"Just be myself?"* I ask blithely.

"Of course."

Sighing heavily. Always a tragedy when good sarcasm goes to waste.)

The folder contains one new item, per my request—a photocopy of the letter Keahi's sister had allegedly written to her. Not the envelope, though, which, in hindsight, I would've liked to inspect as well. Not because I know what I'm looking for, exactly, but as the saying goes, you know it when you see it.

The note is written on a blank piece of printer paper. The writing is large and scrawling, nearly childish. Because seventeen-year-old Lea hasn't had access to schooling? Or because most schools no longer teach basic penmanship? Rather than tangle myself up in wild theories involving graphology, I focus on the wording instead.

Keahi,

I don't know if you'll get this letter. Don't know if I'll have the courage to send it.

I ran that night like you said.

Hid the best I could.

But he found me. He killed Noodles so I'd know better than to run again. He told me he killed you too, but years later I saw your face on the news.

If you did what they say you did, I don't blame you.

You are my kaiku'ana. I remember you always. I miss you forever. I love you to the moon and back.

A hui hou,

Leilani

I read the letter three times through, then rest it on my lap. Keahi had been certain the note had been sent by her sister. I'm guessing the inclusion of both of their "secret" names helped, though I imagine those names became known once they made it to Hawaii. Noodles, however, jumps out at me. I'm guessing it's the name of the kitten MacManus had given to Lea—apparently, just so he had something to punish her with later.

I'm half-prepared to brave my first trip on an airplane just so

I can avenge Noodles the cat's terrible death. Except that single point of specificity in a letter otherwise filled with vague references bugs me. It feels too perfect, almost planted.

Want to get Keahi to believe this letter really came from her long-lost baby sister? Include a little-known personal detail, say the name of her sister's cat.

Except what would be the point? If this letter is bait, who's it supposed to trap? Not Keahi, who will only be leaving death row for one very final journey. Her lawyer, committed to halting her client's upcoming execution, isn't going to suddenly race off to a tropical island. I guess that leaves me, but snaring the attention of a barely employable recovering alcoholic is hardly a prize.

I'm back to my earlier conversation with Twanow. Why this letter now? And I'm stuck with the same answer: there's no obvious upside to pretending to be a serial killer's long-lost sibling.

If I step back from it, the letter doesn't read as a cry for help as much as a simple need for connection, say, a final attempt at closure, from one sister to another on the eve of big sis's execution. Certainly, that would explain the why now.

The fact that Lea doesn't ask for anything from her sister, not *come save me,* not even *please write back,* seems to imply she knows this communication is a one-way street. Again, evidence that she's reaching out for her own sake, versus some ulterior motive?

I look up the final phrase in Hawaiian, *a hui hou,* and learn it means "until we meet again." Often used in parting, as Hawaiians are superstitious of the word *goodbye.* Also, spoken at funerals to maintain a feeling of hope.

The sentimentality of the expression makes me feel guilty for my cynical thoughts. Doesn't stop me from having them, however. Being in a line of work where everyone lies to me has made me a firm believer that everyone lies.

So, two possibilities. This letter is bait of some kind and/or filled with hidden codes. Or Lea, having realized her big sister is still alive just in time for Keahi to be put to death, felt compelled to reach out with one last gesture of love and support. End of story.

I really want it to be option B. Still stuck on option A.

I set the letter aside for now and return to reviewing the dossiers on all my soon-to-be best friends. Nothing like time on a remote, semi-deserted island for getting to know one another. For no reason, the theme song from *Gilligan's Island* keeps running through my head.

And for the first time, picturing that tropical island, I feel myself getting excited. I don't really know anything about coconuts, palm trees, and white, sandy beaches. I know the heat and humidity of the deep South, not to mention the unbearable stickiness of the Bronx in July. But an island retreat...Beautiful blue ocean, waving palm fronds, maybe dolphins frolicking in the distance? Could I swim with dolphins? Could I touch a dolphin?

Now I'm positively giddy.

Which is perfect timing, as a booming voice announces over the sound system that it's time to board. Maybe this will feel like a vacation after all.

En masse, my cell-phone-fixated fellow passengers rise to standing.

This is it. Arrive in Honolulu. Charter my way to a billionaire's personal atoll. Locate Leilani Pierson.

In, out, down. Easy, peasy, lemon breezy.

Whiskey, my brain taunts. *Vodka, gin. Cointreau. Single-serve bottles. Pocket-sized nips. No one to know...*

Fuck you, too, I inform my traitorous cravings, and immediately feel like my old self again.

CHAPTER 5

I GO FROM NEVER HAVING FLOWN to twenty hours later sitting in a small private plane surrounded by buttery leather seats and gleaming wood molding. This cabin, which features two built-in sofas and four captain's seats, is nicer than any place I've ever lived. Period.

I keep stroking the leather, then marvel at a personal light switch, USB ports for my fancy new phone, discreet drink holders for the pleasures awaiting in the well-appointed bar. The captain and first officer appeared long enough to give me the lay of the land, with instructions to make myself comfortable. No flight attendant today as I was their only passenger (and clearly didn't rate high enough). The weekly flights often didn't have passengers at all, I learned, but were still necessary for delivering fresh provisions and removing waste.

Apparently, MacManus really is richer than Croesus if he's using a top-of-the-line private jet for grocery delivery and trash removal. On the other hand, who am I to argue?

I'm giddy and wired and definitely overtired. For all my resolu-
tions, I did a terrible job of sleeping on my first two flights. There
was just so much to see and do. Passengers to watch, new customs
to learn. On my first flight, I sat next to a big guy in a suit—
definitely not headed to Hawaii on vacation. He had his attention
focused on his laptop the entire time, which allowed me to sneak
glances and mimic everything he did. Otherwise I never would've
discovered a tray table folded up inside the armrest. Pretty clever.

Landing at LAX was a blur. I had an easy walk to the gate for
my next flight. Then I folded my increasingly restless and cramped
limbs into yet another airline seat. For someone who was used to
walking everywhere all the time, the twelve hours on a bus combined with another twelve hours on a plane was getting to me.
And at least I'm not a big person. I had no idea how most of the
people on the plane were surviving it.

Honolulu equaled employment office. I had about five minutes to blink at the bright sun, marvel at the waving palm trees
and gorgeous purple and orange flowers, then back inside to complete forms and make a copy of my driver's license. Another quick
reprieve, standing outside, the sun on my face. So warm, but not
too warm. Look at that flower, oh and that one, and ooh, that
one. Is this seriously what it's like here every single day?

Then before I could process the thought, a cab appeared and
whisked me to what appeared to be a small warehouse in the middle of a huge airfield but turned out to be one of apparently dozens of charter companies set up to help people bebop around the
Hawaiian islands.

I giggled a few times, covered my mouth with my hand self-
consciously, giggled some more.

Fortunately, Captain Marilee and First Officer Brent didn't
seem to care. They were all business. This way, ma'am. Please

make yourself comfortable. Seat belt buckled for takeoff. There's water and champagne in the fridge.

I totally giggled again.

Now the door is latched shut, the pilots are situated in the cockpit, and we're off. I can feel the speed and lift as the plane takes to the sky, such an intimate experience compared to my earlier commercial flights. Those takeoffs felt like a bus heaving itself off the ground. This feels like I've grown wings and am personally soaring into the clouds. It's wild and primal and glorious. I officially understand why rich people love their private jets. I would do this every single day if I could.

Once at cruising altitude, which is still low enough to marvel over the endless blue expanse of the ocean rippling beneath us, Copilot Brent appears in the small space.

"How are you doing?"

"I love this I love this I love this. You get to do this for a living? You are the luckiest person in the world!"

He laughs. "First charter flight?"

"Yes."

"Not gonna lie, doesn't get much better than this. MacManus takes care of his people."

I nod, too excited and happy to contemplate darker motivations.

Brent gestures to the bar. Water, wine, and beer are complimentary. As a lowly worker bee, I do have to pay for liquor, so apparently there are limits to MacManus's generosity.

I accept a bottle of water. Ever since Wyoming, I've had new appreciation for agua on demand. Plus, the YouTube guy recommended plenty of fluids to assist with jet lag.

"Your first time to Pomaikai?" Brent asks.

"Yes."

"Don't worry. You'll love it. I mean other than..." His voice drifts off.

"Other than?" I prompt.

"Umm. Nothing. Just been some turnover lately."

"Because not everyone takes to such remote living?"

"Sure," he says in a tone of voice that isn't sure at all. I feel my first twinge of doubt.

"I heard I'm replacing someone who had to leave abruptly?" When in doubt, go with a leading question.

"Chris. Injured her ankle last week. Requires real medical attention."

"Last *week*?" I'm trying not to sound too shocked by the transportation delay.

Brent smiles ruefully. "This flight is hardly a daily commute. Once a week is the goal, however..."

"Because the island is so far away?"

"Distance is definitely a factor, but also the runway is nothing but a crude strip of crushed coral. No lights or tower, which limits when we can land or take off. Also, given its short length, there's only one jet in all of MacManus's fleet nimble enough to make that touchdown."

"This one?"

"Exactly. I'd like to add, also only two pilots in the world skilled enough to make the landing."

"You and Captain Marilee."

"Now you're getting it. Add to that factors such as weather systems, no radio comms for most of the flight, and other random variables—we make it to Pomaikai when we make it to Pomaikai."

"Regardless of a crew member's status." I'm getting it now, though *it* is definitely crushing my vibe.

"Don't worry. I'm sure everything will be fine. How much bad luck can one place have?"

"What?"

"We got about an hour," he continues brightly, "before Captain Marilee begins her descent. I'll let you know when we're in sight of the atoll, but it'll be pretty hard to miss."

Brent disappears back into the cockpit. I'm left alone with increasing levels of worry. Information is power, so I boot up my phone, discover this close to land I still have a signal, and take advantage of my gargantuan data plan to read all about atolls. Based on the explanations, I almost understand what Twanow had been saying earlier. An atoll starts with an underwater volcanic eruption that gushes lava onto the sea floor, building a seamount that eventually breaks the surface. Coral grows on the edges of this new island, forming a ring. As the seamount then slowly subsides, the barrier reef creates a lagoon, now surrounded by lush trees growing on top of the coral walls. And voilà, a mere thirty million years later, you have an atoll.

Most of the pictures feature gorgeous white and green circular to horseshoe-shaped islands with incredible aquamarine water in the middle. Exactly the kind of place you'd expect to find lifestyles of the rich and famous. No doubt about it, I should buy my very own atoll, right after my first private jet.

But none of this quells the dark tendrils of anxiety that start to creep up my spine. My job has taken me all over the country, but always on the fringes. I've been to Boston, but it was inner city Mattapan. I've done New York, but a housing tenement in the Bronx. I spent an entire year in Alabama in a mobile home, which was still nicer than the no-tell motel I had in Miami.

I pride myself on being able to live anywhere. Having said

that, this plane alone is so outside my experience it might as well be another planet. Now, looking at these pics of absolute paradise, a future destination for jet-setters everywhere, I'm more than a little freaked out. This I don't know how to pull off.

Just in time to feel the plane begin to descend. The deep blue waters growing closer and closer.

"On your left," Brent yells from the cockpit.

I quickly shift sides of the plane, and there it is.

It's less a symmetrical circle, more a sprawling, irregular, ghost-shaped island with brilliant white and deep green edges and startling turquoise water in the middle. I press my face against the window, as if that will help me take it all in.

It can't be done.

Pomaikai, the gift.

It defies expectation, definition, any single word I know. It also sits completely alone in the middle of the vast ocean. The last time I went on such a remote search, off the grid, beyond reach of rescue, it didn't go well. I feel a familiar pang for people I'd barely known but then grew to care for, only to lose them in that wilderness.

I sit back, much less enthralled with Pomaikai's incredible beauty and much more concerned about what could happen next.

TRUE TO BRENT's description, the runway turns out to be nothing but a narrow strip of crushed white coral, precariously placed at the atoll's farthest edge. One wrong bounce, endless ocean here we come. Captain Marilee is clearly a pro, however, touching down light as a feather before braking so hard my stomach nearly spills out of my throat. Almost immediately, the plane is powering down, and First Officer Brent is back in the cabin.

"Excited?" he asks me as he yanks back the locking mechanism on the external door.

I'm officially too terrified to answer but scramble to unfasten my seat belt and get moving.

There appear to be a dozen casually dressed people milling about below us, which surprises me. That has to be the entire population of the island. I'd expected to meet everyone, but not necessarily all at once.

"It's a tight turnaround," Brent explains as he lowers the stairs. "We gotta get everything they need off, and everything we need back on, before daylight fades or weather hits."

Captain Marilee materializes behind me.

"Is that Trudy and Ann? God, I miss their tuna poke. Don't we get lunch? Snack? I don't remember our schedule."

She waves to two older women who wave enthusiastically back.

"Depends on how fast they offload. While they're packing us up again..." Brent's voice trails off optimistically.

"Yes!"

Captain Marilee turns her attention to me, staring hard. I realize belatedly that I'm blocking the exit. I sling my messenger bag over my shoulder, then stick my head cautiously out of the door.

The humidity slaps me wetly in the face. Then I register the sounds of birds screeching overhead and waves crashing ashore. Finally, I notice the slight but nearly imperceptible pause among all the people scurrying around the plane's underbelly, clearly curious about the newbie but trying not to show it.

The two ladies, Ann and Trudy, are already drawing closer, gesturing to me to come on down. And just like that.

Ready or not.

Here I come.

CHAPTER 6

I MEET TRUDY AND ANN ON the edge of the landing strip. Both look to be mid-fifties with the kind of fit build and rugged look of born outdoorspeople. They are yin and yang in physical coloring—Trudy appears distinctly Italian with her olive-brown skin and short-cropped dark hair, while Ann is a petite blue-eyed blonde with pale skin that must be a bitch to maintain in this environment. They both wear beaming smiles that crinkle the corners of their eyes and ease the anxiety building in my chest.

I barely make it two steps before they're talking excitedly.

"Welcome, welcome, welcome."

"You must be Frankie. I'm Ann."

"I'm Trudy."

"Forget everyone else, we're the two most important people on this island."

"We're in charge of the food."

"And coffee. And sometimes booze."

"Everyone loves us. Don't worry, they'll love you, too."

I simply nod, the two women continuing almost as a singular unit: "Follow us, we're going to give you a quick tour of the camp; then we'll head to the mess hall to fix lunch."

"Is it tuna poke?" I ask.

"Yes!" Trudy pauses long enough to be impressed. "How did you know?"

"Captain Marilee—"

"Totally her favorite," Ann chimes in.

"What is tuna poke?"

"You don't know tuna poke?"

"She doesn't know tuna poke!"

Trudy and Ann share a look of total shock.

"Do you like sushi?" Trudy asks me.

"I don't know. Hasn't exactly been on the menu of my local establishments lately."

"Where are you from?" Ann asks. They are leading me to a wooden stand at the edge of the runway, topped by a large green-and-white-painted sign that declares, "Welcome to Pomaikai." It's decorated with drawings of turtles and flowers. In the lower right-hand corner, there is a tacked-on sign: "Beware of Crabs."

"Nowhere in particular," I mutter, looking around for crabs with concern—which is how I notice that some of the ground seems to be moving.

"It's true," Trudy agrees. "Nowhere has terrible sushi."

Ann is rummaging around behind the stand where there seems to be some kind of shelf. She emerges with a pale-yellow-painted piece of wood shaped into the form of an arrow. As I watch, she grabs a hammer and nails and deftly pounds the board into place amid a bristle of other arrows, all different colors and bearing different names. Philippines, Big Island, California, Australia. My addition, sure enough, says Nowhere. I honestly didn't know they had a sign for that.

"Why is the ground moving?" I'm a little distracted. The crushed white coral forms a curved path leading away from the runway into what I can only describe as a thick, green jungle topped with towering palms. And all along the ground, pieces of the trail keep moving.

"Hermit crabs. They're everywhere. Try not to step on them. It hurts you, and the crabs don't care for it, either."

"Pomaikai has no mammals," Ann adds. "So the crabs have evolved to occupy all the roles in the food chain, you know, herbivores, omnivores, carnivores."

"The hermit crabs are carnivorous?" I immediately draw back. The shell-wearing crustaceans are definitely tiny, scuttling about the path like scattered pebbles, but what they lack in size, they more than make up for in numbers.

"Not them," Trudy says. "The coconut crabs."

"Don't mess with the coconut crabs," Ann warns. "Their claws aren't powered by muscles like a mammal. Think of them more like hydraulics. Meaning once they snap shut..."

I don't want to think about hydraulic claws.

Ann is flipping a number hanging from a hook below the sign, changing Pomaikai's official population size from twelve to thirteen in my honor. *All well and good till the crabs get me,* I think darkly.

"No." Trudy is already flipping the numbers back. "Still twelve. Chris is leaving, remember?"

"Oh yeah. Also watch for holes in the ground," Ann provides. "The ghost crabs live in underground dens. Again, painful for you, and the crabs don't care for it much, either."

"Is that how Chris hurt her ankle?" I venture.

"Well, that and—"

"Never mind!" Trudy interrupts quickly. "Plenty of time for standing around and yapping later. At the moment, we got work to do. This way!" Trudy starts marching down the path toward the jungle, deftly stepping around hermit crabs that are dropping and tucking into their shells at the sound of her approach.

"My luggage…"

"The contents will find their way to you."

"The contents?"

I don't have time to finish the question. Ann is already on the move, and I scamper to catch up, watching every single step I take while wondering what kind of protection sneakers offer against waving claws. I notice all the crabs seem to favor the same turban-shaped white shell, just in different sizes. Some of their homes seem newer than others, with a few even having worn holes that show hints of the red-colored resident inside.

Ann and Trudy are motoring right along. I have to hurry to keep pace, my brow starting to drip with sweat. This isn't the delightful warmth of Hawaii, but something much hotter and more oppressive. It reminds me of July in the South, though it smells distinctly tropical, a mix of floral notes sprinkled with ocean salt.

Everything is green and greener. We pass lush bushes heavy with orange, purple, and white blossoms, while the edges of the path are lined with a mix of thick grass, heavy ferns, and low-growing shrubs. We arrive at a fork in the road, a small, dark-green structure directly in front, a slightly larger deep-blue building across the way. Both are raised off the ground on stilts, with stairs leading up to the front porches.

"Bathrooms." Trudy points to the smaller unit. "Three units.

Everything is unisex. Keep the doors shut and the lid down. You don't want to know what you'll find in there if you don't."

I nod hastily, the warning ominous enough for me.

"Showers." Ann points to the larger building, painted a rich blue and decorated with some kind of intricate wave mosaic that turns out to be comprised entirely from washed-up flip-flops. Clever.

"When Mr. MacManus gets the resort up and running, there'll be desalination units to provide water," Ann continues. "For now, all our fresh water comes from rainwater collected in a cistern. Meaning we don't waste water. You familiar with a Navy shower?"

I shake my head.

"Turn on the water long enough to get wet. Turn it back off, lather up. Then a couple more seconds of water to rinse. That's it. To be superefficient, brush your teeth as part of the lathering process. If you're doing it right, you should be in and out in a couple minutes. The fact our water isn't heated helps."

Cold water, check. Then again, as sweaty and overheated as I'm feeling right now, a cold shower sounds great.

"There are five stalls." Trudy speaks up. "Each one is outfitted with eco-friendly soap and shampoo. Use that, not whatever chemical crap you brought from the mainland."

"Towels are on a rack at the front." Ann's turn. "You'll notice the other half of the space is our laundry facility. Which will be one of your new chores."

"As well as cleaning the showers."

"Now, your cabin."

They're off again, leading me down the left-forking branch of the trail, more white shells with red bodies scurrying out of our way. I notice rustling coming from the underbrush beside us, which has me veering to the middle of the path. An orange crab appears briefly, freezes, then does a quick side shuffle back into the grass.

"Is that a coconut crab?" I ask, as it's certainly bigger than the hermits.

"Oh, no, you'll know the coconut crab when you see it. They're nocturnal, so not out hunting just yet."

"You'll definitely want a flashlight for after dark."

"You think the path is busy now, just wait till then!"

We've arrived at the residential area, the crushed-coral trail now dotted on either side by small wooden cabins, each painted a rich hue of green or blue and bearing some kind of carved sign, from a perfectly shaped turtle to a leaping dolphin to an impressively detailed blossom. Trudy and Ann turn to the left, climbing the stairs to a green cabin adorned with an orange-and-pink painted hibiscus.

"Home sweet home," Trudy declares, yanking on the screen door. It takes three tugs, then the door groans open, the humidity wreaking havoc on its wooden frame.

I mount the stairs, trying to notice everything all at once. The front porch boasts a single rocking chair, a tall black umbrella, and a row of pegs jutting out below the impressively sized front-facing window. More movement catches my eye, one of the orange crabs disappearing beneath the cabin. Behind us I'd already noticed three or four holes dotting the front yard. Apparently, the orange crabs also come in impressive numbers.

Stepping into the cabin, I'm immediately greeted by a cooling breeze against my flushed face. The ceiling fan, whirring away in the peaked ceiling. I'm still sighing in relief when I notice the rest of the space—whitewashed ceiling and walls, dark-green trim, and a pale-blue-painted floor. It sets the perfect stage for two twin beds, one on each side of the room and both topped with obviously well-worn but still adorable flowered quilts.

Three of the four walls boast large screened windows, designed to let in the maximum amount of air. More hooks dot the corner posts. There is also a plastic shelf unit and bedside reading lights.

"There are wooden storm shutters on the windows, but we took the liberty of opening them for you," Trudy informs me. "You'll want to keep the windows open and the fan running, or this place will turn into an oven. As you can see, no insulation. Good news: the amount of sun we get keeps the solar-powered generators fully juiced. Unless we end up in a prolonged storm, we're good on the electricity front."

"Storms?"

"You've flown south from Hawaii," Ann explains. "You're pretty much at the equator now, where the weather stays a consistent eighty-five degrees with eighty-five percent humidity. Pomaikai is classified as a coastal rainforest, which feels exactly like it sounds. And we're subject to crazy storms. Sheets of rain that can hit for hours or last days."

I take a guess: "Hence the umbrella on the front porch?"

Trudy is nodding. "You'll see 'em everywhere. Though, truth is, once you get used to being wet all the time, it's no big deal. Personally, I like a good storm. I think of it as a long, decadent shower. Aren't people back home forking over a fortune for rain shower heads? See, we're already living a life of luxury, and we're not even having to pay resort fees."

"Pro tip." Ann again. "Take off your shoes outside. Otherwise you'll constantly be sweeping out sand."

"And use the pegs for your shoes!"

"Definitely use the pegs. Toe of shoe pointing up."

"But you should still inspect them before putting them on."

"Otherwise, spiders."

"And geckos," Trudy adds.

"Or possibly a scorpion, but that's not common," Ann reassures me. She points down to a bright pink pair of Crocs encasing her sock-covered feet. "We recommend open shoes. Too many things like the dark."

"I...I have a pair in my luggage." I look around, but my roller bag isn't here.

"Perfect." Trudy points up at a large black knot on a ceiling beam above us. "Don't worry about the wolf spider. They look worse than they are."

"That's a spider?" The thing is nearly the size of my fist. Not the kind of roommate I had in mind, and I once had to share space with a feral cat that routinely bloodied my ankle. "Are there snakes around here? Just tell me. What kind of snakes?"

Ann and Trudy stare at me, obviously sensing my agitation. Finally, Ann pats my arm. "No snakes, dear."

I work on controlling my breathing. I have hardly slept in days and can feel myself starting to crash. I don't want spiders. Or carnivorous crabs. Why can't a tropical paradise be a damn paradise?

"So all of this." I take another breath, gesture to the collection of cabins outside my window. "This is just for the current staff? The forward crew?"

"Exactly."

"And MacManus? Does he stay here?"

"Oh, no." Ann is already shaking her head.

"Definitely not," Trudy agrees. "He has his own massive cabin—"

"More like a lodge—"

"On the other side of the camp. Still rustic, but private shower, bath, and kitchen. You'll see it soon enough."

"I will?"

"You get to clean it. He's due to arrive in three days. Another one of your jobs, housekeeping and provisioning."

"Okay."

"Next we'll show you the mess hall," Ann says brightly. "That's our domain. And the most important place in the camp. Breakfast is seven to eight a.m. Lunch around noon. Happy hour at five with dinner at six. Speaking of which, we need to get moving. Poke doesn't make itself."

Ann is already exiting. Trudy stares at me expectantly. I dump my messenger bag on the far bed and hastily follow. The rustic cabin is definitely more comfortable than the elements, because the second I'm outside, my T-shirt and jeans glue themselves to my body, and sweat once more beads along my brow. Rainforest indeed.

"You'll get used to it," Trudy tells me firmly. "Give it a week, you'll see."

I'm not sure how I'm going to make it a day in this kind of humidity, but I nod gamely. Adaptability is my superpower, I remind myself. Time to activate.

CHAPTER 7

TRUDY AND ANN BUSTLE ABOUT the kitchen with the same kind of crazy simpatico that they have in conversation. The dining hall turns out to be surprisingly large and has the inviting feel of a ginormous screened-in porch. A rectangular box, the front half sits beachside, with gorgeous views of bright-blue sea and a rustic wooden dock. Overhead fans faithfully disperse the fresh ocean air throughout the shaded space filled with long tables and assorted plastic chairs. My temperature drops immediately as I enter, and I think I might live just yet. There are two side doors leading into the dining area from the outside. Both have sinks next to the door and instructions to wash hands upon entering. I notice some maps pinned up above the screened windows, including an aerial shot of the atoll I hope to check out later. There's also a bulletin board for future studying and a whiteboard that appears to be the central organizing hub: there's a list of names, then what appears to be a location across from each one. Some read as beaches, some as buildings. I guess so everyone is accounted for?

My name hasn't made the board yet. I notice next to Trudy's and Ann's names there is an asterisk bearing a note: "Divine Goddesses," while weather for the day is listed as "Too Damn Hot," followed by a humidity reading of "You Gotta Be Fucking Kidding Me." That note is followed by another asterisk: "Yes, I Put a Dollar in the Swear Jar."

This might be fun yet.

Behind the dining space is the back half of the building, which features the kitchen. No windows here, just two rear doors flung open to catch as much breeze as possible. The deep-green walls are lined with a massive stove, a long metal sink topped by shelves groaning beneath the stacked weight of plain white dishes, and a refrigerator that goes on and on. In the middle of the space is a series of stainless steel prep tables. The setup reminds me of most commercial-grade kitchens. Certainly Trudy and Ann buzz about as confidently as any master chefs I've ever encountered.

While I wash my hands, Trudy explains that due to the humidity, almost everything, including bread and spices, is refrigerated. The kitchen features two side-by-side units. A neighboring structure houses a full-size walk-in, not to mention an industrial-size freezer.

Where apparently my luggage is now hanging out.

"Just a precaution," Trudy supplies, grabbing two heads of lettuce and handing them to me. "Chop."

I obediently find a waiting cutting board and a magnetic strip holding sharp knives.

"To reduce cross contamination," Ann is saying. "Your bag could be bearing seed pods, bacteria—"

"Cooties," Trudy calls out.

"Exactly. We don't want cooties on Pomaikai. Not good for the ecosystem."

"Do you have anything with Velcro?" Trudy is asking. "That stuff holds on to everything. Definitely anything with Velcro requires deep freeze."

"Otherwise the rest of your clothing will be dropped off in your cabin."

"Hope you packed your good underwear. Charlie peeks."

I finish chopping lettuce. Trudy produces a cucumber and two tomatoes. I resume my chores, too bewildered to think.

Ann has a stainless steel bowl where she's adding generous pours of soy sauce and sesame oil. Next she tosses in chopped green onions and red pepper flakes.

"That's the poke? What is poke?"

"Hawaiian specialty. Basically a raw tuna salad." Sure enough, watching her stir, I can make out cubes of red tuna meat being mixed around in the bowl. "Everyone has their favorite recipe. This is my secret ingredient." Ann points to another small dish filled with finely chopped nuts. "Macadamia. And then as the final step..." She adds a squeeze of lemon, a dollop of honey, and gives it a final toss. "Voilà. Guarantee you right now, it'll be the best you've ever tasted."

"My specialty is crepes," Trudy supplies. "Or Sunday morning biscuits and gravy."

I keep my attention on chopping salad. Soon enough, we seem to have lunch in order. A green salad supplied by me, a bowl of sticky white rice produced by Trudy, and as the crowning touch, Ann's tuna poke. A timer rings, and Trudy withdraws a basket of warmed, soft white Hawaiian rolls.

Out front, I hear the screen door bang open, followed by water running in the handwashing station. Apparently, the rest of the crew has arrived.

I'm nervous. I'm always anxious meeting so many people at

once. One of the most common things you'll hear at AA meetings is how much most social situations wig us out. We had to have a drink before walking into that crowded room or going on a first date or showing up for morning class at the high school. Certainly that explains most of my misspent youth.

My father had to have a drink to get off the sofa. Does it make me stronger than he was that I only needed one to leave the house?

Now the first two people file into the kitchen. I recognize the man immediately but do my best to school my expression.

"Vaughn," he introduces himself, his light-blue eyes and dark tanned skin a perfect match for the photo in Twanow's dossier. His brown hair was probably once cut military short but now stands up on end, while his cheeks are shadowed with at least a few days' growth. He reaches out a hand. "You must be Frankie Elkin."

"Yes." We shake hands, his calloused fingers rough against my skin. It's possible I hold on a beat too long, but then I'm more than a little jet-lagged.

"Trudy and Ann showing you the ropes?" He has a deep voice to go with his strong handshake. He's wearing a blue T-shirt with a faded red logo, battered gray cargo shorts, and a pair of half-destroyed Crocs. He also has a black strap hanging across his body attached to a radio. It's issuing a low-grade buzz of static, apparently nothing to be concerned about.

"Yes," I manage again.

"Your cabin?"

"Adorable!" The burst of enthusiasm catches us both off guard. He smiles, a bit reluctantly it feels, but I like him better for it.

"Hey there, freshie. Pleased to meet ya," a new voice speaks up merrily. Belatedly, I shake hands with the second man, who sports an overgrown mop of salt-and-pepper curls, heavy on the salt, and cheeks covered by a scruffy gray beard. I peg his age at anywhere between fifty and sixty, with the wiry build of a whippet and fingertips so stained by oil no amount of washing will ever get it off. Sure enough:

"Name's Charlie. Head engineer." I think back to the arrows on the welcome sign and peg him as the Australian. "Which is just a fancy way of saying I fix everything around here. Generally without the proper tools or supplies, mind you, but I get it done."

"You have my luggage."

"Sure thing, mate. Will getya your suitcase back tomorrow, no worries. Contents are already sitting on your bed. And no matter what those lovelies tell you, I don't peek." He winks at Trudy and Ann. Trudy rolls her eyes. Ann, I notice, blushes a charming shade of pink. Well, well.

"Say cheese."

I barely have time to register the words before Charlie is holding up his cell phone and snapping a photo. "For our records," he announces merrily. "Or if need be, to identify your body. Cheerio."

I'm still gaping at him when others appear in the dining room, washing their hands, then materializing in the kitchen to grab a plate and load up. Very quickly the space becomes a blur of faces and names. I recognize Copilot Brent and Captain Marilee—

"Poke! Ann, you shouldn't have. But I'm so glad you did!"

Then an absolutely stunning Hawaiian woman strides into the kitchen, sweat-soaked white tank revealing darkly tanned and toned arms, while dark-blue shorts set off incredibly long legs. Gotta be the architect Aolani. She is every bit as impressive as

Twanow said. Now Aolani offers me a quick handshake, followed by a much longer assessing glance. I have to work hard not to squirm beneath the power of that scrutiny. Finally, she nods once to herself, then hits the food. I want to believe I passed inspection, but it's just as likely I've been dismissed completely.

Behind her comes a leanly built young man with short-cropped black hair and sharply chiseled features. His cheekbones alone, not to mention his deep chocolate eyes, thick brows, perfectly formed lips...Now it's my turn to stare.

A faint, understanding smile, as if he's used to such attention, but not defined by it. "Ronin Katsumoto. Archaeologist. And you are?"

I work on remembering my name while we shake hands. In the end I stutter out something that at least begins with the letter *F*, then watch Katsumoto load up his plate and give Trudy and Ann an appreciative nod before returning to the dining room where he takes a seat next to Aolani. I wonder if they're a couple—one being an architect who wants to develop an environmentally and culturally important atoll and the other who's inspecting the same atoll in terms of preserving and protecting said environment and culture. They should be at odds, but what's that saying about opposites attract? Not to mention, their combined genes would produce gorgeous children whose physical beauty would be a gift to all mankind.

Belatedly, I realize there's a positively tiny woman with thick glasses and a lively smile standing before me.

"I am Emi, an ornithologist. Are you a bird-watcher?"

Her accent nags at me. I think back to the arrows. "Philippines!"

"Yes! Very good. And you?"

"I'm from nowhere."

"I understand that is very beautiful this time of year."

I like these people so much.

"Ooh, tuna poke. Ann, you take such good care of us."

Emi moves on to the food, while I tend to more people, more handshakes, more introductions. It becomes a blur of hungry faces. People fill their plates, make appreciative noises in Trudy and Ann's direction, then head straight for the dining area, where they grab the first available seat and get to it. The rolls disappear almost immediately. Most people, I notice, come back for thirds.

"It's hot, hard work out there," Trudy tells me, noticing my wide eyes. "Trekking through the rainforest to reach undiscovered areas, hacking down new trails. There's a reason we need fresh supplies each week. But it's also what Ann and I like about our jobs. Food is the fuel that keeps a good camp running. We keep our crew happy and satisfied—"

"Crepes!"

"And the wheels keep turning. Hungry, tired workers, on the other hand—"

"Donner party!" Ann states darkly.

"Definitely don't want that," I promise them both. "So what's my role?"

"Prep cook," Trudy rattles off. "Dishwasher. Busboy—"

"Girl."

"Person. Supply management. And laundry. Only machines are the ones you saw, so you're in charge of clothing, linens, and towels for the entire camp. People drop off. You wash and fold, then leave items for pickup."

I consider this for a moment. "So if Charlie was peeking at my underwear..."

"You get to handle his." Trudy grins back at me.

Ann turns more shades of pink. "Our turn to eat. Come on, dish up."

Given everyone's rave reviews of the tuna, I'm excited to give it a try. I do my best to ignore the fact that it's raw, because I'm not sure what I think of that. Most of my meals come from diners or taverns, which is to say, I'm well versed in hot dogs, hamburgers, and french fries. On the other hand, one of the best things I ever ate was a Haitian meat pie in Mattapan, Boston, though there was also the freeze-dried lasagna I had at the top of a mountain in Wyoming that nearly made me weep. So I can be flexible.

First bite, I register a tang of salty soy, followed by heat with a hint of sweet. And the texture—the raw tuna nearly melting on my tongue...That's it, I work my way enthusiastically through my entire portion of poke, as the crew members wander back in one by one, rinse their dishes, then stack them in the sink.

More nods and polite waves, then they disappear back out the door to do whatever official things they are supposed to do.

I'm just starting to relax, thinking I totally got this, when Vaughn reappears in the kitchen.

"Frankie, I need to speak with you."

"Safety briefing." Trudy nods.

"Don't step on crabs!" Ann reminds me.

But there's a look on the project manager's face that seems too stern for a standard lecture. And just like that, my stomach plummets.

He knows. This was all too easy; of course he knows. And being MacManus's right-hand man, now it'll only be a matter of time before MacManus knows as well.

I get up slowly, hands clutching my plate. Do I play dumb? Try to buy enough time for the plane to take off so he's stuck with me till MacManus arrives? Otherwise all of this will have been for nothing, and Lea will once more be abandoned to her fate. Not to mention, I'm kind of curious about paradise. Even if it does include wolf spiders and carnivorous crabs.

"My office," Vaughn says ominously.

I slowly place my dishes into the sink. Then I square my shoulders and, with no other options, follow him out the door.

CHAPTER 8

"YOUR EMPLOYEE FILE IS SHIT." Vaughn leads me out of the dining hall to a path that follows the water's edge toward the dock. Seabirds wheel overhead, a cacophony of noises. We're back in full sun, which has me sweating almost immediately, but the views of rippling blue water, waving palms, and swooping birds are nearly intoxicating. More things are scuttling along the path and rustling in the bordering grass, but I'm too utopia-drunk to care.

"Umm, it is?" I have to work to keep up. Everyone around here walks so fast.

Ahead of us is the dock, which has three boats, one larger enclosed fishing vessel and two very simple plank-seating motorboats. Last time I was on a boat, it was to use sonar to look for a missing woman's car at the bottom of a lake. Sadly, my theory proved to be correct.

"Where's your physical?" Vaughn turns abruptly, catching me

off guard. His blue eyes are piercing. "For that matter, where's your passport?"

"A passport? Aren't we still in the US?"

He's already moving again. I notice more buildings ahead. A large one on the right with a long covered patio. We blow right by it, even though I do my best to peer through the screened windows. Empty except for some basic outdoor furniture and a ping-pong table. Rec center maybe?

We pass the dock, which is festooned with brightly painted old buoys atop each wooden post. Some have been painted with basic abstract designs, others to resemble animals. I also notice more flip-flop mosaics decorating the side of a giant shed built on the edge of the water, not to mention a tree stump that has been carved into some kind of bird. Apparently limited internet access is good for boosting creativity.

Vaughn leaves the path and cuts a direct line through low-cropped grass, even smaller shapes now scurrying from beneath our feet. We arrive at a dark-green building, about the right size for an office.

We enter, and I'm immediately struck by a wall of frigid air.

"You get air-conditioning?" I can't quite keep the outrage from my voice.

"The computer and comm system get air-conditioning. I'm just fortunate enough to share a room with them. Sit." Vaughn points to yet another cheap plastic chair; they must buy the damn things in bulk. I'm a little surprised by the amount of plastic present on an eco-minded development site; then again, the cheap outdoor furnishings are rugged enough to withstand the elements while light enough for easy transport. There's something to be said for that.

Now Vaughn plants himself in the first real chair I've seen

around here, a plush executive business model, then taps the manila folder sitting atop his desk. "Where's your medical report? Annual physical? Signed form from your doctor? Anything?"

"I don't have one?" I venture.

"Why?" His tone is demanding. It makes me shiver a little, though that might also be the air-conditioning.

"I didn't know it was required. Seriously, you have to have a note from your doctor to work here?"

"We're in the middle of the damn ocean where an emergency medical evac can take up to three days, and that's if the Coast Guard is available out of Honolulu. So, yeah, we require yearly physicals and a signed note from a doctor confirming you're physically fit."

"I didn't know—"

"The employment issue should've told you."

"I might have misread the email—"

"They should've demanded to see a signed clean medical report when you checked in."

"It all happened very fast. My plane arrived in Honolulu just in time to catch the charter." I'm blabbering, trying to fabricate a plausible excuse out of thin air. "I barely had time to sign the forms they did have, and then I had to run out the door. They said you were short-staffed, in need of an immediate placement? Maybe that's why they let it go." I continue chattering. "But I'm in good health, if that helps. Right as rain."

"Prescription meds?"

"I'm not on any. Are you allowed to ask that question?"

"Yes, I can, and yes, I will. As the project manager on record, I'm in charge of every single person's health and wellness on this atoll. Think of me as your father, doctor, and confessor. Because around here, our safety depends on one another. Which means we don't screw around and we don't lie."

He no longer sounds stern or ominous, just matter-of-fact. It makes for a much more powerful statement.

"I'm in good health," I repeat levelly. "And I'm sorry about the missing forms. I honestly didn't know."

Though in hindsight, I bet hyperefficient Twanow did. Meaning she purposefully kept that detail from me. Because even she couldn't pull off a signed note from a doctor in such a rushed time frame? And keeping with her theme of just be yourself, she wanted me to be able to honestly say I had no idea?

Clearly, the lawyer manipulated me. Yet another reason I prefer to pick my cases myself and work them alone.

"Any allergies?" Vaughn asks now.

"No."

"Including bee stings? We have some wasps on the island."

"No."

"Pregnant? Risk of being pregnant?" he continues crisply.

"Definitely not."

"FYI, there's a supply of condoms in the rec room. I also have morning-after pills in the locked medicine cabinet. We follow a code of conduct in this camp, but we're humans trapped together on a nearly deserted island. Be smart. If that fails, come see me."

I open my mouth. No words come out.

"Major surgeries?" He's back to his checklist.

"No."

"You still have your appendix?"

I nod. He makes a note. "We'll have to watch that."

My eyes widen further. For the first time I'm starting to realize the seriousness of our remote location. Even when I joined a backcountry search in Wyoming, no one questioned me about having all my internal organs.

"Joint pain?" Vaughn is moving right along. "Ankle, knee, hip, lower back? Bum shoulder?"

I continue to shake my head as he moves down his list. Finally: "Do you have any medical training?" he asks.

I speak before I think. "I know how to stuff a bullet hole with a tampon to stanch the bleeding."

"Field medic?"

"Unfortunate camping trip."

He regards me for a moment, then abandons his forms and clasps his hands on top of the desk. "What's your deal?"

"Deal?"

"What brings you here, not to mention on such short notice? Most of our employees are professional subcontractors. Some, like Charlie, flow from six-month gigs at McMurdo in Antarctica to time here to another research station in Alaska. When they say they're from nowhere, that's because they're literally from nowhere. But you?"

I'm not sure what to say, so I just blink at him.

"Favorite TV show?" he asks abruptly.

"What? I don't...I haven't owned a TV in years." The moment I say the words, I regret them. Now I sound weirder than ever. But if anything, the answer seems to relax him.

"Family?"

"My parents passed away years ago. I don't have anyone else."

"And when you return to the mainland? Where do you stay?"

"In the short term, probably a bus station." I shrug. "While I figure out my next move."

"You're relying on buses in an island state?"

"I literally just arrived in Hawaii this morning. First time." All of this is true. "I haven't figured out the lay of the land just yet."

"Why Hawaii?"

"Have you looked outside? Of course I had to give it a try. Besides, I've been all over America. All forty-eight continental states. This is what comes next."

"What do you think?"

Twanow was right; it's best to just be myself. "I wish your spiders were smaller, and I'm a little concerned about carnivorous crabs."

"The coconut crabs? Just remember, their claws operate like—"

"Hydraulics?"

"I see Trudy and Ann gave you a proper tour."

"They're amazing. Everyone seems very nice. Look." Since the best defense is a good offense, I go with some sincerity of my own: "I've covered a lotta ground and worked a lotta places. I know how these things work. I won't slow you down, and I won't be a problem. I work hard, and I know how to fit in."

Vaughn eyes me seriously. "Around here, we're each other's backup. Anything goes wrong, it's on us to save ourselves."

I shiver slightly. I've heard these words before. Right before our search group started getting picked off by a sniper.

"That means no fraternizing," Vaughn emphasizes.

"Unless I'm human, in which case come see you?" I hear the double entendre at the last minute and promptly blush furiously. For the first time, Vaughn looks taken aback. MacManus's right-hand man colors slightly, his jaw working, no words coming out.

"For condoms," I add hastily to save us both.

"Yes. Exactly. Also, we have rules about alcohol consumption.

Everyone must be prepared to muster at a moment's notice. So while we have some happy hours and social occasions, no one is permitted more than two drinks a night. Is that a problem?"

I shake my head.

"The alcohol is under lock and key in this office. One of your responsibilities will be to distribute it during prescribed functions, while monitoring everyone else's consumption. Is that a problem?"

Now would be a perfect time to mention I'm a recovering alcoholic, or even state that I don't drink. Instead, I once more shake my head.

"I mark the bottles. And at the end of each evening, you should update those markings."

"Okay."

"We also honor everyone's religion, race, and gender identity. How would you like to be addressed?"

"Frankie?" I venture.

He waits.

"She/her," I add, understanding the question better now.

"I encourage you to ask each of your teammates this question and make no assumptions. There's a myriad of reasons people prefer to work in remote locations such as this."

I get it.

"As you may have noticed, our Wi-Fi is shit. Which also reminds me, out of respect for one another, we don't swear. Except when we do, in which case, there's a swear jar." Vaughn now digs into his pocket. As I watch, he pulls out a coin of some sort, eyes both sides of it, shrugs, then drops it into an old mason jar on the corner of his desk, filled with other bright, shiny objects.

"It's important to monitor our behavior, to try to be our best selves at all times. But it's equally important to realize we're human, and this kind of living, cut off, isolated, and facing hours if not days of boredom, takes its toll. We act our best when we can. Practice forgiveness when we can't. If you have concerns about any of your campmates' behaviors or feel uncomfortable or threatened at any time, come see me immediately. In this environment, minor grievances can quickly become major flashpoints. Speak up early and often. It's in everyone's best interest to nip things in the bud."

"How do you select your staff?" I'm genuinely curious. "I mean, plenty of people are cooks, engineers, naturalists, whatever. Why these people here?"

"We look for experienced contract workers, people who move around often and have an established pattern of success."

"People from nowhere," I fill in. Finally, my lifestyle is considered a superpower.

"As you'll notice, we're a camp full of introverts. Extroverts don't want to live this far from civilization, and the few who have tried..."

"Went insane?"

"Were threatened with death by their fellow campmates, who seriously needed them to shut the fuck up."

Vaughn digs around in his front pocket. Another shiny coin goes into the jar. It might be just me, but very few appear to be US mint. Fair enough. Apparently, we're a band of vagabonds and more power to us.

"Eventually, the hope is we'll have a Starlink satellite connecting Pomaikai to the greater universe. For now, we have extremely limited access, which we reserve for official business. Saturdays and Sundays, we grant each person thirty minutes to go online, check email, connect with home, watch cat videos, whatever works for them. But until then, stay off."

"What about phoning home?"

"Good luck with that. We have two sat phones to reach the

mainland in case of emergency. We communicate around the island via radio." He taps the black case dangling around his shoulders. "Everyone works Monday through Saturday. Assigned duties are on the whiteboard in the dining hall. If you leave base camp for any reason, even as part of your assignment, you need to check yourself out and note your destination. It's a matter of safety. Someone, either myself, Charlie, Aolani, or Ronin, will have radio duties. If you leave base camp, you need to take a unit with you and check in on an hourly basis."

"Or you'll wait until the coconut crabs deliver their ransom demands?"

He finally cracks a smile. "Good news, their payment terms can generally be met with tubs of peanut butter."

"Seriously?"

"They love the stuff. Wait till you visit Crab Town."

"They get their own camp?" I'm a little terrified.

"This place has plenty of surprises. You'll see. Now, where's your passport?"

The abrupt change in topic catches me off guard. I blink owl-ishly, then realize that was probably his intent. Good looks aside, the man is smart.

"I don't have a passport," I tell him honestly.

He stares at me with those piercing blue eyes.

"Aren't I still in the United States?"

He continues to stare at me.

I sit. Fidget. Stare at the pile of coins in the swear jar, some bright shiny new, others dull tarnished old. Definitely from many different countries.

"You're saying the employment office never asked for your passport?"

"Never," I agree, which is probably my first lie, as I'm already certain they said something to Twanow, who simply opted not to mention it to me. Again, because not even she could conjure up a passport out of thin air, and rather than be derailed by such details, she went with "it's better to beg for forgiveness than ask for permission."

Note to self: I'm never meeting with a serial killer ever again, not even the ones with super high body counts and very efficient lawyers.

"You don't need a passport to fly into Pomaikai," Vaughn allows. "But you might need one to return to the mainland. That will be up to customs."

"Really? But if I haven't left the US, why do I need a passport to return?"

"Because an atoll such as this lacks border security. Anyone and everyone can arrive on these shores, from shipwrecked pirates who may have buried treasure here hundreds of years ago to drug smugglers whose single-person sub washed up just a few months ago."

"You have a drug-running sub? Can I see it? Was it empty?"

"Do you mean of humans or drugs?"

"Either. Both. How cool is that?"

Vaughn sits back. He regards me a moment longer, then drops his hands from the top of his desk. "You may just fit in around here," he allows.

I wonder if I should clap or if that would be in poor taste.

"I don't like your file," he warns. "The employment agency is generally much more thorough. I don't know why it should be different for you."

I don't say a word.

"But you're here," he allows. "And we do need more hands on deck."

"Because of what happened to Chris?"

"What do you mean? What'd you hear?" He sits up so suddenly, I recoil into my chair. Third time the mention of Chris has led to a less than clear response.

"Umm, twisted ankle, requires medical attention," I try out.

"Oh, that. Of course, accidents happen." Vaughn sits back, stares at me. He has just lied to me. I know it. He knows it. And yet his expression remains cool, calm, and collected. All that talk of openness and honesty, and now this...

More pinpricks of unease. What the hell is going on?

"MacManus and his people will be arriving in just a few days," Vaughn states. "Your duties include general care and cleaning of his lodge, with random moments of being completely and totally at his beck and call. You got a problem with that?"

"Umm, no."

"Whatever you've heard about our billionaire boss, or think you know, let it go. He's not as arrogant as they say, he's worse. So stay the fuck out of his way, do your job, and everything will be fine. Got it?"

"Okay."

"His entourage includes his teenage ward, Lea—"

I open my mouth, then snap it shut, realizing any questions now would be too much, too soon.

"—his personal chef, and his private secretary," Vaughn continues. "They have their own quarters next to his. You'll be in charge of that setup as well."

"Gotcha."

"You can go now."

Now my jaw does hang open. I haven't been so rattled and caught off guard in...forever. Slowly, I rise to standing, my gaze still locked on his, trying to figure him out. Friend or foe? Ally or enemy? I honestly have no idea.

He lied to me. I lied to him.

But which one of our lies will prove more dangerous in the end?

"Thank you," I say at last.

"For what?"

"I don't know yet. I guess we'll both find out."

I leave him sitting behind his desk with a scowl on his face.

I want to think of it as a triumph.

But mostly I think I'm in way over my head.

CHAPTER 9

THE REST OF MY AFTERNOON passes in a jet-lagged blur. Plane departs. Cheering and waving from the Pomaikai crew as they send off their mysteriously injured comrade, Chris.

I find my way back to my cabin, where I send crabs fleeing in all directions. As my new orange property mates scuttle frantically to safety beneath my unit, I feel my first twinge of compassion. As nervous as I am about crustacean life-forms, they are clearly more terrified of me.

That lasts as long as it takes me to walk inside and discover the ginormous wolf spider is now perched on the ceiling beam right above the pile of clothes from my suitcase. I stare at the arachnid, swear I can feel all eight eyes staring back. It's not a great sensation.

I've lived with cockroaches, a feral cat, and, not too long ago, an absolutely adorable SAR dog that specialized in finding human remains. I refuse to be intimidated by a spider. Maybe.

"Here's the deal," I inform Wolfie. "Your side of the room.

My side of the room. I won't interfere with your insect consumption if you promise not to nest in my clothes or hide in my shoes. Capisce?"

The fist-sized black spider doesn't move. I choose to take that for a yes.

Slowly, I sift through the small pile of my worldly goods. Now that I'm on the atoll, the whole Crocs thing makes more sense. Same with the shorts and microfiber shirts. I pull out my new and improved tropical gear, and with a last glance at the stationary wolf spider, I hit the showers.

I hadn't been wrong before—the icy spray is a welcome respite from the heat and humidity. I have to forcefully remind myself of Navy rules. Wet hair. Shut off and lather. Rinse. Get out. It's all way too brief, though refreshing.

Of course, by the time I wrestle on my clothes, I'm hot and bothered all over again.

Good news—there's no chance to marinate in my pain and suffering as I'm already due back to the mess hall for dinner prep. I'm simultaneously exhausted and grateful, since the best solution to bone-deep fatigue is to work, work, and do more work.

Dinner theme is American night, which apparently involves a vat of homemade mac and cheese, accompanied by hamburgers and hot dogs. I get to work grating a copious amount of cheese for Ann's signature dish, then slice up onions, tomatoes, and pickles for Trudy's world-famous burgers. Along the way I throw together a spinach salad with bacon on the side to accommodate the vegetarians.

The entire three hours is an exercise in moving and not thinking. When people show up and start raving about the food, I almost know what's going on. Mostly, I dish up my own plate and shovel in pasta on complete autopilot. Some piece of my brain registers the golden crushed-cracker topping. The rest of me would sell my soul to be asleep right now.

Trudy and Ann seem to understand, patting my shoulder as they bustle about.

"Tomorrow will be better."

"Crepes! What are your thoughts on Nutella?"

I manage a display of semi-exhausted jazz hands to indicate enthusiasm. They laugh.

"We like you."

"You chop fast."

"You will work out."

"Dishes now, then you're done."

"Congrats on surviving day one!"

"Looking forward to morning of day two."

"Crepes!"

"Fresh fruit!"

"Whipped cream!"

I stare at them as if they are creatures from another planet. They giggle and move on.

As it was with the lunch rush, individuals file in after eating, depositing their dirty plates in the sink while dropping their utensils into a plastic bin filled with a cleaning solution. I recognize the modest-size commercial dishwasher from many of my bartending gigs. Basically, load dirty objects onto a plastic tray, buzz tray through a blistering eight-minute cycle, load next tray, and repeat.

Which doesn't explain the gorgeous man standing in front of the sink, rinsing and stacking each plate in the dishwasher bin.

Ronin Katsumoto, the perfectly sculpted archaeologist who should be off making perfectly beautiful babies with Aolani Akamai.

"Isn't that my job?" I venture at last, not sure what to do.

"Yes and no. We take turns assisting with dinner cleanup. It is our way of showing gratitude for the wonderful meals."

"Oh."

This witty response earns me nothing. Ronin slides the loaded tray into the dishwasher, hits start, pulls out a fresh, empty tray, and returns to the stacking process. Belatedly, I gather up prep bowls and serving dishes.

Ronin rinses. Loads. Rinses. Loads. The strong, silent type, then.

"Where are you from?" I venture at last.

"Hawaii. Big Island."

"You're local?"

"Third generation," he confirms.

I do some math, and based on my rudimentary knowledge of US history, arrive at a sad conclusion. "Your grandparents were Japanese immigrants during World War II?"

"My grandfather was sent to a Japanese internment camp. He met my grandmother while incarcerated."

"I'm sorry."

He finally looks up. "History happens. It isn't your responsibility to apologize for what came before you. It is all of our responsibility, however, to do better in the future."

I gather up more bowls. He stacks them in the next available tray.

"How would you like to be addressed?" I remember this from my conversation with Vaughn.

This would be the perfect time for someone with, say, my sensibilities to quip, "Grand Master of the Universe."

Ronin goes with: "He/him."

I nod. Fair enough. Then, as the silence once again drags out: "I understand the naturalists are inspecting the atoll to analyze the possible environmental impact of the proposed development, but what exactly are you assessing as an archaeologist?"

Ronin points the spray nozzle at an oversize stainless-steel prep bowl and scours away. "I'm looking for signs of previous civilization, for elements of Polynesian culture and history that should be preserved and protected. Which could result in anything from a complete halt to the project to a more scaled-down plan to accommodate historic sites. Or, of course, no changes at all."

"You're looking for ancient ruins?"

"Not necessarily. This atoll, like most of the Line Islands, lacks fresh water. Meaning it was never cultivated by early explorers. Instead, it operated more as a way station—a stopover where expeditions would linger long enough to stretch their legs, replenish their food supplies. Just because there's no record of people inhabiting this island, however, doesn't mean it's completely devoid of sites of interest."

I dump out the bucket of silverware and get to work. "Pretend I'm stupid." Again, a perfect opportunity for him to make some sort of smartass comment. He doesn't, and I feel let down. Ronin might be one of the most beautiful humans I've ever encountered, but he seems sadly limited in the witty repartee department. "Define a site of interest."

"Heiau," he replies immediately, which sounds like hey-yow. "Hawaiian temples, where mana is concentrated and transferred through prayer. It wasn't uncommon to erect heiaus overlooking coral reefs to conduct rituals for better fishing, making this a prime location."

"What does a heiau look like?"

"They can be an earthen mound or stone structure. It's less a prescribed form than a feeling of intent, of our need to honor our ancestors and connect with the land and the sea most of us feel in our blood."

"That sounds very beautiful."

Ronin flashes a smile, clearly acknowledging that I'm an ignorant white woman with no true comprehension of what he just said.

"In practical terms, I am mapping the topography of the island for geoformations that seem out of place. Say, a perfectly formed mound where no mound should be. Or an unnaturally straight line cutting through the rainforest. In my line of work, any symmetrical shape is an item of interest. Perhaps indicating an ancient temple or burial mound."

This grabs my attention. "You're looking for human remains?"

"It's possible. This atoll has been known by locals for hundreds of years. It's not unreasonable that an early Polynesian sailor might be buried here. Not to mention European explorers such as Captain Cook in the eighteenth century and whalers in the nineteenth. Of course, there's also the legend of buried treasure."

"Buried treasure?" I give up on washing silverware to stare at the archaeologist in rapt interest.

His smile grows, crinkling the corners of his dark eyes. Seriously, no man should be this pretty. "An infamous pirate ship ran aground in the early nineteenth century, the surviving crew members allegedly burying their ill-gotten gains somewhere on Pomaikai. They spent months living off of coconuts and crab meat before being rescued. Years later, on his deathbed, the last surviving crew member confessed to burying a small fortune in gold between a V-forked tree and an eagle-shaped rock. As you can imagine, many have searched. None have discovered."

"Is that why MacManus bought the property? To find pirate booty?"

Ronin shakes his head. "Legends of buried treasure are generally just that—legend. And given the number of deserted islands in the Pacific alone, not something to be taken too seriously."

"Still..."

He regards me patiently.

"Who doesn't love the idea of hidden gold?" I insist. "I mean if people are willing to pay good money for lottery tickets, why not search for X-marks-the-spot?" I return my attention to the jumble of silverware. "So your job is to map the entire atoll, looking for irregular—or really, too regular—geoformations."

"More or less."

"What happens when you find these perfectly symmetrical shapes? *Have* you discovered any?"

"There's still much ground to cover. The jungle is real. Our progress is slow. Should I find any areas of interest, proper protocol is to mark off the site, then dig a test pit to check for charcoal layers, metal artifacts, or human remains. Any of which would be grounds for delaying development until further excavation and preservation can be done."

I nod, getting the picture. "Which would be a big bummer for the project."

"The law is the law. NAGPRA alone requires due diligence."

"NAGPRA?" I stumble over the awkward word, which I'm already guessing is an acronym for something long and complicated. Sure enough:

"Native American Graves Protection and Repatriation Act. All human remains, funerary objects, sacred objects, or objects of cultural patrimony must be handled with respect and repatriated to the appropriate parties. It is very important legislation, designed to provide Native Americans with more control over their culture and heritage. Mr. MacManus is aware. The purchase of this atoll for future development came with significant risk. That's the way it is."

I'm genuinely curious. "Does that put you in a difficult position? Anything you discover has the potential to cost him millions of dollars."

"I don't work for Sanders MacManus. I work for the state of Hawaii."

"And the architect, Aolani? Because she does work for MacManus, and anything you find could torpedo a career-making project for her, too, right?"

He regards me for a long moment, his features impossible to read. "That would be a question for AO."

"Sorry, I got the impression you two were working together."

"We are."

Now it's my turn to be confused, but Ronin doesn't elaborate. He clearly holds his cards close to his chest. I hastily return my attention to scrubbing silverware, not wanting to raise too many red flags this early on.

The back door bangs open. Trudy pokes her head in. "You two done yet?"

"I think so." I look at Ronin, who nods his agreement.

"Perfect."

"Light's on," Ann calls out from over Trudy's shoulder. "You gotta see this."

"Bert and Ernie have come to play."

"Bert and Ernie?" I glance at Ronin, whose expression has now relaxed.

"You will not want to miss this," he agrees.

"Okay." I dutifully dry off my hands, then head outside, where

Trudy and Ann are holding flashlights and practically vibrating with excitement.

"Come on, come on, come on."

"Everyone loves them."

"They're like our camp mascots."

"Just you wait!"

They hustle me over to the dock, where several other crew members have gathered, shoes off, feet dangling in the water. A spotlight shines over the rippling waves. I notice the undulations form a pattern and in the middle of that pattern are two dark swooping shapes with flashes of white underbelly.

The first massive form crests the lapping ocean, revealing horn-shaped forward fins powered by giant wings, before it slides once more beneath the waves, followed shortly by a second. I catch my breath.

Bert and Ernie. Two enormous manta rays, mesmerizingly alien and impressively majestic. As I watch, they glide near the dock, slipping beneath one person's outstretched toe, then another.

"Don't worry," Trudy whispers in my ear. "They may look scary, but they're basically giant vacuum cleaners, feeding on the tiny organisms attracted by our dock lights. Each manta has distinct markings, so we know who they are."

"How many are there?" I ask breathlessly as one of them dives just off to my left. I hasten to take a seat, slipping off my Crocs to dip my toes into the churning water.

"We're up to a dozen characters from Sesame Street."

"A dozen? And you get to play with them every night?" The mantas look smooth and glossy, but then one brushes delicately against my toes. "It feels like sandpaper!"

"Aren't they amazing?"

"They are beyond amazing!" A second one brushes against my toes. I stretch out my leg to get even closer. I am totally, completely enthralled. Based on the low hum of happiness thrumming through the air around me, so is everyone else.

I think I may be able to handle it here after all.

CHAPTER 10

SURVIVE THE NIGHT. BARELY. IT feels like sleeping in the middle of a Hitchcock movie. The cacophony of a thousand seabirds, swooping through the moonlit sky while a strong breeze tosses the palm fronds and bangs any and all wooden structures. I jerk awake half a dozen times to snap on my flashlight and search for my arachnid roommate. Each time, I catch the enormous wolf spider encroaching closer to the door, no longer flattened against the whitewashed ceiling but now up on all eight legs, startlingly tall.

The first few times I check, a small gecko flees from the unexpected beam of my flashlight. The fifth time, I spy him staying perfectly still, the wolf spider in his line of sight. The sixth time, no gecko, and a now curiously complacent spider. I don't want to know anything more after that.

Having consumed way too much water to combat the stifling heat, I keep having to stumble my way out of my cabin and down the pitch-black path to the latrine. Each time, crabs flee frantically before me, including my side-scuttling orange neighbor. I feel like a human Godzilla, crashing through crab Tokyo.

The guilt lasts till I come to the toilets, where I have to climb darkened stairs and carefully ease open the bathroom door, paranoid about what might lie behind. On one of my return trips, something very large crashes through the underbrush, and the hermit crabs all drop at once, huddling inside their worn turban-toweled shells. I pick my way carefully around them, flashlight trembling in my hand as I wonder what they know that I have yet to find out.

By the time the morning sun washes across the gray-and-purple horizon, I'm positively bleary-eyed. Just in time to start the day.

The second I exit my cabin, the heat strikes me as an oppressive oven. Clearly, ceiling fans offer more relief than I anticipated. I may need to dig out some coins for the swear jar. Currently, I'm doing an excellent job muttering expletives under my breath.

I discover my crab friend standing frozen amid a scattering of orange blossoms, one clutched tightly in his claw.

"For me?" I ask.

Crabby doesn't move.

"Really, you shouldn't have."

Sidestep left. Then another. Another. A final burst of speed as Crabby flees for the underbrush.

"I'll take that as a sign of affection," I call after him, then trudge my way to the mess hall, where I'm sure many chores await.

Rounding the corner, I come upon Ronin and Aolani, huddled near the corner of the bathhouse. Aolani has a blue-and-green towel slung over her shoulder and toiletry bag in her hand, clearly having been intercepted on her way in or out. Ronin, however, has the hyper-alert look of someone who's been up for hours. Possibly having run eight miles and knocked out a hundred push-ups before daybreak. His expression is intense as he relates something in soft tones that has Aolani frowning. She spies my approach first, jerking her head at Ronin to call attention. He immediately falls silent, not looking happy about it.

Lovers' quarrel? Something else? I raise a hand in casual greeting, then make the left-hand turn toward the kitchen. Immediately, I hear the urgent buzz of their voices picking back up behind me.

Something is definitely afoot between the archaeologist and the architect. Again, personal or professional? I wonder if Trudy and Ann have some ideas on the subject. They seem happily all-knowing, good contacts to have in my line of work. Maybe I can get them to tell me more about maybe, maybe not accidentally injured Chris.

I no sooner approach the back stairs, however, than the project manager, Vaughn, comes banging out the screen door.

"There's been a change of plan," he states without preamble.

"Good morning," I counter.

He scowls. Apparently, no one is in the mood to exchange pleasantries this a.m.

"I need you to pack a cooler and join Ronin in the field. Or, more aptly, the jungle. However much water you think you'll need, triple it."

"Umm..."

"Remember that whole conversation you and I had just twelve hours ago about everyone helping everyone else out?"

The one where you lied to me? I go with: "That was only half a day ago?"

This earns me a fresh glare. "Pack the cooler and meet Ronin by the rec hall. If it makes you feel any better, once you return this afternoon, Trudy and Ann will take you to the owner's lodge. MacManus has moved up his schedule. Big storm coming. He's decided to arrive early rather than be delayed."

"Meaning I need to prepare for his arrival today versus tomorrow." I almost know what's going on.

Just in time for Vaughn to stalk away without a backward glance. No doubt about it, something's up.

When I enter the rear of the kitchen, Trudy and Ann are already at work, moving around the space in their unique little dance. Even here, however, I feel tension. Serving platters banged onto the countertop with more force than necessary. Utensils rattling as Ann searches too anxiously. Refrigerator door slamming shut as Trudy snatches fresh fruit too impatiently.

She glances over first. "Sandwich fixings on the counter. Ronin is a vegetarian, prefers a hummus wrap. What's your favorite?"

"Peanut butter and jelly."

"Oldie but goodie," Ann calls out.

"Favorite jelly?" Trudy wants to know.

"Grape!"

"Public school?" Ann asks sagely.

"Better believe it."

Trudy points to the fridge. "Got some in the door. Sliced bread, bottom shelf. You a crusts-cut-off kinda gal?"

"Only when I'm wearing a tiara."

"Knew we'd like you," Ann assures me.

Trudy's already back to whisking a bowl of thin batter. For crepes, I realize. I'm going to miss the special crepes breakfast. Now I'm in the same bad mood as everyone else.

Now doesn't seem to be the time to fish for answers to my growing list of questions, so instead I wash my hands and get to work. I throw together four sandwiches, two for Ronin and two for me, since I gather they're going to be our lunch as well as our non-crepes breakfast. I hunt down chips and oranges. When I return, a soft-sided cooler has magically appeared, as well as some curiously stiff different-sized squares of wax-coated fabric. I hold them up in total confusion.

"To wrap the sandwiches," Trudy calls over her shoulder.

"Just say no to plastic bags," Ann adds.

Huh. I experiment with the squares, discovering that they fold around the food items snugly enough and seal after a bit of pressing with the heat of my fingers.

In lieu of ice packs, the walk-in freezer offers up an array of reusable water bottles, filled to the brim and frozen solid. They are to chill the food at the beginning of the trip, thawing into a hydrating resource by the end, I deduce.

I've stayed on tribal lands that had limited access to indoor plumbing and housing projects that offered up brown sludge as the only showering option. I'm not sure what to make of a place like this that has both a sense of abundance and conservation. It hurts my head, but maybe in a good way.

The cooler is nearly groaning in water weight by the time I sling the strap over my shoulder and careen my way toward the rec center. I still have only the vaguest notion of where things are, but apparently I did a pretty good job of guessing as I spot Ronin loading up gear into the back of a rugged utility vehicle that looks like a cross between a golf cart and a Humvee. He has a machete strapped to his belt. It doesn't make me feel terribly great about our morning plans.

He glances up when I approach, his expressionless features tight around the eyes.

"Vaughn asked me to help you out this morning."

He nods, gestures toward the cooler. "Thank you."

"Trudy and Ann said you were partial to hummus wraps. I made two, heavy on the veggies."

I keep my voice light, nearly chipper. In contrast, Ronin nods curtly.

"Sunscreen, hat, mosquito repellent," he rattles off.

"As in I should bring some?"

"As in you should already be wearing some."

I regard him blankly, having not gotten that far with my thinking.

"Sunscreen on the table near the dock with the snorkeling gear. Should be some mosquito repellent as well. I recommend a hat. Your decision."

I peel away from the vehicle long enough to follow his advice. The sunscreen is mineral based and has the same consistency as Elmer's glue. I smear it around best I can, then top myself off with a heavy misting of pungent-smelling bug spray. Given the speed and focus of Ronin's packing, I opt not to return to my cabin for my hat. I'm too afraid he'll leave without me.

"I haven't seen many mosquitoes," I venture as I return.

"The strong breeze keeps them down near the beach. Where we're going, however, they'll be worse."

"Where are we going?"

"Inland."

I wait, but apparently that's all he's going to offer on the subject. He finishes securing the gear with bungee cords, then climbs behind the wheel. I scamper to catch up.

Just as he lurches the utility task vehicle into drive, I spy Charlie peering at us from a clump of trees ahead. He grins at me as we pass. Then he raises his phone and snaps more photos.

Of our retreating figures? For posterity? I don't get it. Which only increases my unease as Ronin and I leave the semi-groomed path and crash into the overgrown jungle ahead.

———

MINUTES AFTER WE leave the base camp, the vegetation becomes thick, thick, and thicker. Tightly packed palms block out the sun, while a dense underlayer of green foliage and tall grasses threatens to swallow up any and all open space. We veer from the white crushed coral onto a narrow muddy road that weaves deeper into the dark undergrowth while the air grows hotter and heavier. If I wasn't sweating profusely before, I definitely am now.

I can still hear the cries of the seabirds, but the sound is more distant. Clearly, they prefer the beach to this space. I think they have a point.

"Holy shit!"

I'm too caught off guard to bite back the words. Not to mention if this isn't worthy of the swear jar, nothing is.

We've just slid around another muddy turn to discover a positively gigantic crab smack in the middle of the road. Its sapphire-blue body looks as big as an Abrams tank with massive claws four times as scary.

Ronin slows as the crab shows no signs of scuttling away, and in a showdown between hulking crustacean and heavy-duty UTV, it's unclear which would win.

Far from being dismayed, Ronin finally appears relaxed.

"You've never seen a coconut crab?" he asks me.

"That's the coconut crab? Holy... What does it eat, small children?"

"Mostly other crabs. With a side helping of coconuts, of course."

I think of flower-loving Crabby and my tiny hermit crab neighbors and am immediately aghast. "That's terrible! That...that thing is like something straight out of a nightmare. How do hermit crab mommies and daddies tuck their babies into bed at night, knowing there's those kinds of monsters lurking in the dark?"

"Coconut crabs are actually a type of hermit crab."

"They're cannibals as well? Figures!"

"They're delicious. For many island communities they're a traditional source of food, given the sweetness of their meat, though hunting is now restricted due to the crabs' declining numbers."

"Aren't you a vegetarian?"

"I've lived a life," he says simply.

I'm still dubious. "How can you take down a creature of that size?"

"Most hunters try to sneak up from behind, but the crabs have a highly developed sense of smell, which makes it risky. Especially given their claws have a crushing strength twenty times greater than a lobster's."

"They can smell?" I study the creature, from the safety of the UTV, for some kind of nose. In return, it waves a massive blue claw at me in a clearly threatening gesture.

"It's how they hunt at night. They're nicknamed the Robber Crab, based on writings from an English naturalist at the turn of the twentieth century. He observed them stealing saucepans, bottles, and other small items from his tent. Reportedly, one even got away with a bottle of whiskey. Naturalists believe they were attracted to the smells from the campsite."

"Are they violent drunks? Because I think that's the most relevant question."

Ronin finally smiles. It eases more of the tension from his face. "They're territorial. Most likely we interrupted this crab returning home from a long night hunting, and he wants to make sure we know all of this belongs to him before he disappears back into his den."

"He can have it. Jungle, coconuts, and all. Seriously no argument here."

"What do you think of the coloring?"

I glance from Ronin to the crab and back to Ronin. I hadn't really gotten that far, being much more obsessed with the Hulk-sized claws. "I've never seen that shade of purply blue before," I allow. "Kind of pretty."

"You will see them in two colors—either this shade of blue sapphire, or a dark ruby red. But no one knows why. Their shading doesn't seem to be related to diet or gender. It's one of those things that even now, we can't explain."

There's a change to his voice I understand. "You like that. That the world is still full of wonder."

"It is good to still have questions to ask. It is even better to still have answers to discover. It means someone like me will never be bored."

"I like a good mystery, too," I allow.

Our giant roadblock seems to finally be done with its intimidation tactics. Slowly, it turns and starts a lumbering march to the edge of the underbrush. The side view is no less impressive. So this is what I heard last night on my way back from the bathroom. I swear to never pee after dark again. And Crabby, poor Crabby, who must worry about falling prey to this kind of monster each and every night. I vow to protect my property mate at all costs, even if we have just met.

Ronin lurches the UTV back into drive.

"Speaking of mysteries," I say, swatting at mosquitoes that are now buzzing about, "are you going to tell me what we're doing this morning?"

Ronin remains silent for so long, I assume he's not going to answer. But then:

"Remember how I told you all of these islands come with legends of pirate treasure? It's nothing worth taking too seriously."

I nod.

He glances over at me. "I might have been wrong about that."

CHAPTER 11

THE MUDDY ROAD GROWS ROUGHER as the ruts become deeper and deeper. I grip the roll bar tightly as we pound our way along. I now understand why Ronin tied down the gear so tightly. Finally, when my entire body is starting to ache, Ronin rolls to a stop.

I look at him blankly, having no idea where we are, but apparently, it's our destination as he's already climbing out.

I just manage to muffle my moan as my feet hit solid ground. I feel beaten and battered, and we haven't even done anything yet. More mosquitoes appear around my head. I clap my hands long enough to kill two of them, then give up as it requires too much effort.

Now that we're still, I realize the sound of birds has picked back up, as well as feeling a salty breeze across my overheated face. We must be near the ocean. Sure enough, I catch a glimpse of blue between the leaves of some truly impressive trees with massive, silvery smooth trunks that twist into gnarled branches that soar up even higher. They remind me of the manta rays, both majestic and ancient. I stare in rapt fascination. If only trees could talk, the stories I bet these ones have to tell...

More seabirds swoop across the sky. They have large, white bodies with sooty brown wings and appear to travel in packs. Or flocks, I suppose. There's certainly way more of them than us, and I'm happy to remain tucked in the relative safety of tree cover.

"Where are we?"

"They call it Rory's Beach, named after an early explorer's favorite cocker spaniel."

I turn to Ronin, who's releasing the bungees holding down our gear. "By 'they' you mean?"

"Europeans." The way he says it, white men is implied.

"Why name a beach after a dog?"

"Why name anything something it isn't?" Ronin shrugs, pulls out the cooler. "The Polynesians already sailed these waters and knew these islands. They referred to them by their nature— Hāhālua Bay for the mantas that lived in the water, or Puakenikeni Beach for the flowering bushes along the shore. For the Europeans, discovery wasn't about observing the world but claiming it as their own."

"Or on behalf of their canine companions, apparently." I understand what he's saying, though. "Isn't there a movement to return places to their tribal names in recognition of their history? And not just in Hawaii, but on the mainland as well."

"Yes. It's possible MacManus will consider such options here. Though he is under no obligation. Pomaikai has always been privately owned. It has a unique status as an unorganized incorporated possession of the US. Technically, it's not part of Hawaii but falls directly under federal jurisdiction."

I stare at him. "I've never heard of such a thing."

"Because there is no equivalent. Pomaikai is Pomaikai."

"A territory that reports directly to the feds? How does that even work? I mean, if you're working on the environmental impact statement of the proposed development project for the state of Hawaii, and Pomaikai isn't part of Hawaii…"

"We work closely with the US Department of the Interior. It would be unusual for them to ignore our findings."

I catch the nuance. Unusual, not impossible. Meaning a man of MacManus's wealth, status, and power…I regard Ronin, but once again his features are impossible to read.

He's a very smart man, I'm beginning to realize. And definitely the strong and silent type, but maybe for good reason. There are a lot of dynamics at play here. I wonder what Aolani's opinions are on the subject.

"So, umm, pirates?" I ask finally, grabbing the cooler and heaving its strap over my shoulder.

He unsheathes his machete. "This way," he says.

Without any other choice, I follow him into the underbrush.

WE REMAIN IN sight of the beach, but tucked behind the enormous trees with their towering branches and umbrella of waxy green leaves. There's already the imprint of a crushed trail through the carpet of ferns and grasses. It's still slow going, Ronin weighed down with a giant backpack as well as two more black equipment bags, me banging my legs against the cumbersome cooler. Ronin uses his machete not to attack the undergrowth but to bend fronds out of the way before taking the next step. It makes me wonder what lives in the dense vegetation, but I'm too busy trying to maintain my balance to give it much thought.

"How far are we from base camp?" I call out, catching my toe on a fallen branch and just managing to halt my stumble.

"Half a mile."

"You're mapping that far away?"

"I'm inspecting the entire island. I started at the beaches and have been working my way in."

"Because beaches are where ancient people would have first landed." I feel compelled to show off my smarts.

"Yes. But nature is in a constant state of change. What is beach now versus jungle before is a steadily evolving line. Big storms can rip out trees, expanding the beach, just as enormous waves can carve out the sand, narrowing the border."

"So how do you know what you're looking for? Especially..." It's green all around me. And not just green, but Green, as if the undergrowth itself is a monster crab, jealously staking out territory. I have a vision of collapsing where I stand and my entire body disappearing by nightfall, completely absorbed by the plant life around me. Maybe I don't want the trees to talk. They're predators in their own way, or at least opportunistic.

"Experience," Ronin states now.

He has me there.

"What are these giant trees, 'cause they're certainly not palms."

"Pisonia trees. They're the preferred nesting habitat for red-footed boobies, frigates, and noddies. This atoll is a seabird paradise."

"I'm guessing that's a good thing?"

Ronin glances over his shoulder. "Very much. But also the major challenge for developing this island. Most tropical resorts promote ocean views. In this case, that would mean cutting down a significant portion of these trees. It would not only make the beach more susceptible to erosion but it would also vastly reduce the bird population."

I peer to my left, where I can still see dozens of seabirds cartwheeling through the sky in a noisy, jubilant display.

"Maybe not so bad from a tourist perspective," I venture. "The birds are a little...loud...by most standards."

"Hitchcock movie loud?"

"Exactly!" I'm pleased he understands.

But then: "It's not that simple. We've always known that nature is interconnected. Previously, however, scientists still specialized along horizontal lines—ocean life, land habitat, or avian populations. Now we understand there is a strong vertical relationship. These Pisonia trees on land offer nesting grounds to the birds in the sky, which, in turn, nourish the fish and coral in the sea."

"Nourish?"

"Guano."

"Oh!" I can finish connecting those dots on my own. "So cut down the trees, reduce the number of birds, which lowers the amount of bird...guano...leading to the fish and coral suffering, which, of course, diminishes the draw for the other resort activities such as snorkeling, fishing, boating, whatever."

"Exactly."

"This is complicated."

"Exactly." Ronin might be impressed with my smarts after all.

When he finally halts, it's so sudden I almost run into him. He stands perfectly still, face forward, machete held down by his leg. I try to peer around him, to see what he sees, but I don't get it.

"Shh," he murmurs.

Then I hear it. Like a low moan. *Animal,* I think immediately, the hackles rising on the back of my neck.

"What is th—"

"Shhh. We are close."

As in haunted cemetery close? Or get pounced on by a wild animal close? Because any kind of close associated with this sound isn't a good thing.

Then, just as abruptly, the moaning dies down. I stare at Ronin wide-eyed.

"Is that the wind?" I ask softly.

"Maybe."

I shake my head at him. I'm sweating through the clothes I've already soaked through in a state of near panic, and he looks absurdly calm and collected. I don't care how good-looking he is, I want to throttle him on principle.

"I require better than maybe."

"Then you shouldn't have come to a remote atoll." His words are so matter-of-fact, I want to kill him a second time. Mostly because he's right. I hate that trait in other people.

"Where...What do we do?"

He points his machete forward and slightly to the right. "That way. Not much farther. We'll take a water break, then get to work."

Doing what, I want to ask, but am interrupted by a new sound. The flutter of wings and a nasally *cah, cah, cah*. I instinctively raise my arm to ward off the newest intruder, only to discover a little white bird with a gracefully formed head and sleek black bill darting above us. It swoops around; then a second joins it. They dance in midair, flapping their wings and repeating their shrill calls. Then, as quickly as they appeared, they dash away again in a blur of dappled light, and I'm left dazzled by their splendor.

"What was that?" I ask breathlessly.

"Manu-o-Kū. Common white terns; they are a small seabird."

"There was nothing common about that."

"Some call them fairy or angel terns. They also like these trees. They are unique, however, in that they don't build a nest but lay their single egg directly onto a branch. These two must have a chick nearby and are checking us out. Look."

Ronin points higher up, where I make out one of the lovely birds peering down at us from between thick leaves. It cocks its head from side to side, then launches once more, swooping down and around our heads, wings spread exactly like a visiting angel's.

Far from being intimidated, I wish this could go on forever. If the coconut crab was every nightmare I've ever had, then the white terns are every happy dream. And I don't dream very happy anymore. Not since Paul. Or Mattapan. Or Wyoming.

I wonder how the Beautiful Butcher sleeps at night. Is her slumber interrupted by her rage or her pain? Or does someone like her remain unbothered by it all?

This place is impossibly beautiful and incredibly magical, and suddenly my throat has tightened because I've come here for the darkest of reasons—to rescue a young girl who's most likely been kidnapped and abused.

Is there any such thing as paradise anymore? The fascinating, urban appeal of Mattapan with its vibrant Haitian community, where I held a young man while he bled out. The soaring grandeur of the Wyoming mountains, where I watched my friends get shot, my hands still covered in their blood as I fled for my own life.

I've been doing this work for more than a decade. Searching for the missing everyone else has forgotten. I can't imagine quitting, because if someone like me doesn't keep looking, then who will? But I also wonder how much more I can take.

I want to feel the joy of this place. But mostly I'm overwhelmed with a sense of foreboding.

"Are you and Aolani dating?" I blurt out, desperate for distraction. "You seem like a couple."

He doesn't answer for so long, I think he's going to ignore me. Then: "I don't know."

His words are quiet but raw. I nod. Most of my relationships feel like that, too.

"Why ask me to come with you today? I'm new here. You don't know me."

"Yes."

Once again, his tone is honest. I struggle to understand. "Do you truly think you've found long-lost pirate gold?"

He hesitates. "I have found something. I need to dig to understand what. And I need help with that."

"So you brought me along. You don't trust your other campmates?"

"It is imperative such a discovery be kept quiet until I know exactly what it is."

"And you think I won't gossip? Again, you don't even know me."

"I know you weren't here before."

"Before what?" Now I'm even more confused.

"Just before. That is good enough."

I don't understand, and he doesn't seem to be in the mood to explain. Once again, I struggle with the dynamics of this strange place. Where everyone is supposed to be open and honest and trust one another, except that Vaughn has already lied to me, and nobody wants to give a clear accounting of what happened to the recently departed Chris. Not to mention Ronin and Aolani's obviously tense exchange this morning, and Charlie popping up from the bushes like some rabid member of the paparazzi. I scrutinize Ronin, his smooth brown skin, sculpted cheekbones, exotic eyes, willing him to give something—anything—away. But he remains perfectly composed, a man who, even after trekking through an infernally hot and humid jungle, has barely a drop of sweat on his face.

"How did Chris sprain her ankle?" I finally ask.

"I heard she tripped down the stairs."

"Really? Because I was told she stepped into a crab's den."

"Does it matter?"

"I don't know. Does it?"

He smiles faintly. "We should get moving. We're almost there."

"That's not an answer."

"Welcome to Pomaikai. Nothing here is as simple as it first appears."

"And the crew?"

"There is nothing simple about us, either. Just—" He hesitates as if about to say something more. "Trudy and Ann are good souls. You will enjoy working in the kitchen with them."

I have an uncomfortable feeling that this is Ronin's way of saying beware of everyone else. But before I can press further, he resumes his trek forward through the jungle.

I have no choice but to follow, beads of sweat streaking down my overheated face even as I shiver from a new and unexpected chill.

CHAPTER 12

"WHAT DO YOU SEE?"

We've finally arrived at our destination, a gentle rise about five feet above the beach with a massive Pisonia to one side and all sorts of vegetation everywhere else. Spying us this close to the water, the seabirds are going nuts. Dozens and dozens, swooping and calling, with many gliding closer and closer to study us with their dark, beady eyes. If the delicate white terns were magical beings, these large, sooty birds are the goon squad, wanting to know what the hell we're doing on their turf.

I edge back beneath the protective canopy of the tree.

Ronin remains waiting patiently for my answer. We've each downed a bottle of water and inhaled the first of our sandwiches. While I reveled in the salty sweet comfort of a perfectly prepared PB&J, Ronin had started unpacking his bags. I recognize an impressive camera with a multitude of lenses, something much smaller and sleeker that appears to be a recording device, and then tools, lots of tools. Compact shovel, collapsible pail, smaller scoops, brushes, screen mesh, all wedged into a modest-sized equipment bag that apparently holds four times its actual volume in supplies.

Ronin's movements are quick and efficient.

I want a nap. Or a dip in the ocean, or a nice swimming hole. Aren't tropical islands required by law to have a gorgeous, turquoise-colored swimming hole, fed by an equally gorgeous cascading waterfall?

Clearly, the heat and humidity have made me delirious.

"You are overheating," Ronin states.

"No shit." I'm too tired to care about the swear jar.

"Your face is red. You should take a cloth, wet it with cold water, and place it on the back of your neck."

I stare at him. For a terrible moment, I'm not here, but in a valley with a glacier-fed stream where a red giant is patiently showing me how to filter drinking water and soak a bandana to tie around my neck.

I scramble to my feet, furiously batting the memory away. "I'm fine. Just needed a sec. So, what's going on here?"

"What do you see?" Ronin repeats patiently.

"Green. Like I've seen all morning. Everything is green. Lots and lots of green."

"You see a color. What about shapes?"

Belatedly, I remember his earlier lecture. Study the landscape for straight lines, square angles, balanced objects. Nature doesn't do symmetry. People do.

I take a deep breath, peer around me. Then I swallow my pride long enough to place one of the half-frozen water bottles on the back of my neck, sigh in relief, inspect some more.

The landscape around me is hardly flat. The Pisonia tree to my right has a thick, twisted root system that undulates beneath our feet, while the ground drops off sharply ahead and a cluster of tangled debris stretches out to our left.

The debris...At first glance it's helter-skelter, except then it's not. The shape beneath the pile of detritus is too perfectly formed. An elongated mound of rocks with no good reason for being there.

I point my finger. "That. The size and shape, it's not haphazard enough."

He nods soberly.

"You think it's a pirate's grave?" I'm perplexed. "Couldn't it be anyone? You said this island has served as a way station for centuries."

"In traditional Polynesian burials, bodies are placed in the fetal position. The prone position is distinctly Western, as is the stone mound."

"Still a big leap from European sailor to nefarious pirate."

"Agreed. What else do you see?"

I purse my lips and do my best to remember the pirate legend. Something about a V-shaped tree and eagle-shaped rock. Spinning in a slow circle, I get nothing. My turn to stare at Ronin.

He takes a few steps toward the Pisonia, tapping lightly with his machete at a dark circular mark lower on the trunk. Upon closer inspection, it's clearly an old wound, say from where a large upward-reaching branch broke off.

Begrudgingly, I grant his point. "If that limb were still there, the tree would be V-shaped. But plenty of the trees on this island fit that description."

"I would prefer X marks the spot," Ronin agrees. "Trees and habitat change, especially two hundred years later."

"I don't see an eagle-shaped rock."

"That takes a bit more imagination." He moves again, gesturing for me to join him.

When I peer at the rock mound from this angle, I still get nothing. Ronin waves his machete around the general outline of the shape.

"Perhaps an eagle in repose," he suggests.

I arch a brow. "Now which one of us has heat stroke?"

He smiles. "Which is why we are here this morning. Conjecture is a waste of time. Plus, Mr. MacManus is not a fan."

"Pisses him off? Hey, does that count for the swear jar?"

"You're going to be poor by the time we return."

"Do you ever have to toss in a nickel?"

This earns me an enigmatic grin. It's a good look for him.

"We are going to take a peek," he states now. "Pick a spot, remove the debris, then carefully excavate enough rocks to reveal what may or may not lie beneath."

I'm not sure what I think of this. Unearthing pirate treasure sounds like fun. Human remains, not so much so.

"I don't have any experience in grave robbing," I hedge.

"The work is simple. Photograph extensively. Remove first layer of cover. Photograph again, then additional excavation, then additional documentation. When we arrive at the final layer, I'll take over."

I hesitate, still feeling uncertain.

"Have you never seen a dead body before?" Ronin asks gently. "Skeletal remains are nothing to fear. We respect our dead. Everything we do now is with the utmost dignity and respect."

I don't have the heart to tell him I've seen too many corpses. And forget skeletons; it was the mummies that nearly broke me.

He continues to peer at me calmly. God, that face...How does anyone tell this man no?

Ronin tosses me a pair of gloves, and we get to work.

———————

IT'S NOT SO hard. Easy, really, in ways I don't want to think about. Ronin sets up his small GoPro to record away, then unpacks his camera to shoot rapid-fire photos of the site from every conceivable angle. Next up, we untangle the top layer of branches and dead leaves. The first section of the rock mound emerges almost immediately, a rounded pile of dark stone and green vegetation. The rocks are small, roughly the size of my hand. They appear similar to the rubble I've already noticed on sections of the beach, including a pebbly finger of the atoll that juts out fifty yards ahead of us.

More documentation. Some muttering under Ronin's breath as he pauses to dash off a few quick notes and draft a couple of pencil sketches. Then back to modern photography.

I work on my breathing, reminding myself that I'm on a tropical island and these are ancient remains and nothing like what I have experienced before. Historic, not contemporary.

This is not that. I repeat it to myself again and again. *This is not that.*

The beautiful terns appear from time to time, darting overhead. The larger seabirds, however, have grown immune to our presence and drift farther out over the ocean. Periodically, some sort of bird drama seems to erupt, with a flurry of wings and a spike in volume. But mostly the birds do their thing while we do ours.

Then we've completely cleared the debris from the rock pile. The moment of truth.

Ronin stops long enough to show me how to work the camera. Just point and shoot, he instructs. The camera feels heavy, my hands shaking more than I'd like.

"This is not that," I mutter to myself, though I'm having a hard time believing my own words. It's the nature of trauma. Once you've experienced the worst-case scenario, you can never go back to believing bad things won't happen. You can only remind yourself that you were strong enough to survive the first time, and you'll be strong enough to survive again.

Ronin picks a spot near the top of the mound, where the pile of rocks already appears disturbed. Various clumps of vegetation sprout from between the dark stones. While originally the grave had appeared overgrown by the jungle, our work has already separated it from its surroundings.

That spikes my unease higher. Surely a two-hundred-year-old pirate tomb should be more consumed by its surroundings by now, at one with the riotous plant life, pounding waves, and crying birds instead of resting perfectly above ground with barely a stone out of place.

"This is not that," I whisper, even as my body breaks out in a fresh layer of sweat.

Using one of his smaller trowels, Ronin removes a half dozen clumps of greenery, exposing a small section of stones near the top end of the pile. He pauses. I hear him utter a low murmur of lyrical words, something between a song and prayer. A tribute to the deceased, an apology for our trespass? I have no idea. Then Ronin delicately lifts the first rock, laying it on a protective tarp. Followed by the next and the next.

I can feel my anxiety thrumming through my entire body now. I focus harder on the work at hand. Inhale, snap a photo. Exhale, snap a photo. I will not grow hysterical. I will not become a victim of the past.

This is not that.

Ronin removes a final few stones. He sucks in his breath.

A glimmer of light, like the bones are shiny. Then, as Ronin slowly clears a larger hole, an explosion of sparkling red dots where no sparkling red dots should be.

He glances at me immediately, his expression apologetic.

He doesn't say anything. I don't need him to.

And I don't make any comments of my own, because if I open my mouth, I'm going to start screaming, and once I start I doubt I'll be able to stop.

I lift the camera. I point it at our macabre discovery. I snap away.

Then I close my eyes and offer my own prayer for this poor young woman who once upon a time came to a tropical paradise and never made it home again.

"WE SHOULDN'T DISTURB anything else," Ronin says, slowly straightening.

"Okay."

"I have another tarp. We'll cover everything, return to camp. Vaughn will have to contact Honolulu for assistance."

"Okay."

I can't seem to move or look away. Through the small opening is the perfectly shaped lower portion of a human skull, attached to a skeletal neck and pillowed against long, dark hair. The jawbone is no longer bright white but a dark, mottled gray. A sign the remains have been interred for a while? But then there's the matter of the sparkling red dots, the sun reflecting off a cluster of red sequins forming a flower dotting the exposed top. If the skeleton is old, her outfit appears shockingly new, as if she just threw it on for a night of dinner and dancing.

These are definitely not the remains of a European explorer or Polynesian sailor or peg-legged pirate. And they're definitely not historic, based on the sequins alone.

"Frankie," Ronin says quietly. He's staring at me with concern.

Which is when I finally notice my knuckles have turned white on the camera.

Ronin steps forward, gently removing the Nikon from my grasp.

"We should go back to our vehicle. You can sit there. I'll take care of the rest."

"I'll be okay."

"It's only natural to be upset. This isn't what I expected."

I wrap my arms tight around my waist, scouring the woods with my gaze. I'm looking for a glint of light, I realize. A rifle scope. Because that's what comes next. The crack of a rifle. A spray of blood.

"This is not that," I state out loud, fighting against the pull of the past.

"What isn't that?"

"This. This is not that."

Gnarled Pisonia tree. White angel tern. Green ferns. Dark rocks. Red flowered top. I dig my nails into my side to stop the spiraling.

"This is not that," Ronin repeats soothingly. "Whatever that was, this is not that."

"That was worse."

"Okay."

"So many bodies. And I've never been any good with blood." I stare at my hands because I can still see the red staining my finger-tips. I'll always be able to see it. Did this woman have blood on her hands? Did she fight back? Or did she succumb to the exhaustion that follows endless terror?

I can relate. I nearly did so myself.

Then I'm moving. I shouldn't. I know I shouldn't. But I need to get the stones off of her. I need to see her. To tell her I understand, that it's okay now. Even when it hurts, I promise to remember her. I promise to bring her home again.

"Frankie, stop it. Frankie!"

Ronin grabs both of my arms, trying to pull me away from the grave. I fight back.

"She shouldn't be here. Abandoned. Alone. Why do they do that? All those terrible people. They see something beautiful and they crush it."

"I know." His tone is soothing.

"You don't! She is someone's daughter, sister, mother. She didn't deserve—"

"We don't even know that the remains are female."

"Of course they are. They always are!"

I twist out of his grip. Ronin snaps his hand around my wrist, rooting me in place.

"Frankie." He stares at me intently, lets the moment suspend. I'm breathing hard. He is, too. "You are correct," he states softly. "Whatever this is, whatever we've found, it shouldn't have happened."

The rage drains out of me. I find the emptiness worse.

"We can't help her. We need to contact the police. Which means returning to base camp. But first, we must secure what we've found, in order to aid their investigation."

"Do you know her? Recognize the flowery top?"

"No."

"He brought her from elsewhere."

"First rule of science, Frankie." Ronin lets go of my wrist, eases back. "Stick to facts. We don't know who this is, or what happened, or even when it happened."

"This isn't a historic artifact."

"Given the sequins, most likely not."

I remain ragged. And then. And then...

"Fine. Let's do this." I step back and take a final deep, steadying breath. There is only one way forward, and that is through. I prepare to once more get to work.

CHAPTER 13

WE RETURN TO BASE CAMP in total silence. Ronin focuses on driving, while I let my mind drift over everything and nothing at all. The sky has darkened, the wind picking up and starting to toss around the tops of the palm trees. Vaughn had mentioned an incoming storm. Based on the clouds alone, it doesn't seem to be waiting till this afternoon. When we pass close enough to open water, I can see a dark line out over the ocean. A wall of rain, I realize, heading straight for us. Do tropical storms include thunder and lightning? Because speaking of PTSD triggers I've carried with me since Wyoming...

I try to organize my thinking. The body, a female in a red sequined, flowered top. Is it possible that it's Lea and I've already found her? Except the note she may have written her sister arrived just recently. Also, Vaughn clearly knew Lea and was expecting her to appear on Pomaikai in a matter of hours. That seemed to imply she was still in the land of the living.

So, an earlier MacManus victim? If the guy was a predator,

nothing like using his own private atoll as a burial ground. Then again, the minute he decided to develop it, he also knew the entire island would be subject to intense scrutiny. Surely he didn't expect something as basic as a grave to go unnoticed by a trained archaeologist. The location wasn't even hidden, being within eyesight of the beach.

Of all the traits I've heard to describe MacManus, stupid isn't one of them.

Meaning a previous human trafficker? I never asked who owned the island before him, which brings up Vaughn's mention of the recovered drug-smuggling sub. An island this remote could be a logical layover for all sorts of evildoing. The current base camp and forward crew are recent developments, given MacManus's plans for the atoll. And perhaps a terrible inconvenience for other, less luxury-resort-minded folks?

Forget outraged environmentalists, drug dealers really didn't take kindly to loss of habitat.

Now I have too many angles to consider, as well as too many terrors to contemplate. For better or worse, most of the missing persons cases I investigate turn out to be domestic matters. The number of times I've known within five minutes that the vanished young wife or disappeared small child never left the surrounding area. Meaning my job is really just a matter of asking the right questions while listening for the wrong answers.

The things people do to the ones they love are tragic enough. Contemplating criminal enterprises, including sophisticated drug-running or human trafficking operations...

Ronin was right. We need the police. Especially as I'm getting the distinct impression that this discovery is not the only disconcerting thing to happen on this atoll.

A fresh gust of wind brings the first spray of rain.

Ronin parks behind the rec building just as the skies open up. For a moment, we both sit there, staring at the wall of water cascading down in silver sheets. Then, without saying a word, we climb out of the UTV and trudge through the deluge to Vaughn's office.

I LET RONIN do the talking, taking up a position near the back wall with my arms wrapped around my torso for warmth. The air-conditioning that had been so refreshing yesterday now feels positively chilling. I could blame it on the fact I'm soaking wet, but it's also just that kind of morning.

To give Vaughn credit, once Ronin starts talking, the project manager doesn't interrupt. His expression, which had started out with its usual annoyed scowl, has now settled into a look of one hundred percent intensity. He doesn't argue with the basics, and he doesn't disagree with Ronin's conclusion.

"According to NAGPRA," Vaughn states when Ronin finally winds down, "the discovery of any human remains less than fifty years old must be reported to law enforcement. Your expert opinion is that this grave falls within that time frame?"

"The clothing is of modern origin," Ronin states.

"All right, I'll contact Oahu on the sat phone. Our issue is going to be when the feds can get here."

"How so?" I finally speak up.

Vaughn flickers a look in my direction. He frowns at my shivering form, then stands up, grabs a gray sweatshirt off a hook, and tosses it to me. "You're freezing."

I don't say anything. It's not a question. But I accept his offering, slipping the oversize garment over my head. It feels soft against my icy skin and smells faintly of saltwater and sunscreen.

Vaughn continues to study me. I stare back. Does he expect me to break down in tears or erupt into screams? I reserve the right to do both, though now that the initial shock has passed, I've moved beyond my graveside meltdown—which Ronin graciously glossed over.

The archaeologist offers me a bolstering smile. Nothing like exhuming a skeleton to bond two crazy kids.

"This storm," Vaughn says at last. He looks from Ronin to me and back to Ronin again, clearly catching the fresh vibe. His eyes narrow, contemplating. "It's supposed to last at least twenty-four hours."

Ronin grimaces, understanding implications I don't.

"It'll be a bit," Vaughn fills in, "before any planes can attempt the flight."

"MacManus. Wasn't he supposed to arrive today?"

"Not anymore. If the wind and rain weren't challenging enough, the cloud cover is too low. No visibility to make the landing."

"Do you still want me to set up his lodging this afternoon?" I ask.

"No rush. You can take the afternoon off if you'd like. If you need," he adds belatedly.

"What do we tell the others?" Ronin speaks up.

Vaughn purses his lips, frowns. "I'd prefer to say nothing. 'Course, that never works."

"I won't talk," I counter immediately, my voice harsher than intended. "I know how to be discreet."

Vaughn holds up two hands in a placating manner. "Not doubting your or Ronin's character. Just the nature of camp life. We're a captive audience with vast amounts of downtime. Someone will figure out something, and then the whispering will start, and then it's all over. Better to be open and honest."

I shake my head. I don't know why. I'm protective of our find, that poor woman. For her fate to become a salacious tale swapped around the mess hall feels wrong to me. And yet, I get Vaughn's point.

"I'll make an announcement over dinner. Keep it simple. You discovered human remains that may fall within the fifty-year threshold. Bringing in the feds just to be safe. Our job is to hold tight and let the agents do their job. Which brings me to the next salient issue—anyone else know specifically where you were working today?"

Ronin hesitates. "AO," he confesses at last.

Vaughn gives the archaeologist a look. Clearly I'm not the only one who's noticed the air of intimacy between the two.

"We're strictly professional," Ronin protests.

Now Vaughn rolls his eyes. "You're two grown adults. How you plan on navigating this...situation...is on you to figure out; just know I wield a positively nasty I-told-you-so."

"No one should visit the scene," I interject. "It's important to preserve it as much as possible for the investigators."

Vaughn doesn't question my authoritative stance on police procedure, merely looks outside at the deluge and sighs heavily. He's not wrong. Covering the grave with a tarp was a good idea, but given the ferocity of this storm, and that we'd already dramatically disturbed the site...law enforcement is not going to be happy with us. Of course, that's my general experience with them.

We all fall quiet for a bit, digesting this latest implication.

"How are you doing?" Vaughn addresses Ronin first.

"I'll be okay. I'm used to discovering skeletons, though this is more recent than most." Ronin nods in my direction. "I'm sorry I dragged her into it, however."

"Not my first experience, either," I murmur softly.

"More information conspicuously absent from your background interview?" Vaughn drawls.

"What can I tell you? Nowhere isn't always a peaceful place."

He rolls his eyes, but rather than push the point, he sticks to the matter at hand. "What do you think of today's discovery?"

"I think our skeleton is probably female, and hopefully in some missing persons database, but I don't know." I hesitate. "And just for consideration, if someone had the means and forethought to dispose of a body on a remote island, how do we know it was only one? I mean, how much of this atoll has been inspected by now?" I glance over at Ronin, who appears positively aghast.

"Not nearly enough. Certainly..." Ronin's voice sputters out. He looks askance at Vaughn, who appears equally startled.

The project manager exhales slowly, rakes a hand through his dark hair. He gestures to what appears to be a cross between a heavy-duty cordless phone and a two-way radio sitting on the corner of his desk. "Well, on that happy note...Look, all of this is a matter for professionals. I'll reach out to Oahu. They'll come and do their thing. We'll take it from there, after, of course, consulting with Mac. His atoll, his responsibility."

Or his doing, I fill in drolly in the back of my mind. Vaughn eyes Ronin and me with clear dismissal. We take the hint and head for the door. As we step outside, I think I see a flash of light in the distance. Lightning? But there's no thunder to accompany it.

Flash, I register, as in a camera. Charlie, snapping away from behind the bushes again? Why, and what the fuck? Gracefully swooping manta rays aside, I'm really starting to hate this place.

I'm tired beyond words.

Where to go, what to do? I let my feet make my decision for me.

And I am not surprised by where I end up next.

CHAPTER 14

Trudy and Ann appear almost exactly as I left them, bustling around the kitchen. This time, instead of making breakfast, they're cleaning up after lunch. I enter through the back door, take a second to wipe the worst of the rain from my face, then plop down the half-filled cooler. Trudy and Ann both stop mid-motion and gawk shamelessly.

"You need a raincoat."

"Or at least an umbrella."

"Nice sweatshirt, though."

"Ann, haven't we seen that before?"

"Why, yes, Trudy, I do believe—"

I raise a hand in surrender. "Vaughn lent me the sweatshirt. Ronin and I got caught in the downpour on the way to his office. Air-conditioning plus soaked clothes, not a great mix."

"Did Ronin also get a sweatshirt?" Trudy asks politely.

Ann giggles.

I honestly can't decide if I want to throttle them or throw

myself into their arms. Except hugging might make me cry, and this day is hard enough. And now with the storm. I don't do well in storms anymore. Apparently, my job is a gift that keeps on giving.

Trudy, as usual, cuts to the chase. "Coffee or hot cocoa?"

I blink at her. "I haven't had hot chocolate in years."

"Cup of cocoa it is. I'm not even going to ask about marshmallows. You'll thank me later."

She whirls toward the range while Ann comes forward, holding out a towel. "Dry off before taking another step. Don't want water all over the floor. We weren't joking earlier—weather like this, you're gonna want to wear a poncho and grab an umbrella. Remember the giant one on your front porch? We didn't put it there for show."

I nod, too soaked to argue. At least I'm not shivering anymore. While the air-conditioning in Vaughn's office had been freezing, the rest of the atoll remains its usual eighty-five-degree rainforest self. The intense humidity has merely solidified into water droplets. Yippee.

"Successful morning?" Trudy calls out.

I don't know what to say. I don't want to lie, but it's for Vaughn to deliver the news. I go with, "Any chance there's leftover crepes?"

"Never," Ann states cheerfully. "But don't worry, we'll make them again next time we get a shipment of fresh bananas. How was the PB&J?"

"Like childhood all over again."

"Ronin approve of your hummus wrap?" Trudy wants to know.

I shrug, unpacking the cooler, including the two extra sandwiches we never got around to eating, post–grave exhumation.

"He's very polite," Ann hums in approval.

"And handsome," Trudy adds.

"Just ask Aolani," Ann whispers, poking me in the ribs with a wicked smile. Vaughn's right; there are no secrets on this island.

"Doesn't mean a girl can't enjoy the sights," Trudy says knowingly. "I recommend a sunrise walk along Eaton's Beach, where a certain someone starts his morning with tai chi. Or maybe it's tae kwon do. It's shirtless, which is the relevant point."

"So that's why you've been getting up so early!" Ann gawks at her friend.

Trudy grins, snaps off the range, and grabs a white mug from the rack above. I deliver the leftovers to the fridge, then stack the untouched water bottles back into the freezer. Used containers in the sink, cooler positioned next to the utility sink for rinsing, and then Trudy is standing in front of me with a steaming mug of hot chocolate.

I feel like a wet dog, yet just the smell of the cocoa, the waft of sugar from the melting marshmallows, and I'm seven years old again. It's not my mother who's standing at the stove, as she's off working yet another job to keep a roof over our heads, but my father, in a rare moment of sobriety. His hands are shaking, as they do when he's drying out. But he's stirring the saucepan and prattling away about something. The history of cocoa, the first time he ate chocolate, his own mom's recipe for perfect no-bake fudge cookies, whatever.

My father loved to tell stories. And he was one of those great animated narrators. His hands would fly, his body shift and contort, his voice boom, then soften, then boom again. I would lean forward in anticipation of some great reveal, then gasp and whip back, only to lean forward again.

I remember the smell of the cocoa. The warm feel of the kitchen. But mostly, the dazzling wonder that was my father when he wasn't drowned in a bottle of Jack. His sobriety never lasted.

I don't have memory of a time I expected anything different. But unlike my mother, who went through life with a pinched look of disappointment and general air of exhaustion, I accepted each moment as it came. This rare afternoon with my father, his shaking hands scalding the milk but then compensating with a pinch of cinnamon and cayenne as that's how cocoa was meant to be served. And me positively wide-eyed as I took the first sip, loving the sweet, totally shocked by the spicy.

My father roaring with laughter at the look on my face. Attempting his own taste, except his trembling hands spilled his drink, but no matter, I bounced up and grabbed the paper towels just in time to see him pull a small bottle out of his pocket, pour the contents into his mug.

I didn't say a word as, even then, I understood there was nothing to say. I just waited a few years; then I joined him in drunken oblivion. After that, we took turns disappointing my mother.

Till one day they were dead.

My parents were my first lesson that you can genuinely love someone and still not do right by them. While my own downward spiral into alcoholism became my first education in that knowing better doesn't mean you'll behave better.

I've never looked back on my childhood and wished my father were sober; it's beyond my comprehension. I do wish, however, that I had been. That I could've been a source of pride to my mother, who worked so hard. That I could've been a source of inspiration for my father, who was a good man, just weak. At a certain point, I realized they truly loved me the best they could. But they died before I knew if they realized the same about me— that I loved them, too. Drunk, sober. Happy, sad.

They were mine, and I've never figured out how to hold their memory close or let them go. I just keep moving, a rolling stone.

Ann pats my shoulder. I'm holding the mug with tears in my eyes. I catch myself, force a smile.

"It's okay," Trudy says kindly. "Chocolate has the same effect on me."

"Take your time," Ann assures me. "Rain like this slows everything down."

I nod, manage the first sip, almost cry again at the taste. "Cinnamon and cayenne."

"Only way to make it," Trudy assures me.

"Maybe you'd like a nap," Ann offers.

But I shake my head. Downtime has never been good for me, especially when I'm in this kind of mood. Keeping busy is a far better approach. I take a deep breath, exhale, enjoy a few more sips of cocoa.

Then I peer at my friends from over the rim of my mug. "Can you show me the way to the owner's lodge?"

CHAPTER 15

TRUDY DOES THE HONORS OF fetching us a UTV; in this weather we're going to need it. That affords me the opportunity to dash back to my cabin for my raincoat and umbrella. I also hang up Vaughn's sweatshirt to dry, leaving my arachnid roommate with instructions not to touch it. Wolfie doesn't bother with a reply, not being one for daylight.

I'm learning to love my new plastic/rubber/resin—whatever the hell they're made of—Crocs. Splashing through mud, pounding through wet grass, everything rinses right off. And no blisters, which, given the endless wet, is an accomplishment.

When I return to the rear of the mess hall, Ann is armed with a mop and bucket of cleaning supplies. She lists off the contents, then hands them over.

"Clean sheets and towels are in the closet at the lodge. May have to run them through a quick refresh cycle in the dryer, however. The damp makes everything smell musty."

"MacManus has his own laundry room?"

"And kitchen and bathroom. Money has its privileges."

"So does ownership," Trudy calls out, arriving in our glorified golf cart and gesturing for me to climb aboard. Apparently, Ann is staying behind. I pull my hood over my head, then dash out, cleaning supplies in hand.

The rain hasn't relented at all. If anything, it might be coming down harder. The noise of it, thundering against the building, the trees, the ocean, is enough to make me miss the birds.

Trudy hits the accelerator, and the vehicle leaps forward aggressively. She peels out, roaring down the crushed-coral path as water sprays and hermit crabs scamper. I grab the roll bar.

"Do I want to know where you learned how to drive?" I ask.

"Boston."

"Never mind."

We race past the dock, where I spy another raincoat-covered soul working on covering the boats. Charlie looks up as we zip by, slapping both hands against the sides of his face in a dramatic display of horror. Trudy flips him off. He roars with laughter, turns back to his tarp.

"Do you have to throw a coin in the swear jar for that?"

"Maybe. Want to know a secret?"

"Sure."

"Poker night."

"Seriously?"

"Yep. Every other Friday. We generally play for can tabs, but sometimes Vaughn will break out rolls of pennies. He seems to know when our pockets are getting low."

"You like him as a project manager?" What I want to ask is do you think he's trustworthy and/or not dangerous, but I'm thinking I should warm up to the serious stuff.

Trudy shrugs, swinging us around a corner. We're still blazing along the water's edge but are now out of sight of the base camp. The path is rough, up and down and all around. Best not to be prone to motion sickness around here.

"He's better than most, strikes a solid balance between leaving us to our own devices while periodically reining us back in. It's not easy managing a bunch of antisocial introverts. If we played well with others, most of us would have real jobs and permanent addresses. Instead, we do this." Trudy slides me a glance.

"Instead, we do this," I agree. I definitely work best on my own. And yet in a project of this scale, there's gotta be some semblance of overarching strategy and teamwork or the ultimate goal wouldn't be achieved.

Trudy finally slows, approaching an outcropping that affords a two-hundred-and-forty-degree ocean view. In other words, the perfect location for deluxe accommodations. "You ever work with Vaughn before?" I continue to press.

"Nah. But Ann and I often overlap. We like several of the same locations and work well together. Once we got on the same six-month contract schedule, easy enough to apply to the same places for the same term."

"What about Charlie? And is it just me, or is he always snapping photos?"

"True that." Trudy laughs. "I don't actually know Charlie that well. Sounds like he's a regular at McMurdo while I'm more a tropical gal myself. Personally, I think he can be an asshole, and yeah, he does seem to be skulking around half the time, but Ann likes him. And he works hard. Matters in these kinds of places. The bigger the challenge, the happier he seems to be. Something to be said for that."

"Do I want to know how big the challenge?"

"Well, at the moment, we still have electricity, plumbing, and a comm tower."

"As opposed to?"

Trudy grins at me. "Storm's still early yet."

Then she roars up over a small rise, and MacManus's private lodge comes into view.

TRUDY DROPS ME off in front of a spectacular front porch. She promises to check on me in an hour; then she's off in a spray of water. The woman definitely likes to drive.

I mount the front steps with supplies in hand, happy to be on my own where I can gawk and inspect without having to explain my curiosity to others.

Needless to say, this "cabin" is a huge step up from my modest abode, a vast rectangular structure closer in size to the mess hall but twenty times nicer. The overhang of the sprawling front porch is supported by polished tree trunks, which gleam like pillars of gold against the rain-swept sea. On a sunny day, the view from here must be insane. Even in the midst of today's gray-walled downpour, there's something mesmerizing about standing within the shelter of the porch while watching the storm-tossed sea.

A deck this large fairly begs for a row of rocking chairs with bright-patterned pillows. I don't see any, but it's possible they're tucked away given the conditions. The front door appears to be solid wood, the inset panels bearing the carved shapes of island flowers and tropical fish. I run a finger along the flowing designs, marveling at the detailing. This door probably costs more than most people's homes. It is both unbelievably gorgeous and incredibly frivolous, given what this level of heat and humidity will do to it in the end.

The door is framed in dark charcoal-painted trim, set against a deep-red exterior, which makes this the only building on the property I've seen that isn't blue or green.

Apparently, MacManus likes to stand out.

I shed my shoes, raincoat, and umbrella, then square my shoulders and prepare to enter. The door immediately puts up a fight before eventually yielding with a groan. Definitely feeling the impact of its tropical living conditions. Is it a testimony to Mac-Manus's arrogance that he chose such a door? I wonder. Or indifference? And which is worse?

Even though all the exterior walls are essentially windows from halfway up, the inside of the lodge remains heavily shadowed, the storm sucking all the light out of the place. I locate three switches next to the door. The first snaps on two vast overhead lights set in the middle of sleek ceiling fans. The second switch gets the fans swirling. The third makes the lower half of the walls glow. I'm so taken aback I stop and gape.

Unlike my cabin with its exposed stud beams, MacManus's house boasts a completely finished interior, including dark-painted baseboards. Above each trim piece runs a bead of lighting, which I just activated. Ingenius, especially at night, when too much light would impede the exterior view, while not enough could lead to stubbed toes.

If the home makes the man, so far MacManus is elitist, arrogant, indifferent, and brilliant. A dangerous combination.

I set the bucket of cleaning supplies inside the door and get my bearings.

I've entered the main living room. Beautiful hardwood floors striped in red and gold tones stretch before me, while the vaulted ceiling is finished in something equally exotic.

The walls are painted a light sage with dark-gray trim. The furniture is overstuffed and covered with a tropical print, flowers swooping across the cushions in shades of green, blue, and coral. That sets the stage for a massive dining room table with seating for eight and, to its left, a U-shaped kitchen featuring white glazed cabinets and charcoal soapstone.

It looks and feels like a designer showroom. Will this be the model for the luxury resort to come? If so, I'm already disappointed. The whole vibe of the base camp, with its stripped-down aesthetics and quirky charm, is lost here. Frankly, this kind of high-end oceanfront retreat could be on any island anywhere in the world.

I already think a wolf spider would give the place some personality. Maybe I can convince Wolfie to move. But not Crabby. He's grown on me, especially now that I know how much he likes flowers.

Behind the main living area, I discover a hallway leading to three bedrooms. On the right is clearly the main bedroom dominated by a king-size bed and a massive, mirror-topped dresser. The attached bath is modest—tiny vanity, stand-up shower, toilet. Luxury compared to what the rest of us have, but no doubt a step down from the mogul's usual haunts. Across from the main bedroom are two smaller rooms sharing an adjoining bath. One of the rooms offers an efficient double bed, two nightstands, single dresser arrangement. The second room contains a twin bed, a lone nightstand, and that's it. Room for the help, I expect. Or maybe for Lea?

When she's not being summoned to the master's chamber.

I shudder despite the pervasive heat, then return to the entry-way where I left my mop and bucket.

I'm not sure what to do next. All of the beds are stripped bare, decorative quilts folded at the foot of each mattress. Remembering Ann's comment about musty sheets, I search till I discover a small closet bearing a stacked washer and dryer. Shelves to one side reveal stacks of folded linens. I sniff experimentally. Ann definitely has a point. I pop the first batch into the dryer with some kind of lavender-scented sachet. Now that I appear properly engaged if someone drops in, I tend to my real mission—trying to learn more about MacManus and his alleged ward, Lea.

I start in the main living area, searching for personal items—framed photographs, books, artwork. The side tables next to the couch offer up reading lamps and ceramic coasters, that's it. Ditto with the lounge chairs in the other half of the room. The whole design seems to be about taking advantage of the view outside, not promoting the space inside.

The dining room wall offers up three broad shelves, each a lustrous masterpiece of undulating wood that seems less like it's mounted on the wall than flowing across it. The lower two shelves are topped with a collection of crystal glasses, high-end candles, and a wine decanter. Up high, however, is an item of interest—a roughly twenty-four-by-eighteen-inch work of abstract art. I have to climb on a dining room chair to reach it. With a self-conscious glance over my shoulder to make sure Trudy hasn't returned, I grab the painting by its thin wooden frame and drag it down.

At first glance, it's an evocative study of swirling greens and blues. There's something about the shape in the middle that holds my attention, however.

I blur my gaze, blink it into sharp focus, and then I get it. It's Pomaikai, an artistic rendering of the atoll sitting in the middle of the ocean. Upon closer inspection...I see darker colors shading some of the beaches along the perimeter, as well as subtle feather-ings of orange, yellow, and red lining the green vortex.

The proposed development plans. Has to be. The yellow would be the existing base camp, the cluster of red the lodge I'm cur-rently standing in, which makes the streaks of orange dominating the northern space, farthest from the airstrip, the future resort. It's a substantial imprint, dominating nearly a fourth of the atoll. I remember where Ronin's comment about trees most likely being removed to improve the ocean view and the impact on the island's bird and sea life. The proposed size feels too big to me. I already think Crabby and his friends won't approve. The coconut crabs, on the other hand...Maybe tourists taste like chicken.

I'm struck by another thought—is the envisioned resort footprint near the area where Ronin and I were this morning? I'm not that well versed in the island's geography, but I could ask someone else.

I fish out my cell phone and quickly snap a few quick shots. I also check the time, realizing I need to remember to contact Victo-ria today. Still no Wi-Fi, however, so that'll have to wait.

I carefully replace the painting just as the dryer buzzes. First load of freshly fluffed and lavender-scented bedding out, next load in. I carry the still-warm pile of sheets to the main bedroom, where I toss them in the middle of the mattress, then quickly scour the rest of the space. I discover three photos on top of the dresser. One is of MacManus framed by palm trees and holding a giant pair of nov-elty scissors. Ribbon-cutting ceremony for something, maybe the start of construction on the base camp. Next, a tuxedo-clad ver-sion of him with a beautiful young Hawaiian woman in a hot-pink cocktail dress. I'd recognize those rich brown eyes and sculpted cheekbones anywhere. Lea definitely looks like her older sister, sans the air of growling menace.

MacManus is beaming in this photo, his arm around the girl's waist. Lea appears more subdued. She isn't looking directly at the camera, but off to the side. There's nothing untoward in their stance. If anything, it's a pretty standard welcome-to-the-party snapshot. MacManus could very well be some rich dad escorting his self-conscious teen to a formal function.

I don't like it, however. Has anyone ever questioned how Lea became MacManus's responsibility? Who has wards anymore, anyway? Sounds very *Downton Abbey* for a tech mogul.

The third framed photo is smaller, a gritty black-and-white. Two teenage boys next to a boxy desktop computer, definitely not from this decade or maybe even century. One boy is hunched over the giant keyboard. The other stands behind the monitor, arm resting on its frame as he laughs at something the typing kid is saying/doing. It takes me a moment; then I think I have it. The standing figure is a young version of MacManus, which makes the second male most likely his high school buddy and former business partner, Shawn Eastman. Based on the quality, the picture looks like something that might have appeared in a yearbook.

A reminder of better times? Before their joint venture launched them into the stratosphere of the tech elite? And his partner, Shawn, died under questionable circumstances?

Interesting.

A search of the bathroom turns up basic toiletries and nothing more. The shampoo and conditioner in the shower promise to be environmentally friendly and smell like coconuts. It seems feminine to me, another argument Lea spends more time in this room than the tiny single, but maybe in a place such as this, coconut is a given.

The dryer buzzes again. I realize belatedly that Trudy should be returning at any time and quickly make up beds, wipe down countertops, and dust all flat surfaces. I'm just preparing some eco-friendly solution to mop the hardwood floors when I'm struck by a new thought.

Quick, before Trudy comes roaring through the rain, I know one last place I should explore.

CHAPTER 16

I TAKE PRIDE IN MY SEARCH skills. Especially because, as a cold case expert, I arrive late to the party. Whether it's law enforcement engaging in at least a rudimentary investigation or a worried family member desperate for answers, others have generally scoured the premises first. Not to mention, with the passage of time, more and more traces of the individual have vanished. Or, in some very sad instances, there was never much to begin with, merely a whiff of a memory of someone who once was and now is no more.

Generally, I can still discover at least something and almost always more than the police. Cops have a tendency to think like criminals. Where would they hide evidence of a crime? Some of the better detectives will at least play at being the victim. Where would I stash my personal diary or compromising photo?

Me, I try to think like the person. I'm a five-year-old boy with an entire dilapidated farm as my playground. I'm a fifteen-year-old girl, trying to carve out some sense of identity and privacy while sleeping on the sofa in an overcrowded apartment. I'm an exhausted single mom, struggling to preserve a drop of sanity between working three part-time jobs and raising a two-year-old.

I learn about the person first, then do my best to view the world through their eyes.

Which is why this space is throwing me. For one thing, I don't know Lea. I've heard about her five-year-old self from her older sister and possibly read a single note from her teenage version. Neither is particularly illuminating.

Nor does this lodge feel like a home. For personal effects, I basically have one painting, three photographs, and coconut-smelling shampoo. This might as well be a hotel occupied by tourists.

Which is how I need to approach it: not with my usual customized Frankie flair, but with a cop's instincts. If Lea is being held as MacManus's personal plaything, she's a victim. This isn't her home, then, just a particularly well-decorated prison.

Considering she got out one note to her sister, chances are she's made other, more subtle attempts at communication. She wouldn't trust MacManus's full-time staff, assuming they'd be loyal to him. But this island, populated mostly by contract employees who've never worked for MacManus before and don't necessarily plan on working for him again...

This would be a place to drop breadcrumbs.

I'm jittery now. Clock is ticking. I might be able to pull off an awkward excuse if I'm caught snooping by Trudy, but what if Vaughn appears, or Charlie, or even Aolani? They'd be much more suspicious.

I skedaddle for the tiny bedroom—the one that ostensibly belongs to Lea. Even if she does spend most of her time in the main bedroom, that's MacManus's domain; she wouldn't risk leaving anything behind there.

The single bed is wedged kitty-corner to the window-dotted

outside wall, a single nightstand to its left. Not much to work with for a desperate girl looking to stash secret communiqués, but enough to take me more than a few minutes to properly search.

I start with the freshly made mattress, running my hand beneath it. Then I pull the bed away from the wall and inspect behind it, from the headboard down along the far mattress edge to the base. I marvel again at my new and improved phone, which includes a built-in flashlight, perfect for scouring the shadows. I don't find anything notched, taped, or scrawled behind the bed. Next up, the pillows. One decorative, one meant for actual sleeping. I start at the bottom of each and run both of my hands up the sides, squishing as I go. I feel for any inserted object, like a note, personal token—hell—drugs, weapons, cash. Never make assumptions in my line of work.

There's something in the sham pillow, thin, flexible. Maybe paper? I excitedly rip off the quilted cover and unzip the case. Feathers poof out in an annoying cloud. I have to huff and puff to clear them from my face. I thrust my hand inside, churning around with my fingers, more feathers flying as I reach all the way to the bottom. The side of my hand brushes against something thin and rough. Definitely not a feather. Now if only I can get a grip on it. It slides out from between my fingertips a first time. Then a second. I jam my arm in deeper, eyeing the bedroom door, knowing I'm pushing my luck.

Through the window, I can still see pewter-colored rain sluicing off the roof outside, but that only makes it more likely they'll send someone to pick me up. And it's a little hard to come up with a cleaning technique that requires me gutting a feather pillow. Especially as dozens of the tiny white feathers are now scattered across the bed as well as stuck to my hair.

I finally get a grip on the pliable scrap. Tug at it. It doesn't budge. Pull harder. Watch the entire pillow cover bow inward and realize it's only some kind of internal tag.

Great. I've made a mess for absolutely nothing.

A fresh glance out the window. I register nothing but doom and gloom everywhere.

I quickly do my best to catch wayward feathers and return them to their pillow prison. I'm breathing hard by the time I'm done, and there are still random feathers clinging to the bedding, the wall, and me.

I turn to my final target, hands shaking. Nightstand. Simple wooden unit. I already know both drawers are empty, but now I want to examine the pieces themselves. I pull the top one all the way out, which involves a bit of jiggling given the furniture is swollen with the humidity. I turn it around in my hands, inspecting every side. No taped notes or scrawled messages. I set it on the bed, grab the lower module, and repeat the process. Still nothing.

I allow the second drawer to rest on the twin bed next to its mate, feeling deflated. Was I being too paranoid, seeing riddles and danger where none existed? Maybe Lea really was perfectly happy living a life of luxury as MacManus's ward. Maybe she sent a note to her sister because her serial killer sibling was about to be executed, so, you know, some kind of final communication seemed like a good idea. Is there proper etiquette for handling a homicidal family member being put to death? Does Hallmark make a card for such a thing?

I sigh heavily, realizing I've stressed myself out and destroyed the room for nothing. But now is not the time for regrets; now is the time to quickly reassemble and get the hell out of here.

I grab the lower drawer and get down on my knees, preparing for the arduous task of shimmying it back in. And there it is. In my haste, I'd forgotten one of the more basic hiding spots—taped to the back wall of the unit. Sure enough, a ripped scrap of paper gleams white against the dark interior. I reach a hand in and carefully work the corners till I release it.

I draw it out, holding my breath. It looks similar to the note Twanow had shared with me: handwritten in a childish scrawl, simple in tone.

My sister is Kaylee Pierson of Texas. Please tell her I'm sorry and I love her. Leilani Pierson

That's it.

I sit back on my heels, churning the words through my mind. Not a message begging for help. Nothing that obvious. But a statement haunting in its fatalism. *Tell her I'm sorry and I love her.*

I'd assumed Lea had written to Keahi because of her sister's looming execution date. But maybe I had that wrong. *Tell her I'm sorry and I love her* is the kind of message one delivers when they fear the worst. It's their own time that's up.

Lea, who is growing older and older. Who, in a matter of months, will be considered of legal age.

A terrible kind of aging out in an even more terrible system.

I'm just folding up the note as my mind races through various possibilities, each worse than the last, when all of a sudden...

There's a noise behind me. A sudden exhale of breath.

I don't have to turn around to know I've been caught.

A male voice booms out: "Crikey, what the hell are you doing?"

I KNOW IT'S Charlie before I turn around, given the Aussie accent. My heart is pounding, my palms sweating. I can't figure out how to slip Lea's message in my pocket without drawing attention to it, so I tuck it under my hip, then cover the motion by picking up the drawer and slowly twisting around.

No point in denying I've dismantled the nightstand, so how to excuse my behavior? Charlie is an engineer. What might grab his attention?

It comes to me immediately. "I think I broke it."

"What?" He strides into the room, movements impatient. He's shed the blue raincoat he'd been wearing earlier as well as his shoes. But his shaggy salt-and-pepper hair is still wet, and his worn white T-shirt and ripped cargo shorts are soaked through in blotches. There's no way to stay dry in this kind of weather.

"The nightstand." I hold up the empty drawer awkwardly. "I noticed the drawers had crumbs inside. I removed them so I could dump them out. But now...I can't get the drawers back in."

Charlie squats down beside me, taking the lower drawer from my hands and turning it around in his. He smells of wind and rain, with a top note of WD-40. He's clearly been busy with a million projects before coming to fetch me, his fingernails grease stained and bits of grass stuck to his hairy legs.

He scowls while studying the drawer. Then, his face just inches from my own, he turns and scowls harder at me.

"There's feathers in your hair, Frankie girl."

"There's sand in your beard, Charlie dude."

That distracts him long enough to run one hand through the scraggly gray strands. Sure enough, fine particles rain down.

"Hey, I just cleaned this room! Including under the bed. Do you know all the dust and cobwebs and, and, *feathers* that had accumulated under there? I don't know who's been cleaning this place, but it wasn't Mary Poppins."

Charlie's gray eyes widen; he's taken aback by my tirade. I

send up a silent prayer that it wasn't Trudy or Ann I just threw under the bus. That's the problem with lying—you don't have time to think it through.

"Just saying, you're molting around the edges. No need to have a whinge."

"I don't know what that means."

He shakes his head, more sand and water scattering. I bare my teeth at him, ready to go on the offensive on behalf of the room I hardly cleaned but am now fully committed to protecting.

Charlie gives up on the crazy woman, completing his inspection of the drawer, then lining it into position and with the merest of shimmying, sliding it into place.

"How did you—" I don't have to feign my surprise. The drawers definitely weren't that accommodating for me.

"All in the wrist, luv." He gives me a wink. I do my best not to hit him. But my plan seems to work, as he repeats the process with the top drawer, then rises to standing without another word. "Right-o. Time to get a moving. Storm isn't getting any kinder, and I got more work to do."

I point to the sandy mess that's appeared in his wake. "You. Wait by the front door. I'll clean up the trail after both of us."

"Won't you be needing your cleaning supplies for that?" His tone is guileless, but with just enough edge. I'm not out of the woods yet.

"Hey, I thought I was finishing up my last task, not starting a whole new one. I'm on it."

I make a show of lurching to my feet, grabbing the folded note and sliding it into my pocket as I rise to standing. I hope Charlie didn't notice, but given his narrow gaze, can't be sure.

I follow him to the front door, grab my mop and bucket, and

return to the room. I clean up the mess in earnest, then make a show of wiping away our tracks, working my way back toward Charlie.

"Heard you and Ronin made quite a discovery this morning," he calls out.

I pause, not sure what to say. Clearly, he's fishing for more intel. I go with, "Is that right?"

"First body?" he asks. Yep, the camp grapevine is whirring away.

"No." I realize I basically just mopped a clean stripe across the hardwood floor and make a detour into the sitting area.

"What'dya think? Pirate? Native? Maybe a mermaid?"

"I let Ronin do the thinking; I was merely the photographer. But Vaughn's gonna fill everyone in at dinner."

"Ah, yeah. Bloke loves his announcements. Hold the floor and all that."

I pause in my cleaning long enough to regard Charlie. "Do you like him as a camp manager? I heard you have a lot of experience with these kinds of postings. How does he compare?"

A one-shoulder shrug. "Good enough. Does his work, lets me do mine."

Charlie's assessment sounds a lot like Trudy's. Clearly, remote outposts appeal to people who prefer not to play with others.

"Don't know how he stands this one, though." Charlie points in the general direction of the house. MacManus, I realize. He's talking about MacManus.

"How so?"

"Know what these floors are made of?"

I shake my head.

"Tiger wood. Porch out front—Brazilian mahogany. Know what those two woods have in common?"

Another shake of my head.

"Deforestation. As in, these beauties came straight from some rainforest that no longer exists. And those shelves above that table— Hawaiian koa. So rare it's considered the wood of royalty. That's a lot of board feet that won't be growing back anytime soon."

"In other words, the guy who wants to build an eco-lodge crafted his own residence from endangered trees?"

"There's no understanding the rich. Gronks, each and every one of them. Though they know how to sign a good check." He gestures to my mop, clearly impatient to get going. I take the hint, wrapping up what must be the world's most haphazard janitorial job. I dump the bucket, rinse the mop, collect the rest of the supplies, and then follow Charlie out the front door.

The wind hits me immediately, a powerful gust that nearly knocks me off my feet and showers me in a mix of rain and ocean spray. I spit out sand, understanding what happened to Charlie's beard and is about to happen to my ponytail.

We both turn our backs to the storm while we fight to pull on our raincoats within the relative protection of the front porch. I don't bother with the umbrella. No way it's surviving these kinds of conditions.

"Weather's getting a might tetchy," Charlie comments. I nod in agreement, bucket clutched tight in one hand, the other holding my hood on top of my head as the wind tries to snatch it back.

The UTV is parked at the bottom of the porch steps, as close as it can get. It's still a wet, blustery run as we dash down the stairs. The air, land, and sea have seemingly swirled into one heaving mix that's throwing its entire weight against us. Charlie barely pops into the front seat before his door is slammed shut. I have to scrabble to get a grip on the frame and heave my door open with all of my strength.

"Can we really drive in this?" I shout above the uproar. The storm has definitely strengthened since I've been inside MacManus's lodge.

"Can we, luv? Absolutely. Should we? Now that's another story. Buckle up. It's gonna be a ride."

I grab the roll bar as Charlie punches the gas. For a moment, the UTV simply leans forward, as if thinking about it. Then, it leaps ahead, and we're off and running, already soaked to the bone. It's eighty degrees out, but I can't stop myself from shivering, being this wet again, caught in yet another storm. My mind threatens to ping-pong to other places and scarier times. I feel like I'm hanging on by a thread to keep myself in the here and now.

"This has gotta be a little different from Australia," I attempt to scream above the wind. "Do you miss it?"

"Ahh, now and then perhaps. But I'm not a hometown sort of bloke. Spend too much time in one place and my skin starts to itch."

"I don't have a permanent address myself. But I've hardly covered the miles you have. I've never even been outside the US. Well, unless this counts. Does it? I'm still confused on the subject."

I'm hoping he'll elaborate on the situation, show off his knowledge—always a great way to get people to talk—and unwittingly reveal all his deepest and darkest secrets, including but not limited to his photo-snapping tendencies. But he merely chuckles, taking a sharp turn around a fallen palm, then veering again to avoid a pile of debris. We're tossed left, then right, earning a fresh blast of rain and salt across our faces.

"Is it just me or is this place wet, wet, and wetter?" I try again.

"Ahh, just wait a few weeks till the first patches of white start growing on your skin."

"There's going to be something growing on my skin? Why? What?"

"Fungus. Price to be paid for never drying out. Our packaging is pretty good, luv, but not that good."

"I'm going be covered in fungus?" I don't have to fake the horror in my voice.

Charlie flashes a grin. "No worries. Take a bit o' Selsun Blue, rub it straight on the affected areas. Right as rain after that."

This conversation isn't helping me learn anything new, let alone distract me from the current weather pattern. I tighten my grip on the roll bar, anxiety spiking higher.

"You scared of storms?" Charlie asks me as he carelessly zigzags his way around one giant puddle, then another, then another.

I swear to myself I will not vomit, then admit, "I tried to die in a storm once, so not a fan. You?"

"Oh, I love me a good humdinger. Nothing like nature in its purest form. 'Course, cleanup's gonna be a bitch, but whatya gonna do? Even paradise comes with a price."

Ahead of us, three palm trees are blowing so hard they're nearly sideways. I can't even look.

"Hear you're from nowhere," he calls out.

"Yep."

"East or West Coast kinda nowhere?"

"Lately in the middle."

"What brought you to our slice o' heaven?"

"Never been to paradise before." I grimace against a fresh rooster tail of water spraying alongside my door. "I'm feeling a little misled."

That grin again. "No worries, luv. By tomorrow morning, that sunrise, now. That sunrise'll be a peach."

"Okay." I peer at him harder as we careen along. His accent tickles at me. Somewhere between Australian and British and something else. His own version of international stew, I guess.

"Hear you and Ronin…" He waggles his bushy brows. Leers at me.

"No," I say firmly. "Just…no." I give up on fishing and go with the direct approach: "Hey, didn't you take a photo of us when we were leaving this morning?"

"Now, why would I do a thing like that?"

Which is not the same as no, and once again raises my suspicion. Between Charlie's own attempt at not-so-subtle questioning and his accent, which I swear comes and goes—

A palm tree crashes down immediately to our left. Charlie jerks at the wheel, causing the UTV to slide right, then left, then right again. I squeeze my eyes shut until the tires magically dig in and we lurch forward.

Charlie's grinning wildly, his salt-and-pepper hair a riot of curls whipping around his head. I want to be as gleeful as he is, but I don't have that level of crazy in me.

"Had my own near-death experience," Charlie shouts out.

"Where?" I glance around anxiously.

"McMurdo. Somethin' fell outta the sky. Maybe space debris or a meteorite, or equipment from a weather balloon. Space is chockablock full of this and that and plenty of it crash-lands in the Antarctic. We gotta know just what, of course, junk or no junk, so I get sent to check it out. Have shovel, will travel."

"Aren't you an engineer?"

"I'm whatever I need to be, luv. Nature of the job. Let me tell you, this place, I've been a freakin' electrician for months now. What this level of salt does to wiring. Don't even get me started."

"Okay."

"So, I ride around in my snowcat for what feels like forever. Round and round. Waving at all the penguins—"

"Seriously?" I give him a look.

He flashes me a fresh grin. "Finally find me a hole punched into the ice. Definitely something big crashed down. So I get my shovel and start digging."

"Were the penguins around for this?"

"Always, luv. Best part of Antarctica. Penguins, penguins, and more penguins. Now, I'm a-digging and a-digging and then...I'm flat on my back, unable to move. Pain shooting up my leg so bad, I can fair hear it, screaming through my nerves."

"What did you do?"

"What I had to do, luv. No cavalry gonna reach me before the cold digs into my bones. I crawl inch by inch back to the snowcat. Then I force myself up into the cab, cursing and swearing and shrieking like a lunatic. Have you ever wondered if penguins can blush? Take it from me, luv. Yes, they can."

"Okay, now I know you're pulling my leg."

That hundred-watt smile again. But edgy, too. There's something going on here; I just can't put my finger on it, which leaves me both intrigued and wary. Is Charlie merely a character, which seems a strong possibility, or something else?

"I might be telling a furphy, but then again...My back had locked up. There's a special term for it, comes on from digging trenches. Don't remember much of the return to base, but if I hadn't done it, would've died on the ice instead. As it was, they had to medevac me out of there and all sorts of nonsense. So that's my story. You have yours. I have mine. And we're both still here to tell the tale."

He pulls up outside the mess hall on that triumphant note. I have to shake my head, like a person awaking from a weird dream.

"How long have you been here?" I ask as I climb out.

"Long enough, luv, to know next time you tell a furphy—say about cleaning under a bed—you best clean under the bed."

I open my mouth, but before I can stutter some kind of excuse, Charlie is off again. I stand in the torrential downpour, watching his retreat and wondering what the hell just happened. This day, this afternoon...

I feel Lea's note burning a hole in my pocket. *Tell my sister I love her.*

I don't need the storm to feel terrified anymore.

Because this island isn't paradise. And at this point, I have no idea who to trust, let alone what to do next.

CHAPTER 17

"Have either of you met MacManus's ward?" I ask Trudy and Ann fifteen minutes later as I peel my way through a bag of potatoes.

"Lea? How do you know Lea?" Trudy works on setting up two gigantic pots of water to boil.

"Vaughn mentioned her. Then, cleaning the lodge, I saw her picture. She's beautiful."

"She's gorgeous!" Ann chimes in. "That skin, that hair. Oh, to be young again."

"How old is she?"

"I don't know." Trudy turns to her cooking partner. "What'dya think, Ann?"

"Well, she's obviously not a child, but also not a legal adult. So there you have it. She's teen years old." Ann is very pleased with herself.

"How did MacManus end up with a ward? That seems... old-fashioned."

"Friend of the family," Trudy answers promptly. "Died when Lea was young. MacManus took her in afterward."

"Have you met Lea?"

"Coupla times," Ann provides. "She doesn't always come, only when he stays overnight. And even then, they rarely take their meals with us. He has his own private cook that travels with him, Chef Kiki." Ann's voice pitches up in an ooh-la-la sort of tone, so I know exactly how chichi this cook must be. She drops to her regular tone. "Plus, you've seen his place."

"Those floors," Trudy sighs admiringly.

"Charlie said they came from deforestation. Is it weird that the same person who wants to develop an eco-lodge built the first official residence with non-sustainable materials?"

"We don't judge the house," Trudy advises me. "We just clean it."

"Or send you to clean it!" Ann chortles.

I hesitate, wanting to get back on topic without drawing too much attention. "In the picture, Lea...she looked sad. I don't know. MacManus had his arm around her. But she didn't look very comfortable with that."

Immediately, the atmosphere in the kitchen changes. We're three women, after all. We don't need everything spelled out to know what we're discussing.

"I've never really talked to her," Trudy starts.

"I've never heard her talk," Ann interjects. "She's quiet. Shy, maybe."

"But you never see her without him." Trudy is looking at Ann now.

"And he always stays close," Ann agrees. "Maybe protective, fatherlylike, but maybe..."

They exchange a glance, then turn toward me. "You have a

reason for concern?" Trudy asks me point blank. "This relationship between two people you've never met?"

I peel off a few more strips of potato skins, weighing my next words carefully. Trudy raises an excellent point. How best to proceed? "I roam about. Come from nowhere, remember?"

Both nod.

"Sometimes, living on the fringes, I've encountered certain... situations. Something about the photo, a rich white guy with his arm around a pretty underage Hawaiian girl...Maybe it's just an image capturing a particular moment, or maybe there's a reason stereotypes such as lecherous old man taking advantage of vulnerable teen exist."

"Which is an overgeneralization you damn well better keep to yourself."

Vaughn has materialized in the doorway between the dining hall and the kitchen. His hands are planted on his hips, and he's scowling at me with a swear-jar-worthy look on his face.

I start peeling very rapidly, while Trudy becomes obsessed with boiling water and Ann breads pork chops with renewed vigor.

Vaughn stalks into the room. "I've known Mac since he first brought Lea home after she lost her parents. If you'd seen how frightened she was then, compared to the graceful young woman she is now, you'd know he's done right by her. And he doesn't deserve you or anyone else twisting his good deed into something sordid."

I glance at Vaughn's stormy face. I believe he believes what he's saying. Doesn't mean I have to. Especially his remark about Lea having lost her parents, which I already know is pure fiction. I give Vaughn a mutinous look as I finish with the potato in my hand and drop it in the container in front of me. Trudy ventures close enough to snag the bowl, dump its contents into the first pot of boiling water, then ease it back in front of me without interrupting our staring contest.

"Why the hell are you asking so many questions anyway?" Vaughn demands now. "What business is it of yours?"

"What business is it of mine? What business is it of *mine*?" Now I am pissed off. And it feels good. After spending the day feeling exhausted, anxious, and overwhelmed, rage is exactly the break I've needed.

I toss down the potato peeler and march up to him. "According to you"—I jab a finger into his chest—"I'm working on an island so remote my own appendix is a danger to me. Add to that, I've spent my first morning discovering recent human remains—"

"You found a body?"

"Is it a pirate's?"

"Wait, recent remains…"

I ignore Trudy and Ann, who are standing wide-eyed in front of the stove. I poke Vaughn a second time. "Then, I get sent to clean the ritzy home of this island's billionaire developer—"

"Your boss," Vaughn growls.

"Who's supposedly planning an eco-friendly resort, but whose own abode is a testimony to extravagant excess. And, oh yeah, while I'm dusting, I happen to notice a framed photo that, frankly, made me uncomfortable and concerned about the young girl involved. So yeah, I'm asking questions. I would be stupid not to!"

I stab him a third time. Which I'd like a whole lot better if his chest didn't feel like granite.

"Are you done?" Vaughn asks me.

"I don't know yet." My outburst did feel good. But now, with the last of my anger draining, I'm tired. And really wishing it would just please, for the love of God, stop raining.

"If you have questions," Vaughn states, his face inches from mine, "talk to me. But none of this gossiping in the kitchen. And especially no bad-mouthing a man you haven't even met yet."

That does make me feel slightly guilty. I concede his point with a single step back.

In return, he acknowledges: "You've had an unusual first day."

"Difficult," I correct. "Some might even say awful."

"Less than ideal."

"Seriously? I do not like you right now!"

"Umm, hello?" Ann has raised her hand behind us. "Human remains?"

"Recent," Trudy adds.

Vaughn sighs heavily, raking a hand through wet hair already sticking out in every which direction, then sighs again. Based on the tired look in his blue eyes, it's possible he's had a difficult day, too. He is the one responsible for everything that happens on this atoll, though I'm still not ready to forgive him just yet.

"I'll make an announcement at dinner," he informs Trudy and Ann. "That way I can tell everyone at once, and put an end to unnecessary conversational churn."

"Conversational churn." Ann turns to Trudy. "Does he mean gossip?"

"No, I think that's unauthorized speculations."

"Or maybe salacious musings?"

"Oh, I know what he means—rumormongering. Definitely we should stop the unfounded chattering."

Vaughn closes his eyes, inhales deeply through his nose, exhales all the way out. Then he turns on his heel and exits the kitchen.

"I still don't like you," I call out after him. Then I turn back to Trudy and Ann. "Though you two I love very much."

They beam at me. Ann pats my arm. "You raise good questions. We don't really know the girl."

"Which maybe proves your point," Trudy adds.

"We could probably find a way to get her on her own."

"Encourage her to speak."

"Learn more about how she truly feels."

Trudy peers at me: "Are you always this suspicious?"

"You have no idea."

"You don't need to be," Ann states. "People who do this kind of work, live this kind of life, most of us are content to do our own thing. We're eccentric and antisocial—"

"But not bodies-buried-in-the-basement antisocial," Trudy assures me.

"Not to mention Pomaikai has no basements!"

I study both of them. "I would feel better about that statement if I hadn't spent my morning discovering a body."

"Oh," Trudy says.

"Oh dear," Ann agrees. "Umm…"

"Back to dinner prep!" Trudy declares.

"Food fixes everything," Ann extols.

Based on my first twenty-four hours alone, I think they are both incredibly optimistic.

LIKE THE PREVIOUS night, we're the last to join the party. The meal is amazing: platters of fried pork chops for the carnivores and breaded eggplant for the vegetarians, accompanied by mounds of mashed potatoes, boats of gravy, and some kind of quinoa harvest salad that might be one of the best things I've ever tasted. People help themselves to seconds and thirds. I don't blame them, though having the inside track on Ann's surprise dessert—fresh-baked brownies—I pace myself accordingly.

Upon entering the dining hall, I look for Ronin first. He's deep in conversation with Vaughn and, given the grim looks on both their faces, I take a pass. Next up I search for Aolani, but her table is already full.

Which brings me to Emi, the petite ornithologist. She glances up at my approach, gives me a huge smile, and pats the empty seat next to her. It's so unexpectedly kind, I almost embarrass myself by breaking into tears. I hide my rush of emotion by busying myself with the exact placement of my plate and silverware.

"How was your first day?" she wants to know.

It takes me a second, then: "I saw the most beautiful white birds. Angel terns? They were just...magical."

Emi beams. "There is a chick not far from the rear of this building. Tomorrow, when the rain stops, I can show you. It looks like a puff of cotton perched on top of a tree limb. I shouldn't play favorites, but between you and me, I love the common terns. They remind me that miracles can always happen."

She turns to the older woman sitting across from her, who has beautiful silver-gray hair cut in a shoulder-length bob framing her brilliant blue eyes. "Have you met Tannis? Tannis, Frankie. Frankie, Tannis."

I reach across the table to shake her hand.

"Are you also an ornithologist?"

"Oh, no, no. I'm not nearly that smart." She flashes Emi a warm look. Clearly, they're friends. "I'm a landscape architect."

"Landscape architect...as in designing the grounds around the new resort? Flowers, plants, that kind of thing?"

"And hardscapes, walking paths, patios, porticos. The options are endless in a setting this beautiful."

"Isn't it a little early to be contemplating the gardens when the building hasn't even been started yet?"

"It's never too early to involve someone like myself." She has a bit of a lilting accent. Canadian, maybe. MacManus has certainly assembled an international team. Apparently, hiring the best money can buy involves global cherry-picking.

"How a building is situated on a property is the first step in the design process, particularly a resort that must both dazzle upon first glance and yet blend seamlessly into its natural surroundings. For a project such as this, it's imperative to be on-site. I couldn't do my job otherwise."

"And we get to torture her," Emi chimes in. "She thinks in terms of sunlight and curving inlets and perfect views. Then I discover nesting sites and it's all, 'No disturbing there. Or there. Or over there.'"

"The boobies are tough taskmasters," Tannis agrees, but she doesn't sound angry about it.

"From what I can tell, the birds own this place," I say. "Certainly, that's what it sounds like at night. How do you work with that?"

"I'm thinking along the lines of a fluid mix of natural habitat and human ingenuity."

"I have no idea what that means, but it sounds good."

Emi giggles. "She already has you figured out!"

"We don't have all the answers yet," Tannis concedes. "The naturalists are still making discoveries. But in the end, there's always a way. It's just a matter of thinking creatively and strategically."

She sounds very sure of herself. I'm sure if I had access to her résumé, I would see why. For now, I return to Emi.

"If nesting sites impact where the resort can be placed, is there anything you might discover that could derail the project completely?" *Other than a dead body*, I add in the back of my mind.

"Rare and endangered species," Emi provides promptly. "Hawaii is often referred to as the endangered species capital of the world, given the number of unique birds, animals, and plants that exist only on those islands. Unfortunately, many of the bird species are now succumbing to avian malaria, as warming temperatures enable mosquitoes to survive at higher elevations. It is a huge tragedy. So many species have already vanished, and many, many more are down to less than a hundred pairs in the wild. It's referred to as the silent forest. Where once there were mountains filled with birdsong, now you hear nothing at all."

"That sounds unbelievably sad."

I want to ask her more about it, but we're interrupted from further discussion as Vaughn rises to standing and raps his knuckles against the table. I already know what's coming, so I turn around more slowly than the others.

"I have an announcement," Vaughn begins. "A discovery was made earlier today..."

He keeps it matter-of-fact. The finding of a grave containing remains that probably aren't historic. Notifying the authorities in Honolulu, who will take over handling of the burial site. Whenever they get here. Which might be a few days or a few weeks, as flying special agents and forensic professionals to a remote island takes some coordination.

Ann's hand is already in the air, as her earlier question has never been answered. "What does 'not historical' mean?"

Ronin fields the question. "NAGPRA specifies within the past fifty years. Based on the clothing, I'm presuming that time frame is accurate."

Ann waves her hand again. "You're an archaeologist. You've seen plenty of skeletons. You can't do better than that?"

"No." Ronin doesn't elaborate. Ann looks peeved.

I raise my hand, as that seems to be protocol. "How long has this base camp been operating?"

"Depends." Vaughn this time. "It's been fully staffed for the past eight months. But in terms of first boots hitting the ground, fleshing out the infrastructure, more like a year and a half."

"So lots of people coming and going, to bring in all the supplies?"

"Literally by the boatloads. We can't fly in lumber, comm towers, heavy equipment. It was all shipped over on charter boats. They spent a week sailing over from Oahu. Returned with our building debris."

"How many people on the boats? Same crew every time?"

Vaughn arches a brow at the specificity of my questions. I shrug, still wanting the answers.

"Three different companies, given the volume. Four-to-six-man crews each."

I nod, sit back.

Ronin stares at me. "There's no reason to believe the remains are that recent. They appear skeletonized."

Trudy snorts in disbelief. "Please. In these conditions? Crabs alone can strip you down to spare parts in a matter of hours. Crab Town anyone?"

Everyone nods in agreement. I still haven't seen this alleged Crab Town but make a mental note to stay away. The murmuring starts building in earnest.

Vaughn raises his hand for silence. "We're getting ahead of ourselves. Look, the whole point of this operation is to fully explore and document this atoll. Well, today two of our people made an unexpected discovery. Our job now is to stay away and wait for the feds. That simple."

"Where is it?" Tannis asks.

"Oh no, you're not getting that out of me. I know what a curious lot all of you are. Second this meeting is done, you'll go check it out for yourselves. So that's that. Subject closed."

More muttering. Emi regards me curiously. "Weren't you with Ronin this morning?"

"Yes, but I have no idea where we were. Honest truth. I can barely find the mess hall."

Emi doesn't appear convinced. I can guess the number one question I'll be asked from here on out.

"Now, the good news." This grabs everyone's attention. They turn back to Vaughn. "Given the rain, we're going to have movie night. And—I'll allow public use of Wi-Fi."

Excited chatter now. I'm one of them. Finally I can check in with Victoria Twanow.

"We'll follow our usual protocol. Last names ending *A* through *H* get first hour. *I* through *P* next sixty minutes. Which leaves *Q* through *Z* for the end."

Groans from two people, I'm guessing the *Q* through *Z* crowd.

Vaughn is already waving away the complaint. "Come on, you've spent your entire lives sitting in the back of the classroom. You know you're used to it. Plus, I have one more surprise." He pauses for dramatic effect. "Homemade brownies, baked by Ann this afternoon."

This earns actual applause. Ann stands up, takes a bow. More clapping.

"And popcorn?" someone wants to know.

"And popcorn," Trudy answers over the noise. She glances slyly at Vaughn. "Drinks?"

Vaughn debates it for a second, but even I know he's going to cave. First rule of toddler management: distract them with treats. "Fine," he says. "Beer and wine. One drink per person maximum. Weather like this, we need our wits about us. Everyone got it?" He glances around the room. When no one else speaks up, he raps the table, apparently signaling the end of the meeting. "Rec hall, thirty minutes."

As one, people push back from the tables and scurry into the kitchen to drop off their dirty dishes. I scramble to my feet, as that means work for me. I can tell by Trudy's and Ann's rushed movements that they're anxious to complete cleanup so they can enjoy movie night.

Vaughn materializes at my shoulder just as I start loading the first dishwasher tray.

"My office, ten minutes."

"I'm in trouble again?"

"Oh, I have a feeling you're in trouble always. Or maybe you *are* trouble always." With that, he stalks off.

"Busted," Ann stage-whispers.

I shake my head, quickly scouring the pile of plates, then grab my already soaked rain jacket and head into the deluge.

CHAPTER 18

VAUGHN IS LEANING BACK IN his deluxe executive chair when I enter, his feet propped on the edge of his desk. His radio is no longer worn as a leash around his neck but tossed next to the keyboard in front of him. I wonder if that's his idea of cutting loose.

I take up position across from him, the air-conditioning hitting my damp clothes and making me shiver. Belatedly, we both glance at the empty hook where his sweatshirt had been—the sweatshirt I now have hanging up in my cabin.

A weird vibe hums through the space between us. I shift restlessly from side to side. I don't want vibing or humming. Sleep, on the other hand...

"I did some digging into your background after this morning's development," Vaughn states after a moment.

I stiffen, say nothing. First rule of thumb, make them come to you.

"Seems like nowhere features quite a few missing people. And your name is attached to most of those investigations."

I remain silent.

"Are you law enforcement?"

"No."

"Private investigator."

"Definitely not."

"There's no way one woman is randomly connected to over a dozen missing persons cases."

"And yet..." I shrug. "Personally, I consider myself to be a woman with an unusual hobby. Or a self-destructive streak. The line between the two gets a little blurry."

Vaughn's feet hit the ground. "Remember what I said about the importance of open and honest communication? That we don't keep secrets in this camp, because we need to trust one another. Our safety depends on it."

"Seriously? I started my day discovering a woman's grave. Recent remains, to use your own words. So you want to talk about trust? Here it is: I don't trust any of you. Not a single person on this atoll."

"Jesus. Do you ever back down from a fight?"

"No."

He scowls, rakes his hand through his brown hair. I'm beginning to understand that the motion is one of his tells. He's disturbed about something, and it's not just me.

"Why are you here?" he asks tersely. "The real reason, this time."

"Because this is what I do. Travel from place to place, picking up work as I go. You've seen my résumé. I don't have a permanent address or, quote, unquote, real job. I'm restless. Always have been."

"But you've gotten involved in searching for missing people. You've assisted the police?"

"That's not how they see it." Now I'm being perfectly honest. No cop likes a layperson getting involved in their investigation. Let alone the time a local sheriff and his two deputies, Redneck 1 and Redneck 2, tried to chase me out of town with shotguns.

Vaughn thins his lips, clearly annoyed by my opaque answers. He's tired, I realize, fatigued in a way that goes beyond the usual stress of managing a camp of this size and complexity.

"You're concerned about something." My turn to issue a statement of fact.

"Welcome to project management. I'm always concerned about something."

"How many of these assignments have you done?"

"Four."

"Always with MacManus?"

"Mac's a good guy. We go way back."

"To when Lea was young?"

"There you go again, asking questions."

"Clearly I drove my parents crazy from a young age. Come on, Vaughn, what do you really want to ask me?"

He grimaces, looking up and away. More hair pulling, face rubbing. Something is definitely eating away at him. I remain silent, the best interrogation technique I know.

"Do you have opinions on the skeleton?" he asks abruptly. "You said it wasn't your first body. And based on what I read, it sounds like many of your cases...don't result in locating the living."

I don't love his euphemism but can't argue with it, either. I contemplate him for a moment. We are at an impasse, I realize, where he knows more than I'd like him to know, and I need someone to trust more than I'd like to need someone to trust. I decide turnabout is fair play.

"Tell me about Chris. How did she really sprain her ankle? Answer my question and I'll answer yours."

"She stepped into a crab—"

"You can stop right now." I raise a hand. "When I said answer my question, I meant truthfully. You're the one who keeps talking about the importance of open and honest communication. And yet, you lied to me first, and we both know it."

"I didn't lie first—"

"So you admit you lied!"

He sits back, scowls at me. "You're fucking annoying."

"Thank you. I consider it one of my superpowers. Right up there with once I ask a question, I don't quit till I get the answer."

"Chris sprained her ankle," he allows.

I give him a look.

"She stumbled down the front steps of her cabin, into a crab den."

I narrow my gaze.

"The crab den part was accidental enough. The stairs..."

My eyes widen.

"They'd come loose from the cabin. Upon close inspection, most of the screws were missing."

"Someone had removed the screws?"

"Hydraulic claws aside, I doubt the ghost crabs possess the necessary tools."

Sarcasm. Score one for the sexy project manager.

"You suspect foul play?"

"I suspect the stairs were once screwed to the cabin frame, and somehow, someway, were removed. Other than that..."

"What did Chris have to say?"

"I want to go home," he intoned. It takes me a second to realize he's speaking as Chris.

"Did the other crew members like Chris?"

"Yeah. She was solid. No issues, no complaints."

"Umm, any chance she was dipping into the condom/morning-after pill supply?"

"More likely to be robbing the strap-on supply, except we don't have a strap-on supply."

"Oh." I get it. A little slow on the uptake, but still.

"Everyone liked Chris. No hint of trouble. No idea what happened. Which made it especially..."

"Unnerving?"

"Folks were rattled."

I thought of Ronin and his claim to have picked me for his expedition because I hadn't been here before. As in I hadn't been on the atoll earlier to sabotage a fellow campmate's stairs.

"Okay," I allow.

"Okay?"

"Okay, you showed me yours, so I'll show you mine. I do have a particular...interest...hobby...obsession...with missing persons cold cases. But," I add hastily, "I'm no expert. I can get people to talk, and I'm pretty good at listening to their answers. However, forensics, mad computer skills, real-world investigative techniques, not my thing. So while I have encountered skeletal remains before, I'm no forensic anthropologist. Not to mention, Ronin and I only cleared a small window into the grave. If not for the sequined flower on the clothing, I don't think we could've given you an estimated time of death at all."

"But you must have some thoughts on the subject."

I take a deep breath, consider the matter. I don't feel like I can trust Vaughn concerning Lea. He's clearly Team MacManus. On the other hand, he clearly knows enough about my background. Surely it doesn't hurt to partner with him on this matter, maybe even reach a point of mutual respect that might come in handy later.

"From what you've described, this atoll may be remote, but in the past year and a half, it's been a hub of activity, including dozens upon dozens of people passing through."

"Probably close to a hundred," he allows.

"And those are the ones you know about. Consider the single-person submersible that ran ashore. It's possible there are other individuals, say less law-abiding folks, who've also used this place as a stopover."

Vaughn pauses, taps a lone finger against the top of his desk. "I hadn't thought about that, but sure. A deserted island in these waters would come in handy for a variety of activities."

"Hawaii is a major hub for human trafficking."

"You think that's what happened to this woman? She was a victim of human trafficking?"

"Her top. The sparkling flower. When I saw it, my first thought was that it looked like something she'd thrown on to go dancing. Though given our location, it could also be a swimsuit cover-up, I suppose."

"You're thinking prostitution."

"Possible. What did you say about not getting ahead of ourselves?"

That sigh again. There's more to this story. Once again, I wait.

"We've had some...issues." Vaughn addresses these words to the ceiling. "Beyond missing screws and suddenly detached front steps."

Now we're getting to the good stuff. Fascinating. Or terrifying, given that I live in a cabin with screws and front steps.

"Mostly minor accidents, or unfortunate occurrences," Vaughn continues. "Maybe random bad luck."

"For the love of God, just spill it, man."

"Fine. For example, the electric board frying on the brand-new comm tower. Not to mention a major crack appearing in the cistern. And a hole in the fiberglass hull of the fishing boat we use not just to study the waters around this atoll but to catch dinner most weekends. None of these individual incidents are exactly dire, but they're enough to keep Charlie overworked and the rest of us behind schedule."

I blink my eyes several times, considering. "What do you think it means?"

"Well, I thought it meant this was the project from hell. Which, for the record, I also thought about my last project and the project before that. But now…maybe someone is deliberately trying to delay our efforts."

"If it's sabotage, don't you think the perpetrator would be conducting bigger acts to get you off the atoll once and for all, versus extending everyone's time here?"

"Depends. One, does the person in question understand the size of Mac's wallet and the depth of his determination? The person might have assumed a little bit would go a long way. Of course, retreat has never been Mac's style." Vaughn pauses, stares at me. "Now that I think about it, given your own obstinate streak, I'm not sure the two of you should be on the same island together. Or the same planet."

"Tomorrow afternoon, we'll find out."

Vaughn doesn't dispute the time frame, so hopefully Mac-Manus is still on track to arrive. At this point, I'd like nothing more than to grab an aside with Lea, hear what she has to say, and then, Victoria Twanow willing, get the hell off this island.

"Also," Vaughn continues now, "I'm not exaggerating when I say this camp is a self-enclosed, dependent system. Can't hurt one of us without hurting all of us. Limits the ability to pack a punch, if you know what I mean. An act too aggressive might unwittingly harm the perpetrator as well."

Hence the new approach of targeting a specific cabin, I wonder. Which did result in someone leaving the atoll.

"Interesting point," I allow. "You're saying it's Charlie's skills that have gotten you this far?" I'm very curious, given Charlie's own puzzling behavior.

Vaughn seems emphatic: "The man's seriously one of the most gifted and resourceful engineers I've ever worked with. Had to pay a pretty penny to lure him away from his next term at McMurdo."

"Did you know him from McMurdo?"

"No, this is my first time working with him. But he came highly recommended."

"And he's been at the camp since the beginning?"

"No. Had a different crew for installation. Once we got the first cabins built, Ronin and Aolani arrived. Ronin because he's got an entire atoll to inspect for possible environmental impact; AO because she's not letting some state archaeologist run amok with her career-making design. Charlie arrived shortly thereafter. Been here the past six months."

"And when did the issues, I mean unfortunate accidents, first start happening?"

Vaughn has to think about it. "Probably four to five months back."

In other words, shortly after Charlie's arrival. The official fixer? Or maybe the arsonist who also worked as a firefighter?

"Is everyone here from the original research party?"

"No. Trudy and Ann are our second mess hall attendants. We had a dedicated boat pilot, but she had to move on to another gig, and I haven't found a replacement yet. Charlie's been doing that duty, too. Let's see...Tannis, the landscape architect—"

"I met her tonight."

"She arrived just a few weeks ago. Umm, most of the naturalists have arrived over the course of the past few months, each with their responsibility for some aspect of reporting. Honestly, I can't keep track of all the scientists. I just make sure they have what they need to get their job done and don't hurt themselves or others while they're at it."

"Which up to this point—"

"Project from hell," Vaughn reports. "But no more hellish than the past few. Well, maybe a bit more. God, I'm tired."

I eye him curiously. "Do you think the proposed resort will happen?"

"Haven't seen anything to convince me otherwise."

"Even the discovery of recent remains?"

"Especially not that. Historic remains would've involved a delay. This...The feds will arrive, ask questions, remove bones, and that'll be that."

"So probably not related to the sabotage, then?" I surmise. "Because if this was another delay tactic, surely there are some kind of ancient relics somewhere that could be planted here for show."

"When you put it like that..." Vaughn sighs. "So this project has now been subject to both bad luck and a dead body."

"Which technically means, she's had some bad luck, too."

He gives me a look. "You know I don't mean—"

"Look." I'm tired, cold, and desperately want a brownie. "You're an experienced project manager. Off the top of your head, is the base camp suffering from bad juju, or something more?"

He opens his mouth. Closes it. Opens it. "Something more," he concedes abruptly.

"Agreed. Now, according to you, Charlie's above-average skills have gotten you this far. Meaning maybe the next thing to go wrong will either be something he can't fix or outside of his purview altogether."

"Comforting thought."

"Think of it more as proof of concept. Next unfortunate incident, we'll know for sure."

Vaughn rolls his eyes. He seems calmer, though. I've hardly fixed his problems but maybe it's enough to have someone to talk to. As head of this enterprise, he can hardly confide in the others.

"What's your biggest fear?" I ask him now. "Like, the worst thing that could happen?"

He stares at me in apprehension. "Why?"

"Because if you're that worried about a saboteur, it might be something to start protecting against."

"Well, a storm of this magnitude, which can inflict damage while hindering evacuation, certainly rates up there. Though wind speeds aren't something a person can control."

"Good point. Outside a natural disaster."

"The cistern collapsing, which would cost us our fresh water supply. On the other hand, Charlie could probably rig a makeshift desalination tank to get us through. Plus, we have bottled water stored in the freezer."

"Keep going."

"Injury. Some kind of mass casualty event that would impede our ability to aid one another and/or evac. Also, the loss of the comm tower, which would cut us off even more from civilization."

"Are there guns or weapons around?" I ask sharply, because

this certainly rates as one of my top three fears. Make that the top one.

"One rifle, one shotgun, both secured in a locker." He nods his chin toward a tall metal structure in the corner of his office. "I have the only key."

"I saw Ronin with a machete," I prod.

"In terms of blades, there are plenty, from pocketknives to hacksaws to utility blades. Hard to do much work around here without one."

"That is not going to help me sleep better at night. Speaking of which, do you have a night watch?"

"No, just twenty-four-hour coverage of the radios. I always have one; Charlie, Ronin, and AO take turns with the second."

"What about starting some kind of nighttime security measures...?"

"Would probably raise a bunch of questions and concerns I don't want raised right now."

"What about asking someone like Charlie?"

"I can't ask the man to work all night, then save our asses repairing broken items all day."

I nod. "When MacManus gets here, tell him it's time to mine those deep pockets and pony up for extra help. Or when the police arrive to inspect the grave...They might have something to offer. But if your suspicions are correct, you could use more resources. You're the project manager. Manage."

Vaughn rolls his eyes again. He's back to his mussed hair, preoccupied expression. He is carrying the weight of this camp on his shoulders. He seems to take the responsibility seriously.

He rises to standing. "Thanks for the pep talk." His tone might be sarcastic. "I've kept you from the movie long enough."

I nod, then find myself saying, "Look, I'm no expert, but I have some relevant experience. If you want to even…just talk…you know, whatever. Whenever." I should shut up. And still the words pour out. "I'm here for you."

Night or day seems implied. It's the faint undertone of dressed or undressed that has me horrified. Though I don't take it back. It's been a while. And he's a good-looking guy, in a super fit, brilliant blue eyes sort of way.

"Drinks," he says.

"Right now?" Well, so much for having to wonder.

"Beer and wine. For movie night. You're in charge, remember?"

Belatedly, I recall my job description. "Umm, yes. One drink apiece. Where's the stash?"

Vaughn points to a European-size fridge churning away in a darkened corner, producing a chain dangling beneath his shirt that bears several keys. As he selects one to unlock the fridge, he rattles off: "Don't underestimate the inmates in the asylum. Ronin doesn't drink at all. AO only drinks on occasion. The rest of them, you better keep count. Especially Trudy and Ann. They like to do this trick where they pretend to be fetching a drink for someone else, except they're not. Apparently, they think if someone passes on their designated drink, that beer is now available for them, versus that whole 'one drink per person,' means they are the person who only gets one drink."

I can almost follow that. Vaughn pulls out two boxes of wine, one red, one white, then piles a six-pack on top. Given all my years as a bartender, the size and weight of the load doesn't faze me. Given all my years as a hardcore drinker, it also makes me a little giddy.

Now would be a good time to mention I'm a friend of Bill.

And yet I don't. I'm playing with fire. I can't even say why I'm so anxious to burn.

I depart the office with my illicit stash. Outside it's still pouring but so much warmer than the bone-biting air-conditioning that I actually welcome it. It's only a short distance to the rec hall. When I appear with an armful of booze, people literally cheer. Just like that, I'm one of the cool kids.

I pass out booze, feeling very much in my element, while Aolani starts fiddling with some device that appears to house every movie ever made as a computer file. Except for the good ones, Trudy informs me with a wink as she snags a beer. Then again, when stranded on a deserted island, is there such a thing as a bad movie?

I stay in the back, not just to monitor/moon over the booze but because I remember the second boon of the night—Wi-Fi access. As Twanow had anticipated, I haven't had enough reception to call. But with the gift of Wi-Fi, I can at least attempt my first check-in via text. I start with:

"*Hi mom! Made it safe and sound. Already met some nice people, with new friends arriving tomorrow.*"

That sounds innocuous enough. I think of the morning's events, from the grave to Lea's note. I'm not sure how to communicate all that without giving too much away in case I am being monitored. I finally go with:

"*Sad start to the day. Archaeologist made a discovery that might not be historic. Police will arrive later in the week to determine. We could all use answers to what happened. Feeling a little concerned right now. Is this the right choice for me? I and some of my friends might want to come home sooner versus later.*"

Too vague? I honestly don't know. I've never tried coded

communiqués before. And compared to the *Get me the hell off this island* command I truly want to send, this feels tame.

I hit send, stuff my phone back in my pocket, then settle in to count heads and bottles/glasses of booze while watching some movie involving Betty White and a supersize prehistoric alligator. It engenders equal parts laughs and gasps, the right notes for a group of people dealing with news no one is talking about and yet everyone is worrying over.

The only staff members missing are Vaughn and Charlie. As the two busiest men in camp, maybe they can't afford such luxuries. The rest of us enjoy it in their stead.

Afterward, I cart the leftover booze to Vaughn's office. He's left his key on the desk. I take it and, without giving myself a chance to think, unlock the fridge, refill, relock, then stash the key in the center drawer and flee without a backward glance.

Rain lashes. Wind howls. I huddle inside my raincoat, splashing through puddles, scrambling crabs as I dash for my cabin. I don't think about Wyoming, or final moments, or a flask of Maker's Mark when no one would've been the wiser.

I keep going. And maybe that's a giant coconut crab crashing through the tall grass. And maybe that's Crabby, fleeing for safety beneath my little slice of paradise. I'm too damn grateful to finally arrive home to contemplate anything else.

I barely have time to strip off my soaking wet clothes and towel off my hair. Still no answer from Twanow when I plug in my phone to charge. I collapse on my bed face-first.

I'm asleep before I even know it.

Banging wakes me up some time later. Minutes? Hours? I stagger groggily to the front door. I open it, already expecting it to be Vaughn. Is this when we have mad, passionate sex? If only I wasn't so genuinely exhausted.

Except it's Ronin, with his perfect cheekbones. I'm so confused I almost say, "No, no, you belong to Aolani."

But before I totally embarrass myself, I register his grave
expression.

"Get dressed. Grab a flashlight. Meet in the rec hall. Whole
camp is now activated for duty. Charlie's gone missing."

CHAPTER 19

VAUGHN IS ALREADY BARKING OUT orders when I enter the rec hall, assembling staff members into groups of two and assigning them designated search areas. The pairs cycle through a table manned by Ronin and Aolani to gear up with heavy-duty flashlights, red safety whistles, and extra rain ponchos. Then they're out the door.

I stumble slightly at the sight of the safety whistles, catch myself, soldier on.

I'm last in line. When I appear in front of the gray folding table that just hours ago held our movie projector, Vaughn points at a section on the map without looking up. "Runway. Watch your footing—the green patches are slippery in this weather."

I don't move. He taps the map. I remain stationary. He finally peers up. "What?" Then he notices it's me, and his scowl deepens. I glance around. Most of the crew have now departed. Just Ronin and Aolani remain.

"When was Charlie last seen?" After my last conversation

with Vaughn, I don't feel a need to explain my line of questioning. "I never saw him at movie night."

"Dinner."

"Does he have a radio?"

"No. He signed back in right before dinner, returning the radio to its charger."

"How did you discover he was missing?"

"I did." Ronin appears beside us, Aolani in tow. "I had a question, went to his cabin, but he wasn't there. Odd for this time of night. I did some more checking around. I can't find him anywhere."

I'm confused. "Isn't it one in the morning?"

Ronin nods.

"So you went to his cabin at what, midnight? With a work question?"

"Charlie's a night owl," Ronin informs me. Given the lack of reaction on Vaughn's and Aolani's faces, apparently this is common knowledge.

"Vaughn says you have experience searching for missing persons," Aolani speaks up. It's the first time she's spoken directly to me beyond a basic greeting. Her tone is cool. I don't know if that's how she always sounds or if she's miffed about having to hear about my hobbies from someone else. Am I supposed to apologize? Offer an explanation? I don't do my best thinking at one a.m. Finally, I nod in acknowledgment, and then I'm saved by Ronin continuing with his story.

"I checked his cabin—Charlie's cell phone, raincoat, and Crocs are missing."

"Maybe he hit the latrine or returned to the mess hall for a midnight snack?"

"I checked. I toured the bathrooms, dock, and maintenance

shed when I didn't find him in his cabin. Then, when he still hadn't returned, I covered all the outbuildings. There's no sign of him, and it's been over an hour. In this weather, this late at night... Something's wrong."

"What about the UTVs?"

"One is missing." Ronin and Vaughn exchange a look.

"Charlie wouldn't take a UTV and not a radio," Ronin begins, talking more to Vaughn than to me. Clearly, they've been over this. "He always follows proper safety protocols. He helped write them."

Vaughn shakes his head. "The body, burial mound, whatever we're calling it. It's the one new development, and Charlie had a lot of questions on the subject—he drilled me with them walking out of the dining hall."

"You think he headed to where Ronin and I were this morning?" My turn. "But how would he know the location?"

"Charlie knows everything," Aolani speaks up, her tone possibly admiring, possibly derisive. I can't get a bead on her.

"Charlie's a smart guy," Vaughn agrees. "I'm sure he has plenty of ideas from his own travels around the atoll. He'd trust himself to figure out the rest on his own. Frankly, that's what he does best."

I raise my hand. "There's a second option, now that we're talking drive distance. MacManus's lodge. When Charlie picked me up this afternoon, he had plenty of questions about that place as well."

"About what?" Aolani stares at me.

I'm not sure how to answer that question without giving too much away. "About what's under the bed."

"There's something under one of the beds?"

"Exactly."

Vaughn blinks at me. Aolani gives me a clearly annoyed look; this expression I can read.

"I will go to the burial site," Ronin states.

"No." Aolani utters the single word in a tone that has both Vaughn and me rocking back on our heels. "I'll go to the grave."

"AO, this is not the time—"

"This is exactly the time."

"You don't know where it is."

"I know enough. She can lead me the rest of the way." Aolani jerks her head in my direction.

"Umm, I'm not so sure—"

"You'll be fine."

I glance wide-eyed at Vaughn, searching for rescue. Vaughn, however, keeps his gaze fixed on the ceiling.

"Coward," I mutter. "Look." I make an attempt at reason: "Say for a moment that Charlie has taken one of the UTVs out to the burial mound or over to the owner's lodge. What does it matter? Can't we just wait for his return and then give him a thorough talking-to?"

Vaughn exhales. "Fuck."

I still don't get it. "The dude can drive. And, according to you, can MacGyver his way out of just about anything. I'm sure he'll be back shortly. Then you put him in time-out, or lock him in the gallows, or whatever you do to bad engineers who break camp rules."

But the other three are exchanging worried glances. "*What?*" God, I hate one a.m. discussions.

"It's not safe," Aolani states. "To be out alone without any means of contact at this time of night and in this weather."

"The coconut crabs will get him?"

"Many things could go wrong," Ronin supplies quietly. "And without a radio to call for assistance...In a place this remote, minor injuries can quickly turn into major ones."

"Small problems become big problems," Aolani intones.

Ronin looks up, holds her gaze. Entire conversations flow between them. Grand declarations made and rebuffed. Epic poems written and erased. Deeper understandings reached, then unraveled, then reached again. Meanwhile, Vaughn returns to studying the ceiling. I examine the floor. Finally:

Ronin exhales slowly. "You and Frankie head for the burial mound. I will check out the owner's lodge."

"Do I get a vote in this?"

"No," all three inform me. Well, well.

As the dead woman walking, I have one final request. "Radio. I'll carry it."

Vaughn removes the one hanging around his own neck and drapes it over mine. It feels like a formal, if not ominous, changing of the guard.

"I can grab another from my office," he mutters.

He shows me how to work the volume and channel selection. I nod while telling myself that radios have no odor, hence it's impossible that the one dangling across my chest smells like him.

We now have a plan of attack, but nobody seems happy about it. If anything, Aolani appears more subdued, while Ronin has that tight, shuttered look on his face.

I recall my earlier conversation with Vaughn regarding the string of accidents. My prediction that something worse would happen soon, probably something Charlie couldn't fix. Charlie's sudden disappearance certainly fits the bill. That makes me glance sideways at Vaughn. What are the odds I say something like that to him and only him, and then it comes true?

"Get moving," Vaughn commands gruffly. "Sooner we know, sooner we know."

He moves to the supply table, handing me two backup flash-lights, extra rain ponchos, an entire medical kit—nothing to worry about there—and emergency warming blankets.

"Just in case," he says.

Yeah, definitely nothing to worry about.

I follow Aolani out to the row of parked UTVs. Where there were once three, there are now two, meaning once we take one and Ronin the other, the rest of the camp will have no means of transportation. And if none of us return?

I so want off this fucking island.

Aolani turns the key, firing up the first jungle-grade golf cart. I climb inside, arranging the supplies at my feet. At the last moment, Aolani pauses, then exits the vehicle long enough to return with two hefty walking sticks, which she lays in the back.

"To keep us from slipping and falling," I deduce.

"That, and for the coconut crabs. This is the time of night they like to hunt."

And on that cheery note, we are off and running.

THE RAIN AND wind seem to have calmed, but that's to say they've gone from hurricane to gale force. Palm fronds snap above, while whipping gusts pelt our faces with rain and debris. My hair starts out in a ponytail but quickly turns into a free-flowing mane. Beside me, Aolani isn't having any better luck, her own dark strands lashing across her face. I keep my eyes half shut and a tight grip on the door as she careens around one muddy corner, plows through a vast puddle, then heaves us forward.

It's still eighty degrees outside, but my teeth are chattering while each jostling motion of the UTV grates against my bones.

"So," I say at last, trying to break the mood. Aolani is definitely operating on the angry side of midnight. Is that because she's worried about Charlie, mad in general, or perhaps pissed about me spending yesterday on a private adventure with the boyfriend she swears isn't her boyfriend? That's the question. "I know of you," I forge ahead now. "You know of me. But we've never really spoken, so just to catch up, how about I tell you all my deep, dark secrets, then you can tell me yours?"

Aolani doesn't answer, gaze fixed straight ahead as the jungle waves wildly around us.

"I'll go first. My name is Frankie Elkin. I go by she/her. I'm a Virgo. Let's see, I was born in California but now live nowhere at all. I prefer the life of a rolling stone, moving from town to town picking up bartending gigs and working missing persons cold cases. Mostly, I search for people no one else is looking for. And you?"

Aolani finally flicks a glance in my direction. "None of that is secret; I'd already heard as much from Vaughn."

"Oh. Then...I'm afraid of snakes."

She gives me a look, then has to quickly refocus as she jerks us around a fallen branch. I grab the 'Oh shit' handle, muttering under my breath. Are we close? It feels like we've already been out in the storm forever. But the ride had seemed a solid distance the first time around, so I'm assuming that puts tonight's trek somewhere around the length of eternity.

"Your name is Aolani Akamai, AO to your friends?"

She doesn't take the bait. I forge ahead. "Architect, working what I'm guessing would be a career-making project. If it isn't blocked by any findings made by Ronin, the state's investigating archaeologist who is definitely more than a friend."

Now she huffs from the driver's seat. "It's no one's business."

"At this point, I think it's everyone's business. And hardly a secret," I add.

"We are both professionals. Shit!" She slams on the brakes. We slide to a stop before a giant blue beast that waves two massive claws at us. Aolani flickers the headlights at the coconut crab. It seems to take the hint and lumber to the side, where it takes a final moment to shake its fist. I shudder and lean away. She guns us forward.

"My new deep, dark secret is that I'm terrified of coconut crabs," I mutter.

"You really want to know my secret?" Aolani says abruptly. "My most terrible thought that keeps me awake at night?"

"Yes!"

"This is a career-making project."

"Yes?"

"A luxury eco-lodge, funded by a world-renowned billionaire in one of the places I love most. This is everything I've ever dreamed of. Challenging, inspiring, and if I get it right, game changing. The advances in environmentally friendly, sustainable development practices alone..."

"I'm not getting the terrible part."

"And I don't want to do it anymore," Aolani states flatly. "I don't care if Ronin or the naturalists discover something that kills this project. I hope they do."

"Because you don't like working for MacManus?"

"No. He is merely an arrogant haole. You can't work on the

islands without encountering his type. At a certain point, it doesn't matter if one is ten times or even a hundred times wealthier than another. An asshole is an asshole."

I can't fault that logic.

"It's Pomaikai itself."

"You don't think it should be developed? It's too ecologically fragile."

"I think *it* doesn't want to be developed. When I first arrived, I could feel the beauty, the purity of such untouched land. It spoke to me, and I promised I would do right by it. But there have been too many frightening accidents, more than seem probable. Lately, when I hear the trees rustling in the breeze, see the shadows collecting along the shore...I can feel a shift in the energy here. Ronin has, too. Pomaikai might have welcomed us once, but now, there's a change in its intent, a dark turn of its own heart. Pomaikai doesn't want us here anymore. And you can't fight with nature. One way or another, it'll have its way."

CHAPTER 20

W<small>E'VE JUST SPRAYED OUR WAY</small> through another enormous puddle when the missing UTV comes into view. Aolani slams on the brakes. Our vehicle has barely come to a full stop, and we're both out, flashlights bobbing through the rain. No sign of Charlie. I radio in the news, get a staticky confirmation from Vaughn, while Aolani grabs the walking sticks and medical kit. She doesn't have to tell me to hurry up. The discovery of an abandoned vehicle on a dark and stormy night is enough to kick my sense of urgency into high gear.

It takes me a few seconds before I discover the trail of trampled grass Ronin and I followed earlier in the day. I catch the bright reflection of a glistening ruby-red shell, hear more scuttling from over there. I don't want to enter the underbrush at this time of night and in these conditions, but I don't have a choice. Clearly, Charlie came to check out the grave site on his own. Why? And what happened to cause him to be gone this long? Surely he was thinking he'd be in and out before anyone discovered that he was missing.

The downpour batters against my Gore-Tex hood, reducing my world to a single thunderous sound, while my flashlight carves out a narrow beam of light. I take a deep breath, then, as the designated guide, plunge forward. I immediately start slipping and sliding. If I thought the trail was challenging the first time around, the conditions have only made it trickier. I can feel Aolani pressing impatiently behind me. We need to find Charlie and we need to find him now.

I use the walking stick to sweep the underbrush before me as more eyes appear in the dark. Then, a resounding thwack as I connect with something solid and send it reeling.

Please don't let coconut crabs be the vengeful type.

I careen down a small dip, tripping over roots, sloshing into mud. I right myself just in time to catch movement at the base of one of the Pisonia trees. A ruckus as two bodies collide. I frantically flick my flashlight to the right in time to catch a giant coconut crab dragging a smaller, still flailing orange ghost crab away.

Don't think about it. Forward momentum. Eyes straight ahead.

I slip over another root, go down on one knee, Aolani nearly falling over me. For a second, my foot is caught. I kick frantically, rip free from the tangle of plants, then surge to standing. I spy more evidence of trampled underbrush and power forward.

Rain, mud, muck. Giant crabs, vicious predators, hydraulic claws.

Just move.

I can tell the moment we're close. The rain now tastes of salt as we stagger up the small knoll overlooking the ocean. No sign of the angel terns or sound of raucous seabirds as I head to the right, scooching under the umbrella of two trees.

And then...

I wave my arm frantically to grab Aolani's attention.

"I've found him, I've found him, I've found him."

I twist around.

"And he doesn't look good."

I TRY TO raise Vaughn on the radio. No matter what I do, however, I only hear static. After a half dozen attempts, I give up and join Aolani in tending to Charlie.

"We have to get the tree limb off him," she murmurs. She wipes gently at the dark curls plastered against his pale cheek. Charlie's eyelids flutter slightly. That's it.

He's landed facedown in the mud, the falling branch having caught him from behind. There's blood on the back of his head, where maybe the bough hit him first. Now it rests across his back, a massive, leafy obstruction of considerable weight.

"How long do you think he's been like this?" I ask Aolani.

"Too long. His cheek feels cool to the touch. It's possible he's suffering from exposure. We need to get him back to base camp ASAP."

Aolani rises to standing. She studies the downed branch, paces left, paces right, points a finger at me.

"You, stand there."

I do.

"Grab the branching limbs closest to you as near to the base as you can get."

I do.

"On the count of three."

She counts. We heave. The log moves incrementally.

"Again."

We repeat, the wind gusting our hoods back from our faces, allowing the rain to cascade inside our coats, down our backs. I don't notice it anymore. I'm too intent on watching the prone form on the ground, willing Charlie to groan, twitch, scream. Something. Anything.

Please still be alive.

After the fourth attempt, Aolani steps away—it's clear we don't have enough brute strength between us. I play with the radio once more while she stalks around the target. I can tell from the expression on her face she will get this done or die trying.

I looked like that once. But then the dying part became too real and involved too many other people. How many bullets have I escaped now? Some part of me has always assumed there's still one out there bearing my name. It'll find me someday, and when it does, I won't protest. I'll remember cradling Paul's head on my lap as I tried to stanch the flow of blood blooming across his stomach. I'll remember my new friend in the wilds of Wyoming and how sure I was I could save him. Until I didn't.

The ledger of my life is filled with red. The Beautiful Butcher hadn't been wrong; I'm desperate for a win.

The radio is still filled with nothing but static. I give Aolani a helpless shrug. She nods once, then bends down, positioning two rocks beneath the leafy branch on Charlie's right, then after a bit of hunting, repeats the process on his left. She picks up the walking sticks and tosses one to me.

"Leverage," she states.

I get it. Moving behind him, we each wedge the end of our walking stick into the narrow space between the stones and the branch. On the count of three, I plant my feet and push down for all I'm worth.

A shudder from the branch. A groan from the man on the ground.

"More," Aolani grunts through the rain.

I put my back into it, gritting my teeth, cursing, praying, cursing some more. Slowly, the limb lifts.

"Come on, come on, come on," Aolani chants. The limb hovers an inch or two off Charlie's back. It's enough to ease the weight off him, but not enough to shift the branch itself. We arrive at the same conclusion at the same time. If we can't move the obstacle any more, then we have to move him.

"I've got it," Aolani barks out. "Go!"

No time to argue. I drop my walking stick, leaving Aolani shuddering with the strain as I dash around to Charlie's head, slip both my hands under his shoulders, and pull hard. Immediate resistance. Maybe his clothes are caught? I wrestle with his body, trying to wiggle him side to side.

"Now," Aolani screams at me, her arms shaking.

I dig in my heels and heave back a second time. This time Charlie's hips pop free and his body slides toward mine. I just have time to scramble backward and yank his entire form free. Then, with a cascade of green leaves, the oversize limb collapses onto the ground.

A loud groan. Aolani, I think, then realize it's too close to be coming from her. A second sound escapes from Charlie's lips. I nearly cry in relief, cupping his cheeks with my hands.

"Come on, you crazy bastard. Wake up!"

A fresh moan from him as Aolani slides into place beside me, med kit in hand. I grab the warming blankets and start spreading silver foil thermal wraps over Charlie's inert form while she digs through the kit for bandages.

I've just reached Charlie's waist with the blankets when his fingers suddenly snap around mine.

"It's okay," I murmur into his ear. "We got you. You're safe now."

"Frankie—"

"Shh..." I wipe smears of dirt from his face with my thumb, trying to soothe him with my touch. His gray eyes flutter open. I can't tell if he's actually conscious or floating somewhere in between.

"Don't let them take me off the atoll," he whispers hoarsely. His words are hard to catch over the noise of the storm. I lean closer.

"It's okay—"

"I can't leave."

"Everything will be just fine."

"Promise me." His voice is stronger, demanding. I glance over at Aolani, but she's still playing with bandages.

"You've been hit in the head," I try to explain.

But he's shaking his head in agitation, his grip now an iron clasp around my wrist. "Promise me!"

Aolani looks up.

Charlie peers straight at me. "I can't leave. Not before she gets here. She's the key. I know it."

Then his eyes drift shut, and I'm left wondering what the hell he just said. And what it means that he spoke without a single trace of an Australian accent.

"We're going to need help to get him out of here," Aolani

states. "Run back to the UTV and see if you can radio base camp from there."

I do, slipping and sliding through the wet greens, ignoring beady eyes and snapping claws. And when Vaughn's voice finally crackles over the airwaves, I dig my fingernails into the palms of my hands to stop the shudders of relief racking my body.

MUCH LATER, WE have Charlie back at camp. Ronin and Vaughn take over inspecting the damage. Charlie's eyes are open again. He almost seems alert. But he remains silent as he slides an arm around each of his friends' shoulders and lets them assist him back to his cabin.

With him tended to, Aolani and I finally have our turn in the showers. We don't talk. We are soaked to the bone, covered in mud and leaves, and streaked with salt from the ocean spray. A three-minute Navy shower isn't nearly enough. With the water off, I scrub and scrub. But it's all so sticky, and my hair...good God, my hair. I hear sounds from the stall next to me. Aolani crying. Frustration? Rage? Relief?

I'm having a hard time choosing myself.

A final rinse of cold water that still feels better than the rain, then I do the best I can to wrestle a dry T-shirt and cotton shorts over my still damp skin. The material feels so soft and warm, I choke back my own sob.

I'm running on fumes by the time I stagger back to my cabin. As I crawl onto my bed, hair still dripping, I hear a chime.

My cell. It takes me a minute to remember where it is, what I've done with it.

Charger. Nightstand. I fumble around till I manage to get my phone in hand, peering tiredly at the screen. Against all odds, a text has managed to get through.

It's from Victoria Twanow. A single-word reply to my earlier message: *Sorry.*

I have no idea what that means.

I collapse back onto the bed, and within moments I'm sound asleep.

CHAPTER 21

THE NEXT MORNING, EVERY MUSCLE in my body aches as I drag myself out of bed and trudge out of my cabin. It's late, midmorning, and entirely too bright as the storm has evaporated, leaving a blazing hot sun behind. I swear I can see the steam rising from the vegetation around me. There are bent trees, shredded leaves, and downed branches everywhere. The entire camp looks like a bomb went off.

I discover Crabby in the middle of the walkway, surrounded by a treasure trove of orange blossoms. For once, he doesn't scuttle away upon my approach. Maybe he thinks he's safely camouflaged. Or he's petal drunk.

I wish him good morning. The words come out hoarse and croaky. He immediately bolts. I don't blame him. If I look as good as I sound, I'm beyond disaster.

I head to the mess hall for coffee and to apologize for oversleeping the breakfast shift. It's well past time for me to be doing whatever Ann and Trudy tell me to do, though I'm not sure I can lift my arms today, let alone follow intelligent instructions.

The kitchen is shockingly empty. The serving table is covered in an assortment of offerings. Bread. Yogurt. Cereal. Fruit. Clearly a DIY affair. Apparently, my fellow campmates are equally exhausted by last night's drama.

It makes me feel better as I pour my first mug of coffee. I'm already sweating from the humidity, my T-shirt clinging to my skin, but it doesn't stop me from welcoming the piping hot brew. I have a vague memory of reading somewhere that it's better to drink warm beverages in the heat. Something about it requires less energy for your body to process, blah, blah, blah.

I carry my mug into the dining room, looking forward to enjoying my caffeine fix in peace.

Of course, Vaughn is sitting there.

"You look as good as I feel," I say, pulling out the plastic chair across from him.

He grunts, his attention off in the horizon. This morning's faded blue T-shirt has a hole next to the rounded collar and some kind of stain on the shoulder. It fits his unruly whiskers and mussed hair. I wonder if he's slept at all, because he certainly doesn't look like it.

On the other hand, if he doesn't want to talk, I'm down with that. I pick up my mug and take my first sip while gazing out over the ocean. The lapping waves sparkle in the sun, the birds back out in full force, cartwheeling across the sky and cawing raucously. I imagine the atoll is now bustling with various life-forms, emerging from the storm and busily scavenging food. Everything is alive and joyful. Except for the humans.

I've never seen the base camp so empty. The dining hall feels positively eerie without Trudy and Ann's chattering presence.

"How is Charlie?" Maybe I don't do silence well.

"I don't know."

I cock my head at this. That doesn't sound like the circus master I've come to know.

Vaughn sighs at last, pulls his gaze away from the distance and focuses on me instead. "He probably has a concussion. Compressed neck, cracked skull. Hell if I know. Either way, he's suffering from injuries well beyond the scope of a basic first aid kit. Policy 101, he's off the island. Time for the man to head to Honolulu for real medical care."

"Before little problems become big problems," I recall from last night.

"Exactly."

"Is he refusing? Can he? Aren't you the boss?"

"Exactly!" Now Vaughn sounds more like himself. "But in case you haven't noticed, Charlie's one stubborn SOB."

I've noticed. I remember what Charlie had said last night, that he couldn't leave before she arrived. The only "she" I can think of is Lea. Which brings me to my next question:

"Is MacManus on track to arrive today?"

"Yeah." Vaughn sighs again, sits upright. "Which is my next problem. We got a helluva lot of cleanup to get done. At least we have some extra time. Some mixup with his catering order, so they're delayed till midafternoon."

"Catering order?"

"Man travels with all his own food. Apparently, they forgot his kale."

"Seriously?"

"Yep. Also travels with his own chef and personal assistant. Fortunately, they're a married couple and already have a designated cabin. However..."

I set down my coffee cup and lean forward. "However?"

"Problem three. He's bringing a couple of guys."

"The extra resources you requested? That was fast!"

"I didn't request them." Vaughn stares at me.

I need a moment. "You didn't mention the camp accidents, Charlie's injuries, the need for reinforcements?"

"I didn't have a chance. Mac started by announcing the additional passengers. And he didn't refer to them as scientists or engineers or experts A, B, or C. He said he was bringing two of his men."

"Two of his men? As in security?" Now I am intrigued.

"That's what it sounded like. Which, given the circumstances, is helpful. Except, of course, I gotta find lodging for two extra people, and it's not like there's a rental market on a deserted atoll. Only thing I can think of is me moving into my office and giving them my cabin. Fuck it all."

I blink my eyes, trying to process this development. "Hang on, lodging inconveniences aside, what does it mean that MacManus was already bringing security personnel? Did he mention this yesterday when he first planned on arriving?"

Vaughn shakes his head.

"So sometime between yesterday morning and this morning, he hired two guards. The biggest events in between being the discovery of the burial mound and Charlie's midnight misadventure."

"I'd informed Mac about the discovery of the recent human remains. He didn't seem especially worried, at least not on a personal level. Future of the project." Vaughn shrugged. "Not gonna lie, the fact Ronin estimates the grave to be of modern origin was received as good news. As much as unearthing a dead body can be considered good news."

I understand what he's saying. An ancient burial would result in an almost immediate work stop as well as jeopardize MacManus's development plans. Finding some poor recently missing woman, however...Bad for her, not so relevant to the MacManuses of the world.

"You don't think the security personnel have anything to do with the grave, then. But maybe after Charlie disappeared? Do we even know why Charlie went out to the gravesite in the middle of the night, in the midst of a hurricane?"

"Curiosity." Vaughn's flat tone indicates he believes that answer as much as I do.

"Do you consider Charlie a danger?" I ask curiously.

"Given that, currently, he can barely stand upright..."

"Have you ever noticed his accent coming and going? Like maybe he's faking it?"

"Charlie?" Vaughn frowns at me, clearly surprised by my question. "His résumé says he's from Australia. When I first met him, he certainly sounded like he was from down under. Not sure I ever thought of it much after that. Does he have the heaviest accent? No. But he hasn't lived at home in decades. If he sometimes sounds more Yank than Aussie, well, he's been hanging out with the riffraff for a while now."

"Maybe." I don't mention the other details from last night. I want to talk to Charlie first. I want to know exactly what he meant by "her," not to mention what he was really doing at the burial site.

"But either way," Vaughn is saying now, "Mac arranged for security personnel before I told him about last night."

"Before *you* told him. But what about someone else? As the architect, Aolani must be comfortable contacting him directly. Or maybe Ronin?"

"They didn't. I asked."

"Oh." Now I'm a little stumped, too. "Is there something else going on?" I venture at last. "Something that happened in Mac-Manus's world, versus our little slice of paradise?"

Vaughn tilts his head to the side. "Possible," he allows. "Mac didn't mention anything. But . . . possible. I can ask him more when he arrives. Speaking of which." Vaughn rises to standing. "I gotta move into my office. You"—he smiles pointedly—"get to change over my cabin for two new visitors. And the entire crew"—he heads toward the dinner bell—"gets to play pick-up sticks."

He rings the bell, summoning the rest of the inmates. Midnight drama over; we're officially back to work.

Before MacManus arrives in a matter of hours.

With Lea.

And my true mission begins.

I HIT THE bathhouse to pick up clean linens for Vaughn's cabin. There, I confront the growing pile of laundry that apparently hasn't done itself while I've been running around the atoll. Whether I'm here under false pretenses or not, washing is my responsibility, so I get the first load of whites chugging away.

Then, armed with a pile of sheets and towels, I follow the leaf-strewn path to Vaughn's dark-green cabin all the way at the end. It's larger than the others, with an expansive front porch and an absolutely stunning two-hundred-and-seventy-degree view of the ocean, framed by drooping palm fronds. Definitely the boss's house.

I knock first, not sure if Vaughn has had time to clear out yet. When no one responds, I let myself in, already curious.

The interior is similar to mine, whitewashed exposed framing with a churning ceiling fan and gray-painted floor. The window trim is a cheery aqua color, while a small, parlor-size table with seating for two sits by the window, perfect for a morning cup of coffee.

The right side of the space is dominated by a pair of twin beds, which I'm guessing are generally pushed together but now have been awkwardly separated to accommodate the two new residents. I set down the pile of fresh bedding on the closest mattress, but then I am immediately distracted by a floor-to-ceiling bookcase. I spy well-thumbed paperbacks with sci-fi-looking covers. Glossy hardcovers cataloging everything from fish life to seashells to flora and fauna. Travel guides from an assortment of countries. Places Vaughn has gone, wants to go?

And framed photos. Vaughn, with his arm around a beautiful dark-haired woman, in sweat-stained safari clothing. Vaughn with a group of six, laughing in the middle of an undulating red desert. Vaughn and the same woman again, except now he's all cleaned up in a white dress shirt, unbuttoned to expose the bronze column of his throat, while she's in a black graduation gown. Girlfriend? Sister? I'm desperate to know. Workday Vaughn is ridiculously sexy enough. Well-groomed Vaughn with his lean cheeks freshly shaved and vivid blue eyes practically popping out of his head...

I force myself to walk away.

There's a small dresser near the table. The top is covered with random piles of paperwork and a reading lamp. Of course he brings his work home at night. I give a cursory glance, but even by my standards it feels invasive to sort through the stacks or tug open drawers. A pity, because I'm itching to learn more.

I drag my attention back to the beds, engaging in various acts of gymnastics to wrestle on fresh sheets in such a limited space. By the time I smooth out the seashell-embroidered quilts topping each bed, I'm all hot and bothered.

I blow clinging strands of hair away from my sweaty face, roll up the dirty sheets, and trudge out into the blistering sun. Crabs scatter at the base of the stairs, while small fish go shooting through the clear water at the edge of the point. I eye the ocean longingly, then turn around and march back to the bathhouse.

And I spot Charlie sitting in front of a neighboring cabin. I don't even think about it. Sharp turn right and I'm standing in front of him, laundry still in hand. He's settled into his front rocker, nursing a steaming mug of something fragrant. He appears freshly showered, his wild salt-and-pepper hair briefly subdued in damp curls around his face, while a clean strip of bandages wraps around the top of his head, holding a giant square of gauze in place. He watches my approach with the eye that isn't swollen half shut.

"How do you feel?" I ask at last.

"Skull's a bit hammery," he allows, "but nothing that can't be fixed by a proper cup o' tea."

"Jasmine?" I finally deduce the flowery scent.

"Yessiree, Bob."

I take it he's back to Aussie speak this morning, or some variation thereof. I lean against the railing, settling the dirty sheets more comfortably in my arms. Then I regard him for a bit.

Charlie raises his mug, takes another sip. I stare at him. He stares at me. Even injured, the man refuses to blink.

"You're going to make me ask?" I break first.

"Whatever would you need me to be telling you, luv?"

"Why were you out there last night? Disturbing a grave in the middle of a tropical storm?"

"Wasn't disturbing no grave. Just out for a frolic. No better way to feel alive, man versus Mother Nature. 'Course, Mother Nature's a right bitch." He grimaces, gingerly fingers the patch of gauze.

"Liar."

Charlie's gray eyes widen at the direct accusation. He takes another sip of tea.

"If you were out just to have fun, you would've taken a radio."

"Forgot."

"You're not that stupid. Not a man with your experience. What, you thought the penguins were going to save you?"

He finally cracks a smile. For all his bravado, he looks like hell. He may be doing his best to play his usual devil-may-care self, but he isn't feeling it. Something's going on with him, and it's serious enough to keep him from leaving a remote island in order to seek proper medical attention. Which even he would agree is a very dangerous decision.

I go with a different approach.

"MacManus is scheduled to arrive this afternoon."

"Right-o. Heard the same from the boss man."

"Running late, though. They forgot his kale." I whisper the second part in a scandalized tone.

Charlie snorts. Then, proving once again he's a hard man to fool, he lowers his mug to his knee, stares me straight in the eye, and states: "I'm not returning to Honolulu on that plane, boss man's orders or not. So if Vaughn sent you to work your feminine wiles, you can sod off now and save yourself the trouble. I'm staying. You can't have a team stationed on this remote outpost without a proper engineer. Even one with a touch of the loopies is better than none at all."

"You're serious."

"Deadly so. Which is what I've told Vaughn three times

already this morning. Not going, no way, no how. Skull's already mending. By tomorrow, right as rain." He nods firmly. We both pretend the motion doesn't cause him to wince.

"Clear enough. So. Tell me about Lea."

I'd hoped to catch Charlie off guard with the abrupt change in topic. It seems to work, as he blinks at me in confusion.

"Lea? You mean Mac's ward?"

"Yes." I study the engineer intently, looking for some hint of his relationship to her, why he'd been so insistent last night he couldn't leave before she got here.

"What about her?" Charlie asks, expression wary.

"You've met her, right?"

"Aye. Super shy. I've barely heard her speak."

"She sticks with MacManus?"

"Mostly stays with the hired help in the owner's quarters. I've fetched a paddleboard for her a time or two. Taken her and Mac out boating. But her attention is always on him, not the rest of us." Charlie shrugs. "Mac and his entourage are all here today, gone tomorrow. Man has an entire globe to jet about, you know."

I nod. Charlie's description of Lea matches what Trudy and Ann had said. MacManus and his crew remain separate from the main base camp. Blow in. Blast out.

"Last night, when I was busy saving your life," I add pointedly, "you told me you couldn't leave before she got here. Because she is the key, you just know it. Who were you talking about, Charlie? Why are you really staying on the island?"

He stills mid-rock—only for a microsecond, but enough to make me notice. He tries to cover the blip by raising his mug, blowing on his no-longer-steaming tea.

"Can't hold a bloke accountable for what he says while his brains are leaking out of his ears," he defers.

I don't buy it for a minute. "Where are you from? What city in Australia?"

"No place you'd know."

"Try me."

Another staring contest, but this time I can see his pulse pounding at the base of his throat. He's not as calm as he appears.

"Katoomba."

"What?"

"Katoomba. Where I passed my tender years. Ninety minutes outside of Sydney and right beautiful if you fancy a visit."

He's lying to me. Worse, I can tell he knows that I know that he's lying. But I have nothing concrete to press him on. Whatever secrets he's protecting, he's doing a damn good job of it.

"Did you know the woman in the burial mound?" My last-ditch effort, the only other angle I can think of pursuing. "Or did you think you might?"

"Just went adventuring in the storm," he states. "Learned a valuable lesson about remembering to take a radio along. Won't happen again."

"That's not an answer."

"Right-o. Just like jawing with me doesn't get that dirty laundry any closer to clean." He nods his chin at the linens in my arms in clear dismissal. I don't want to give up the fight, and I absolutely hate being outplayed. But at the moment, he has me.

"Fine," I grumble, and just resist motioning with two fingers that I'm keeping my eyes on him.

He grins, looking like the Charlie I met for the very first time. Insult to injury, as it's clear now that Charlie is a total fake. Him, his accent, his purpose for being here. Forget MacManus's private lodge or Vaughn's executive cabin—Charlie's shack is the one I'm desperate to search.

For now, I straighten from the railing, giving him a last prob-ing starc. Who is this man and are his lies for good or for evil? He could be some kind of international criminal, using this remote outpost to hide from the law. Or maybe he was once wronged in one of MacManus's various business dealings and is now plotting his revenge?

He could be crazy. He could be dangerous.

Or he could be exactly who he says he is, an engineer who by all accounts has kept this place running with dental floss and chewing gum.

He takes another sip of tea, expression giving nothing away.

I force myself to walk away.

CHAPTER 22

THE BUZZ OF THE INCOMING aircraft draws everyone to the landing strip in an excited rush. We're all hot and sweaty from hours of hard-core cleanup. Sticks gathered, debris raked, stoops swept. After changing out Vaughn's linens, I made an emergency run to MacManus's lodge with Trudy and Ann in tow. Sure enough, there was an entire set of outdoor furniture and brightly colored pillows to be arranged on the front porch. Not to mention more pick-up sticks.

I feel like we're an army of soldiers, frantically preparing for the four-star general's arrival. Now, waiting for the sleek little Cessna to land, I have a hard time not standing at attention with my chest puffed out. Beside me, Trudy and Ann are bouncing up and down on their toes. Whether they're that excited to see their billionaire boss or it's just fresh guests in general is hard to tell.

The charter jet touches down as light as a feather, the side hatch popping open the second the engines cut out. I expect Copilot Brent to poke his head out and lower the stairs. Instead, a buzz-cut blond guy appears. His sharp gaze scours our collected group, then moves up and down the runway. He disappears back inside the cabin.

Brent emerges, his expression remote. He lowers the stairs, then retreats without so much as a wave.

Ann, who had her hand half-raised, quickly lowers it. She and Trudy exchange a look, while a low murmur works its way through the crowd.

"The first man wasn't MacManus, was it?" I whisper to them.

"Never seen him," Trudy confirms.

"So one of the two extra guys he brought with him. Hired muscle," I provide absently. "No doubt about it."

Trudy and Ann turn to stare at me. "Like, security guards? Why?"

"I have no idea." And I don't. Especially as, according to Vaughn, MacManus had hired them before hearing about Charlie's misadventure.

The first man reappears. He descends the steps, taking up position at the base, arms clasped before him. He's wearing tan trousers and a white linen dress shirt that does little to conceal the handgun holstered at his waist.

More buzzing from our group.

Vaughn takes the first step forward and promptly gets skewered by a thousand-yard stare. He wisely halts in his tracks.

Fresh person at the top of the stairs. I recognize MacManus instantly from his photo. In contrast to the camp's collective wardrobe of sweat-stained grunge, he's sporting tight-fitting linen slacks and a red, tropical-print designer shirt that probably cost more than most people's monthly rent.

I do my best not to stare as he nimbly rat-a-tats down the steps, then turns back toward the top.

There she is. Leilani Pierson. Younger sister of Keahi Pierson, aka the Beautiful Butcher. Possible kidnapped teen, forced to stay with her sister's abusive ex-boyfriend against her will. Possible adopted charge, now living a life of wealth and privilege with same ex-boyfriend.

In person, she's even more beautiful than her photo.

Like MacManus, she's dressed in five-star resort wear. A wraparound sleeveless dress in shades of red and yellow that complement MacManus's own attire. Wedge sandals with delicate straps. A single bracelet that flashes something brilliant and sparkly in the sun.

Given her footwear, she descends more carefully. After her comes the second security professional. He's dressed similarly to the first guard, with milk-chocolate skin, a perfectly shaved head, and a sharply groomed goatee.

He waits for Lea to join MacManus on the runway. MacManus holds out his hand to his young charge. When she takes it, offering a small smile but keeping her gaze down, I feel myself shudder. For all intents and purposes, they look like a couple—rich mogul and his trophy wife. I don't understand how anyone else can see this and not feel as uncomfortable as I do.

The first guard moves forward, MacManus and Lea falling in step behind him. The second security expert brings up the rear. Our normally rowdy and enthusiastic crew has fallen silent. Even Vaughn hasn't moved a muscle, simply watching MacManus and his men approach.

Belatedly, I realize two more people are now exiting the jet: an older man and woman. Must be the couple that serve as MacManus's personal chef and private secretary. Finally, Brent reappears with Captain Marilee. Both look uptight.

Definitely a big difference from my landing just two days prior.

"Vaughn," MacManus greets his project manager.

"Mac."

They don't shake hands, but nod in acknowledgment. Vaughn's gaze remains locked on the two new men. We're all staring. Given our highly informal summer camp vibe, the arrival of two stony-faced professionals is disorienting.

"Shall we?"

Apparently, MacManus isn't one to dally. He gestures impatiently toward the waiting UTV. Vaughn shakes his head, clearly unhappy with what he's seeing. But he leads the way, with security goon one, MacManus, Lea, and security goon two all in tow.

We all continue to gawk as the group of five arrives at a vehicle that only holds four. Low muttering. General maneuvering, followed by more muttering. Finally, Vaughn takes the wheel with blond bodyguard beside him, MacManus and Lea in the back. The second bodyguard prepares to hoof it after them.

The UTV lurches forward, and just like that, our group bursts to life in an explosion of chatter and general *what the fuck?* No doubt about it, the swear jar is going to be full tonight. Trudy and Ann scamper ahead to welcome Brent and Marilee while no doubt pumping them for the inside scoop. Everyone else heads for the cargo hatch to start the unloading process.

I go with my first instinct and chase after the lone bodyguard with the impressively groomed goatee.

"Let me show you the way," I declare brightly, falling in step beside him.

He skewers me with his deep, dark eyes. Why are the best eyelashes always wasted on men?

I hold out my hand. "Frankie Elkin. I'm in charge of housekeeping, laundry, and food prep. In practical terms, I know where all the good snacks are hidden."

"Elias Jackson," he allows.

"I set up the project manager's cabin for you and your buddy to use."

"Jason Tamworth," he supplies. "Location?"

It takes me a moment to realize he's referring to Vaughn's cabin, where they'll be staying. "Umm, at the edge of base camp. Set out on a knoll. Absolutely stunning view," I assure him. "Second only to MacManus's private lodge."

"Which is?"

"At the other end of things? Maybe fifteen minutes away."

"No."

"No?"

"We will require closer accommodations. A neighboring hut."

"There isn't any neighboring hut. Well, the cabin used by Mac-Manus's chef and personal assistant is near there."

"We'll take it."

I blink, realizing belatedly that even knowing some sort of private security team was arriving, Vaughn hadn't completely understood that a private security team was arriving. As in they'd want to have eyes on their charge at all times. And MacManus probably expected that as well.

"I will make it happen." I offer another bright smile, determined to break the ice.

Elias doesn't so much as glance my way. His determined strides are much longer than mine, leaving me to scamper beside him like a toy poodle. Somehow, I doubt that bothers him.

We reach the intersection with the latrine and the bathhouse. I point out both, then spy the UTV now parked at the rear of the mess hall and lead us in that direction. After walking so fast in the heat and humidity, I welcome the relief of the fan-cooled kitchen.

Vaughn and company are in the dining room, MacManus and

Lea seated with glasses of water before them, Vaughn and the first bodyguard—Jason—standing next to the table. Jason looks up sharply at our approach.

Seeing Elias, he moves from the center of the space to take up position next to the side door. Jason smoothly inserts himself in the cutout between the kitchen and dining area, guarding the rear. No doubt about it, these two are hard-core. Well trained and, most likely, extremely expensive.

What the fuck, indeed.

I busy myself filling two more glasses of water and offering them to the security professionals in order to justify my presence in the room. Both refuse. I barely notice, already eavesdropping away.

"Don't you think this is a bit much?" Vaughn is asking.

"Not your problem."

"The hell it isn't. Half of my job is camp dynamics. These two"—he skewers the stony-faced guards—"don't exactly blend in."

"And yet, here they are. Get over it."

Vaughn scowls, rakes his hair. I see a small smile form around MacManus's lips. Clearly he knows his friend well and understands the level of aggravation communicated in that single gesture.

"Captain Marilee and Copilot Brent are staying as well."

"What?" Now Vaughn doesn't bother to hide his frustration. "You know this isn't actually a resort yet. I can't just pull extra lodging out of my ass."

That smirk again. "No worries. They'll sleep on the plane."

"What the hell is going on, Mac?"

"Just some extra precautions. You know, nothing like success to paint a target on a man's back."

"Oh, come on. You've been successful for as long as I've known you. You've never had private security before."

MacManus merely shrugs. Lea, I notice, keeps her gaze on the table. But there's a set to her shoulders that tells me she's paying attention to every word spoken. Like a lot of quiet people, she's an excellent listener.

"How long?" Vaughn asks now. "Extra people means extra work, extra food. I need some sort of timeline."

"I haven't decided yet."

"So help me God, Mac—"

"I brought extra food."

"You know, just because we're friends and I work for you doesn't mean I won't kill you."

Both bodyguards immediately step forward.

"Oh, for Chrissake." Now Vaughn is losing it.

MacManus holds up a hand to still his men. His smile has grown into a full grin. He's good-looking in a privileged white guy sort of way. I can see where younger Keahi Pierson would be drawn to him. But there's something about him that puts me on edge. And not just that I'm biased from the stories I've been told; he's a little too well groomed, a little too smirky. I could know nothing at all about this man, and I still wouldn't trust him.

Now Lea places a dainty hand over MacManus's on the table.

"Please," she says quietly.

"I know. It's been a long day. Just a bit longer, then we can retreat to the lodge."

"I can take her," I speak up immediately.

MacManus looks over at me and frowns, as if realizing for the first time there's waitstaff in the room. "That won't be necessary."

"Please," Lea states again.

He returns his attention to her, his tone soothing. "Given the circumstances, it's best for us to stay together."

"Even here, at one of the most inaccessible places on earth?" Lea fingers her brow. "My head. I'd just like to rest. Please."

In response, MacManus squeezes her hand gently. His look is surprisingly sympathetic. "Are you sure?" He splits his attention between Lea and me. She nods, I go with:

"No problem. I'll take her straight to your lodge."

Another moment of reluctance. Then:

"Fine. Go on ahead. I'll be there shortly."

Lea rises gracefully. I don't waste a moment, leading her promptly out the back of the mess hall to the waiting UTV. She doesn't say a word as she awkwardly climbs aboard, then smooths a hand over the skirt of her tight dress.

I can barely believe my luck in engineering an opportunity for a private conversation so quickly. My hand is fairly shaking with adrenaline as I start the engine.

"My name's Frankie," I inform her, hitting the path.

"Lea MacManus," she replies quietly.

So she's already taken his name. Crazy.

This is it. The moment I've been waiting for. Where to begin, how to ask. I'm not going to have many chances to get this right. I wait till we pass the dock, clear the edge of the base camp. Then I turn to her, take a deep breath, and call out over the noise of the crashing waves: "I know what happened to Noodles the cat."

CHAPTER 23

LEA RECOILS IN THE SEAT beside me. Her hand goes to the door as if she's preparing to bail from the moving vehicle, while her eyes widen in fear. Of all the reactions, this isn't one I'd been expecting.

"Who are you? What do you want?" Her fingers scrabble with the handle.

"Hey, hey, hey. I'm here to help. Honestly, I swear. I'm a friend. Come in peace." I'm babbling, her own anxiety triggering mine.

"How do you know about Noodles?"

"I read the letter you sent to your sister."

"My sister?"

"Kaylee Pierson? Well, Keahi Pierson now."

If anything, Lea's eyes grow wider. "You! You helped her? You're in on this."

Now I'm totally confused. "In on what?"

"*Who* are you?"

"Frankie Elkin. I search for missing people. Your family, well, your sister, reached out to me. They've never stopped looking for you, Leilani. They want you home safe."

"You're a private investigator?"

"No. Just a woman with a weird hobby, not being good at sports or skilled at crafts." I'm still babbling. Honestly, it's like I've never done this before. But Lea's response is throwing me for a loop. No relief or even denial. Just terror. In ever-increasing amounts.

"Stop. Just, let me go. Release me now, and I won't tell Mac anything. I promise."

"You don't need to be afraid of him."

"*Afraid* of him? What's wrong with you?"

I have totally lost control of this conversation. I take a deep breath, slowing the UTV just in case Lea decides to jump out. Given the size of MacManus's bodyguards, I don't want to discover what will happen to me if Lea winds up injured on my watch.

"Keahi received your note. The one explaining how you ended up with MacManus. That you just realized she was still alive, and that you forgave her and loved her. She'd thought she'd lost you, too. You have no idea."

"I don't know what you're talking about."

"Keahi Pierson is your older sister, right? AKA the Beautiful Butcher?"

"Yes." Lea's tone is hushed, guarded, like revealing a secret told only in dark corners after midnight.

"I found a second note. In your bedroom here. Well, the tiny room across from the master."

Lea shakes her head. "Please just leave me alone. Whatever it is you want, I can't help you."

"It's okay. You can trust me. I don't care about Keahi. I won't betray you to MacManus. I work for the missing. And that's you, Leilani. You are my focus."

"Then why did you help her?"

"Who?"

"Keahi. Why did you help my sister escape?"

And just like that, I get it. The new security personnel, Mac-Manus's now indefinite stay on a remote atoll that in Lea's own words is one of the most inaccessible places on earth. I hit the brakes, bringing us to a full stop in the middle of the path, with the brilliant sun above and sparkling ocean to the left and waving palm fronds on our right. Paradise. Absolute, complete paradise.

Except it isn't.

"Keahi broke out of prison?"

"Yesterday morning."

I close my eyes. "It's okay," I attempt. "I'll contact her lawyer, Victoria Twanow. I'm sure she can still help us. We'll make some excuse to return to Honolulu, and Twanow will take it from there."

"No, she won't."

"Yes, she will. She cares, Leilani. You deserve a chance—"

"Keahi's attorney is in the hospital. Keahi beat her half to death, then stole her clothes and fled with some prison guard. They don't expect the lawyer woman to live."

I gape like a fish. I instruct my mouth to close, but it won't cooperate. I want to argue that there's no way such a thing could happen. But several thoughts strike me at once, including the first time I saw Victoria Twanow and noted how much she resembled her notorious client. Tucked away in a private room, it would be easy for Keahi to attack her idealist lawyer and steal her clothes, particularly with the assistance of some stupidly enamored corrections officer. I wonder about the one who'd greeted Twanow when I was there. Had his friendliness already been an act, a way to further lower the lawyer's defenses?

The text I received last night. A single word: *Sorry*. I'd assumed it had come from Twanow, but now I get it. Keahi, stealing her lawyer's phone, intercepting her messages. The closest she could come to revealing the truth. Of course, that leads to an interesting question. Sorry for lying to me or sorry for what's about to happen next?

Somehow, I doubt Keahi worries much about dishonesty, meaning...

"She can't really get all the way out here, can she?" I ask without thinking.

Beside me, Lea shrugs. My immediate concern seems to have eased hers. "Why do you think we're staying? We would've arrived even earlier if not for the storm."

I nod. "Only two ways to access this atoll, right? Private jet."

"I don't think Mac will send one for her," Lea assures me.

"Or boat. But that takes a week or something like that."

"Mac has ordered a restriction on all shipping traffic in this area."

"He can do that?"

She shrugs again. "He's Mac."

Enough said. But that still leaves me with questions. "You didn't send a note to your sister?"

"No."

"Did you know she was alive, that she's on death row?"

"Yes."

"For how long?"

"Since the day she was arrested. Mac told me."

I give up on all pretense of driving and turn sideways to face her. "Do you feel safe with him?"

"Of course."

"Even after what he did to your sister?"

"You mean, did they fight? Was it physical?"

"Yes."

Lea nods shortly. Her dark eyes are hard to read. "He hit her; she beat him. I don't remember everything, but I remember enough. All my memories of my sister involve blood and violence. When Mac told me what she had done, the men she'd murdered...I wasn't surprised that she'd killed so many. Only that she'd been caught."

"Does he hit you?"

"I'm not my sister."

Which I think is an interesting answer. "And Noodles the cat?"

"I had a kitten named Noodles. But she ran away a long time ago. How do you know about Noodles?"

"She was mentioned in the note. That Mac had killed Noodles to discourage you from leaving him."

"The message I didn't write," Lea clarifies. For all of her meekness in MacManus's company, she certainly seems direct enough now. It makes me wonder if it's a show she puts on for Mac's benefit, a way to manage a man she knows can be violent when challenged directly, as her sister did.

"Who else would know about Noodles?" I ask now.

"Keahi, of course."

"Is that how you think of your sister, Keahi versus Kaylee?"

"I know I was born in Texas, but I don't remember much of those days or my parents. I remember Hawaii, and in Hawaii, she was Keahi and I was Leilani."

"Then why did you return to using the name Lea?"

"Mac thought it was best, after Keahi had disappeared."

"She disappeared?" Now I arch a brow. "Because in her version of events, *you* disappeared."

Lea shakes her head. "No. I was with Mac. I was always with Mac. I don't know what happened to Keahi."

"According to her, you tried to interfere one night when Mac attacked her. He flung you against a wall. When she retaliated, he beat her so badly she ended up in the hospital. By the time she got out, you were gone. She and the rest of your family—your auntie and cousins?—searched everywhere for you, including Mac's house, but you were nowhere to be found."

Lea shakes her head. "I have no memory of such a night."

"You simply woke up one morning and your sister was gone?"

"Yes."

"And you never questioned that?"

Lea shrugs, apparently unmoved by her sister's account. "I did ask. Mac said she left. The cook agreed. And I was sad, but not surprised. I was young, but already old enough to sense my sister's rage. She could be terrifying, and that was before she'd met Mac. Learning that she'd disappeared, I mostly felt relieved, like I could breathe again. And Mac took good care of me. He promised I would always be safe with him, and he's held true to his word."

"You're not afraid of him?"

"No."

"He's not violent with you?"

"Never."

"And when did he first start sleeping with you?" I ask the question matter-of-factly. I want to see her reaction.

She doesn't respond immediately. Her thickly fringed eyes peer over my shoulder, to the rippling ocean beyond. Her face is perfectly beautiful, and smoothly expressionless. I've seen such looks before, on survivors of long-term abuse who've learned to completely mask their emotions in order to avoid future punishment.

"He has not touched me."

There's just enough inflection for me to catch what she isn't saying. "Yet," I fill in. I do some considering of my own, reach a logical conclusion: "Your eighteenth birthday?"

"Given Mac's profile, it's important for everything to be perfectly proper."

"Proper as in waiting to have sex with the barely legal girl who should be like a daughter to him?"

"My body, my choice."

She states the words calmly. They still break my heart. The depth of naivety, of believing she's the one making the decision, when someone older and smarter has been manipulating her all along. There's a saying that the devil's greatest trick was convincing the world he didn't exist. That's what MacManus, like so many other abusers, has done—convinced his victim he's not evil.

Between Keahi's and Lea's stories, I don't know who to believe, but I know this much is true: MacManus is taking advantage of his position of power.

"I'm here for you," I repeat to Lea, trying to drill into her the depth of my sincerity. "Keahi may have asked me to start this search, but I don't work for the family; I work for the missing. I care about you."

"There's no need."

"And yet, here I am." I restart the UTV, resume our bouncing journey to the owner's lodge. I need to think. She said versus she said. Both probably with some truth, and both probably with a few lies. Of all the pieces, the lies will be the most telling and what I need to figure out first.

Especially as Keahi Pierson has escaped from death row.

While my lifeline to the mainland, Victoria Twanow, is now at death's door.

———

I AGREE WITH MacManus's assessment: one way or another, Keahi will do her best to find him and Leilani. Given the difficulty of accessing this island, we should have some time to prepare. Except I have another troubling fact still to consider.

We pull up to the lodge, the freshly furnished front porch beckoning cheerfully. I don't say a word as I lead Lea up the steps. I open the front door first, noticing she has no problem remaining tucked behind me as I make a brief inspection of the space. When I confirm all rooms are empty, Lea takes a hesitant step through the door and seems to eye the main room for herself before finally walking into the kitchen. She takes down a glass and fills it with water.

She doesn't offer me one, a pointed reminder it's time for me to go.

I have one last card to play. I gesture to the notepad tucked beside the refrigerator.

"Give me your phone number. If I learn anything about Keahi, I promise to contact you immediately."

After a moment, Lea picks up the pen and complies.

At the last minute: "Anyone else I should contact? A friend from home? Someone to notify in case of emergency?"

Her expression is more unsettled, but once again, she jots down the info. I take the piece of paper from her, give a nod of acknowledgment.

"Hope you feel better soon." Then I'm out the door, note still clutched in my hand. I wait till I'm back in the UTV before I dare to look at it. It's not the information I care about. It's how it's written.

In small, precise lettering, so straight it might have been penned using a ruler.

In other words, the exact opposite of the large, childish script used for both the messages I'd seen signed by Leilani Pierson. Meaning someone else had authored those notes.

Who? To what end?

And where are they now?

Because I'd discovered the second note in this house. On this remote atoll.

One of the most inaccessible places on earth.

Which doesn't matter, if the threat is already here.

CHAPTER 24

PARK THE UTV AT THE rear of the mess hall, entering the kitchen with my mind a million miles away, and immediately come to a halt. There are three people now working the prep space, and it doesn't take a rocket scientist to determine none of them are happy about it.

Trudy has a very large knife in her hands and is dicing carrots in a dazzling display of speed and force. Ann stands across from her at the giant mixer, where she's dumping ingredients into the bowl in massive puffs of white flour. Both appear thin-lipped with barely contained fury.

Meanwhile, a petite woman with a halo of riotous brown curls is busily rearranging the contents of the refrigerator while clucking under her tongue.

Rat-a-tat-tat goes Trudy's oversize knife across the cutting board, while whack-whack goes Ann's measuring cup against the metal mixer.

I stay perfectly still, a gazelle caught out in the open, pretty sure I've been spotted, unsure which predator will pounce first.

The dark-haired woman pulls back from the refrigerator. She eyes me up and down.

"Chef Kiki," she declares with a French flare. "Et vous?"

"Uhhh, Frankie." I'm already guessing she's MacManus's personal chef. Her husband must be the private secretary who's currently sitting in the dining room. Except I thought they kept to themselves.

"What do you do, Frankie?" Chef Kiki hits the last syllable of my name with enough trill to turn it into a carnival ride. I've never felt so exotic.

"Umm, prep cook?"

"Non! I already have two prep cooks. I do not need a third."

"MacManus has decided we should all eat together," Ann declares tightly.

"Meaning we should all cook together." Trudy jabs the air with her knife. I have no illusions who she's fantasizing about stabbing.

"I, uh, I have other responsibilities." Though I'd been hoping to catch up with Trudy and Ann about whatever intel they'd gleaned from the pilots, Brent and Marilee, now, however, definitely isn't the time. "Laundry!" I manage, remembering—sadly—the piles I still haven't gotten to.

"Oui. Laundry. Something that is not here. Parfait. Au revoir."

Okay then. I give Trudy and Ann a sympathetic shrug, then hightail it out of the lion's den. Vaughn's right: MacManus is messing with our camp dynamics. If he's not careful, outside attack will be the least of his concerns. So far, Trudy is ready to go Sweeney Todd at any moment.

Laundry is an excellent idea and one of my required duties. Making a left and heading to the bathhouse would be a highly responsible choice. Of course, I turn right and follow the path toward the cluster of cabins that serve as resident housing. I'm not sure what I'm hoping to find, but it only takes me minutes to have success.

Vaughn, MacManus, and the goon squad have all gathered before Charlie's cabin—Vaughn and MacManus crowding the tiny front porch, Elias and Jason in position at the base of the steps below. They immediately register my approach, following me with their narrowed eyes. I keep on walking, nice and steady, as if I have a very good reason for strolling along, scattering hermit crabs before me.

The moment I round the bend, I duck behind a clump of bushes. I have to strain to hear from this distance, especially over the rustling palm fronds and lapping ocean, but where there's a will, there's a way.

"If you were really stationed at McMurdo, why hasn't Esperanza heard of you?" MacManus is demanding to know.

"Don't know any Esperanza, mate. I worked with Abigail Gibbens, if that name means anything to you."

"Esperanza signed your reports."

"Right-o. But I never met any Esperanza. Could be some administrative bloke. The boss men aren't always in the field, you know. Prefer their cushy offices, versus mucking about."

The last words are a not-so-subtle jab at MacManus. Yes, everyone is in fine spirits now.

"I think you're lying."

"Cuz I got felled by a tree? Sorry my bleeding skull offends you."

"Why were you out in the storm? Just be honest." Vaughn now, sounding less hostile than MacManus but equally impatient.

"Told ya. Drive about. Stupid me. Regret it plenty."

A low growl of frustration from MacManus. "I don't trust you."

"Makes you feel better, I don't trust you, either."

"I want him locked up." MacManus, clearly having had enough.

"Like under house arrest?" Vaughn asks.

"Exactly. Watched at all times."

"Uh, Mac. Look around you. We don't exactly have the facilities or the manpower to be incarcerating the crew. Unless, of course, you're volunteering your guys."

Silence, which I take to mean no.

"Move him to your office. You got a lock on that door, don't you?"

"Lock him in with the main computer, comm control, and gun cabinet? Sure, let's do that." Vaughn doesn't bother to hide his sarcasm.

"The plane, then. He can stay with Marilee and Brent."

"There's not enough room for three people on that plane. Hell, Marilee and Brent shouldn't even be staying there. If you're this concerned, have them fly him back to Honolulu. We could use the empty cabin."

"The Cessna doesn't leave without me."

"Perfect. You can go with them." This time, Vaughn is not sarcastic.

"Lone. Engineer." Charlie is speaking up in clear, clipped tones. "Don't care what you think of me, mate." I take it he's addressing MacManus. "But I've kept this camp running on a wing and a prayer. Despite ocean air that corrodes wiring almost as fast as I can replace it, and a dingy comm tower half the size and power of what we really need. Your guys good with plumbing, electrical, and fiberglass hull repair? Are they boat captains and crack fishermen, capable of bringing home fresh dinner for the masses? Cuz if not, sending me home leaves this place right fucked."

"I'm sure we can manage."

"Uh, Mac—"

"I'm not tying up the plane with a lone reprobate," Mac continues. "But he can stay, as long as he does exactly as we say and remains under constant supervision. Is that clear?"

"Right-o, boss man. Have rocker, will enjoy the view."

"No. *Constant* supervision. Vaughn?"

"Hell no, I'm not babysitting; I got an entire camp to run. Like I said, we don't have the manpower—"

"Busiest place in the camp? One with nearly constant activity? Mess hall, I'm assuming."

"Sure, the kitchen—"

"He can remain there. There's enough space for an extra body to be hanging out."

"I can't ask my camp caretakers to serve as prison wardens—"

"Then don't. I will."

"They're cooks, not guards. How are they supposed to protect themselves if he decides to pull something?"

"Easy, mate!" Charlie, sounding insulted.

"Please. Chef Kiki is there now. Don't let her small size fool you. She knows more than how to debone a chicken with a knife."

Complete silence, as if no one, especially Vaughn and Charlie, know what to make of that statement.

"It's decided. Elias, escort Charlie to the mess hall. Explain the situation. Come nightfall, Vaughn can bunk with Charlie in this cabin. Case closed."

"Oh, for the love of God." Vaughn, no doubt raking a hand through his hair.

"Do I need an escort to hit the head?" Charlie drawls now. "Or just piss in a cup when the need arises?"

"Someone will take you." MacManus, still irritated.

"Fuck this!" Vaughn, more irritated. "This camp runs on trust. Our safety depends on it. You don't trust this man. Fine. Then send him back to Oahu. But to do this—put one of our own under constant guard? The camp will grind to a halt. Hell, we might as well all go home."

Rustling beside me. I jerk around, expecting to discover myself busted by one of the bodyguards. Instead, it's Tannis, the landscape architect. She holds a finger to her lips to silence me. Has she been here all along, also eavesdropping, or is she new to the party? Now is not the time to ask, but her presence proves Vaughn's point. Forget work. Trying to sort out the latest developments in this unfolding drama will become everyone's full-time job.

"Plane stays. Conversation over."

More noise. MacManus descends the front steps. Belatedly, I pull back; Tannis as well. We hustle to the path and fall in step as if it's the most natural thing in the world, just two campmates out for a stroll. Tannis doesn't turn to the right, however, and head back toward the mess hall. She takes a left instead, leading us deeper into the row of crew cabins.

"Do you really think Charlie is a threat?" she asks the moment we're out of hearing.

"I'm not sure. You've known him longer than I have."

"He's always been nice. Goofy maybe, but when something breaks—and around here something is always breaking—he's the one you want. I can't believe..." She sounds shocked, a sentiment I'm sure many share.

"You ever notice his accent coming and going?"

Tannis eyes me warily. "He's...got an interesting way of speaking. But he travels all over. I figured it was the chicken soup of it all."

"Maybe." I hedge my bets. "MacManus seems to think there's a problem with Charlie's backstory—his time at McMurdo."

Clearly Tannis had heard as much as I did, because she immediately counters with: "But to Charlie's point, his checks from here are signed by MacManus, and yet how often do we see the guy?"

"How often do you see the guy?"

"Since I've been here, maybe a couple times a quarter, tops. And never for long. He flies in, flies out. We're the worker bees. He's the queen, if you can forgive the analogy."

"I kinda like it. Okay, worker bee. I have a question for you. I hear a single-person drug-smuggling sub washed ashore somewhere on the atoll. Can you show me where?"

"I can do better than that," Tannis assures me. "I can bring you to the sub."

TURNS OUT, THERE'S a whole labyrinth of trails around the base camp I had known nothing about. Tannis leads me past Vaughn's cabin, which I always assumed was the end of the line, to a small break in the bordering wall of underbrush. Two steps in, and we're on a thin, muddy trail that seems to curve around in an endless arc until, lo and behold, we're back on the main pathway, halfway between the bathhouse to our left and the landing strip to our right. Tannis heads toward the camp, then forks left onto another muddy path. This one is much wider, cleared enough for the UTVs to traverse, but not beautified like the main pathways, maybe a testimony to its more utilitarian role.

I follow her around muddy ruts and interconnecting puddles, fattened from yesterday's storm. No hermit crabs bustle before us, but the thick green brush on both sides rustles loudly as we pass. Shortly, I spy a huge concrete structure, cube shaped and at least two stories tall.

"The water cistern," Tannis informs me as she mucks past it.

"That's our fresh water supply?"

"Yes." It's impressively large, which I find reassuring. Then: "I heard it sprung a leak that Charlie had to fix?"

"A crack developed near the base. Charlie filled it with caulking. When that didn't hold, he used some of the fiberglass he has for boat repair. Ingenious, really."

I have to scramble to catch up. Caulking and fiberglass. Charlie may be lying about some things, but apparently the man can truly engineer.

"Is it common for a structure that solid to develop a crack? I mean, isn't it new?"

Before me, Tannis shrugs. "Even the best structures can fail, but *common* would be a strong word. I don't really know, to tell the truth. The cistern was installed before I arrived. Vaughn might be able to tell you more."

We come to a fork in the muddy path. I note the sign to the right and immediately halt in my tracks. A brightly painted red crab holds a banner declaring Crab Town—where, according to Trudy, crabs can strip anything or anyone down to bones.

"Uhh, we're not going that way, right?" I point to the sign.

"You haven't been to Crab Town yet?" Tannis draws up short.
"No."

"Fascinating operation. That's where all the food scraps go. Between herbivore and omnivore crabs it disappears in a matter of hours, significantly reducing our waste footprint. It will be a critical component of the eco-lodge. I can't decide if it should remain here, out of sight, or perhaps be incorporated closer to the lodge with a viewing platform. It's genuinely mesmerizing to watch hundreds of crabs crawling over each other in a feeding frenzy. And an excellent example of how to use the local crustacean population to our advantage."

"Hundreds of crabs?"

Tannis pins me with her bright-blue eyes. "Want to see?"

"Nope. I'm good. Very good. So, uh, drug sub?"

Tannis heads left, thank goodness. We're moving back in the direction of the shore, slipping and sliding our way along the rutted path. Shortly, a giant structure comes into view. It's open on all sides, basically an enormous corrugated-metal shed. I see an assortment of tools and equipment in half the space, then a pile of rusted metal bric-a-brac on the other side.

"Town dump," Tannis declares.

"We have a dump?"

"Welcome to island life. As the landscape architect, I'm still working on this problem. So: the miscellaneous building waste that comes from creating new structures—leftover wood, metal, plastic, etc.—all gets returned to Oahu on the same ships that bring in the raw materials. However, this atoll sits in the middle of a variety of currents. Factor in storms such as yesterday's humdinger—"

"Humdinger. Nice."

"New items wash ashore almost daily. Debris knocked loose

from cargo ships, commercial fishing boats, miscellaneous trash—no doubt you've noticed our fine collection of flip-flops, not to mention plastic bags, water bottles, drinking straws." She shudders. "The ocean is a busy place, and this island is a natural collection point. One of Charlie's duties is to make the rounds every few days to identify what's come ashore. Then either Vaughn, or sometimes an entire contingent of us, go fetch it and bring it here."

"Including a single-person submersible," I fill in.

"Including a drug sub," she agrees.

She brings me around the enormous garage to a corner where larger items have been piled up. I don't immediately see anything that screams *Red October*, but then Tannis points to a slender strip of aquamarine metal thrusting out from beside the pile. Upon closer inspection, it bears the same shape as a kayak, though it is roughly three times larger in size. I can't get over the color of the exterior, which I'd expected to be gunmetal gray but instead is tropical blue.

"Because a dark shape would be noticeable in these waters," I deduce.

"Yes. And possibly attacked by a shark."

"Seriously?" This draws me up short.

"The only dark shapes in the ocean are predators or prey. Hence the need to blend."

"Okay then." I'd thought of a drug-running submersible as needing to hide from law enforcement. I'd never considered the other dangers inherent in such an activity.

"Most likely, this sub was abandoned elsewhere and simply washed up on these shores," Tannis supplies. "But it indicates the way the currents move through the Line Islands, that an item can be abandoned hundreds of miles away and still wind up here."

"Or launched," I murmur, thinking of the Beautiful Butcher

and her obvious goal of reaching this atoll. I wonder if a sub is faster than a ship, which in theory takes seven days to reach this island. It would definitely be more covert. Apparently, MacManus can shut down shipping lanes, but he can't stop all the currents heading here.

"Do you know how the sub works? I mean, how hard is it to operate?"

"I imagine there's some training involved; it can't be that safe to cross the ocean in something barely larger than a coffin. But if you look inside, you'll see this is nothing but a shell. Whatever electronics, engine, whatnot, were used to power this beauty are long gone, so it's hard to know."

A small top hatch—barely large enough for a slender adult to slip through—is open. I peer down inside the sub. True to Tannis's report, the stark interior might as well be the same as a kayak's. There's a rough, single-person seat and some padding along the edges, as well as dangling strips of duct tape—maybe from securing the drugs to the sides? That's it.

"Do you know anything about drug smuggling?" I purse my lips, still considering the matter. "I mean, how useful, really, is it to land drugs on a remote atoll? You'd still have to get the entire stash into Hawaii, the mainland, somewhere."

"I can't see how bringing anything to Pomaikai would be useful in terms of entry; you'd still have to go through passport control and customs in Honolulu. However, this would make an excellent exit point."

I turn to Tannis, genuinely curious. "How so?"

"Well, you don't have to be an expert in missing persons"— she slides me a glance; the camp rumor mill has definitely been churning away—"to know human trafficking is a big issue on the islands. The number of local girls who disappear, not to mention males kidnapped to staff the enormous Chinese fishing fleets that basically set up camp on the ocean, catching, harvesting, and processing fish twenty-four seven. The need for manpower to work those boats, and even more tragically, to supply entertainment for that manpower...It wouldn't be so hard to smuggle people from, say, Honolulu to here, where the kidnapped victims could be picked up on larger boats and taken directly out to the fishing fleets."

"That's...clever. Yeah, Pomaikai as an entry point, not so helpful. But as an exit port...Interesting."

"The grave," Tannis asks me directly. "Do you think...?"

"A victim of human trafficking?" I recall the sequined flower. A small spark of brightness, maybe even hope, in a life that ended so darkly. "I don't know. But it's possible. The acts of sabotage going on at base camp..."

"Someone doesn't want us here."

"Yeah, and even more relevant, given there are no strangers camping in the jungle around us..."

"That person has to be one of us."

"Yeah." I eye her, willing her to volunteer a name, some suspicions, anything. But in response to my unasked question, she merely shakes her head. It's frustrating. The only person I know who's obviously behaving strangely is Charlie, but he's also the one repairing the issues and keeping the camp running. Those seem like two mutually exclusive goals.

"At the moment," I declare finally, my thoughts whirring away, "we have a bigger problem. One very specific predator who definitely wants to be here. Any chance you're approved for Wi-Fi?"

"Does this have to do with Charlie's predicament and our new, uninvited, highly armed guests?"

"Exactly."

Tannis considers me for a minute, her blue eyes unblinking. I return her look just as sincerely. If there's one thing I learned from my last adventure, when it comes to remote locations, Vaughn is correct. We're all in it together. As in, we can survive together.

Or we can die, one by one.

"I've used up my minutes for the day," Tannis says abruptly. "But I know someone who can help. Follow me."

CHAPTER 25

TANNIS LEADS US BACK TO the collection of staff cabins. When she knocks discreetly on the front door of one, I'm not sure if it's Aolani's or Ronin's residence, but am not surprised when they both appear. Tannis exchanges a few words with them in a low voice. They look at me, back at her, then slip out of the unit and follow her down the stairs. A single nod in silent greeting, then we are on our way to Vaughn's office.

No one speaks. Even our footsteps are measured against the crushed coral, leading to some confusion for the pointy-shelled hermit crabs, who can't seem to decide if they should run for it or shelter in place. We've adopted the air of a clandestine operation, even though it's broad daylight and the sun is already baking us out.

AO leads the way. She walks with catlike grace that speaks to hours of some kind of training. I'm guessing martial arts, probably both her and Ronin, given his movement patterns. My new goal is to stay close to them at all times. Should Keahi suddenly appear, I want to be surrounded by the island's resident ninjas.

Vaughn's office is empty. The heavily chilled, deeply shadowed space only adds to the general atmosphere as AO takes a seat in front of his computer.

"I haven't logged in today," she murmurs to Ronin.

He nods as if that means something to him. "I did this morning, so your user ID would be preferred."

"Not just anyone can access the internet," Aolani explains, her fingers flying across the keyboard. "You have to be assigned a user ID and password, which serves as a basic security precaution but also reinforces prioritizing Wi-Fi resources for the staff who truly need them."

She finishes clicking the mouse, then turns to face me fully. "So, what are we doing?"

"We're looking for articles related to the escape of a serial killer from a Texas prison. Keahi Pierson, aka the Beautiful Butcher. I believe it was early yesterday morning or the night before."

"Isn't she the woman about to be executed?" Tannis speaks up.

"Not anymore."

"Why?" Aolani again, her tone clipped. She definitely isn't a small-talk kind of gal.

"Why was she being executed? I'm assuming that had something to do with chopping up eighteen men and serving them to her pigs."

"No, why do we care that she's on the loose?"

"Because she's Lea MacManus's older sister who believes MacManus kidnapped Lea when she was five years old and has been holding Lea hostage ever since."

"Do you have proof of this?" Ronin asks me with a frown.

"Well, when I confronted Lea with the news an hour ago, she

didn't deny it. More like MacManus has been good to her. Her older, violent sister, not so much so. From what I can tell, Lea believes she's traded up."

"So is Lea actually MacManus's ward?" Ronin is trying to sort it out.

"Legally, I have no idea. Keahi thought she'd lost her sister, so she returned to Texas, where... well, we all know how that went. So ostensibly Lea has been living with MacManus ever since. Her parents are dead. Did that allow him to legally adopt her? I can't be sure, but I sincerely doubt it."

"Why?" Aolani again.

"Among other things, Lea informed me that MacManus is planning on having sex with her when she turns eighteen. She's not his charity case. She's his future wife."

Ronin and Tannis recoil slightly. Aolani simply frowns in distaste. Her fingers have been steadily tapping at keys. Now she sits back and studies the monitor. I quickly understand their point about the limited Wi-Fi. Where usually article after article would already be loading up, all I see is the spinning wheel of doom.

"It'll happen," Tannis murmurs beside me. "Generally, right as you're ready to whack it with a hammer."

"I don't understand what this means." Ronin again. "If what you're saying is true, MacManus's relationship with Lea is inappropriate. But what does that and some escaped prisoner from Texas have to do with Charlie being put under house arrest?"

I walk them through it best I can. My meeting with Keahi. Her insistence her sister needs to be rescued. Her lawyer, Victoria Twanow, arranging for me to work on Pomaikai in order to personally confront Lea and hopefully arrange a means of escape.

"Keahi wants her sister back," I wrap up now. "One way or another, she's coming for Lea and MacManus. Hence MacManus flees to a remote island in the middle of the Pacific with two bodyguards in tow. He's safer here than anywhere else, and he knows it."

"That's his plan? Hide out here forever? Because sooner or later the plane will have to resume carrying people and supplies. We need to eat, which means the atoll will become accessible again."

I shrug. "Not sure MacManus has thought that far ahead yet. Dunno. My focus has been Lea. Get her alone, hear her side of the story, then phone home to Keahi's lawyer, Victoria, for instructions on how to get Lea off the atoll. So far, I consider this mission a total fail. These things happen."

"Here we go." Aolani. She turns the monitor slightly so we can all see it. There's a list of matches for our search. Most appear to be news articles bearing titles such as "The Beautiful Butcher Strikes Again" or "Infamous Femme Fatale Fatally Flees." That one has me blinking my eyes.

"Which one would you like to read first?" Aolani asks me.

"Something with images. Keahi was supposedly assisted by a corrections officer. I want to know who."

Aolani clicks on an image button. More spinning wheel of doom. Then, just as I'm itching to grab a hammer, the screen once more fills with results, including several photos. One is clearly a mug shot of Keahi Pierson, staring defiantly into the camera. The second appears to be from an employee security badge and bears a man's face. Sure enough, Joe Lacchei is the same officer who had seemed so friendly with Twanow just days before.

Had the entire thing been a ruse? A concerted effort on his part to lower her defenses? And why? Did he fancy himself in love with Keahi Pierson and truly believe for a minute that a woman nicknamed the Beautiful Butcher might be capable of loving him back?

A third picture fills the screen. Victoria Twanow, posed with a thoughtful smile, long, dark hair clipped back at her nape, hammered silver necklace accentuating her graceful neck. I can just make out the caption below the image. "Young attorney, working pro bono in an effort to save her client from execution, now hospitalized in critical condition."

"That's the lawyer who got you here and was supposed to help Lea escape?" Aolani is tapping the image.

"Yes."

"Based on what I'm reading, they don't expect her to make it."

"That's what Lea said."

"What are you supposed to do next?" Ronin asks, staring at me.

"No idea. But first off, the corrections officer, Joe Lacchei. Does he look familiar to any of you?"

They all peer more closely at the image, then one by one they shake their heads.

"Does he have any ties to Hawaii?" I ask Aolani, as she's driving the computer bus. "I'm curious if he has any connection to Pomaikai."

"Hmm." She starts scrolling, a process that is painfully slow as she keeps having to wait for information to load. Finally. "Yes. He's originally from Waikiki. He studied criminal justice at a university in Texas. Never moved back."

I sigh. "In other words, he could have family, friends within MacManus's operations. Catering company, tech services, property management, whatever. MacManus owns major real estate holdings on the islands, correct?"

Ronin nods first.

"So not that difficult for there to be some kind of overlap. I'll bet that's why Keahi targeted him. Not just because he had the power to help get her out of prison, but because he has the connections to get her here."

"In other words, MacManus is right to be paranoid," Ronin fills in.

"And you no longer have someone to call for backup," Aolani adds.

"The police are coming," Tannis speaks up. "That's gotta be a good thing."

"Maybe. But here's another thing. Last night when we rescued Charlie"—I glance at Aolani—"he muttered some words in my ear. Basically that he had to stay on the island until *she* came. *She* was the key. At the time the only 'she' I could think of was Lea. But now, knowing the Beautiful Butcher has escaped and is headed here…"

My sentence trails off awkwardly. I don't want to suspect Charlie of working with a serial killer, I really don't. Except.

Ronin and Aolani exchange troubled glances. Tannis goes with a look of reproach—how dare I question her friend's integrity.

I reach into my back pocket for my final piece to this headache-inducing riddle when—

The office door flies open. Vaughn fills the space. His gaze goes from me to Tannis to Ronin to Aolani sitting at his desk.

"What. The. Fuck."

He stalks into his office. And I start talking very, very fast.

CHAPTER 26

To give Vaughn credit, he doesn't interrupt. His expression grows darker, and he starts to jangle some loose change in his shorts pocket before slowly pinging coin after coin into the swear jar as I prattle on. Apparently, cursing inside one's mind counts.

When I finally wrap up, he has a single summary assessment: "Fuck."

We all glance automatically at the swear jar, then shrug. Given the fistful of change the man just dumped in, he's probably paid enough.

Vaughn's attention bounces to Aolani next, as she's the one camped in front of his computer. "You found articles on the jail escape? Proof that this serial killer is Lea's older sister?"

Aolani turns the monitor toward him. The original images are still on the screen, but now dimmer, while the spinning wheel of doom takes front and center. Aolani whacks the frame, as if to force it back to life, but it doesn't make a difference. Apparently the computer has lost its signal. At least we still have residual results to work with.

"The articles don't list Keahi Pierson as having a sister, but according to Frankie, Lea didn't deny it."

"Just look at the photo," I urge. "You can see the family resemblance. I mean, if you discount that Lea walks around looking like a Disney princess, versus Keahi's decidedly...harsher demeanor. But you know, cut of the cheekbones, same noses, similar eyes. The real stuff."

I'm babbling. It shouldn't matter to me if Vaughn believes my story or not, but it does.

For now, he studies the grayed-out images, then grunts, which could mean most anything. I focus on more salient points: "Look at the CO—Joe Lacchei. Recognize him? Is it possible he or anyone named Lacchei was part of the construction crew, prior worker, anything?"

Vaughn scratches his whiskered jaw. Finally, he shakes his head. "You think Keahi Pierson and the CO will both come here?"

"Keahi and her lawyer got me here in less than twenty-four hours. So, yeah, where there's a will, there's a way."

"But then she turned on her lawyer."

"Apparently serial killers aren't the loyal type. Look, I only met the Beautiful Butcher once, so I'm no expert, but I can tell you she's genuinely obsessed with Leilani. As in she wants to save her younger sister from the clutches of her diabolical, abusive ex, Sanders MacManus. She and her lawyer, Victoria Twanow, had already concluded that the easiest way to gain access to MacManus is right here on Pomaikai, where he can't hide in a gated community or behind an army of workers. Keahi will focus on this location once again, I'm sure. How she'll get here, I'm less certain, especially now that MacManus has his guard up. But I'm thinking that's the CO Lacchei's job. If we can tie him to MacManus's operations or Pomaikai, that'll tell us what we need to know."

"I doubt he has any connection to the atoll. I've never seen that man before in my life."

"Directly," I argue. "But what about the company that operates the charter jet, or the distributor supplying all your food? You know all their employees and their family and friends?"

Vaughn scowls. His hand sneaks up to his hair.

"It's already standing on end," I assure him.

I don't need his deposit in the swear jar to understand his next look. Tannis starts chuckling, turning it into a quick cough when he directs that same glare at her.

"There's also the matter of Charlie," I begin, earning a fresh glower. I shrug. "In his post-concussion delirium, he was adamant he needed to stay on the atoll long enough for some woman to arrive. I assumed he meant Leilani. However, given this latest news..."

Vaughn sighs, shakes his head, sighs some more. I don't blame him. This entire conversation is overwhelming me, and I've had more time to consider the angles.

"Charlie is taken care of for the moment," Vaughn announces finally. "MacManus has him under constant supervision. Let's remove him from the equation for now, move on to more pressing issues."

"Great, because we have one more problem."

"Another problem?" Ronin interjects. He's standing near Aolani's shoulder. I can see him just resist the urge to give her arm a reassuring squeeze.

"I um, well, so my job has been to make contact with Leilani—Lea—who may be held against her will. So of course, I searched MacManus's lodge to see what I could learn."

"You have been busy," Vaughn drawls.

"And I found something." I hold up the slip of paper from my back pocket. "This is a note I recovered from the nightstand in Lea's room. It's a message to her sister, sounding rather . . . fatalistic."

I pass it around the room for everyone to judge for themselves.

"But you said Lea's happy to be with MacManus," Aolani states sharply, handing the scrap of paper to Ronin.

"Which is the problem. According to Lea, she never wrote this note, or the message to her sister that got Keahi's attention after all these years. I asked Lea to write down something for me. Her handwriting is small and precise—not a match for what you see here."

"I don't understand." Aolani again. "You don't think she wrote this, a hidden message in her own room?"

I shrug. "It doesn't seem so." Which is as precise as I can be.

"But why? Who?" Ronin now.

"I jumped to a different question—"

"Where," Vaughn states bluntly, his mind having gone the same direction as mine. "If that note is on this atoll, then by definition, the person who wrote it is, as well."

"Don't suppose the script looks familiar to anyone?" I ask hopefully.

Tannis is already shaking her head as she hands the paper scrap back to me. "But we don't exactly sit around writing notes. Well, the daily board, I suppose. That's handwritten in dry erase marker. But normally you two handle the majority of the grid." She nods at Vaughn and Ronin. "With others filling in just a spot or two. Not enough to truly judge penmanship. At least not for me."

"This script is large and childish," Ronin supplies. "I would notice it if I saw it elsewhere. I haven't. And for the record—it doesn't match Charlie's. His scrawl is microscopic and almost impossible to decipher."

"Could this note be disguised?" Aolani asks. "The script seems distinctive in a distracting sort of way."

"Sure. But that doesn't change the main implication—someone still had to place it in the owner's lodge. Meaning that person is someone here, or was here."

"Fuck." Tannis swears this time, sounding way more cheerful than Vaughn when he does it. He actually frowns at her, as if that's no way to drop the f-bomb. She shrugs back, unapologetic.

Vaughn presses his lips into a thin line. I can tell from the look on his face that he's been thinking, thinking, thinking this whole time. He's the project manager; problem solving and logistical planning are his bread and butter. Now:

"In the short term, I think it matters less what we don't know and more what we do. Fact one, a convicted murderer has escaped who has incentive to come here in search of Mac and her younger sister."

I nod.

"Everyone should know this," Vaughn states firmly. "And everyone should have a choice whether to stay or go. If MacManus wants to hide here with his security guards, good for him. But this isn't what anyone else signed up for, and I won't ask people to take on additional risk. This location is dangerous enough."

"You will make an announcement at dinner?" Ronin prompts.

Vaughn nods. "Makes the most sense. Camp meeting."

"And how to get people back to Oahu?"

"There's the plane," Vaughn provides, "though MacManus is currently opposed to it leaving, and it's not big enough to transport everyone. We may just have to demand that it charter the people who want to leave, in multiple trips if that's what it takes."

"What about the authorities?" Tannis asks. "If investigators from Oahu are coming to check out the human remains, couldn't some folks return with them?"

"Possibly." Vaughn reaches for the corner of his desk. His hand halts midair. "Dammit."

I don't understand, but Ronin does. "Where's the sat phone?" he speaks up.

I have a vague memory of a rugged black radio/phone thingamabob charging on Vaughn's desk. Sure enough, both the thingamabob and the charger are gone.

"Mac." Vaughn practically swears the word. "His goons apparently didn't understand the remote part of a remote atoll, and thought they could still communicate with Honolulu using their cell phones. When they figured out otherwise . . . Mac asked me to bring them the backup sat phone. I should've known they'd simply help themselves."

He mutters under his breath, crossing his office to a shelf in the corner. Then he draws up short. "Fuck me, they took the backup as well. Goddammit, this is no way to run operations. Their lack of planning is not our emergency. I don't even want them here!"

Now his hand is running through his hair, over and over again. The rest of us remain silent.

"Fine," he bites out at last. "Here's the deal. It's about to be dinner. Everyone will be present, including Mac and his people. I don't care if the idiot is my boss and friend. Safety comes first. I'll make an announcement of the situation—"

"Are you going to talk to MacManus first?" I interrupt.

Vaughn looks so troubled on the subject, I genuinely feel for him. "No," he determines at last. "If I tell him I know all this and he demands I say nothing, then I'll be violating a direct order when I speak up. Better to beg for forgiveness than ask for permission."

Standing beside him, Ronin nods his agreement; Aolani as well.

I'm impressed. There's a strength of character to this group I don't encounter often. Maybe that's what it takes to work this far off the grid, where safety and security really are your own responsibility. Bad decisions will cost you directly. Good decisions will keep you alive. I respect the straightforward math of such an existence. If I wasn't from nowhere, I'd be tempted to be from somewhere like here.

"People can have till the morning to decide. Depending on the numbers, I'll return to Mac with next steps. He'll simply have to permit the use of his plane. I'm not the only one responsible for everyone's well-being; he is, too."

"And the authorities?" Tannis again.

"I'll reach out. When I can get my hands on my damn phone again." More hair raking.

"I can't find any additional information here," Aolani announces, rising to standing. "Wi-Fi is having one of its moments."

"Or Mac is tying it up checking stock prices," Vaughn grumbles. "I keep trying to explain to him..." Another heavy sigh.

"And Charlie?" Tannis speaks up, a challenging tilt to her head. "He just remains under house arrest. Guilty until proven innocent?"

Vaughn is clearly not pleased to return to a discussion of the man's fate. "Look, I can't answer the Charlie question. I like the guy, I've always liked the guy. But him heading out into the storm, without a radio...Does that sound like Charlie to you?"

Tannis's expression falters.

"Something's up there," Vaughn continues. "I might not know what, but I know my responsibility to everyone else in this camp, which is when in doubt, play it safe. Personally, I think

Charlie should be the first one on a plane to Oahu. Once you've lost trust..."

"Hey, stop staring at me!" I'm genuinely insulted.

Vaughn could clearly not care less. "The rest of you, out. You have better things to do than rehash old news in my office. You, on the other hand"—he pins me with his blue eyes—"you stay."

I get looks from Aolani, Ronin, and Tannis ranging from open sympathy to "better you than me." "Cowards," I call out to their retreating backs as they file out of the office.

Then, it's just Vaughn and me. He makes a show of taking a seat before his desk, then leaning back and propping his feet at the edge. He gestures to the chair across from him.

"Sit. Then tell me what the fuck is really going on."

I take a seat. I'm tired all of a sudden. Exhausted, really, from the lack of sleep, and the unrelenting stress of trying to adapt to a new place where it really is wet twenty-four seven and I can practically feel the mold growing on my skin and I just want to be dry and comfortable and not lost on some remote island surrounded by people I can't decide are friend or foe.

I want a break. From this place. From this situation. From me, and my mind that never shuts up, even when I want it to.

My gaze drifts to the locked cabinet of booze in the corner of the office. Then I contemplate the key worn on the chain around Vaughn's neck, its outline just visible beneath his sweat-soaked T-shirt. I could hint in the right direction. Something casual but heartfelt—God, what I'd give for a drink after the day I've had...

He'd fetch us one. I know it with absolute certainty. Vaughn's had a bad day, too. And he wants me to talk. So why not grab a bottle of whiskey, rum, tequila, and pour us both a shot.

I've spent so much of my life in this moment. Wavering on

a precipice. Wanting what I know I shouldn't want. Wanting it anyway.

I need a meeting. The comfort of a church basement where the only thing bitterer than the coffee is the brutally honest confessions: I promised my daughter I wouldn't drink on her wedding day. So I stole a bottle of booze from the limo and downed the whole thing in the ladies' room before staggering down the aisle and throwing up on the altar. I promised myself I'd have one drink with my friends, before staying till closing downing pitchers of beer. Then I got behind the wheel of my car, squeezing my eyes against the blinding headlights till I swerved to avoid hitting a deer. Except it wasn't a deer, it was some poor dude walking home from his dishwashing job, and while I missed him, I plowed into his three closest friends.

I promised my children. My parents. My spouse. My friends.

I promised myself that this time, I wouldn't do it.

Then I looked in the mirror and did it anyway. Just like me and myself knew I would.

I'm sweating again, and it's not the heat and humidity given the air-conditioned space. It's need. It's hunger. Just a shot or two. Then Vaughn will lock it back up and save me from myself. Other people, when they have bad days ...

I want to be like other people.

Because I've never really enjoyed being me.

"Charlie's definitely lying," Vaughn states.

I'm so befuddled I don't immediately reply. I force my attention from the cabinet, back to the man sitting before me.

"I thought you told Tannis not to worry—"

"I didn't want to upset her. But you're right. Now that I'm listening, his accent is shit. And his background details don't hold up. I'm guessing the man at least has some training as an engineer, given he's been able to save our asses. But other than that...wouldn't be surprised if even his name's a lie. Whole time Mac was grilling him, Charlie wouldn't make eye contact with me. He knows he's caught."

"Is that why you want him off the atoll?"

"At this point, I think we should all depart. This deployment is done."

"Will MacManus agree to such a thing?"

"No. That's the problem with geniuses. They generally became successful by doing something people told them couldn't be done. Having been rewarded once for going against prevailing wisdom, they're not apt to listen ever again."

Vaughn drums his fingertips against his armrest. "Do you think Charlie could really be working with this Beautiful Butcher woman?"

"It's possible. She has a certain charm. Though I'm not sure why that would make him head out in the storm to see a recently discovered grave. Keahi definitely had nothing to do with that, given she was on death row at the time. Morbid curiosity?"

"Or someone who got wind of their plan and had to be silenced?"

I pin him with a look. "Any of your workers gone missing lately?"

"No."

"Others from the construction and contractor crews? One of the hundreds of people you said helped build this base camp?"

"Of course not. And I would know."

"Exactly. Chances are, the body predates all this recent activity and has more to do with your friend MacManus. A human trafficking victim or something of that nature. Or do you always insist on missing the obvious?"

"We have no way of knowing—"

"The man's a pedophile!"

"Not if he's waiting for his charge to turn eighteen. That would be the opposite, in fact."

"It's still an abuse of power! Why are you defending him?"

"Why are you so convinced he's evil? You still haven't spoken to him. An admitted killer, yes. But Mac? Why not just talk to him?"

"I already know what he's going to say, and I don't need him lying to my face." I cross my arms over my chest in a huff. I mean it. I've spoken to enough MacManuses in my life. They always have rationales and excuses. And it's always their needs that matter the most in the end. I return to what I don't know: "Why are you so loyal to him? Especially when even you concede that he's an arrogant ass."

"Because he can be loyal, too. Ever think of that?" Vaughn drops his feet to the ground, leans forward intently. "Fifteen years ago, I was project manager of a research station in Alaska. Needless to say, there was a storm, things went sideways. Two people died. After that, I wasn't project manager material anymore. I wasn't anything...anymore. It took me years to come to terms, regain my footing. Mac gave me my first job back. He'd seen my work. He believed. And, yeah, he drives me crazy most of the time, but I've never seen him doing anything I thought was morally repugnant."

"Except groom his ward to become his lover."

"So she says. Again, have you asked him?"

"Why would she lie?"

"I don't know. Why is he automatically the Antichrist? Isn't the basic tenet everyone is innocent till proven guilty? Where's the proof?"

"I don't think Keahi Pierson is waiting for a court of law."

"Yes, the woman who confessed to murdering an entire string of men. Absolutely, let's let her play judge and jury."

I'm breathing hard. And my eyes sting. I'm tired, and my chest is too tight. I'm sliding down into the abyss, where the only thing that seems like a good idea is to pour a drink, then let the booze sort it out. Why be in charge of my own life when good ol' Jack would feel so much better?

I climb to my feet. I need away from the booze cabinet. "What happened to MacManus's first business partner?"

"What?"

"His software developer friend. The one that actually made them gazillionaires. Wasn't he the true genius? MacManus was just the face of operations, till his friend died. Then MacManus inherited his partner's shares and proceeded to sell the whole kit and caboodle for half a billion. Isn't that how the story goes?"

"I never met Shawn Eastman. That was before my time. Mac doesn't even talk about those days. You're right, he's no tech wunderkind. Property development is more his speed. But what does that—"

"I don't know! Point is, neither do you. So maybe I haven't asked MacManus the right questions yet. But maybe, neither have you."

"Are you going to leave the atoll?"

"What?" Now it's my turn to be confused.

"After our camp meeting. Will you choose to stay, or choose to go?"

"I...I..." My arms fall to my sides. I don't know. I haven't gotten that far. "I guess I'll have to figure it out. You?"

"I'm the leader. If others stay, I will, too."

I nod. I'm not a leader, but I'm a woman with a self-destructive hobby. If Lea stays, I guess I do, too. Do I have something to fear from Keahi, should she arrive? After all, she's the one who sent me here. Then again, given what she did to her lawyer...

I scrub at my face. I gotta get outta here.

"I am powerless over alcohol. I've come to believe a higher power can help restore me to sanity."

For a moment, I'm too stunned to move.

"That's what I learned," Vaughn says softly. "Fifteen years ago. That's what I had to accept to get my life back. I see the way your gaze keeps going to the liquor cabinet, the key around my neck. I'm guessing you've had some hard learning you had to do yourself."

I know the word I need to say. And yet it refuses to rise to my lips.

"I'm here if you want to talk," he continues quietly. "None of us is alone."

"You will be. When I step out that door. You'll be alone with the booze stash. Is that a good idea?"

"I'm okay for this moment. When I'm not, I hand Ronin the key. None of us is alone," he repeats.

"Thank you."

"Anytime."

Then, because I can't help myself: "If Keahi gets to this atoll...she'll grab her sister. Then she'll kill everyone who chooses to stay behind. She's never repented for her crimes, and take it from someone who saw her just days ago, her homicidal rage has not decreased since being incarcerated. If she gets here before the authorities, none of us will survive."

"We're not entirely defenseless; we have a rifle, shotgun, a few other resources."

"Yes. But she prefers blades. And how many of those did you say were on this island?"

Vaughn doesn't have an answer for that. He nods once in acknowledgment.

I think he's very handsome for someone who looks as exhausted as I feel.

"Things are going to get worse before they get better," I tell him honestly.

"Welcome to project management."

He flashes me a fleeting smile. Then, because that smile makes him even more ridiculously attractive, I play to my own strengths.

And run like hell.

CHAPTER 27

GIVEN IT'S NEARLY DINNERTIME, I allow myself ten whole minutes for a cold shower and change of clothes. Though the act of trying to drag a sports bra over my wet skin leaves me so frustrated and sweaty, I'm not sure why I bothered.

I enter the mess hall just in time to take in three arguments occurring at once. Trudy and Ann, standing in front of Chef Kiki, who is waving a bottle of champagne like she knows how to use it.

"Cocktail hour. Monsieur MacManus wants it, brought these lovely bottles to share."

"And Vaughn said no!" Trudy, arms in the air. "He's the boss. He ixnays the booze, we ixnay the booze."

"Non!" Chef Kiki is equally outraged. "I will do no such thing. This champagne is the perfect accompaniment for the charcuterie—"

"I'll show you charcuterie!" Ann moves in to block the French-woman's advance.

Meanwhile, the pilots Marilee and Brent are on the other side of the dining hall with MacManus's bodyguard Elias. "We're telling you we need to speak to him, immediately. As in right now, not after dinner!"

Meanwhile, Vaughn and Ronin are standing in front of a seated Charlie, whose face looks even worse than it did a few hours ago.

"What did you do to the comm tower?" Ronin demands to know.

"Nothing, mate. Telling you—been sitting right here. Boss man's orders."

"Come on, Charlie. This is serious." Vaughn is struggling to sound reasonable.

"Yeah, like a blow to the head."

"Tell us, Charlie." Ronin's voice is dangerously calm. "What did you do to the battery?"

"Don't know, mate."

"Charlie—"

Crash. First bottle of champagne hits the floor, followed shortly by a second. Trudy and Ann appear triumphant, Chef Kiki aghast. One crisis averted, I think. Just as Kiki launches herself at her two sous chefs.

All three go down, followed by a tray of sliced cheeses and assorted crackers. The cooks roll into a table, taking out two chairs. Another crash as they knock down more serving dishes.

Everyone in the dining room shuts up, shocked by the carnage.

I nod thoughtfully at Vaughn during the brief moment of silence. "You're right—MacManus's people are definitely messing with our vibe."

Then Chef Kiki starts shrieking again.

———

IT TAKES FIFTEEN minutes to sort it out. Trudy and Ann sweep up glass; I mop up champagne. Kiki flounces into the dining room and throws herself into a seat across from Charlie and Ronin. She takes in Charlie's bruised face, offers up two words of advice.

"Raw steak."

"Heavens no, luv. Waste of sirloin."

Captain Marilee and First Officer Brent give up on Elias and plant themselves in front of Vaughn. "Someone rifled through our plane," states Marilee, hands on her hips. "We demand answers!"

"What do you mean 'rifled'?"

"When we returned from showering, someone had clearly entered the jet. Storage bins opened, the cockpit searched."

"You left the plane unattended?" Elias materializes beside them.

"Of course we left it unattended." Brent scowls at the bodyguard. "Why wouldn't we?"

"You were told to stay with the plane."

"No," Marilee interjects crisply. "We were told to *sleep* on the plane. Which is hardly SOP—"

"All right!" Vaughn holds up a silencing hand. "Trudy," he calls out. "Ring the bell. I want everyone assembled right here, right now. And that includes Mac." He glares at Elias, who calmly raises a discreet handheld radio to his lips, clicks a button, and murmurs something low and indistinct before frowning and repeating the process.

"Elias to base, Elias to base. Base come in." His frown deepens. "Elias to base, I repeat—"

"Comm tower is down," Ronin informs him. "The lead-acid battery has been drained." Another piercing stare at Charlie.

"Telling you, mate, been sitting here so long, I've rooted in place. Just ask Sergeant Smiley."

Charlie points at stone-faced Elias, who mostly seems confused by the reference.

"He has been under my watch, per Mr. MacManus's orders," Elias confirms. "What does it mean that the comm tower is down?"

"There goes our radio signal as well as Wi-Fi," Ronin supplies.

"Can it be repaired?"

Charlie smiles faintly. Given his alibi, I'm willing to believe he wasn't the one who tampered with the equipment. But he also doesn't appear surprised. Because he's in cahoots with someone else? As in there's more than one member of this twelve-person camp out to get us?

The screen door slams open; others start to file in, whether drawn by the smell of food or the sound of the bell. One by one they take in the obvious tension, then walk slowly down the side of the dining hall before taking up positions on the perimeter, safely out of the line of fire.

Tannis enters with Emi, both eyeing Charlie with worry. Given his battered face and obviously drawn features, I don't blame them. The optics of three larger men looming over his seated form don't help.

"We have backup batteries," Vaughn directs at Charlie. "In the workshop, right?"

"Right-o."

"Then where are they, because I didn't see any," Ronin accuses. He and Vaughn exchange another concerned glance.

I think I'm starting to get a bead on the situation. Someone—not Charlie—disabled the battery powering the comm tower, effectively cutting the atoll off from accessing the main islands via

Wi-Fi, and from communicating with one another via radio. The same person, I'm guessing, also hit the plane. Because the jet has a communications system as well? And the goal is to completely cut us off from civilization?

The sound of a low motor and crunching gravel. MacManus and Lea have arrived with the second bodyguard, Jason, and the personal assistant. MacManus is still wearing rich-man resort wear, but Lea has changed into khaki shorts, a lightweight linen top over a deep-rose tank, and in a nod to practicality, canvas sneakers in a matching shade of dusky red. I've never thought to coordinate my tennis shoes with my tops. Now I know.

"What's going on with the radios?" MacManus demands to know, striding through the door without so much as a backward glance at his entourage.

"Oh, good, you're here." Vaughn sounds as droll as MacManus sounds angry.

"Well?"

"Everyone, have a seat. Camp meeting is officially in session."

"Meeting? What the hell, Vaughn?"

"Excellent. I'll go first. Frankie, please join me."

I DO NOT like standing in front of a group. I'm pretty sure I started drinking heavily in high school just to avoid the anxiety of these situations. Knowing my audience doesn't help. Trudy and Ann appear curious, Tannis and Emi encouraging. Ronin has taken up position next to Aolani, the ultimate power couple of incredible physical beauty, catlike prowess, and impossible-to-read features. Even their cool, assessing gazes match.

Lea, I notice, has taken a seat beside MacManus. Her hands are folded on her lap. His arm is slung loosely around the back of her chair. Not overtly possessive, but close enough to be a reminder to her, if not everyone else in the room, of who is in charge.

Vaughn is better at these things than I am. He goes through the motions of welcoming MacManus and Lea, then introducing the entire entourage to the rest of the camp crew. He mentions that Mac is planning to stay for a bit and had suggested this evening's feast, even supplying his personal chef for the effort.

A smattering of applause, mostly for politeness' sake as everyone can tell there's another shoe still to drop. Chef Kiki scowls in displeasure. She's probably used to making grown men weep in anticipation of her cooking. Whatever.

My turn.

Vaughn hadn't consulted me on this impromptu show. Standing in front of MacManus and Lea, I don't feel like I can point a finger directly at them and say, hey, you did this, and she did that, and now she says that, and you say this, and shame on both of you.

So instead I focus on my story. My background. Meeting with the Beautiful Butcher. Her accounting of her beloved sister who disappeared as a young child. Her request for me to find Leilani and assure her safety before the Butcher's upcoming execution date. How after all these years, Keahi had finally received a lead on her sister's location, which led me here.

I pause to let everyone absorb that much. Lea won't meet my gaze. MacManus is already on his feet.

"That's enough! I will not sit here and have you slander me."

My turn: "Slander you? I haven't even mentioned your name. Guilty conscience much?"

"This is an outrage!"

"No, outrage is a serial killer breaking out of prison after nearly beating her attorney to death. Outrage is you responding to the news of the Beautiful Butcher's escape by grabbing her younger sister and hightailing it all the way out here—"

"I own this property!"

"Where you are now putting the rest of us in danger!" I rest on my laurels, which is just as well, as the room has exploded into shouted questions and gasps of horror.

MacManus's face has turned bright red. If looks could kill, I'd be dead eight ways to Sunday. As it is, bodyguard Elias takes a step closer to me.

I keep my attention on Lea, still sitting demurely, hands on her lap, gaze on the floor. And I feel the first ripple of unease pass through me. No shock. No fear. Not even rage. If I were to judge her by her posture right now, I'd score her emotional state at a complete zero. Maybe even a negative number—she isn't just neutral about the unfolding chaos. She's indifferent.

And yet, just a matter of hours ago, she practically quaked in her boots at the mention of her big, bad older sister. Eyes wide with terror. The whole "don't hurt me, don't hurt me" vibe. Like she was auditioning for a part in a horror movie. Which would make me her audience.

A second uneasy ripple. The beginnings of a dark, disturbing thought.

Her behavior around MacManus: all demure glances, light touches of her hand. Compared to her one-on-one with me, where she made direct eye contact and issued blunt statements.

The two faces of Leilani Pierson—who can apparently change up her entire emotional makeup at a moment's notice. All the better to manipulate everyone else. Because...

I really don't want to be thinking what I'm thinking. Please let me be wrong. Pretty, pretty please.

Leilani glances up. Her deep almond eyes meet mine. A faint curve lifts the corner of her mouth.

And just like that, I know I'm right.

"You did it!" I blurt out. "You helped your sister escape. This whole thing, it's been your plan from the very beginning. Why? Why would you do such a thing?" Then, on the heels of that thought: "We gotta get off this island. Everyone. Right now. If Lea's involved, forget waiting for Keahi to get here—she's already arrived."

Bedlam. It takes several minutes for Vaughn to bring order to the room, partly because MacManus has gone full coronary, shouting insults at me and anyone who tries to interrupt. Jason and Elias have taken up position flanking him, their hands on their sidearms as if they're moments away from drawing down on a group of overworked, unarmed researchers. Aolani and Ronin respond with some body language of their own, making it clear the burly outsiders will have to go through them first.

And that's not even the craziest part.

Charlie.

After I take in Lea's response, my gaze automatically goes to Charlie, who may or may not be an accessory. He is also staring straight at Leilani. Except...

In his gaze, I see nothing but pure, unadulterated hatred, as if he'd like to grab her by the throat right now. Stab her through the heart with a rusty knife. Kill her with his bare hands.

In response, she gives him the same toying smile she gave me.

A third and final chill shivers up my spine. Based on that expression alone, Keahi and Leilani Pierson are definitely sisters.

I am so far out of my league. I don't think either one of them is a victim. From the very beginning, none of this was as it seemed. And now, Victoria Twanow isn't the only idealist about to pay with her life.

CHAPTER 28

I WANT TO KNOW WHAT'S GOING on with the plane!" Vaughn has to shout his demand three times to be heard over the din. Pilots Marilee and Brent acknowledge him first; then MacManus stops roaring long enough to register the valid concern. As the room finally quiets, Vaughn continues.

"Captain, you and your first officer, go inspect the Cessna again. Take additional help—"

"I'll go," MacManus interjects immediately. "It's my jet. I want to know if there's something wrong with it."

"The comm system," I speak up. "If the atoll's tower is down and the satellite phones are missing, the plane's radio is the next logical thing to disable."

Captain Marilee shakes her head. "The Cessna's radio wouldn't make a difference—Honolulu is well beyond our transmission range. We fly NORDO for over half the trip. It's part of the challenge of serving such a remote location."

"You don't have a satellite system?" Vaughn pushes.

"Not on this craft. Though..." Marilee pauses, glances at Brent.

"The ELT," he murmurs.

"What's an ELT?" I ask on behalf of the technologically ignorant.

"An emergency locator transmitter. It automatically deploys after a crash to help rescuers find the aircraft, but we can also activate ours via a manual switch in the cockpit. The ELT does use satellite technology and would alert the closest search and rescue agency while providing our GPS coordinates."

"Flip the switch and help is on the way," I summarize.

Both pilots nod.

I sigh heavily. "I would check on the ELT. I'm assuming it's not that hard to access, maybe even remove?"

"Fuck." MacManus is already on his feet. He gestures to his bodyguards. "With me."

He heads for the door, Elias having to scramble to get in front of him in order to take the bullet. Does it matter that Keahi prefers knives? I'm feeling a little lightheaded. Maybe even hysterical. Take a job for a serial killer, and this is what happens. What the hell was I thinking?

That a seventeen-year-old girl might be in jeopardy. The same one now standing up and meekly following the parade of bodyguards, pilots, and anxious personal staff out the door. MacManus's team empties out. The rest of us don't know what to do.

Tannis and Emi cross to where Charlie remains seated. Trudy and Ann are already there, Vaughn, too, though he's scowling off into the distance as if he's mentally working through a particularly complex calculus equation. In many ways, I'm sure he is.

"You need to get off the island." Charlie speaks up, his voice low. "If MacManus won't agree, make the pilots do it anyway.

Transport as many people as possible, get to Oahu. Quickly, while there's still enough daylight for taking off."

"Nice accent," I say. Because all trace of Australia is gone. He sounds as plain old American as I do.

Tannis eyes him worriedly, as if losing one's accent is a side effect of a concussion.

"Who are you, really?" Ann demands to know, half angry, half hurt. Trudy is shaking her head, clearly disappointed in the man they thought was their friend.

"You need to get off the atoll. As many of you as possible."

"The Cessna is designated for eight passengers, and that includes using the toilet as an extra seat." Vaughn is paying more attention than we'd realized. "Given the short runway, the atoll can only accommodate a light jet, hence the size restriction. We might be able to sit two more on the floor, but then the extra weight will start messing with the plane's ability to gain enough lift before plowing into the ocean."

"As many as you can," Charlie repeats. "Forget radioing for assistance. Arrive in Honolulu and make the request in person."

I decide to go about this a different way. "Is there anyone specific we should contact?"

Charlie flickers a glance in my direction. "Special Agent Clara Gehweiler, FBI."

"Tell her Charlie sent us?"

"That'll work."

"Who *are* you?" Ann gives up on anger, leans heavy into the hurt.

Charlie directs his attention to Vaughn. "Captain Marilee probably has a sidearm. Get it from her before she departs. We're gonna need more than the rifle and shotgun in your office."

"You want to tell me what's going on here? Threat assessment?"

"MacManus, Leilani Pierson, or Keahi Pierson, or all three?"
I pile on.

Charlie doesn't answer, so much as his gaze travels around the
dining room, the others still gathered at the far table.

"Someone else? Or more?" My voice is now as low as his, but
higher on the fear factor. "Is this about the sabotage, which I'm
assuming wasn't your handiwork, as you had to fix everything?"

"That's the problem," he whispers urgently. "I haven't figured everything out yet. Why the sabotage, how does it figure in,
who's doing it. I have just as many questions as the rest of you. It's
just…"

"The burial mound," I deduce. "That's where you were headed
in the storm. Do you at least have some theories on that subject?
She's a human trafficking victim? You were sent here to investigate?" An organized criminal enterprise would certainly merit
the involvement of the FBI, while confirming my suspicion about
Charlie's real occupation and why he's been lying to us.

We huddle closer, awaiting his reply. Charlie licks his lips,
appearing torn between his professional marching orders and his
obligation to the rest of us.

"You need to tell us," Vaughn hisses at him. "That plane can't
take everyone. Those of us left behind deserve to know."

"I wasn't able to get close enough to the site. Not before I got
hit by the tree. But…the first agent sent in undercover…she went
missing nine months ago."

"Jesus!" Vaughn explodes, spinning away from the table.

"You're with the FBI," Ann exhales. "You're a special agent!"

"Do not tell them!" Charlie orders urgently, and none of us
need a translator to fill in who "them" is. MacManus and his people. The FBI is investigating them.

And one agent has already lost her life over it.

I'm with Vaughn. Fuck.

Ronin and Aolani appear, looking at Vaughn questioningly. Before they can join the fray:

"Hey. Everyone. I want your attention." Vaughn snaps his fingers. The few stragglers stop whispering among themselves and look up. "Grab your passports, cash, bare essentials. Then head to the runway. You're flying to Honolulu in ten minutes. Go!"

A screech of plastic chairs as the first group pushes back, still uncertain. Vaughn's glare hurries them along. Our gathering, however, is slower to respond.

"All of you as well," Vaughn instructs. "I'll stay. Charlie stays. The rest of you are on that plane."

"You're assuming MacManus will let it depart."

"He no longer has a choice. There are more of us than him."

Ronin, coming up to speed: "You're ordering an immediate evacuation."

"Yes."

"There aren't enough seats—"

"Everyone. Grab passports, head to the runway. I mean it."

I peer at him intently. I can't decide if he's stubborn, suicidal, or has some grand master plan.

"As many as we can," he states softly, which I guess says enough.

One by one, we head toward the door. Ronin already has his hand on Aolani's arm, whispering to her intently. The rest of us are silent.

I'm the last one to file out. When I glance back, I see Vaughn taking a seat next to Charlie, heads ducked close. I can hear Vaughn murmuring.

"I'm not leaving. You're not leaving. And like hell I'm letting

Mac and his bodyguards fly off into the sunset. Now, tell me everything."

Which is how I know we're going to war.

HOW DO YOU picture yourself in your mind? Do you see your child self, all wide eyes, beaming smile, and chubby cheeks? Or are you forever your high school photo, rocking the best skin, hair, figure of your life. Maybe you see yourself on your wedding day, or focus on your identity as a young parent, holding your toddler's hand?

At a certain point, we continue to physically change in real life, while slowly but surely freezing into a single static image in our heads. The identity we liked the best? The person we wished we were still? Or some amalgamation, a fleeting moment when all of the pieces of ourselves, the different roles from different ages all lock into place and we feel our most true. *Yes,* some voice whispers in the back of your mind. *This is me.*

And having achieved such nirvana, we hold it tight, while averting our gaze from any reflective surface that might tell us differently.

This is one of those questions that haunts me as I make my way to my cabin to grab…nothing at all. I don't have a passport. And while I could pocket my license and small stash of folded bills, what would be the point?

I already know what I'm going to do. I just wish I understood why.

These days, I don't recognize the person I see peering back at me from the mirror. Who is this too-thin woman with her hollowed-out cheeks, bruised eyes, and creased forehead? She looks strung out. Exhausted. Haunted.

She looks like an addict.

When I first started investigating missing persons, it was on a whim. A woman in my AA group's adult daughter had disappeared, and given the girl's history with drug abuse, the police couldn't be bothered. Sitting in a room surrounded by twelve-steppers, I felt the swell of mutual indignation that we should be dismissed based on our worst moments, thrown away because of our disease.

So I took it upon myself to search. And I found the girl, eventually, though it wasn't a happy ending. But my AA friend still thanked me. One way or another, I'd brought her baby home.

Which got me reading about more cases and visiting online forums and soon becoming aware of an entire world where hundreds of thousands of people went missing each year, and particularly if their skin color was anything other than white, a person of color, most likely no one had bothered to start looking.

I felt empowered by my outrage, vindicated for all the hours I now poured into my new hobby, while I drifted further and further away from Paul and his genuine conviction that a good life involved a house, a steady job, and eventually, hopefully, a child. Didn't I want a good life, too?

I never said no. I just stopped saying yes.

Paul accused me of being a dry drunk, of substituting my desperate need for alcohol with an urgent need to save the world. My obsessive nature was driving the bus, and like all obsessions, it would only lead to destruction in the end.

We fought about it bitterly right up until I left, raging that he didn't know me at all. It was good to have mission and purpose. It gave me focus, kept me from drinking. Not to mention the walls were closing in, and the longer I stayed, the more I didn't understand how people could get up and do the same thing day after day. Same house, same job, same commute, hobby, restaurant, friends. I felt like I was losing my mind, and then I truly did want a beer.

I felt liberated leaving Paul. Terrified and heartbroken, but still...I was going to stand on my own two feet. I was going to be me! A woman who fought for the world's forgotten.

And I did. And I did not.

Like most recovering alcoholics, I stumbled. I walked into a liquor store one night, thinking, *Just one bottle.* It had been so long. What could a little tequila hurt? At the last minute, I came to my senses long enough to call Paul. And even though he was happily married now, he came. At the same time as a kid wielding a loaded gun.

Paul died in my arms, his hands cradling his blood-soaked stomach, a look of total surprise on his face. Sometimes I still dream of our beginning, the feel of his fingertips rippling through my hair. The way his lips dancing upon my neck could ignite my entire body.

But mostly, I have nightmares involving blood and gunpowder and the last words he whispered in my ear.

How did I look when he died? Like a self-righteous soldier with smooth features, bright eyes, and softly rounded cheeks? Or had I already begun transitioning to the thinner, harsher woman who haunts my reflection now?

It's so hard to know, and there's no one to ask.

My parents' deaths erased my childhood. My drunk self I don't remember. And my twenty-something freshly sober version, the one who fell madly and passionately in love with Paul, who spent entire weekends rolling around in bed, with just short breaks for takeout before we flung ourselves at each other again...

Those days feel like moments that happened to someone else.

A movie I watched, a story I read, a witness's recollection I heard. My memories have grown so much darker since.

I had parents once. I loved a man once. And now...I'm just a shadow passing through other people's lives. One time there was this crazy woman who asked a lot of questions. You don't remember her? Me neither.

I want to be seen again. Not in pieces and not as a shadow. I want to be really, truly *seen*. All of me. The lonely child, the grieving lover, the struggling alcoholic. The adult who still feels like an outsider in every room. The person who now cries when it rains. The woman who still longs for the feel of a man's fingertips sliding down her body.

I want someone to know me. At least enough to miss me when I'm gone.

And yet, I will never allow it to happen. Forget self-sabotage. I'm now roaring full speed ahead toward total death and destruction, with the pedal to the metal and both hands on the wheel.

I don't know any other way to live.

My ten minutes are up. I rise to my feet and exit my cabin with absolutely nothing in my hands, just as I knew I would.

My name is Frankie Elkin. I go where I'm needed most, but I never stay. I'm an excellent listener, but a terrible sharer. I've run from bullets. I've held total strangers while they died. I've fought to save people I barely knew. And I've sobbed hysterically when I failed in that mission.

I miss a detective in Boston. I mourn a man in Wyoming.

One day, much as Paul predicted, my current obsession probably will kill me.

And then I will be the one who vanishes without a trace.

CHAPTER 29

THE SCENE AT THE RUNWAY is chaotic. Vaughn has pulled Mac-Manus to the side, where they are having an animated discussion under the watchful gaze of the bodyguards, plus Leilani.

Meanwhile Ronin stands next to the plane in deep conversation with the pilots. Captain Marilee is frowning heavily, while First Officer Brent mostly appears concerned. I notice Marilee now has a pistol holstered on her hip. Proof, I'm guessing, that the ELT has vanished and the situation is officially dire.

Aolani casually assumes head position at the front of our crew. While Vaughn and MacManus argue and Ronin and the pilots negotiate, AO slowly but surely starts leading everyone toward the plane's boarding stairs.

Elias notices first. "Hey," the security expert booms out. "Stop right there." He reaches for his sidearm, Jason immediately following suit.

"What the hell? Are you trying to steal my jet from behind my back?" MacManus rounds on Vaughn furiously.

"I'm not stealing it. I'm commandeering it. For the safety and security of the personnel under my care."

"You and everyone else on Pomaikai fall under my care. Not to mention, it's *my fucking plane*."

"We have no ability to communicate with the outside world, an unacceptable level of risk. Safest course of action is for the pilots to fly back to Honolulu with as many of our people on board as possible. Once the Cessna has landed, Marilee and Brent can apprise authorities of our situation. If you're still so damn insistent about having a plane hang out here, they can return tomorrow with a ham radio."

"A ham radio?" MacManus is briefly distracted by the specificity. Aolani continues to usher people forward, up the stairs. "Why a ham radio?"

"Bigger broadcast range without requiring a comm tower. We'll need a license. Any chance you have an extra amateur license lying around? No problem. With your resources, I'm sure someone can rustle up one on your behalf. Let the Cessna complete one trip, and in return you'll gain worldwide communications access. Honestly, we should've thought of it sooner."

"It's too close to dusk for the plane to be taking off," MacManus states. "Better to wait for morning. We'll go then."

A compromise of sorts. Fortunately, Vaughn isn't buying it. He turns toward Ronin and the pilots. "It can be done," Captain Marilee calls back. "But we have to leave immediately. As in right now."

Aolani nods, having already waved the first few people up the stairs. More quickly follow suit, Trudy and Ann delivering sad little waves of goodbye before disappearing into the cabin. Emi and Tannis duck in behind them.

MacManus opens and closes his mouth, as if he's determined to protest but running out of ways to say no.

Vaughn focuses on Lea, who is literally standing in MacManus's shadow. A brilliant piece of staging for her shy and retiring act, I think.

"Are you truly MacManus's legal ward?" Vaughn asks her.

Lea's head comes up, thickly lashed eyes widening in bewilderment. "Of course. That's what he's always said—"

"What happened to your parents?"

"They're dead."

"But not your older sister, this Beautiful Butcher woman?"

"I barely remember her. She took off when I was just a kid. Clearly, she wouldn't have been a suitable guardian."

"Does she know you're okay and living with Mac of your own volition?"

"I haven't had any contact with my sister since I was four or five. I have no idea—"

"What about written notes?"

"No. Never."

"And your eighteenth birthday. What's going to happen on your eighteenth birthday?" Vaughn whirls on MacManus, not bothering to disguise the anger in his voice. "You really going to sleep with her? That's what this has been about this whole time? Grooming yourself the perfect little wife?"

"No!" MacManus sounds so outraged even I'm taken aback. "Who told you that?"

"She did." Vaughn points at Lea.

"I did not," she protests.

"This is crazy. How long have you known me, Vaughn? How many years have we worked together? In that entire time..."

MacManus continues his tirade, but I've stopped paying attention, noting instead that the plane is now fully loaded. Aolani has even shepherded a distressed Chef Kiki and spouse aboard. With Ronin, Vaughn, Charlie, and me staying behind, there are exactly enough seats for everyone else, including AO.

Ronin has his hand on the captain's shoulder, urging her to board.

They're going to get away with this, I realize. Vaughn's mission was to distract MacManus while Ronin and Aolani got the job done. It's a master class in covert operations.

Aolani reappears. She rat-a-tats back down the steps, capturing MacManus's attention. Too late, he realizes the plane is fully boarded, leaving him shut out on the runway.

"I order you to cease and desist," he shouts belatedly, shoving past Vaughn to stride forward. "I did not authorize this trip. Disembark right now! I command you!"

Captain Marilee hesitates, clearly torn. Ronin murmurs more low, urgent words. After a brief nod, she squares her shoulders, regards her employer.

"Sir, this is clearly an example of extraordinary circumstances. The safety and well-being of these people must come first, and staying on this atoll without any means of outside contact isn't it."

"That plane takes off, there's no coming back from this," MacManus warns. "I'll see to it that neither of you ever work in aviation again. And you." He turns to Vaughn. "We're through. I took a chance on you when no one would. This is how you repay me? Going against my explicit instructions all because you believe some pack of lies?"

"This is the right thing to do," Vaughn repeats steadily. Captain Marilee heads toward the boarding stairs. Two steps, three, almost at the base.

Ronin falls back, his mission accomplished.

And Brent, following in Marilee's wake, casually leans forward, wraps his fingers around the handle of her pistol and slips it from her holster.

"Sorry about this," he says. Then he pulls the trigger.

Pandemonium. Ronin leaps forward to catch Marilee's collapsing form. Brent ducks under the plane and races to the other side. Jason and Elias both raise their pistols to return fire.

MacManus knocks the gun from the bodyguard closest to him. "The wings," he snaps. "Hit the fuel tanks and we'll lose our only way off this island."

Elias belatedly drops his arm. He and Jason bend low, trying to get a bead on Brent's retreating form.

"There!" I cry, spying him disappearing into the brush on the other side of the runway.

"You." MacManus whirls on Jason. "After him. You." He stabs a finger at Elias. "Come with me. We gotta get everyone out of here. Safest place to retreat?" He looks at Vaughn.

"The mess hall. Open lines of sight, secured on two sides. Everyone, move."

Jason takes off after Brent's fleeing form, while MacManus pivots back toward the base camp, Lea tucked protectively at his side. Aolani is already clambering onboard the Cessna and ordering everyone to evacuate. I can hear muffled crying and demands for information. They all heard the shot. Only some could see what happened.

"Captain Marilee will be all right," AO assures everyone, ushering each person down the steps as I bound forward to help any way I can.

Vaughn has reached Ronin now. They shield Marilee's body with their own, making it impossible to tell the extent of her injuries.

"Did he shoot her?" Ann demands to know the second her feet hit the runway. "Did one of those evil bodyguards shoot our Marilee?"

"Brent did," I supply quickly, ushering them toward the crushed-coral path.

"What?" Trudy gasps.

"Not possible!" Ann seconds.

"Brent is armed and on the run. Head to the mess hall immediately. We're taking cover there."

For once, they're speechless. Finally, both squeeze my hands, then take off down the trail leading to the camp, casting furtive glances over their shoulders.

The urgency of the situation has communicated itself through the group, people moving faster and faster for the relative safety of the buildings we'd decided to abandon just thirty minutes prior.

Ronin stands up, Marilee's body slung over his back in a fireman's carry.

There is so much blood. On the ground, her shirt, Ronin's hands. I smell it now. Blood. Gunpowder. Terror. It tastes metallic on my tongue, a flavor both alien and familiar. Time for feminine hygiene products to soak up the blood, stanch the bleeding. Except you have to treat the entrance and exit wounds; that's what I learned the hard way. Stemming the bleeding from one side isn't enough. Never enough.

I promised I would save him. I cursed at the universe, screamed that it owed me that much. But the universe just didn't care.

A moan from Marilee's dangling form.

Another form bursts from the bushes up ahead. Charlie races into view, shotgun in hands.

"Move, move, move," he shouts at me. "Got you covered."

Then he's scrambling into flanking position, a wild vision of bloody bandages and battered visage as he waves his shotgun at the space behind us.

Ronin hits the path, moving at a light jog even with Marilee slung over his shoulders. Vaughn's on his heels.

At the last moment, Vaughn turns toward me. "Now, Frankie."

Then, when I still can't seem to find my feet, he takes three long strides in my direction, grabs my hand, and pulls hard.

"Whatever the fuck it is, let it go. There'll be time enough later. Now, *go!*"

Then we're running, Charlie bringing up the rear.

Another gunshot, this time from behind the plane. A startled flock of seabirds takes flight while white shelled hermit crabs scatter at our feet.

And I catch, just for a second, another face peering at us from the jungle.

Keahi Pierson.

The Beautiful Butcher gives me a wink.

Then she fades once more into the lush greenery as I sprint in earnest.

CHAPTER 30

MacManus is already barking orders by the time Vaughn, Charlie, and I careen through the rear doors of the mess hall.

"On the table. Everyone, clear space!"

It takes me a moment to realize he means for Marilee, whose prone body Ronin is depositing on the closest table, face up. Trudy is already scrambling for a first aid kit.

"Elias, rear doors." MacManus points in the direction from which we came. "Ronin, right side door." He pauses, glances up at our chaotic arrival. "Why does that man have a shotgun?" He stares at Charlie.

"Because I gave it to him." Vaughn is equally curt.

"What the fuck is your play?" MacManus is still staring at Charlie, while Elias lingers in the middle, hand on his own weapon.

"Get us off this atoll safely. Sir." Charlie drawls the last word with just enough attitude to make me and everyone else want to hug him.

"Fine, you get the left side door."

"No. I'll take the rear, seeing as I'm the one with the shotgun. Your man should take the east position, which has the second-most access. Ronin, your thoughts on rifles?"

"I don't do guns."

"I'll take it." Aolani steps forward.

Charlie nods at Vaughn, who produces a bolt-action rifle from the shelf above the sink. Clearly, these two had coordinated efforts before all hell broke loose.

"West door. Bear in mind, while we have two long guns, ammo is limited. You there." Charlie turns to Elias. "What'd ya have?"

"CZ seventy-five SP zero one Phantom. Plus two magazines. Total of fifty-five rounds," he rattles off. The rest of us stare at him wide-eyed.

"Seriously? I thought you security guys carried Glock nineteens."

"I prefer hammer fired—smoother trigger pull."

Charlie nods as if this means something to him. "Backup piece?"

"Smith and Wesson Bodyguard thirty-eight."

Charlie rolls his eyes. "You're not going to hit much with that short barrel."

"Better than a knife in a gunfight," Elias deadpans.

Charlie snorts, turns away.

"Who *is* that man?" Ann whispers beside me, still in shock over this new version of her favorite devil-may-care engineer.

Captain Marilee moans again.

Belatedly, my attention returns to her. Vaughn is already there, a pair of scissors magically in hand as he slices away her shirt.

"Son of a bitch," she groans.

"Easy. We got you."

"Four years in a cockpit together. Asshole."

Vaughn pulls away enough of her top to expose an angry furrow along the right side of her ribs. Again, my fingers spasm. Must stop the bleeding. Can't look at just the front, must check the back.

I turn to the side and quietly dry heave.

"Good news," Vaughn claims. "Missed the important stuff."

"Define... important," Marilee mutters.

Trudy is back with the first aid kit. Alcohol wipes, bundles of gauze, rolls of tape. I know it all too well.

I hone in on other very important matters. "You've never had reason to suspect Brent of anything?"

"Hell... no."

"Who oversees loading the plane?" I press. "Like, gives the final approval before you guys depart?"

"We vary. This time... Brent. His turn."

Vaughn hits her wound with the first disinfectant towelette. Marilee hisses sharply but manages not to scream.

"Brent shot you up close and personal."

"You think... I... don't know... that?"

"And yet, didn't kill you."

Marilee turns her head enough to glare at me. Not to mention the looks of reproach I'm getting from the rest of the room. Vaughn frowns but doesn't intervene.

"He could've blown off the back of your skull," I state. "Or fired a shot directly into your chest. Instead, he manages to only graze your ribs?"

Marilee's expression falters. For a moment, she appears horrified, as if just now understanding how close she came to a terrible and sudden death. "I have a daughter," she murmurs. "Six years old. I keep a photo of her... pinned in the cockpit. Maybe..."

"He's not a total monster?" I shake my head. "I'm not so sure about that. Did you two socialize, have a relationship outside of work?"

"I'm married—"

Vaughn hits her with a second towelette, cutting off her reply.

"But you've known each other for years."

"As colleagues. Two pilots...busting each other's chops in the cockpit. I never...He's younger than me. Living the...single scene. No family. Never...met...any friends. Gambling..."

"Gambling?" I press.

"I think. On his phone. Sometimes...saw him checking baseball scores. Obsessively. But he never...talked the game."

"He could've been bought? Or vulnerable to pressure?"

"Guess...so. But didn't..." She stares at me with bright brown eyes now glassy with pain. "Didn't see it coming."

I nod. I understand her level of betrayal. I've been there myself. I turn my attention to MacManus, who remains standing with Lea hovering at his side. "Brent's working with Keahi," I announce.

"How the hell do you know?"

"I saw her. Not five minutes ago. She's here, on the atoll. She's coming for you."

I watch MacManus for his reaction. Guilt, shame, anything. Mostly, he appears confused. "That's not possible—"

"If Brent was in charge of the final check, he could've hidden Keahi on board. Then, upon landing...Today's acts of sabotage, from the damaged comm tower to the missing ELT; it would be difficult for one person to cover so much ground all at once, especially without anyone noticing. But Brent plus a homicidal maniac..." I turn my attention to Leilani. "Got anything to add?"

She shrinks into MacManus's side, clasping his arm. "I haven't seen my sister since I was five. And given everything I heard about her afterward...I wouldn't welcome her. I know what she's done."

"Slaughter eighteen men?"

Lea drops her gaze. "Our father," she murmurs.

Now this is interesting. I step closer, studying her beneath MacManus's wrathful stare. "How do you know about what she did to your father?"

"I just know."

"She contacted you after she returned to Texas?"

"No, I watched some interviews. I'm sorry," she adds quickly, looking at MacManus. "I remember our father. I remember... enough. And in the interviews, I heard what Keahi said, and didn't say. I filled in the blanks from there."

"Because you're sisters."

"I barely remember her—"

"But you were compelled to look her up, read news articles, listen to her in her own words."

"She's my only living flesh and blood!"

"Exactly."

"That's enough!" MacManus fires at me. But I'm not having it.

"No, it's not! Keahi Pierson is on this atoll. A woman who killed grown men because feeling their blood on her hands made her feel alive. And she has an equally violent partner running around with a loaded gun who's not afraid to use it. We deserve to know what's going on. All of our lives are now at stake."

A low murmur from around the dining hall. MacManus might be our wealthy billionaire boss, but there's nothing like the threat of imminent death to level the playing field. Everyone is now regarding Lea with fresh suspicion.

She holds up her hands in a placating motion. "I had nothing to do with this. Honestly... If I knew how to end this, I would. I remember enough of where I came from. I don't want to go back."

She sounds so damn sincere, I have no choice but to glare at her. This whole situation, all the various parties involved, from serial killer Keahi to oh-so-innocent Leilani to arrogant and entitled MacManus to shockingly homicidal First Officer Brent...

"What did she tell you?" Leilani asks now.

"What?" Everyone's attention swings to me.

"You said you met with her."

"Well, yeah—"

"Just a few days ago."

"Her lawyer reached out—"

"Right before she escaped. And sent this lawyer to the hospital."

Wow, as traps go, this is a good one. I can already feel a wave of suspicion starting to build around me. "I'm an expert at finding missing persons. Keahi summoned me to talk about one thing and one thing only—locating you."

"You brought her here."

"*She* brought *me* here. Big difference. You and MacManus have hardly kept a low profile. She knew all about your relationship with him and this project. She predicted you'd be here, and look, you are."

"Just two days after you arrived."

I'm a little pissed off now. "Maybe because she was anxious to get to you before your eighteenth birthday, when you become this sicko's child bride."

"How dare you—" MacManus now.

"Oh, shut up. Big rich guy; young, beautiful ward. What did you think people were going to assume? Come on, I know it's standard practice for über-successful businessmen to be real-world stupid, but try to break the mold."

"You need to back off—"

"I have no idea what you're talking about," Lea interrupts

primly. "Mac has been nothing but a kind and generous father figure to me. Though I know it's standard practice for some people to be jealous of what they can't have."

"Seriously? You're the who told me about your relationship and what would happen on your birthday—"

"I said no such thing. You did. You assumed. You accused. You look at me and see a victim. Which says more about you than it does me."

She sounds so perfectly self-righteous, I'm flabbergasted. My mouth opens, closes, opens again. "Liar, liar, pants on fire," I manage at last.

But it's too late. I can feel the uncertainty in the room. In the battle of she said, she said, we're both strangers to this group, where I'm the stranger who has admitted to consorting with a convicted serial killer, while Leilani is the sweet young orphan who's never said boo to anyone.

I'm not a violent person, but my hands have fisted by my sides. This family, this whole fucking family.

"Now is not the time," Vaughn interrupts curtly from his position beside Marilee. "We have a seriously injured woman, no means of reaching outside help, and at least one identifiable threat. We need a plan."

I expect MacManus to argue more, but if anything, he relents first. "Jason?" he asks his other bodyguard, Elias.

"No sign of him yet."

"I heard a gunshot," I provide. "Right before heading back to camp."

"If it was Jason," Trudy speaks up hesitantly, "and he shot Brent, wouldn't he be back by now?"

Another low murmur as we follow the line of thought. Unless it was Brent who shot Jason, in which case...

"Let's not get ahead of ourselves." Vaughn again. "They could still be chasing each other around the atoll."

"Brent..." Marilee gasps from the table, "knows the island... well. Always goes for a walk...wanders about...when we're here."

Charlie and Vaughn exchange a glance. I can fill in those blanks. Meaning not only is Brent familiar with the territory, but he also could've stashed other supplies, additional weaponry. He probably committed the previous acts of sabotage. And it's possible he's also the one who hid the just-discovered body.

I turn to Charlie, take a deep breath. "Look, it's time to put all our cards on the table. At this point, we're all in this together. Please, what's the deal with the burial mound? What do those remains have to do with what's going on now?"

I don't think he's going to answer, given MacManus's presence, but then he must've agreed with my assessment that the current crisis trumps long-term objectives. "FBI Special Agent Sherry George," he states abruptly. "She joined one of the supply ships ferrying materials to and from Pomaikai as an undercover agent. Developing a hotel on an island so remote caught our attention. Her job was to determine the validity of this project, as fake development deals have long been used as covers for money laundering operations."

MacManus starts to huff in outrage. Charlie cuts him off.

"Nine months ago, Special Agent George disappeared. Completely. Haven't seen or heard from her since."

The room falls silent. Even MacManus appears stunned by the announcement.

"You think the body belongs to her," I say quietly.

"I think it's a strong possibility. Career agent, mother of two kids. Her husband's with the bureau as well. These kinds of things, they're not supposed to happen. And yet it did."

His gaze returns to MacManus.

"As I'm sure you discovered," he blusters, "my business deal-ings are entirely on the up-and-up."

"I wouldn't say that."

"I would never condone the killing of a federal law enforce-ment officer!"

"Maybe." Charlie's gaze cuts to Leilani. I don't know if other people catch it, but I'm certainly interested. I'm expecting another smirk, but her expression remains passive. Given Char-lie's earlier look of genuine hatred toward Lea, I'm guessing he suspects her in the death of the missing FBI agent. Why, however, has me genuinely stymied. Could it be that a seventeen-year-old girl is the true power behind MacManus's enterprise? And already coldhearted enough to be killing off threats to her world order?

Then again, Keahi was barely in her twenties when she started slitting throats. Maybe, when it comes to the Pierson family, no horrible act is beyond consideration.

"You're not an engineer." Ann addresses Charlie, her feelings clearly still hurt.

"I am," Charlie clarifies. "And I've worked on McMurdo. I just happen to be an FBI agent as well."

"But not Australian!"

"I went to school in Sydney. Bummed around a few extra years. In my heart, luv, I'm forever part Aussie."

It's a nice bit of poetry, but based on Ann's expression, she's not buying it.

There's a growing swell of unease rippling around the room. From learning of Charlie's deception to the news the discovered remains might belong to a murdered FBI agent, this conversation is sending a bunch of already scared people's anxiety sky-high.

I try to get us back on track. "We need a plan. Clearly, staying on Pomaikai isn't good for our future safety and security. So. Options?"

I turn to Vaughn. The man's hair is once again standing on end, and his hands are stained with blood, but he's still the most capable guy I know.

"Can you fly?" he asks Marilee now.

She winces, laboring through another inhale. "I don't know. But I could...advise."

"Someone else at the controls, you provide backup."

"Maybe. But it'd...be risky. This kind of flying...short runway... no lights...out of radio range...Don't let my natural skill fool you. Not...for the...faint of heart."

"Not everyone can fit on the plane," Ronin speaks up quietly, bringing us back to our earlier discussion.

"But it's at least an option involving some people," Vaughn counters. I get his line of thinking. We used it in Wyoming as well. We might not all make it, but at least some of us would. It made sense then, too, right until the bullets started flying, and the ones who didn't make it were the ones we couldn't bear to lose.

I hate this place, but mostly, I hate Leilani Pierson, because at least her sister has the decency to be honest about her homicidal tendencies, whereas there's no way this smug little bitch isn't up to something.

And just like that, I have it.

"Parlay," I speak up.

Everyone's attention swings to me.

"Keahi Pierson is here—I saw her. Most likely, Brent is working with her. So let's send out a member of our party to negotiate safe passage for those of us they don't want to kill."

MacManus is frowning. But now, he squares his shoulders, heroically clears his throat. "If it's me she wants—"

"No. Not you. Her." I zero in on Lea. "One way or another, this is all about you. So. Go forth and make nice with your butcherous big sister. You deal with your family and get the rest of us the hell off this island. Sound like a plan?"

I glance around the dining hall. Everyone else is already nodding.

My turn for a smug smile.

"Good luck," I inform her. Then, under my breath, "Game on."

She doesn't deny it.

CHAPTER 31

"WE WILL COOK DINNER," ANN announces.

"Everything is better with food," Trudy agrees. "I'm thinking spaghetti with garlic bread."

"Petits fours." Chef Kiki rises magnificently to her feet. "I will make lemon petits fours."

"Won't that take hours?" Trudy asks.

"Yes! Or all night, if necessary."

"I can make frosting." Tannis raises her hand. She turns toward Chef Kiki. "Petits fours were my mother's favorite."

"I'll prep the salad," I offer up. Certainly, anything would be better than staying in an overly exposed screened-in dining room, waiting for two homicidal maniacs to show up while their earlier victim bleeds out on the table. MacManus has already ixnayed any chance of his precious ward seeking contact with her monstrous big sis, leaving us right back where we started—no place to go, no plan for survival. I already know this is the quickest way to die.

"You will stay right here," Vaughn orders sharply.

"What? Just because I've knowingly consorted with a serial killer, suddenly I'm under house arrest?"

"Exactly. Have a seat."

I remain standing belligerently. Vaughn remains unmoved. For all my bravado, his words hurt my feelings. In a matter of minutes, Lea has sowed enough doubt about my motives to undermine everyone's trust in me. We need to be a united front. Instead...

Vaughn at least should know better, I think resentfully.

"I will help with dinner." Emi raises her hand.

"Hired!" Ann declares, motioning all her helpers back to the kitchen.

Traitor, I mouth at her.

Sorry, she mouths back before following them into the galley. That single word gives me hope.

"It's been over an hour," Vaughn states abruptly to MacManus—meaning over an hour since MacManus's other bodyguard took off in pursuit of Brent. If Jason had caught his target, he certainly would've reported in by now. Same if he lost sight of him. Which leaves...

No one speaks the conclusion out loud, but everyone is thinking it. I keep my gaze on Lea, who is glued to MacManus's side like the poster child for helplessness. Faker.

"It'll be dark soon," Vaughn continues. "Turn on lights, this becomes a fishbowl. We can't look out, but they can definitely look in."

"Dock lights," I suggest. "That would illuminate a whole section of the enemies' approach. Speaking of which, do manta rays eat evildoers, because that would come in handy right about now."

Vaughn gives me that look like he's barely restraining himself from doing bodily harm.

You're welcome, I beam at him broadly, just so I can watch his face turn three shades of red. I might not be capable of violence myself, but my ability to drive other people batshit crazy is a point of personal pride. Especially right now, when my limbs are twitchy and my body jittery, and I'm not sure whether to burst into screams or break down sobbing.

Which puts me on par with about everyone else in the room.

"My lodge," MacManus says, also thinking out loud. "That's an even more defensible position, being surrounded by the ocean on three sides, while providing more comfort." He gestures toward Marilee, who remains flat on the table, breathing heavily. Vaughn's first aid efforts appear to have stanched the bleeding from her gunshot wound, but she still appears pale and clammy. Shock, most likely.

"We're eighteen people," Vaughn counters. "How to safely transport a group of that size from here to there?"

"Fifteen. Minus Brent. Minus Jason." MacManus's throat works at the mention of his personal security. Lea pats his arm soothingly.

As if it's not her sister who's going to kill us all in the end.

They're in it together. I'm nearly certain of it. But why, how? This elaborate ruse—from Leilani's fake notes begging for help to Keahi reaching out for my personal assistance. It seems needlessly dramatic for a prison break. Unless it was the law of unintended consequence—Keahi's lawyer, Victoria, insisting on involving me, others getting caught up in Lea's ruse. But that feels overly random.

There's a master plan here. I just can't see it yet, which is unfortunate, as I'm already certain cracking that strategy will keep us safer than any piece of real estate.

Night is falling. Fifteen souls. A large screened-in porch. Three armed guards. And when people need to use the facilities, or start falling asleep? I can tell others are asking themselves the same questions and reaching equally terrifying conclusions.

"How long before someone comes looking for you?" Vaughn directs this question to MacManus, the only in-demand international mogul present.

"Given all my dealings, I regularly check in by sat phone even when I'm here. By later tonight, my COO, Francis, will start wondering. But midday tomorrow, he'll grow worried. Day two might bring some kind of proactive outreach. Day three at worst."

"And what would proactive outreach look like?"

"I already have the private jet, told them I'd be keeping it for a bit. My other plane—"

"Your other plane?" I can't keep the edge out of my voice.

"My other corporate jet," MacManus continues steadily, "is too big for this runway. So my best guest—Francis would contact the Coast Guard. They'd make an attempt to radio. Failing that, maybe send a ship."

"Which takes a week to get here from Honolulu," Vaughn supplies. He rakes a bloody hand through his hair, immediately grimaces. He crosses to the sink to wash up, while the mood in the room trends from grim to grimmer.

Based on that math, we have one week plus three days to hold out. That doesn't feel highly probable.

"Parlay," I state again. I like saying the word just to gauge Lea's reaction. She hunkers closer to MacManus, all whimpering, simpering phoniness. He pats her arm reassuringly.

"What would that even look like?" He shakes his head at me.

"Send one of us out, waving a white flag? Calling, 'Here, killer, killer, killer'?"

"We could bring French pastries."

MacManus scowls, but I notice Ronin and Aolani taking the idea seriously. It gives me the courage to forge ahead.

"Look, we can't just hang out here for ten days. We don't even know what they want. Shouldn't we at least try to negotiate terms? Isn't that corporate 101?"

"What terms?" he challenges back. "Hand over Lea, or someone else?"

"You," I volunteer sweetly.

"Not going to happen," Vaughn interjects flatly, returning from the sink. "We're not selling out our own. We're in this together. Are we clear?"

Vaughn has mastered the kind of tone that brooks no argument. He dictates, we follow, some of us more grudgingly than others.

"However," he continues now, "a conversation isn't a bad idea. What else do we have that they might want?"

"Food," Aolani speaks up from her position guarding the side door. "They can draw drinking water straight from the cistern. But we have the kitchen and all its provisions."

"They can access the outside walk-in fridge and freezer," Ronin counters. "We don't have the manpower to guard there and here. It is an incomplete mix of supplies, but enough to get them through."

"What's their end game?" I murmur, my gaze on Leilani. "Brent got Keahi all the way here. Now what?"

"The plane," Captain Marilee gasps from the table. "He shot me...Now...he's...only pilot."

"He can fly himself, Keahi, and whomever"—again I stare at

Leilani—"back to Oahu when this is over. What is Brent's connection to Keahi?" I zero in on Leilani.

"How would I know? I've never spoken to my sister."

"But she is your sister. And Brent is your pilot. Maybe your
favorite pilot?" This is an interesting thought. I glance at Marilee
to see if it jogs anything for her, but her eyes have drifted shut. I go
with: "One way or another, you're the crux of this."

Leilani raises her chin stubbornly. "I don't know anything!"

"Bullshit!"

MacManus practically growls at me, while the rest of the
room shifts in growing unease. No one knows what to believe, but
everyone has plenty to fear. Not a great combo.

My attention returns to grumbling MacManus. Could it be
as simple as turning him over to Keahi and letting her have her
revenge? I don't like the guy, but I'm not sure I can get behind cal-
lously sending him to his death. I also doubt that would be the
end of things. I'm guessing that, having escaped from prison once,
Keahi has no intention of going back. Meaning she and Brent would
have little interest in leaving behind more than a dozen witnesses.

When they're done, they're going to fly the plane off into the
sunset. Brent could pilot, Leilani by his side, Keahi hidden somewhere in the cargo hold. Upon landing, easy enough to deliver
some tale of woe: the island was beset by pirates, or one of us went
all *The Shining* on the others. Hell, we were attacked by rabid
coconut crabs. If there are only two survivors, they can get away
with what they want to get away with, including helping Keahi
along her merry way.

It all works as long as none of us is alive to say differently.

We are so fucked.

The smell of simmering tomato sauce and baking garlic bread
wafts into the room. It's enough to make stomachs rumble and

faces relax. Briefly, the tension lifts. We still don't have a plan, but at least we have dinner. Ann was right on that subject.

Which gives me my next not so great but hopefully good enough idea.

Maybe food can be helpful after all.

I WAIT TILL I'm in the rear of the kitchen, as I don't want Leilani to overhear. Vaughn's not around, which will get me in trouble later, but he's not the relevant expert. Instead, I commandeer Trudy and Ann, within earshot of Charlie.

"How easy would it be to sabotage the food? Slip something in the spaghetti sauce that would at least incapacitate our intruders? Say some kind of poison?"

From his vantage point next to the rear screen doors, Charlie drifts closer, actively listening.

"What do you have in mind?" he asks.

"We can't just stay here and wait for Brent and Keahi to do whatever they're going to do. We're literally sitting ducks."

Holding a shotgun, Charlie doesn't dispute my point.

"Our advantage—we hold the kitchen. They can raid supplies from the outside fridge and freezer, but that gives them ingredients, not an actual meal."

Trudy and Ann nod in agreement.

I eye the two of them. "Since I've been here, you've made a big deal over the fact you're the most important members of this team. Good food equals happy crew. Even tonight, you're preparing a full pasta dinner...Honestly, it's one of the only things holding everyone together right now."

More sage nods. These two know their superpower.

"Keahi just escaped death row. What's the one thing she hasn't had in over seven years?"

Ann gets it immediately. "A home-cooked meal."

"Exactly. I want to offer up dinner. Like a peace offering."

"Or tribute to an angry God," Trudy adds.

"Yes. But I'm also an angry God, so I'd like to make them fucking pay."

Trudy and Ann brighten immediately.

"There used to be some rat poison." Ann looks at Trudy. "Also useful: antifreeze or eye drops. But it would take a lotta eye drops."

I blink at the woman. I honestly had no idea.

"The rat poison is stored in the shed. More accessible to them than us." Trudy ponders. "Can't think of any antifreeze or eye drops readily available."

"What about the first aid kit?"

"Saline solution for eye rinse. Not the same. But it does have—"

Both women get it at the same time. "Laxatives!"

They turn to me. "Would that work?"

"Umm, incapacitate? I would think most definitely. Can you slip laxatives into a tomato sauce?"

"A little extra garlic, we can disguise just about anything." Trudy waves a confident hand.

"How are you gonna deliver?" Charlie asks, his gaze on the lengthening shadows outside.

"Good question. I'm thinking keep it simple. I'll load up a tray, then walk next door to the storage shed with the refrigeration units. We can turn on that outside light from here, yes?"

All three nod.

"Then I guess I'll just stand there, make some kind of loud

proclamation that we have some dinner for them. They must be watching us, right? At least in hearing distance?"

"I would be," Charlie agrees. He shifts, the light catching him across one side. His face is a terrible patchwork of dark purple bruises, fiery red scratches, and pasty white pallor. He's exhausted. You can tell it just by looking at him. But he has a firm grip on the shotgun and a resolved set to his shoulders. He's not standing down anytime soon.

"Even better, smelling distance." I'm warming to my plan now. "Maybe sitting in the bush, getting wafts of this wonderful feast we're all about to have and not them..."

"If I were them," Ann speaks up, "I would question free food. Assume it was poisoned. Does Brent know we have rat poison?" she asks Trudy.

"He's seen all the bill of lading receipts involved in transport. In theory he knows everything."

Ann turns back to me. "I wouldn't eat the food."

"Okay...How about I make a big show of taking a bite? Proving it's edible. One bite of laxative sauce can't hurt me that much, right?"

"We can put a little of the untampered sauce on one corner," Trudy suggests.

"Perfect. I eat that one corner. Then set the tray down...Wait, if I put it on the ground, the crabs will have it in minutes." Now I'm struggling again. I have no idea what effect laxatives have on hermit crabs, but it seems a mean thing to do to Crabby and his friends.

"There's a shelf, on the outside wall. Take off whatever's there, put your tray on." Ann glances at Trudy. "Crabs can still climb up, but it will take them more time."

"While providing pressure for Brent or Keahi to grab the meal sooner versus later," Trudy seconds.

Charlie offers up: "I can cover you from the rear porch, as long as you stay beneath the floodlights. But the minute we step outside we both make ourselves targets. Meaning it's not the safest plan, though not the craziest, either. And if you can get them to take the food, weaken them in any way..."

I nod, addressing Ann and Trudy. "Start prepping. Keep it on the DL. I'll smooth over food delivery with Vaughn and Mac-Manus."

"But you're not going to tell them about the special sauce?" Trudy and Ann shift uncomfortably.

"I don't want Leilani to know."

"You said she was the victim."

"I think I got played on that subject." I glance at Charlie. "You seem to have opinions about Leilani. I saw the way you were staring at her earlier—with a nearly visceral level of hatred."

Trudy and Ann study him with renewed interest. He scowls at all three of us, then winces as it pulls at the scab on his forehead.

"Brent was probably the saboteur, don't you think?" I push harder. "He's also part of MacManus's organization, though I'm getting the impression he's not terribly loyal to MacManus. Is it possible Brent and Leilani are in this together? This is all some sort of criminal enterprise coup?"

"I don't know," Charlie mutters abruptly. "As I said, this whole thing started as a money laundering investigation, sparked by MacManus's extensive real estate dealings and questionable taste in business associates. Sherry was sent to see if the proposed eco-lodge was truly being constructed, and how it was being managed. But once she disappeared..."

"I'm sorry about the loss of your friend," I offer softly.

Charlie nods once, eyes on the floor. "I never understood the acts of sabotage. Not who and not why. And I definitely never suspected Brent. Though given what just happened, obviously he's part of it. Whatever the hell 'it' is." Charlie grimaces, clearly still puzzled on several issues. I don't blame him; so am I.

"And your deep, personal hatred of Leilani?" I prod again. "You think she's part of MacManus's misdeeds? As in actively involved with his criminal dealings, including the possible murder of a special agent?"

"Originally, 'course not. But then I caught her in a lie. And not just any lie. A big one."

Trudy and Ann immediately lean closer. I do, too.

"I was chatting her up," Charlie murmurs in our ears. "Had just delivered paddleboards to the owner's lodge. Was trying to see if she'd ever spotted someone matching Sherry's description working on the atoll. Lea was doing her shy act, all headshakes and downward glances. I gave up, returned to the UTV, then realized I still had the life jackets. Grabbed 'em, headed back around the house, where I spied Lea standing there, looking out over the water. Except she wasn't standing like Lea anymore. She had her shoulders back, chin up, all strong and boss-like. Then I heard her mutter, "Figures someone would miss that bitch.""

I recoil slightly. " 'Someone would miss that bitch'?"

"Clear as day. Second she saw me, her face blanked, shoulders slumped, like a switch had been thrown. If I hadn't seen, hadn't heard... Tried a few more times to trap her, but she's clever. Worst part—she knows that I know. It fucking amuses her."

"She's not a victim; she's a perpetrator." I exhale. Dammit, sometimes I hate it when I'm right.

"Bet my soul on it. But I can't prove a damn thing."

"I think she plays him," I volunteer at last. "MacManus thinks he's in charge, but her whole needy act is just that, an act." I think back to earlier today, when she first arrived on the island. Her delicate touches of his arm, pleading looks as she begged to slip away to the owner's lodge. I'd thought she wanted to get away from her overbearing guardian. But now, knowing Keahi had arrived on the island on the same plane—Leilani was trying to get away from all of us to meet up with her sister. MacManus was never the wiser, while I foolishly assumed I was aiding a poor, kidnapped girl. Forget manipulating him, she's manipulated all of us just fine.

"I also think Leilani's in on it with Keahi," I continue, thinking out loud. "She engineered her sister's escape and, with Brent's help, brought her here. Keahi's motives are obvious—she escaped lethal injection and can now have her revenge on a man she says beat her and kidnapped her sister. Leilani is more of a mystery to me. She made it pretty clear life with MacManus was a big step up. Eliminating her legal guardian while she's still a minor seems a risky move. Just puts someone else in charge of her future."

"Matter of months," Charlie counters. "Then she's free and clear. And like you said, her sister didn't have months to wait. Gonna happen, had to be now."

That makes sense. But I still feel like there's more to this story. Leilani had fallen madly in love with Brent, was determined to run away with her new lover, but knew MacManus would stop them as long as he was alive?

I already doubted Leilani possessed that level of genuine emotion. I think she and her sister shared the same use 'em and lose 'em approach to men, butcher knives optional.

People are starting to notice our huddle. Time to stop scheming and start putting our plan in motion. Trudy and Ann are already on it.

"We'll start preparing the tray," Trudy whispers.

"Perfect. I'll finesse the bosses. Charlie, back on guard duty. We got this."

The words come out more hollowly than I intended.

Ann pats my arm in understanding. "When this is over, you should get a new job, dear. You make an excellent sous chef. Maybe you can also take up contract work, spend more time traveling the world like Trudy and me."

"Head to McMurdo? Play with penguins?" I smile wistfully, my gaze going outside, where the sky is dimming, the shadows lengthening. Night is finally coming, and with it...

"We need to get the fuck off this atoll," Charlie states roughly.

"My thoughts exactly."

CHAPTER 32

Vaughn and MacManus greet my announcement that I'm bringing a food tray to our enemies with equal parts scorn and suspicion. Leilani, I notice, studies my face very carefully, while Aolani and Ronin are actually the first on board.

"Charlie assumes they must be watching us," I explain. This much is true. "He wants a better bead on their position. Getting them to show themselves long enough to grab a hot meal will do that."

MacManus is more worried about us having enough food. By feeding the enemy, are we depriving ourselves of anything? Sure, I want to tell him, an immediate and terrible death. But I need to get back to the galley to complete my mission, so mostly I bite my tongue.

If anything, it makes Vaughn even more suspicious.

In the end, no one has any clear grounds for telling me no, though if anyone thought I was a sane, rational person before, they're definitely over it now.

I report back to the kitchen, where Tannis and Emi are starting to set out the buffet of piping hot Italian food. A giant bowl
of spaghetti. Hot pots with two kinds of sauce, one veggie, one
meat. Baskets of garlic bread. A beautiful green salad. In the background, Chef Kiki is still furiously working away on her famed
petits fours.

My stomach rumbles, and my footsteps falter. It would be so
much easier to stay here. Dish up a plate, enjoy the company of
friends. Forget for a moment what lurks just outside our door.

Maybe that's my problem, my fundamental source of anxiety that once drove me to drink too much and now drives me
to work so obsessively. Once I know something, I can't unknow
it. There's so much danger in the world. So many people who
go unseen in life, based solely on the color of their skin, and
then when something bad happens, are ignored completely by
the powers that be.

I can't sit here, in this inner circle of bright light, cheerful
noise, and hot food. My mind is already outside, worrying about
the rustling coming from that bush, the sudden quiet of the always
raucous seabirds overhead, the hulking shadow slipping between
those two buildings.

As long as I'm terrified, I might as well do something about it.

Trudy and Ann have a tray waiting for me. The single plate
bears an impressive mound of spaghetti, topped with grated cheese.
Smack in the center of the cheese is a spot that remains bright red.

"That's your target," Trudy whispers.

"We thought it would look better," Ann adds in a low voice,
"if you took the bite right from the middle of the dish. Less suspicious."

"You two ever want a career change, I recommend espionage.
You're good at this."

Tucked to the side of the screen doors, Charlie grunts his agreement.

Half a loaf of garlic bread sits next to the spaghetti. A pile of silverware is on the other side. Two of everything, I notice, in case Keahi and Brent decide to share.

Would they? What are the dynamics between the two? Given Keahi's victim preference, Brent has selected a risky partner in crime. I'm already certain her corrections officer consort has come to a bloody end. Too hard to get both of them smuggled onto a tiny Cessna bound for Keahi's target. And given what Keahi did to her own lawyer, she clearly doesn't hold loyalty in high regard.

Maybe Brent will reach for a bite of spaghetti and she'll kill him on principle. This feeding the enemy idea might be even better than I'd hoped.

Which doesn't explain why I'm trembling uncontrollably and having a hard time wrapping my fingers around the edge of the tray.

"Are you sure, luv?" Charlie murmurs softly. "You don't—"

"I got this!"

"Maybe we should take it. There are two of us." Ann and Trudy square their shoulders in mutual resolve.

"No!" That as much as anything gives me strength. If they went out there and something happened to them—I couldn't bear it.

Deep breath. I tighten my grip, lift up the tray, get it in position on my left shoulder just as Vaughn appears.

He looks at me, then at my crack assistants. He doesn't have to say anything for us to know that he knows we're up to something.

He focuses his attention on me. "You will drop off the tray, then get right back in here."

I nod.

"No lingering, no side trips, no rash or impulsive acts."

He might as well be asking me not to breathe. I raise my chin a notch. Then I nod.

"I don't like this."

None of us say a word.

"But I'm going to trust you on this."

Low blow. Good thing I'm already shaking.

Last deep breath. I turn toward the rear door. Ann hustles forward to open it. Trudy finds the switch to snap on the outdoor floodlights in front of the storage shed. Charlie raises his shotgun. And under the watchful gazes of my friends, I step into the night.

IT IS QUIET. Way too quiet. Inside, with all the whispered musings, side conversations, and banging pots and pans, it had been difficult to judge, but now that I'm outside, feeling the humidity press against my entire body, the sweat already building on my brow, I can register all the differences.

The eerie silence of a jungle that's never noiseless, especially this time of night. The total lack of movement, not even a light breeze rustling the palm fronds overhead. The pools of inky black that seem impossibly deep all around me, even as the distant horizon offers up lighter bands of gold, faded orange, and starlight blue.

I step off the porch onto the crushed-coral path, and not a single hermit crab scuttles away. That, more than anything, unnerves me.

The storage building is immediately to my left, a beacon of glaring floodlights. Twenty feet, then I'll arrive at the long structure bearing three doors—one for the walk-in freezer, one for the walk-in fridge, and one for miscellaneous supplies.

Generally, there are more crabs milling about beneath the lights. But tonight...

I take another fortifying breath, the tray growing heavy on my shoulder. Twenty feet. Anyone can walk twenty feet. I wonder if this is how Keahi contemplated her final march to the execution chamber, dead woman walking. Or if she always knew she'd find a way out.

I take the first step, find my bearings, and go for it. *One, two, three, four, five, six, seven, eight, nine, ten...*

Then I'm there, standing beneath the glare of twin floodlights. I spy the shoulder-high shelf that will be my final target before turning to face the vast darkness before me.

Being lit up like a Christmas tree makes everything worse. I'm the one exposed and vulnerable. Dead woman standing. Whereas they have the jungle on their side.

I clear my throat, get to it.

"We...um...we brought you dinner. Think of it as a peace offering. We don't want there to be any more violence. Whatever you want, just tell us. There are a lot of people here who deserve to make it home safely."

I'm not sure what else to say. This piece I hadn't thought through. I fumble about, then add belatedly: "Keahi, your sister sends her regards. She wants you to know she's happy." Which I'm pretty sure is a waste of breath, as the two of them are in this together. Which then drives me to open my mouth and continue brashly.

"And I want you to know, you're a fucking bitch. There was no reason to drag me into this. No reason to beat your lawyer half to death or take an entire island hostage. You want to stop feeling so empty inside, load up on carbs like the rest of us!"

Then, to prove my point, I hoist the tray up on the shelf, pull down the plate of spaghetti long enough to furiously twirl a fork in the middle of the red target, then shovel a load of noodles in my mouth. Chew, chew, swallow. Now I'm outta here.

"Look, Ma, no poison!" I declare, holding out the pasta to demonstrate its edibleness.

For the first time, I hear a sound. The low chuckle of laughter coming from somewhere in front of me. The direction of the bathhouse.

A light snaps on, nearly blinding me. I have to turn my head to the side, as my entire body tenses, prepares to run.

But I still don't see anyone. Not the silhouette of Keahi or the shadow of her partner.

Except peering more closely, I do make out a form, the top of someone slumped down on the back porch of the structure.

Despite myself, I take a step forward, trying to understand. First Officer Brent, already eliminated from the picture? Or bodyguard Jason, grievously injured and needing help?

The night, still so damn silent. Not a single rustling tree, breaking branch.

She's here. I can feel her. A predator tucked in the bushes, gleefully watching her prey. And yet I take another step out away from the protection of the storage shed and Charlie's line of sight.

"Frankie!" he barks at me.

But I need to know what I'm seeing. The figure isn't moving. I can just make out his head above the railing. It's going to be Jason, I'm certain of it. Keahi wants me to find him. Wants to make a show of what she's done, like a cat, proudly showing off her latest kill.

It doesn't prepare me.

Nothing could prepare me.

I get just close enough. And then.

I open my mouth, but no scream comes out. The horror is beyond words. It is everything the jungle had been warning me about.

The plate of spaghetti drops from my nerveless fingers. I stay rooted in place. Staring, staring, staring. I need to look away. I can't look away.

More laughter floats around me.

The night, so inky black.

This sight, lit up so garishly bright.

Footsteps, crashing toward me. I need to move, need to flee, need to do something.

Staring, staring, staring.

Jason's severed head. Looking right at me. Eyes milky white.

Then: "Jesus fucking Christ."

Vaughn barrels into me, snapping an arm around my waist.

"Close your eyes," he orders as he drags me furiously back to the mess hall.

But I don't. I can't.

My mouth is still open.

I am still screaming.

And I still don't make a sound.

CHAPTER 33

WE WILL NEVER SPEAK OF it to the others. We don't have a discussion on the subject, never make any explicit agreement. We just know. What we saw was terrible enough. The others shouldn't have to learn of it. It would sow too much panic.

It would allow Keahi to win.

Standing on top of the steps, shotgun to his shoulder, Charlie spies us first. He takes one look at our faces, clenches his jaw.

"Tell MacManus his man Jason won't be coming back," Vaughn orders curtly.

Charlie steps back to inform Ann of the message. I'm trying to get up the stairs, my legs trembling so hard it takes Vaughn's arm around my side to move me up each step.

I'm shaking. Hot, cold, sweaty, dry heaving. I want to curl up in the fetal position with my hands over my head. I want to plunge into the ocean, start swimming, and never look back. I want to live in a world where monsters like Keahi Pierson don't exist.

"Sit here," Vaughn is murmuring. He guides me to a plastic

chair in the corner of the porch, positioning himself to block my body from others' view. He has to hide me. No one could look at my face right now and think things went according to plan.

I rock back and forth, arms tight around my waist. I'm trying hard to breathe, but my mouth still isn't working right. Opening, closing, but nothing happening. No sound. No oxygen. I'm suffocating, I'm drowning. It's all the same in this fucking humidity.

Vaughn pulls my arms from my waist. He takes my hands and plants my palms against his cheeks.

"Look at me, look at me, look at me."

His beard is both prickly and soft. I curl my fingers into it. This close I can smell the tang of salt and sea breeze upon his skin. I work my fingers again, tracing the line of his jaw, the ridge of his brow, the crinkles at the corners of his eyes. His skin is warm and real. I find the pulse at the side of his neck, feel his heartbeat against my thumb.

He's still holding my wrists. Maybe his fingertips are registering my own pulse. Now he breathes in deeply, one, two, three, four. Holds the air in his lungs, one, two, three, four, five, six, seven. Exhales, one, two, three, four, five, six, seven, eight.

I follow along with him. Steady inhale, hold, slow exhale. Again and again. Till the world rights itself and I register his clear blue eyes, perpetually rucked-up hair. I drift my thumb over his lower lip, exploring the fullness. The curve of his ear, the softness of his earlobe.

I pet him, my own personal comfort human. Raking my fingers through his hair, down his neck. Then I feel my eyes start to sting, and I know it's coming, the scream locked in my chest. He seems to know it, too, pulling me hard into his chest just as the sound wells up and explodes.

I press my lips against the salt of his throat, stifling the bursting horror into muffled whimpers he soothes away with a hand down my back. I'm rocking against him. As if I would like to immerse myself into him, disappear completely, no longer be.

And maybe I would like that. But it's not an option.

Another long, rippling shudder, until finally I still. I merely rest against him. He makes no move to untangle, his hand still stroking my hair. I would like to close my eyes and stay here forever. There are so few moments in my life when I've truly leaned on another. He is strong enough to handle me, world-weary enough to understand me. It is a potent, heartbreaking combination given I'm not the right woman for either of us.

The sound is slowly returning to the jungle around us. That, as much as anything, rouses me back to action.

I am only human, so I take a tiny little lick of his throat before pushing myself away and figuring out how to sit upright in my own space again.

Charlie is still on guard on the other side of the porch, shotgun in hand, resolutely looking at anything but us.

Vaughn remains kneeling before me. His blue eyes are concerned, but also dark with other emotion.

"You okay?" he asks at last, his voice husky.

"I will be."

"Another unfortunate camping trip?"

"Something like that. You?"

His throat works. "I don't need to see that ever again."

"I didn't deliver the spaghetti. I failed."

"We'll come up with another plan."

"It's dark out."

"Yes."

"Nothing good happens in the dark."

"There's that."

A rap on the wooden frame of the screened doors. MacManus stands on the other side, taking in our tightly huddled form, Vaughn's hands upon my knees.

"Brent killed Jason?" he asks.

"Keahi killed Jason," I correct him.

"How can you possibly know—"

"It involved a knife." Or machete. I shiver again.

MacManus nods shortly. His gaze goes to Vaughn. "We have another problem—people need to use the facilities. Except..."

We all turn to the total darkness now surrounding the mess hall. The kind of pitch black that hides just about anything and anyone.

"All right." Vaughn pulls away, rises to standing. "You'll be okay?" he asks me.

"I'll be okay."

"Well, then. Let's figure this out." He strides back into the kitchen, once again the project manager extraordinaire.

I take another moment to sit on the back porch with Charlie.

"What do you put our odds at?" I ask him presently.

"This is when it all goes to shit," he drawls.

"I think they'll kill us all. Whatever their play is, they can't afford any witnesses."

He doesn't disagree.

"I only wish I knew what we were dying for."

"Way of the world, luv. Very few people do."

"And on that cheery note." I climb to my feet, order my limbs to start working again. I reach for the door just as Charlie speaks up again.

"Watch your back, Frankie."

"Do me a favor, save one of those rounds for her."

"Which her?"

"Honestly, I don't fucking care anymore."

———

WHEN I WALK into the kitchen, Trudy and Ann come bustling over immediately, twin looks of worry on their faces.

"I'm okay," I assure them. "But I kinda dropped the plate of spaghetti. I'm sorry."

They don't ask questions, merely pat my arm. We move together into the dining hall, where Marilee has made it up from the table into a chair, her feet propped up in front of her. Her color is still awful and her eyes glassy, but they are open and focused on Vaughn, who is making an announcement.

"Here's the deal. People need comfort breaks."

A bunch of furious nods.

"I think we can all agree, making trips to the camp latrine is out of the question. Too much ground between here and there, and walking the paths with flashlights is only going to turn each person into a target."

More anxious nods.

"So, to my left." Vaughn gestures to the side door, where Elias remains on guard. If the bodyguard has any emotional response to the news of his comrade's death, none of it shows on his sharply groomed face. "As many of you may know, there's a narrow strip of vegetation between the mess hall and the ocean. It should be dense enough to offer a bit of privacy, while already being protected on two sides. We'll cover the rest using our guards. Basically, welcome to your new latrine. You're all outdoorspeople. You got this."

General murmurs of surprise followed by approval.

"Okay." Vaughn claps his hands again to recapture attention. "We're going to divide into groups. Ladies first. Who needs to head out?"

Hands shoot into the air, including Trudy and Ann beside me. Personally, I'm too tired to contemplate the logistics involved. Plus, there's another key hand in the air: Leilani's.

Now here's an activity MacManus can't micromanage. I already got Leilani alone for a bit, though fat lot of good it did me. This time, I set my gaze on him. He's the man of the hour, and I'm starting to realize how little I truly know about him.

He's murmuring something in Leilani's ear. Whatever it is, she remains obstinate. Vaughn starts organizing parties of three, and she steps away from MacManus to take up position.

Which I use as an opportunity to sidle closer.

His once perfectly pressed Hawaiian shirt is now wrinkled and stained with sweat. I can feel heat and nervousness radiating from him. He's afraid, I realize, genuinely and truly terrified. And yet, he's holding his shit together. I'm not sure if I admire that or am even more annoyed.

His gaze is fixed on Leilani. I try to read the look. Possessive? Obsessive? Mostly, he looks worried. Like any father, I suppose, looking out for his charge.

"Did you love her?" I ask softly, my shoulder nearly touching his.

"Of course I care about Leilani. I'm her guardian—"

"Not Leilani. Keahi."

The name stops him in his tracks. A parade of emotions flickers across his face. Surprise. Irritation. Sadness. Fleeting, then gone.

"She said she met you at a farm stand. Immediately fell for your charm. She told me she loved you, right up to the moment you started beating her. Then, the dark twisted part of her loved you even more."

He flinches noticeably, his hands curling into fists down at his sides. I wonder if he knows he's doing it.

"She was beautiful," he allows finally. "One of the most beautiful women I'd ever met."

Girl, I want to correct him. Keahi had been barely legal at the time.

"But beautiful women are a dime a dozen. For a man like me." He turns to stare at me. There's no apology in his eyes. I gotta give the man some credit. He knows who he is. "I did love Keahi. But it wasn't her beauty that captivated me. I saw something in her that I recognized, that I felt in myself."

"A propensity for violence?"

"Loneliness. She was haunted by it. And I'd suffered a hard loss of my own. Her pain called to me."

I regard him for a moment, trying to think who he could be referring to. "Your business partner, Shawn?" I guess at last. "You mourned him?"

"Shawn Eastman, and he wasn't just my business partner; he was my best friend. We grew up together. Built a business together. Became filthy rich together. People assume wealthy assholes don't have friends. But trust me, rich pricks like me need best buds the most. No one else in our lives is going to tell us how it is. No one else understands."

"I heard you killed him."

"You heard wrong."

"His death made you richer."

"Everything I touch makes me richer. Not my fault. And with a gift like that, I certainly don't need to resort to murder to fatten my offshore bank accounts."

"Wow, arrogant much?"

"All the damn time, so what's the point of apologizing for it?"

"Did you hit her? Keahi? Did you beat her senseless? Earn the very painful death she's planning for you?"

"I hit her." At his sides, his fists spasm. "I regret it. Always. I'd never so much as slapped a woman before. I've never smacked one since. But there was something about her, once we got going...Keahi would push me. Plant her hands against my chest and shove. Again and again, with this certain look in her eyes, until I...It took me years to realize she was goading me. And every time I gave in and lashed out, she got off on it. Seriously. The sex was mind-blowing if you want to know the truth."

"You have earned that painful death."

"Maybe." His easy admission surprises me. "But I've tried to make amends in the years since. One night, Leilani saw us fighting. Keahi had already smashed a number of vases, lamps, a TV. She was on one side of the sofa, preparing to pounce, I was crouched on the other side, readying for the counterattack, and then Leilani was standing there. This sweet little girl. Staring at us both. Taking it all in. The bruises darkening her sister's eye, the blood dripping from my forehead. And I saw myself. Through her eyes. I saw exactly who I'd become. And for the first time, I felt like a bad person."

"What did you do?"

"I ordered my driver to take Keahi to the ER for the medical attention she clearly needed. Then, after a brief visit from Keahi's aunt when I assured her she should be grateful *I* wasn't pressing charges against Keahi, I grabbed Lea and flew my private jet to New York. I knew Keahi and her family lacked the means to find us there."

"You did kidnap Leilani!"

"And thank God, don't you think? Can you imagine what her life would've been like, being raised by her big sister, the serial killer?"

"When Keahi got out of the hospital, she came looking for her sister. She wanted her back."

"I'm sure she did. And then she dealt with her pain by butchering over a dozen men. Gee, so sorry to have removed Leilani from that kind of loving family."

I honestly don't have a reply for that. "Leilani implied you plan on sleeping with her on her eighteenth birthday."

"I sincerely doubt she meant any such thing."

"She did."

"Just stop—"

"No, you stop. Are you looking around you right now? Do you realize the level of danger we're all in? Keahi is here, on the atoll. And she came on your plane. How do you think that happened?"

"Brent, obviously."

"All by himself? And why, why is she here?"

"You said it yourself: she wants her sister back."

"So why isn't Leilani afraid? You've been around her all afternoon. That girl's been many things, but not terrified."

"She's stoic."

"Holy shit. I thought you were an abusive asshole, but you're nothing but a lousy mark. The rich idiot they've both taken advantage of."

"Shut up!" MacManus's face has turned a mottled red. He takes a step closer, shaking a finger at me.

If I want to prove he really hits women, I'm probably one smartass retort away. But Leilani's going to be back at any moment, and now that I realize the depth of everything I didn't know, I have many more questions to go.

"Leilani and Brent. Did she spend time with him on her own? Could they have a relationship?"

"She's seventeen—"

"Exactly the way you like them. Trips alone or not? Answer me."

"Sometimes. Yeah. I'd fly out first, she'd join me later. She would've been with just Marilee and Brent on those flights."

And as first officer, Brent was the one who came back to spend time in the cabin. "How long, how often?"

"He's been working for me for four years, at least two dozen trips a year—"

"Yeah, they're an item. Okay, next up. What happens when she turns eighteen?"

"For the love of God, I'm not planning to have sex with a girl who's like a daughter to me!"

"Yeah, but going on the principle that every lie contains a kernel of truth, what else might be significant about her eighteenth birthday?"

"I don't know. She's been looking at colleges. But she's already received such an intensive education traveling the world while assisting me with my business, formal study seems a step down. She hasn't decided anything yet."

"Does she come into money?"

"She doesn't have any money."

"But you do."

"Yeah—"

"Is she your heir?"

For the first time, MacManus pauses. I can see the wheels churning behind his eyes. "There's a trust," he states abruptly. "I established it in her name. She'd come into that, in a series of laddered payouts."

"So not all of your billions, but probably millions."

"It's a generous trust."

"What about life insurance?"

His throat works. "She is my designated beneficiary. Look, Lea went through a phase where she'd have these horrible panic attacks. It was important for her to know she'd be safe and secure, no matter what."

I can only shake my head at his naivety. MacManus, however, isn't having it.

"You don't get it. You see who Lea is now, but not the traumatized child she was back then. For years she woke up screaming from some nightmare or another involving her sister. She refused to go outside because she was convinced her sister would appear and snatch her. She'd disappear for hours at a time till eventually I'd find her huddled in the back of some closet or hiding under the bed. She's genuinely, deeply, totally terrified of Keahi. Which makes this whole situation her greatest fear come to life."

I scowl. I don't want to believe him, but his words echo something Vaughn had said earlier: if I'd met the anxious girl Leilani had been ten years ago, I'd understand how good MacManus had been for her.

"All right," I allow, then narrow my eyes. "Final question. Tell me about Noodles the cat."

CHAPTER 34

"WHAT NOODLES THE CAT?"

"The kitten you gave Leilani when you first met her."

"I gave her some fluffy little ginger thing. But she named it Orange Kitty, being five at the time."

"Which she later nicknamed Noodles?"

"Never happened."

"You don't know anything about Noodles? Maybe a nickname she had for something, someone?"

"No. Where are you getting your information from, anyway?"

"From Leilani! In a note she wrote to Keahi..." My voice trails off. In handwriting that doesn't match hers. God, this is giving me a headache. "Fine, tell me about your money laundering enterprise."

More denial ensues, MacManus going through the motions of being insulted and defensive. His real estate dealings are perfectly legal. This is what happens when people are successful; others try to tear them down. Blah, blah, blah.

I find the whole tirade exhausting, especially given the circumstances. If there's ever a time to lose the bullshit and cut straight to the truth, impending doom should be it. I manage to get out of him there's no one person who oversees his entire empire. He prefers to operate each development project as a separate silo. In fact, the only person who probably knows the full scope of his dealings is Lea as she's always at his side.

MacManus seems to understand the implications of that statement at the same moment Leilani reenters the mess hall and makes a beeline for his side, her damsel-in-distress act on full display.

She casts me a quick, uneasy glance, given my chummy position next to MacManus. When she cozies up to him and his arm doesn't automatically wrap around her shoulders, she gives me a second, edgier look.

I feel my work here is done—though to be fair, I'm now as confused and troubled as MacManus, so maybe our conversational duel was a draw. Neither of us knows what to think anymore.

I make my way to Captain Marilee, who's pale and clammy, but still sitting upright.

"Can I get you anything?" I offer.

"Rescue...chopper?"

"I was thinking Coast Guard Uber, myself. If they don't have an app for that, they should."

She manages a smile, points to her water glass on the table. I grab it for her. Then, after she's had a few sips: "When you and Brent were winging Leilani through the skies to meet up with MacManus, did Brent spend a lot of time back in the cabin with her? Like more than he ordinarily does?"

Marilee's gaze cuts to the side where Leilani is once again plastered against her legal guardian.

"You think...Lea and Brent?" She grimaces.

"You tell me."

"Career . . . suicide."

"But is Brent the kind to heed the warning or take the bait?"

She closes her eyes, exhales slowly. "He likes money. Why he was always mingling . . . hoping for the right contact. Or betting on stupid ball games. Our job is good . . . but compared to the lifestyles . . . of the insanely wealthy . . . Yeah, he'd take the bait."

I nod, feeling officially comfortable with my theory.

"What does it mean," Marilee struggles through another breath, "that she's in here . . . he's out there? Shouldn't she . . . walk out . . . join him? They fly away. We get rescued."

"I think in order to disappear with Brent, she first has to deal with MacManus."

"That . . . her sister's job?"

"Maybe."

"Still, if Lea left the mess hall . . . Mac would follow. Her sister then gets what . . . she wants. Brent, Lea gain their freedom."

And a lot of money, I think.

"They fly away. We get . . . rescued."

I like the way the captain thinks, especially as all her scenarios end with us being saved. I don't think it's that simple, however. Lea can't collect life insurance on a man a bunch of witnesses saw her help murder, especially after her lover shot another person in cold blood. Meaning all of us must perish as well.

Though given that . . . why doesn't Lea just walk out of here? Or take off while outside for her comfort break? What's the point of perpetuating this elaborate ruse in front of a bunch of people already marked for death?

I contemplate Marilee. "Brent is doing this for Lea."

"Asshole."

"Keahi is here for Leilani."

"If you...say so."

"And to murder MacManus."

"Sure."

"What does Lea want from Keahi? She doesn't actually need Keahi to kill MacManus. Brent could've done it easily enough. Hell, he shot you."

"Ass...hole."

"So why Keahi? Leilani spent years terrified of her big sister, then suddenly broke her out of prison to serve as a particularly brutal hitwoman? And what the fuck is the deal with Noodles the cat?"

Marilee regards me blearily.

"Exactly!" I agree.

I rise to standing just as the darkness outside is suddenly flooded with light. We turn as one toward the glow coming from the dock, where the silhouette of a woman has appeared.

And I squeeze my eyes shut, because I don't want to see what the Beautiful Butcher has done now.

"DID YOU GET my present?" she calls out from her position between the dock and the rec hall. No one is gasping or screaming, so I risk peering out.

"Shoot her!" MacManus strides toward Aolani, who has the rifle. "Right now. She's an escaped killer, for God's sake. Do it."

Aolani moves to the front of the dining hall, but I can already see the uncertainty on her face. It takes a certain type of person to coldly take aim at another human being and then pull the trigger. I don't blame Aolani for not being that kind of soul.

"What's beside her?" Vaughn asks sharply.

We all squint harder, captive audience to a show none of us wanted to attend. I spot what he's talking about almost immediately. There's a line of red containers organized in a neat row beside her.

"Fuel cans," Ronin supplies.

"Shit." Vaughn and Ronin exchange glances while MacManus, failing with Aolani, jerks the rifle from her grasp and holds it out for his man, Elias.

"You do it."

Elias steps forward quickly enough, but there's a frown on his face. "I don't fire guns I haven't inspected and loaded myself."

"For fuck's sake. She took a knife to Jason. Shoot the bitch."

"Machete actually," Keahi calls out. Her tone is light, laced with laughter, like this is the most fun she's had in ages. After seven years in prison, I suppose it is. She's no longer in death-row white, but wearing an outfit shockingly similar to Leilani's khaki shorts and pale linen top. Because it was supplied by her as well?

I sneak a peek at Leilani. She stands on her own, MacManus having left her to commandeer his own personal firing squad. She's no longer cowering, but holding herself perfectly erect, shoulders back, body language intent. From this angle, I can see only part of her face. Her expression is hard to decipher. Fear. Curiosity. Anger. But also...admiration? For her big sister, who, no doubt about it, is one tough and scary chick.

According to Keahi, she protected Leilani when they were younger. Does Leilani remember those days, too, or only that final moment, her feral sister about to pounce on her already battered boyfriend?

All family relationships are complicated. But I think theirs rates a step above traditional sibling dynamics.

"Hello, Mac," Keahi calls out. "Long time no see. Miss me?"

MacManus doesn't take the bait. He drags Elias to the screens facing the dock, where the bodyguard makes a quick inspection of the rifle, Aolani standing mutely to the side.

"Ahh, you're going to put a bullet in my brain? From all the way over there? Where's the fun in that?" Keahi simpers, batting her eyes coquettishly. "I miss our little spats, Mac. You should know you were the only man that ever offered up a challenge.

"But you never should've touched my sister."

Elias works the bolt action, squeezes the trigger. We all recoil at the sharp retort. Beside Keahi, the light pole splinters on impact.

"Sight's off." Elias hastily lowers the rifle, starts fiddling.

"Too little, too late," Keahi calls out. She hasn't so much as flinched. I return my attention to Leilani, who is practically vibrating with stress, excitement, something. Now's the moment for her to make a break for it. MacManus is distracted, we're all distracted, her sister is right there.

Instead, Leilani fists her hands at her sides. She can't take her eyes off big sis. But she doesn't make any move to join her.

Something is wrong here. I sense it. Vaughn and Ronin are antsy as well. But what, how...

Elias settles the rifle against his shoulder. Racks the next bullet into the chamber.

Charlie bursts into the dining area from the kitchen. "Run! Now! Get out, get out, get out."

Just in time for a wall of flame to explode in the kitchen with a giant whoosh. The gas cans, I realize. She wasn't going to use them. She already had.

Vaughn and Ronin leap to Marilee's side, hoisting her up between them, while Aolani quickly ushers everyone toward the left side exit. Charlie races out before them, shotgun at the ready, as people begin to pour into the exposed strip of land between the mess hall and the jungle-fringed ocean.

At the front of the dining room, Elias remains poised with the rifle, MacManus at his shoulder. Elias pulls the trigger. Another sharp retort, causing screams from the remaining people still scrambling for the exit.

The sound of Keahi's laughter floats above the thick black smoke.

"You forgot, Mac. I've always been an ambush predator. Now, welcome to the main event."

At which point more gunfire erupts from outside.

CHAPTER 35

CHARLIE'S DOWN.

I can just make out his crumpled form at the rear corner of the building. More screaming. With that way blocked, people have only two options: head toward the front, which brings them closer to Keahi, or crash into the narrow border of palm trees and vegetation between the mess hall and the water, which had just been used for comfort breaks. People barrel deeper into the underbrush.

Aolani sprints toward Charlie, bending down swiftly to check on him, then grabbing the fallen shotgun. She casts me a glance over her shoulder, and I nod in response. She is now point, while I tend to the wounded man as medic.

Charlie is gasping, so at least I know he's alive. "Brent," he gets out. "Waiting for me. Shoulda...fired faster."

All the activity has triggered the outdoor floodlights. Tucked beside the building, we're in a vector of half light, half shadow. I can see Charlie's face. I have to feel for his wound. His right shoulder, soaking wet. I can already smell the blood.

I will not panic. I will not break down. This is not that.

Shut up and focus.

Aolani is crouched low before me. She creeps forward a first step, then another, slowly peering around the corner of the building. "Where?" she whispers over her shoulder.

"Tree. Nine o'clock," Charlie manages.

She rotates in that direction. I know what Charlie's talking about. The triangle of palm trees and greenery marking the apex between the main path and forking trail leading to the rear of the mess hall. I cough as the first acrid wave of smoke hits me.

From this position, I can feel the heat but not see any flames from the explosion, which started on the other side of the building. Visibility, however, is reducing quickly as waves of heavy gray smoke funnel across. I'm not sure what's making the blaze so smoky but I am guessing it has something to do with accelerant-fed fire versus damp and moldy wood.

Good news: the smoke works to our advantage as much as theirs.

Vaughn has crept up beside me. "How is he?"

"Just ducky," Charlie gasps out.

"Gunshot wound right shoulder," I clarify.

"Charlie, man, we gotta move."

"Right-o. On that. In a minute."

Aolani materializes in front of us. "I don't see any sign of either of them." She looks questioningly at Vaughn.

"My cabin. Can hold the most people and is surrounded by water on three sides. Gather whomever you can find, and let them know."

She strides behind us, where I can hear her whispering urgent instructions into the bushes, followed by the rustling of leaves and crackling of branches as the crew begins to move toward us.

"Not gonna make it," Charlie gasps out.

I'm offended. "You just said you were ducky."

"Vaughn's cabin, luv. Too far...for me to walk."

Ronin is now beside us, Marilee deposited off to the side. I understand Charlie's point. The able-bodied should have no problem making the ten-minute traverse to Vaughn's lodge, perched at the far end of the barracks. Our two wounded comrades, however...

"Bathhouse," Ronin suggests. "Has first aid supplies."

"Not an option," Vaughn informs him. He glances up. "That's where Jason is."

I can see Ronin processing, then arriving at the suitably horrible conclusion.

"My cabin is close," I whisper. "And I have some first aid materials. Maybe not enough, but something."

Ever since Wyoming, I've traveled with the essentials. Maybe a symptom of my PTSD. Maybe learning curve. When it comes to survival, preparedness is key.

More forms emerge behind us. Elias, shepherding MacManus and Leilani, who are tucked behind him.

"Did you shoot her?" Vaughn asks Elias.

"No. She bolted last minute. Moves faster than you'd think."

"Dammit. You still got your pistol? Give the Remington back to Aolani; we need to spread out our firepower among as many of us as possible. Aolani, here."

Vaughn holds out his hand. She gifts him the shotgun, while taking the rifle from Elias.

"Here's the deal," Vaughn clips out. The air is growing hot as the fire tears its way from the far edge of the mess hall to our rear corner huddle. It's also incredibly thick, more and more of us coughing as fiery grit collects on our faces, in the back of our throats.

"Aolani: head to my cabin. Collect as many of our crew as you can and hunker down. There's only one approach, and you have the high ground. You see anything move outside, fire first, question later.

"Ronin: you, me, and Frankie are going to get Marilee and Charlie to Frankie's cabin, quickly, while we still have the haze to cover our tracks."

Vaughn turns to MacManus and his group. "You're welcome at either location. My cabin is more comfortable, but more ground to cover between here and there."

"We'll be fine," MacManus coughs out.

"We should stick together," Vaughn urges. "There's more of us than them. That's our only competitive advantage."

"We gather in one place so they can burn us down together? I don't think so."

"That was it for gasoline cans," Ronin supplies. "And I am guessing our backup propane tank was used to start the explosion."

"Yep," Charlie rasps out. "Saw Brent...last minute. Scurrying out from the shed. Went to shoot, then smelled gas...Turned. Saw propane tank, lit rag as a fuse..."

"We're going for the plane," MacManus states. He stares at Elias as if daring his bodyguard to protest. "We can hole up, sit tight. Brent won't attack because he can't risk losing his only way off this atoll. And Keahi won't risk injuring her sister."

"You're using your ward as a human shield?" I wish I sounded surprised, but I'm not.

"I'm making a tactical decision that will keep us all safe."

I glance at Leilani, but her face has returned to its expression-less mask, like she's here, but not here. I have no doubt that behind that façade her mind is whirring away on its own strategic plan, but I'll be damned if I can figure her out.

Vaughn is over it. "You do what you gotta do," he says simply. Then to the rest of us, "Let's move."

I follow Ronin back to Marilee, who's propped against the building. This far from the light, I can't see her face, but she doesn't sound good, her breath reduced to a whistling wheeze. It's possible the bullet splintered a rib, dislodged a fragment into her lungs. There are so many things that could be going wrong. She doesn't need a first aid kit, she needs an emergency room and trained medical response.

But here we go instead.

I get on one side, Ronin the other. As gently as we can, we guide her to her feet. She hisses in a sharp breath, staggers between us. For a second, I think she's going to collapse, and I'm not sure I can bear the dead weight, but then she finds her feet, slowly shuffling between us.

Ahead of us, Vaughn seems to be having better luck with Charlie. He has the man up, one arm supporting him, the other gripping the shotgun.

We stagger through the thick smoke, coughing and hacking as hot embers float around our heads and sear our lips.

Vaguely, I'm aware of Elias, MacManus, and Lea veering away from us toward the airstrip. A lot of ground to cover with a blood-thirsty, machete-armed killer on the loose.

Is now when Keahi will make her move?

A shadow materializes ahead of us. We jerk to a halt, standing perfectly still. Chef Kiki appears in the gloom, her face a mask of soot.

"I don't know. Where? Where to go? What to do?"

"With us," Vaughn orders crisply. She falls in gratefully as we continue to my cabin.

The approach is trickier. The front clearing between my cabin steps and the water is pocked with a half dozen holes, dens for Crabby and his friends. We have no choice but to turn on a flashlight to pick our way through them. I think I see Crabby hunkered down to the side, watching us. I will him to be a good guard crab. Protect us and I will shower him in flower petals. I swear it.

Finally, I yank open the screen door with an earsplitting screech. If Keahi or Brent wondered where we were, they should be well informed by now.

Once inside, I swiftly dump my pile of clothes from the second bed onto the floor. Ronin deposits Marilee on the first twin bed. Charlie gets the second. That leaves standing room only for me, Ronin, Vaughn, and Chef Kiki. Nobody complains.

I scramble around for my ziplock bag of supplies. I pull out four maxi pads, two tampons, and a pile of alcohol wipes, plus one instant cold pack, a sewing kit, and waterproof matches.

Vaughn studies the collection. "Bad camping trip indeed."

"The tampons can also be used to start a fire. Pull apart the cotton into a pile of fluff, light the cord," I babble. "If you have Vaseline to add to the mix, even better."

"All right then."

Vaughn and Ronin get busy with their patients. I stay back with Chef Kiki. The diminutive French chef is trembling all over. But she holds herself together, sharp eyes taking in the scene.

"Pneumothorax," she declares, jerking her head toward Marilee, who is gasping for air. "That one. Something has punctured her lung. Oxygen is flowing out, creating too much pressure in her chest and collapsing the lung. See the bluish tint to her skin?"

Ronin stares at her. "Do you know what to do?"

"Needle aspiration. It is not hard, but I will need supplies, starting with a knife."

Vaughn produces a pocket knife from his shorts. "Will that work?"

"No. But we will make do. Aspiration needle?"

We all shake our heads.

"You're taking medical instructions from a cook," Charlie moans from the bed. "Whatever you do, keep her away from me."

"I am many things, not just a chef. And today, you should thank your fortunate stars for that."

"I don't have any needles, aspiration or other," I confess.

"Drinking straw?"

I shake my head.

"Ballpoint pen? Hollow tube of any kind?"

I bow my head in shame. All these lessons later, how can I still be caught short?

She huffs out a breath. "We must get one. I cannot help her otherwise."

"First aid kit, bathhouse," Ronin states again, looking at Vaughn. "It's significantly bigger than the one in the kitchen and better stocked. I'll go. I can make it."

"No—" Vaughn begins. Because I know why, I raise my own hand.

"I'll go. I know where it is. In charge of laundry, remember?"

Vaughn and Ronin frown at me. They don't need to say it out loud for me to know they doubt my odds of success. Or survival.

"I can do this. I'm well versed in creeping around places I'm not supposed to be. Plus...I think I have the best shot if I encounter Keahi. One, I'm not male. Two, I met her before. I wouldn't say she likes me, but she has an interest in me. Might be enough to keep me off her hit list while she stalks bigger game."

"Go." The chef is already waving her hand. No time to argue. Since I agree, I pivot on my heel and head out the door.

I CAN HEAR the birds again, squawking about the dark smoke, stupid humans, all of the above. I try to find comfort in the familiar noise while I snap on my pen flashlight to work my way to the central path.

The fire might be dying down, but the smoke remains heavy. Rather than walk through the ember-ridden cloud, I cut across the trail and weave my way through the wall of bushes and palm trees on the other side. I hold my flashlight down low, enough light to guide my steps, while hopefully remaining hidden by the thick undergrowth.

It's slower going this way. I stumble upon two coconut crabs, one that clicks angrily at me and waves a meaty claw. I detour even more, then begin to panic that I'm taking too much time. All the risk, only to return with the prize too late.

I hasten along, finally coming to the edge of the clearing around the bathhouse. Jason's head is still sitting on the back railing. Looping around to the front entrance will bring me into the open longer, but in the end, I don't have a choice. I can't bring myself to take one step closer to that terrible trophy.

I just step out of the brush into the clearing when a figure appears on the main crushed-coral thoroughfare.

Brent, coming straight at me, gun at his side.

I freeze. Suck in my gut. Will myself to disappear into the night.

But I forgot about my pen flashlight, glowing next to my leg.

Three strides and he's on me, gun barrel pressed straight into my forehead. "Give me one good reason not to shoot you."

I can't think of a single response.

CHAPTER 36

WHERE DID THEY GO? MAC and Lea? Where are they?" Brent brandishes his firearm at me for added emphasis. I step away slightly, enough to put a solid three inches between myself and the wrong end of a gun barrel. It's not enough, but it's something.

"You and Leilani are lovers. How long?"

"Doesn't matter. Now tell me."

I peer at him in the dark. A waft of smoke drifts across us. We both cough.

"I don't think you're a killer," I say at last.

A grimace crosses his face. "You don't know anything."

I study him again, trying to slow down the moment, buy me some time to think. "You could've taken out Marilee. You were close enough to put a bullet through her brain. But you didn't."

He doesn't answer, his face once again contorting in a wave of emotions. "In case I need a copilot in order to leave," he allows at last.

"You could've taken out Charlie—"

"He pointed a shotgun at me!"

"Exactly. You fired in self-defense. You're no killer. A gambling addict, bad friend, and sex predator, maybe, but not a cold-blooded murderer."

"I'm not a sex predator!" Now he's offended.

"Leilani is only seventeen."

"Please, she came on to me. And it's not like I'm her first. I'm the one saving her."

"From MacManus?"

"Exactly!"

Damn, she's good.

"Why isn't she with you, Brent? Shouldn't she have run to your side by now? I mean, if you're truly in this together."

"She has her own job to do."

This catches my attention. "And what is that?"

"Where are Mac and Lea? Tell me!"

I continue as if I haven't heard him: "I'm assuming Keahi is here to kill MacManus. Which makes you what, the backup band? You know she'll slit your throat the minute she's done with him. She didn't break out of prison just to share her sister with someone else."

"She won't. She needs me to get off this atoll."

"I'm sorry. She'll slit your throat the minute you three touch down in Honolulu."

"I wouldn't be so sure of that. I don't need *her* to get off the atoll."

"Ah, the classic double cross. You wait for Keahi to butcher MacManus, then you shoot Keahi. Does Leilani know about this little plan?"

He smirks, and suddenly I get it. The realization nearly rocks me back on my heels.

"That's what Leilani wants? She organized all of this to kill her sister? But why? The good state of Texas was going to do that in a matter of weeks." Then, in the next instant I realize the answers to my own questions. "But this way she gets to use Keahi first. No one will question an escaped serial killer taking out Mac-Manus, or for that matter, a dozen people on a remote island. Leilani's wielding her sister like a weapon. And once that weapon has served its purpose...Damn, that's brilliant. Sure this is the woman you want to spend your forever with? I'm thinking she'll take that until-death-do-us-part promise much more literally than you."

"Shut up. Just shut the fuck up. You have no idea—"

"Did you see what Keahi did to Jason? Were you there while she carved him up? How much did he scream before she was done?" Just saying the words churns my stomach. But they turn Brent positively green, the pistol now trembling in his hand. He did see. And it was as horrible as it sounds.

"You're not a killer," I repeat softly.

"But I am!"

"No. Marilee is still alive. I'm here for the first aid kit. We need some kind of needle thingy to fix her collapsed lung. Let me get it for her. She can still be your copilot for the flight home."

He just stares at me, lips pressed into a mutinous line. In his silence, I recall the other terrible happenings on the atoll.

"The body Ronin and I found. That was you? You killed her?"

"I didn't mean to."

"It was an accident," I assure him, my mind racing ahead, trying to remember if Brent was present when Charlie revealed the woman was an undercover FBI agent. Because if Brent knew he killed a cop, that's it, there's no going back for him. But if he hasn't figured that much out yet...

"She caught me," he adds in a rush now. "I was trying to tamper with the solar panels' wiring, and then, there she was. She demanded to know what I was doing, how involved I was in the criminal enterprise...I don't know. I panicked and shoved her. She fell back and hit her head on a rock."

"See, an accident."

"Then she started to sit up, so I grabbed another rock and bashed in her skull."

"Not so much an accident."

"She was a crew member on one of the supply boats. I thought for sure they'd report her missing, and a bunch of cops would descend to investigate. That would be it, game over. But...nothing happened. So we continued on."

I pretend to nod sympathetically. The boat captain had reported Sherry George missing. Except once the FBI realized their undercover agent had disappeared, they sent in another agent, Charlie, to try to locate her, versus compromising their investigation or scaring off MacManus's dealings with a full-scale missing persons search.

"But why the sabotage, Brent? If all of this was about getting Keahi here and murdering MacManus so you and Leilani can live happily after ever, why the whole sabotage bit?"

"To get people off the atoll! If the power went down, or we lost drinking water, conditions would be too harsh for most to want to stay. They'd leave before...Well, you know. But fucking Charlie kept fixing everything! Dammit, I was trying to limit the damage. I was!"

"Because you're not really a killer."

"It doesn't matter anymore. Here we are, and we both know what's gonna happen next. Now, where are Lea and Mac?"

He steadies his arm, takes fresh aim.

I open my mouth, trying to think of one more stall tactic.

Vaughn materializes from the bushes, shotgun at the ready.

"I'd step away if I were you."

But Brent just looks at him and laughs.

"YOU'VE BEEN GONE so long, I thought I should come check on you," Vaughn informs me, moving closer. I nod in gratitude, though given I still have a pistol pointed at my head, it's limited.

"Step away," he commands Brent again.

Brent shakes his head. "Not gonna happen. You can't risk taking me out. Then you really are stuck here with a woman nicknamed the Beautiful Butcher."

"I have faith in Captain Marilee's ability to recover."

"You also can't risk hurting her." Brent nods his chin toward me. "I already know your shotgun is loaded with bird shot. The spray will hit both of us."

"As long as she's alive."

I'm not really enjoying this conversation.

"You shoot her, I take you out next," Vaughn continues. "Or maybe I just risk it. You're planning on killing her, right? Better chance of recovery from a scattering pellet than a bullet to the brain."

Brent scowls. I shift nervously from side to side. In an action movie, I'd suddenly knock away his arm, or rush him, or drop to the ground. But with the barrel of a gun mere inches from my face, none of those ideas sound appealing to me. As it is, I'm worried another cloud of smoke will cause him to accidentally pull the trigger during a fit of coughing.

"I think we have a standoff," I offer tentatively. "As the person in the middle, can I make a suggestion?"

Both armed men turn to me. Great.

"I know where Mac and Lea are," I supply. "Which cabin." I cast a pointed look at Vaughn.

"Tell me," Brent demands immediately.

"No. I tell you, then there's nothing stopping you from shooting me. I'll take you."

"Hey now," Vaughn starts to protest.

"Marilee needs the first aid supplies," I interject, tone genuinely pleading. "I'll take Brent to MacManus and Leilani. You save Marilee."

Vaughn pins his stare on Brent.

"Works for me," Brent responds.

"Fine," Vaughn clips out.

Brent grabs my arm, twists me against him as a human shield. Slowly he steps away from Vaughn. I have no choice but to stagger back with him.

"Don't be stupid," he calls out to Vaughn.

"Likewise."

I will myself to remain calm, go with the flow. Step by step we retreat from Vaughn, back onto the main path.

"Which way?" Brent growls in my ear.

Another steadying breath. "Follow me."

BRENT FORCES ME to walk in front of him, pistol dug into the small of my back. It's not particularly comfortable. I'm in charge of illuminating our path with the flashlight, doing my best to dodge scattering hermit crabs and threatening coconut crabs. I shouldn't mind the coconut crabs so much anymore. They have nothing on the evil humans.

"So," I start conversationally, as we stumble along, "tell me about Noodles the cat."

"Noodles the cat? What the hell?"

"Noodles. Leilani's favorite kitten when she was little? I thought you two were close."

"You're making that up."

"I'm not. Seriously. Keahi told me all about it, and Leilani confirmed Noodles when I spoke to her earlier. Doesn't Lea talk to you about her childhood?"

"She prefers not to dwell on the past. You can't blame her. Everyone knows what a monster her father was."

Yes, the man who produced one serial killer and one stone-cold psychopath. People always wonder, is evil a function of nature or nurture? In the Pierson family, I have a feeling it's n squared.

"Does she remember him?"

"Abusive son of a bitch. Liked to get drunk, pound on his wife and kids."

"Keahi claims she took the brunt of it; she went out of her way to protect Leilani any way she could."

I sense his shrug behind me.

"What does Lea say about her sister?" I prod, searching for any information I can use.

"She doesn't."

"Come on, she's the one who brought her sister into this. Mentioned Keahi would be the perfect predator—and patsy—for eliminating Mac. She must've said something."

"She said her sister was terrifying. Her father was callous and cruel. But her sister was worse. Her father lashed out in anger. Her sister hurt others for sport."

"And you still agreed to break her out of prison?"

"I had nothing to do with that. Lea arranged it. Did some research on the corrections officers at Keahi's facility. Found one with ties to Hawaii and a crushing load of overdue child support. Leilani offered him cash to get her sister out and all the way to Honolulu, though it sounds like Keahi added some incentive of her own." I can already tell Brent is smiling. "Keahi met us at the airport this morning—"

"Just like that?"

"Hey, 100K buys good help."

"And the CO? Did he personally deliver her?"

"Never saw him."

"Gee, wonder why..."

I let my voice trail off. If Brent caught the dangerous innuendo, he doesn't seem to care. "Hey, I just helped smuggle Keahi onto the Cessna. Not so hard to do. Once the food was loaded, not like anyone's paying attention to a private charter. I walked her out looking like another passenger, then at the last second, slipped her into the back. Lea kept MacManus and his people distracted. And then we hit the skies."

This does not make me think highly of airport security. Though again, given my own experience accessing a private charter, there really isn't any.

"What happens at the end of all this?" I ask curiously. "We're all dead, I'm assuming. You, Lea, and Keahi are the only ones left standing. You, what, somehow manage to kill a woman twenty times deadlier than a viper. Then you and Lea fly back to Honolulu? Make up some tale of woe, take over Mac's operations—illegal and otherwise—and have two point two children and never speak of this again?"

"Where are we going? You said they were in one of the cabins!" Brent digs his gun hard enough into my lower back to make me wince.

"They are! We're going in the back way. Other end of the U. I'm assuming it's our best option for approaching without being seen."

"Oh." He concedes my point as we step off the main artery onto a lesser-used dirt trail that snakes through overgrown bushes and densely packed palms. I'd learned of this secret passageway from Tannis when we made our escape after eavesdropping on MacManus's conversation with Charlie. It is narrow and muddy, but connects with the barracks from the rear, arriving at Vaughn's cabin first.

We veer around a corner. I come to an abrupt halt, Brent nearly colliding into me. A giant sapphire-blue coconut crab blocks the trail in front of us. I pin my light on it. It takes a menacing step forward.

"Step over it," Brent commands.

"You step over it. That thing's huge. Did you know the claws work like hydraulics?"

"Shut up!"

I fall silent, waving my flashlight at the beast, trying to tempt it into moving. It hunkers down in full blockade stance. Ronin had said they were territorial.

"Just give it a second," I say at last. I don't know what else to do. We need the crab to move. We need to reach the end of this trail. I need us to come out the other side. My heart is pounding too hard in my chest, my eyes beginning to sting with tears. And now is not the time. I can't afford to lose it.

What had Vaughn said just hours before on the runway? Whatever it is, let it go. You can deal with it later.

Whatever the damage.

Whatever the horror.

Whatever the cost to your soul.

The crab finally shifts. One last fierce look, then it lumbers off into the underbrush. I force myself to move forward, eyeing its exit path warily.

In a matter of moments, this muddy little trail will connect with the main path. Brent will recognize immediately where we are. The question is, what will he do then? Once he can guess our destination, he won't need me anymore.

"Shhh," I murmur to him now. "We need to slow down, move quietly, so we don't alert them."

"Where are we— Vaughn's cabin. Of course Mac commandeered it. I'm surprised he didn't bolt from the mess hall to his private lodge in the very beginning."

"He wanted to. Couldn't figure out how to get *everyone* there safely." I turn slightly, peering over my shoulder. "MacManus didn't abandon us. He's been working with Vaughn trying to save us all."

Based on the look on Brent's face, my words are too little, too late. He's had four years to judge MacManus for himself. Combined with the stories Leilani has been feeding him... He's not doubting his target anytime soon.

This is it. The thick growth on either side of us ends. The cleared opening around Vaughn's cabin begins.

No lights are on. It sits forty feet from us, situated out on the point. A darker shadow in the already dark night.

"Are you sure you want to do this?" I can't help myself from asking.

"Move."

"What about Elias? He's still armed. And professionally trained."

"I'm not worried about Elias."

"How can you not—" My words sputter to a stop. "Lea," I deduce. "That's her role. She's the inside man. Take out the bodyguard when they least expect it. Clear the way for you and Keahi to do your part."

Brent pokes me with his pistol, urging me forward.

"She is a logistical marvel. Cold and calculating and clever. And only seventeen. N squared indeed."

"Silence," Brent hisses at me.

We move closer, the rear screened window looming larger and larger before us. No sounds come from inside. No sign of movement. My nerves ratchet up another notch. Somewhere on the other side of those walls, Aolani stands guard over Ann, Trudy, Tannis, Emi, and the others.

Please don't let him shoot me right in front of them. Technically, there's no reason for Brent not to eliminate me at this point. I've led him to his purported target. He could pull the trigger at any moment.

No reason to wait.

Unless my first point still stands.

"You don't have to do this," I try one last time. "We could turn around, right now. Grab the others, hightail it to the plane. Let Leilani, Keahi, and Mac work it out for themselves. This is their drama, not ours."

"Shut up!"

"You're not a killer, Brent. No matter what you say, you're not—"

"*Shut up!*" He stops jabbing the pistol into my spine, presses it against the back of my skull.

"You're not a killer," I whisper one last time. Then I drop to the ground, twisting as I roll to light up his form with my flashlight.

Inside Vaughn's cabin, Aolani pulls the trigger.

A single crack. Brent crumples where he stands.

"But now I am," I finish.

Vaughn appears, helping me to my feet. I peer toward his cabin. I still can't see Aolani, but I can feel her standing there, Remington rifle once again slung over her shoulder. I hold up a hand in gratitude. I can almost make out her nod of acknowledgment.

Then a choking sob from inside. Maybe from Ann. Or Trudy. Or Tannis. Emi.

Whatever the damage...

I turn away from the body on the ground.

CHAPTER 37

L EILANI IS THE INSIDE MAN," I murmur to Vaughn as he leads me away from his cabin to the side of the trail. "Brent said it's her job to take out the bodyguards. We need to warn Elias and MacManus."

Vaughn's expression is troubled. "She's really working with Keahi and Brent?"

"Working with? She's the ringleader. This is her...I don't know, teenage rebellion. Overthrow her guardian, take over his operations, and inherit both a trust fund and life insurance bequest. What's not to love?"

Vaughn shakes his head. "The Lea I saw as a little girl, the Lea I thought I knew...Never would've seen this coming."

"Still waters run homicidally deep."

"What do you propose?"

My turn to sigh. "MacManus's plan was to hole up in the jet. Easy to defend from outside intruders, not so much so from inside traitors. I guess we head there. Try to see if we can make contact with him or Elias."

Vaughn has the shotgun down by his side. "All right," he concedes. "We need to be careful, though. Keahi—"

"Is also looking for them." I hesitate. "Marilee?"

"I delivered the first aid supplies to Chef Kiki. Last I saw, she was getting busy with alcohol wipes."

"And Charlie?"

"Still cranky."

"Well, go us. We're harder to kill than they think."

Vaughn leads the way to the muddy ribbon of trail Brent and I had just used to approach the rear of his cabin. It's the most direct route to the landing strip, but also not obvious to outsiders. I admire his thinking as I fall in step behind him.

I'm shaking. I'm aware of it in an abstract way. Later, when the dust settles, should we survive this...There is a giant wave of horror locked down deep inside me. An endless ocean of agony and self-recrimination and regret that comes from leading a man step by step toward his execution.

I can't think about it now.

The night sounds are back. Crazy birds and crashing waves. The air remains humid and thick, but soothing against my tearstained cheeks. We don't pass any more coconut crabs before arriving once more at the main path. To our right, the landing strip. To our left, base camp.

It's very tempting to retreat. Find my cabin, hunker down with my arms over my head. While we wait for the sounds of distant gunshots or aborted screams or approaching footsteps?

I'd rather face my fate head-on than endure that kind of drawn-out horror. Whatever happens next, at least it's a choice I made.

We stick to one side of the path. I keep the flashlight pointed low, enough light to guide our feet without broadcasting our position. I lead us forward. Vaughn, shotgun at the ready, guards our sides and rear.

Bit by bit we make it to the runway. The Cessna glows like a sleek white arrow in the middle of an inky-black field.

It looks exactly as it did last time I saw it. Side door still open, stairs spilling down to the runway.

The first hairs prickle at the back of my neck. This doesn't look like a buttoned-up hidey hole.

Vaughn and I exchange a glance. Slowly, we move into the cleared strip, exposing our position, becoming more and more vulnerable.

No faces appear in the windows of the jet. No forms materialize from the thick brush behind us. No human voices compete with the calls of the birds.

In the end, I climb the stairs and peer inside the cabin, just to confirm what we already know: no one's here.

We're too late.

"WE SHOULD GO back to your cabin," Vaughn whispers. We've retreated to the main path. "Given I have the shotgun, Charlie, Marilee, Kiki, and Ronin are completely defenseless."

"I wouldn't call Ronin defenseless."

"He's not faster than a speeding bullet."

I acknowledge his point with a short nod. But then: "If Leilani had made her move...I think we'd see it. Signs of a struggle. Elias's body, something. There's nothing here at all."

"You don't think they made it this far."

"They could've changed their minds. Or been intercepted. Or had to change their minds because they were about to be intercepted."

Vaughn doesn't argue with my vague possibilities.

"Brent set the mess hall on fire," I murmur now. "We all scattered. Keahi watched us go. So what does she know right now?"

"We're not in the mess hall?"

"Yeah. Her targets fled deeper into the camp barracks or out toward the runway. Meaning..."

Vaughn gets it. "She would head out as well. Leaving the dock and rec building area unattended." He stares at me. "And the UTVs."

"I think we should grab one. We can cover ground much faster, and it's harder to ambush a moving target."

"We're not exactly stealthy in a motorized vehicle."

"Versus now? Crunching and snapping with every other footstep? If you wanted to glide like a ghost around this atoll, you shouldn't have covered the trails with crushed coral. We might as well be walking around on bubble wrap."

"I'll pass along your complaints to management," he answers dryly. "Wait, I already have a reply. Bite me. And now that's out of the way, let's go."

He hefts the shotgun, and we return to our tight little formation. I illuminate before us; he guards behind us.

We do our best to move steady and silent. It's still shockingly loud to our ears, though the squawking cries and beating wings of dozens upon dozens of seabirds help drown out the worst of it.

We make it to the bathhouse, where the smoke from the mess

hall fire lingers in sooty, black waves. We hold our breath to pass through, looping around till we're approaching the rec hall from the back, our eyes on the line of UTVs parked beside it.

There should be three vehicles. Now I count two.

And I spy a dark lump on the ground.

"Stay," Vaughn murmurs.

I don't need any encouragement to remain rooted in place.

Vaughn advances to the fallen form, crouching down to inspect. He turns away, left hand pressed over his mouth. On much shakier legs he returns to me.

"Elias," I guess.

He nods.

"Keahi? Or Leilani?" Knife or gun?

"Keahi. Most definitely."

I don't ask any more questions. I don't want to know. Instead, I step into him, drawing his arms around me, my turn to let him sag against me. We take a second, two, three, four. Listening to each other's heartbeats. Feeding each other strength. Then he steps back, draws a final shaky breath.

"Looks like they returned here, for whatever reason. Keahi ambushed them."

"Did you, um . . . Elias's gun?"

"Not there."

"They took it. And MacManus. And a UTV." I peer in the opposite direction of the cabins. There's only one place they could've gone.

"Mac's place," Vaughn provides. "Maybe some kind of rendezvous point. They're waiting for Brent? But why not just . . . If this is all about killing Mac, why haven't they just done it by now?"

"Oh, I can think of a few reasons."

Judging by the sudden pallor of his face, he can, too. "Ah, shit."

"Keahi's waited a long time for this moment." I shrug. "I don't think she means to be quick about it."

"Okay." Vaughn pulls himself together. "So, we're down to one angry teenager, armed with a gun, and one extremely violent serial predator, bearing a machete."

"In the good news department, they're not exactly trained professionals."

"Have you met us lately?"

"Yes. And so did Brent." I wait a beat. "Do you want to retreat to the cabins? Wait to see what will happen next?"

"No. You?"

"I've never been good at patience."

"Well, they're probably pretty distracted at the moment."

Torturing a grown man and all.

"Ronin and Aolani are manning the defenses," Vaughn continues. "I guess that makes us the tip of the spear. You want the shotgun?"

"I'm no good with guns. It's what makes my witty repartee so sharp and cutting."

He nods, rakes a hand through his hair, the motion so touchingly normal I find myself smiling. He catches my expression.

"When we get out of this," he states roughly.

"When we get out of this."

On that note, we pick a UTV, fire up the engine, and head toward the owner's lodge to take on a serial killer and her sister.

Or die trying.

CHAPTER 38

W E CAN HEAR THE FIRST scream before we ever see the residence. A low moaning carried by the wind that builds and builds to a high-pitched crescendo. Wordlessly, Vaughn pulls over the UTV. We run from there.

MacManus's residence is lit up like a beacon in the night. No need for secrecy anymore; the inmates have taken control of the asylum. A fresh round of screams. Clearly male. Keahi must've started already.

We crouch low as we jog across the cleared expanse toward the house. Between MacManus's guttural shrieks and the ocean's pounding waves, we don't have to worry about noise.

Vaughn carries the shotgun down by his side. We don't have a plan and are probably lacking in common sense, but at least one of us is armed.

We arrive at the exterior wall of the lodge and press ourselves against it. The front half of the lodge is basically a giant screened-in porch, similar to the mess hall's setup, designed to show off the water view while allowing in the maximum amount of cooling breeze. It also enables us to see and hear everything, as we tuck ourselves to the left of the expansive side window.

"Just give me the account numbers and passwords," Leilani is ordering crisply. I risk peering in long enough to get the lay of the land.

MacManus is tied to a dining room chair and already dripping so much blood it hurts to look at him. Keahi is standing behind him with a savage-looking butcher knife. Leilani sits casually on the tropical-print love seat across from him. In front of her, on the coffee table, rests a bloody machete, a handgun—probably from Elias—and even more importantly, the two missing sat phones.

"I don't know," MacManus gasps out, "what...you're... talking about."

"Oh, please. Francis figured out a year ago you were skimming funds."

Francis? I've heard that name before. I glance at Vaughn, who nods in recognition. It comes to me, MacManus's CEO. Mac had mentioned calling him daily even from the atoll. When Mac didn't make contact, Francis would be the first to realize something was wrong and send help. Or not.

"You know as well as I do, these are not men you steal money from."

"I didn't want...their money! Shawn. He did it. Wanted the company to grow faster. More research. More innovation. More...everything. I tried to warn him. Be patient. We'd be okay. But no. He took their *investment* funds. Poor...stupid...bastard."

"And then you kept taking their money."

"Couldn't...say no. Especially after...what they did to Shawn."

"Exactly. He paid for the sin of trying to end the arrangement the first time, and now you'll pay for messing it up the second time around."

I hear movement, risk another glance. Leilani has risen off the sofa, coming to kneel at eye level before the bloody wreckage that is her guardian.

I don't see any horror or sympathy on her face. More like indifference, which I find more terrifying than the smile I see on Keahi as she fingers her blade.

Leilani continues to do the talking. "It's over, Mac. You got sloppy. Stealing from your business partners. Calling too much attention to operations. The FBI has been investigating you for years—"

"No big deal," MacManus wheezes out. "Always...looking. Price of...success."

"Yes, but now there's a slain undercover agent buried on Pomaikai. That's going to be a little harder to dismiss."

"Not...my fault."

"Doesn't matter. Brent confessed to me what happened—she discovered him during one of his misguided acts of sabotage, and he bashed in her skull. Idiot was convinced he was going to be arrested at any moment. But then...nothing happened. Which might have been good luck, but since I don't believe in such things, I did some asking around, reached out to our associates. They'd already caught wind of an undercover agent being inserted into your operations. They were very unhappy about that development. Learning the agent had been murdered made them even unhappier.

"Consider this their vote of no confidence. Account numbers. Passwords for the offshore accounts. I want them. More importantly, Keahi wants them."

Another gurgling scream. I screw my eyes shut. I don't want

to see; hearing is awful enough. Vaughn places his hand in mine, squeezing hard. I can feel his body trembling.

It feels like it's going on and on and on, and then, a sudden, gasping break.

"Account numbers. Passwords."

"How...can you...do this?"

"You chose a tough business. Failure has consequences. And I'm not paying for your mistakes."

"I...raised you...like a daughter."

"You kidnapped me!" For the first time, there's real emotion in Leilani's voice. "You snatched me away from my sister, just like she—" Leilani bites off the words, but her sentence isn't hard to finish.

Just like Keahi snatched her away from her parents. Or more precisely, Keahi snatched her away from her mother, who braided her hair, and sang her songs, and kept her safe with her in the kitchen.

Clearly, Leilani remembers more of her childhood than she's let on. And has her own opinion on her sister's role as savior. Interesting.

"I've never been real to you," Leilani accuses now. "I was always just a prop. Proof of your generous heart. You can't be a total arrogant ass, look at the poor little orphan you're heroically raising as your own.

"But guess what, Mac? You've never been real to me, either. Just some tool my sister brought home one day. She used you first. I used you last. And now you're done. Account numbers. Passwords."

A sharp yelp as Keahi no doubt punctuates the demand with her blade.

"At this point, we have at least a week for Keahi to play with you. This atoll is ours; no one to interrupt, no one to save you. Meaning the sooner you give me what I need, the sooner this can end. We both know you're not that tough. Just be done with it, Mac. Tell me what I need to know."

Silence. But not the good kind. A knuckles-whitening kind of tension that builds and builds.

Then:

Shrieking. Gurgling. More agonizing screaming in pitches and volume I didn't know were possible. I try to cover my ears. I hunch my shoulders as if that will block the sound. But nothing works. It's inside my head, searing my nerves, vibrating my limbs, straining my chest.

Vaughn's arm is around me. We stand together in the midst of the most agonizing kind of hurricane.

Then, I simply can't take it anymore.

Maybe MacManus hasn't broken, but I have.

I push myself away from Vaughn. Before he can stop me, I pound up the porch steps and bang loudly on the front door.

The shrieking ends abruptly. And then the silence gets very interesting.

KEAHI OPENS THE door. She's holding a dripping knife and peering at me quizzically.

"You," she states.

"Me," I agree. "May I come in?"

She scowls at me, trying to figure me out. I stand there and take it. I remember this much from our prison chat. Keahi judges her opponents based on strength. If I'm going to survive this, I absolutely, positively can't appear weak.

The tremors snaking up my spine aren't helping.

"I have a message from Brent," I volunteer, just to move matters along.

Keahi steps back. I enter the living room, leaving the door slightly ajar behind me. I take in Leilani and the items on the coffee table, including the gun and sat phones, as if seeing them for the first time. I keep my gaze away from MacManus, not just because of the gore, but because I can't handle the flicker of hope in his eyes.

"Where is Brent?" Leilani asks sharply, while giving me a look that clearly questions why I'm still alive.

"Are you okay?" I ask her softly.

"Of course. What do you mean?" Her forehead furrows into a frown.

"The first time we spoke, I told you I was here for you. I work for you. Do you remember that?"

Slowly, she nods.

"Keahi sent me to find you." I turn toward the murderess. "Though you didn't really send me, did you? Your lawyer, Victoria, did that."

"She always prided herself on her initiative." Keahi smiles. It doesn't reach her dark eyes. Her pale linen shirt is streaked with blood. Her hands and forearms look like she bathed in gore. Let alone the smears on her cheek, the splatters in her hair.

The Beautiful Butcher back to her full glory.

"The notes. I still don't understand. You claimed they were from Leilani, but she denied sending them, and the handwriting doesn't match."

"I lied." Leilani does the honor. "I wrote them with my left hand to make them seem childish and sloppy."

"But why?" I'm still confused.

"Props. Later, when the police investigate the terrible mass tragedy that occurred here, they'll want to know how Keahi knew where to find me. What motivated her escape. Hence, she received a note informing her that her long-lost sister needed her. Certainly, it was convincing enough for the lawyer woman."

Leilani gives another small shrug. As in too bad, so sad that lawyer lady then had to die and oh, yeah, now me, too.

"But you even hid a note here."

"Details matter." Now Leilani gives MacManus a pointed look. "Investigators will scour this atoll, as well as search all the cabins. A few ominous messages tucked here and there, more proof that poor little me lived in fear of my controlling guardian and his nefarious intentions. Thank heavens my sister broke out of prison to save me. Though, of course, I regret the full extent of the carnage."

"I never—" Mac gargles.

"Shut up." Keahi points her blade at him. I watch in macabre fascination as a single drop of blood beads at the tip, then splashes down onto the ridiculously gorgeous hardwood floor.

"If your goal was to seed suspicion about Mac's motives, why lie about you writing the notes to me? Wouldn't it be better to get the ball rolling by acknowledging your cries for help?"

"No!" Now Leilani is completely exasperated. "It was too soon! The notes are for after the fact. I couldn't have you raising a fuss and compelling others to 'rescue' me beforehand. Honest to God. I'm a complete stranger to you. How hard is it to just walk away?"

She has me there. So much so I feel profoundly stupid. Even ashamed. During all my years trying to save the world, I never once bothered to ask the world if it wanted to be saved. Never thought, for even a moment, it might be better for everyone else if I just stayed out of it.

I guess MacManus hasn't been the only arrogant asshole on this island.

"Noodles the cat," I prompt finally. "For my own sake. Please tell me—what the hell is the deal with Noodles the cat?"

For the first time, Keahi smiles. It's so spontaneous it lights up her face, a macabre contrast to the blood smeared across her cheeks.

"Noodles was Leilani's favorite barn cat back home. She tamed it as a kitten. It followed her everywhere."

I sneak a peek at Leilani's face, which has once more gone blank. She doesn't like this story, I realize. Hence screwing her mask firmly in place.

"One day, Noodles attacked her. I heard her screaming and came running. The cat had gone mad—"

"Distemper," Leilani supplies crisply. "Daddy didn't believe in vet care for the animals."

"Or doctor's care for the humans," Keahi adds. "I couldn't shoo the cat away. I had to put it down."

"*You* shot Noodles? You killed your sister's favorite kitten?"

Keahi glares at me. "I had no choice. It'd gone feral. I was protecting Leilani."

"A fake code in your fake note." I consider the matter. "Later when questioned by the police"—I wave in Leilani's direction—"you'll deliver this tale of childhood tragedy and how you were, in your own way, telling your sister what you needed. For her to come put down the animal abusing you."

"Details matter," Leilani confirms. "Now, the message from Brent?"

"Absolutely." I turn back to Keahi. "You know he's going to kill you when this is all over? He told me about it. Leilani knows and approves."

I'm going for shock, or at the very least, divide and conquer. Instead, Keahi responds with a playful grin. She and her sister exchange a glance.

"Which apparently you know all about," I fill in. This is not going well.

"For some reason, he was nervous about partnering with me on this little operation." Keahi runs her thumb down the side of the bloody knife. "Leilani had to tell him something to soothe his nerves."

"Do you have a spreadsheet for all of this?" I ask Leilani, genuinely curious. I drift closer to the coffee table. "I mean, you telling Brent he can kill your sister when this is over, while no doubt assuring Keahi she can kill your lover when it's done. How do you track so many lies? And do either of them realize MacManus isn't the only tool in all this? They're nothing but marks to you as well."

My body feels jittery, my limbs quaking with a flood of adrenaline as I make it within two feet of my goal.

I peer at Leilani intently. "I'm just trying to figure out—is this your version of teenage rebellion, finally taking control of your life? Or is this purely professional—a hostile takeover?"

Leilani picks up the handgun, points it right at me. "This is me saying shut the fuck up. Now, what is Brent's message, and why isn't he here himself?"

"Maybe it doesn't matter," I continue softly. "Either way, you're broken. Keahi murdered grown men trying to fill the hollowness inside her. You, you're about to slaughter an entire island in order to make a few bucks. Just remember, if your sister is anything to go by, it won't be enough. We aren't the ones standing in the way of your happiness. You are."

"What the hell is the message?!"

"Oh, yes, that. My apologies: Brent regrets to inform you that he's kinda dead. Because I lured him into a trap. And a rifle blew off his head."

I bolt forward, snatch up the closest sat phone, then run like hell toward the door.

Keahi lurches toward me with her knife. Leilani is no doubt taking aim at my back.

Then a shattering boom as Vaughn materializes in the side window and blasts his shotgun.

Screaming. Maybe theirs. Definitely mine.

A searing pain in my lower leg. I don't stop. I keep on chugging as Keahi roars in outrage and sprints after me.

CHAPTER 39

A SECOND BELCH FROM THE SHOTGUN. Vaughn firing at Keahi's back as she pelts after me. I don't know where I'm going or what I'm doing. Acting purely on instinct, I head for the pounding ocean surf on the beach below.

She's stronger than I am. Definitely angrier and deadlier. I have to hope I'm faster.

I head closer to the water, not just because it's easier to run on the packed sand, but because higher up the beach is pocked with crab dens. I don't have time to turn on my flashlight, and I can't afford to break an ankle in one of the holes.

Behind me, I hear the retort of gunfire. Leilani shooting at Vaughn? I can't worry about it. If I can just get away, find someplace to hide long enough to phone for help. What had Vaughn said that first day in his office? It takes three to five days to get emergency medical evac?

I have a hard time believing I'm going to survive for the next thirty minutes, but reducing our rescue window to a matter of days might be enough to save the others. I'll take whatever hope I can get.

I hear more noise from behind me. Maybe panting. Closing footsteps. Hard to determine above the crash of the waves and crying of the birds.

I risk a quick glance over my shoulder, nearly trip and fall.

In the dim glow of the moonlight, I spy Keahi closing the gap between us at a frightening pace. I don't know how the woman managed to stay so fit while incarcerated, but I'm definitely not outrunning her. Forget living another thirty minutes. I'm down to about three.

I don't know what to do. Continue in a straight line, most likely get hacked down in the surf? If I could just make it to the tree line, find someplace to hide.

Fuck it. I make a hard right toward the jungle's beckoning edge. The sand quickly goes from firm to soft to nearly unmanageable. Scuttling sounds. Crabs racing for cover. I try to track the noise above the terrified beating of my heart. Crabs fleeing left to their dens means zigging right. Sounds from the right have me zagging left.

A thick Pisonia tree looms straight ahead, the nesting boobies scattering as I lurch toward it.

I don't even register the sound of Keahi's angry scream until I nearly face-plant on the ground beneath the leafy branches.

"Goddammit!" she howls.

I manage to get up on all fours, tentatively peer out.

She's down in the sand, blade abandoned somewhere in front of her. As I watch, she drags her left foot out of a hole, then cradles her knee against her chest. Crab den. She might know more ways to kill a man with a knife, but she's woefully ignorant of the atoll's local population.

I've dropped the sat phone. I reach out blindly with my hand, patting the ground around me as I watch Keahi carefully, waiting for her to shake it off and relaunch her pursuit.

She's not rising to her feet, however. I can't make out the state of her ankle in the dark, but whatever she did, it seems to have incapacitated her for the moment.

I realize my own leg is on fire. I reach down tentatively. My right calf is wet from the surf and coated in sand. But then, in the thickest part of the muscle...

I can feel a distinct hole, pouring liquid. Blood. Bullet hole. Shotgun pellet hole? I've been shot.

My vision grays. I stay on all fours.

Just as a second form materializes on the beach beside Keahi.

Please let it be Vaughn, please let it be Vaughn, please let it be...

Leilani walks into view, handgun poised before her as she closes the distance between us.

"WHAT HAPPENED?" LEILANI asks her sister, eyes scouring the space around them. I hunker down, willing myself to disappear beneath the leafy canopy of the Pisonia tree.

"Twisted...my fucking ankle. Damn beach."

"The crabs dig dens underground. The sand is riddled with holes."

"Well then, fucking damn crabs. Who was that, back there, with the shotgun?"

"Vaughn. One of Mac's friends and project manager. It's okay. I shot him."

Pressed against the ground, I flinch, will myself not to make a sound. Leilani is still standing there, holding the gun while Keahi remains curled on the beach, clutching her leg.

"This is a shit show," Keahi groans at last.

Leilani doesn't dispute that. "Do you think I'm broken?" she asks.

I watch Keahi still, regard her younger sister more carefully, maybe notice for the first time that Leilani isn't magically pocketing her weapon.

"I think you are amazing," Keahi replies steadily. "I think you're the best thing that ever happened to me. When I got out of the hospital, when I couldn't find you...I tore Oahu apart, pua lei. I would've done anything to get you back."

"He kept me away. In New York. The noise, the smells I missed Hawaii so much. I missed you."

"I never forgot. I never forgave. All of it, including every single day of incarceration, it was worth it because it brought me back to you."

"I didn't lie to Brent," Leilani informs her sister. "I lied to you. I told him to kill you. And I meant it."

Keahi doesn't move. Doesn't speak. I risk scooting forward a few inches for a better view. There, in a ray of moonlight: One younger sister, standing, armed. One older sister, curled against the sand, clearly injured. Both staring across the space between them, as the ocean pounds behind them.

"I know what you did to Mama." For the first time, the gun in Leilani's hand trembles. "You told me to stay, you just had to run back for one last thing. But I was scared. I didn't want to stand at the end of the driveway all alone. So I followed you back to the house. I saw you, your hands wrapped around her throat. You snapped her neck. And she just stood there and let you."

"Daddy would've killed her for letting us go. If you remember anything at all, you must realize that. Except he would've beat her within an inch of her life first. My way was less painful. She knew that, too."

"What kind of child kills her mother?" Leilani murmurs.

There's a sudden heightened tension between the two. I suck in my breath as I suddenly get it. Then from Leilani:

"You are not my sister."

"No."

"Fourteen-year age gap. As if Mama never conceived, never bore any more babies. And then magically, she had me."

"I have always loved you—" Keahi's voice, clear and steady.

"Is he my father? He and you? Making him my daddy and my granddaddy. He was that sick and twisted?"

"He's gone now, that's all that matters."

"Why didn't you kill him first? Why start with Mama?"

"Because I didn't know how!" Keahi explodes. "Because I was just a kid, too. And I did the best I could, and I got us both out of there."

"After Mama got us tickets and then you snapped her neck!"

"I got us out of there—"

"Straight into Mac's arms."

"He was never as bad as Daddy—"

"Exactly. So you kept beating him until he was. You are broken. Without violence, you don't know how to live."

Keahi doesn't respond.

"And I'm the answer to a terrible riddle," Leilani continues. "What do you get when two monsters mate? You get me. Empty, emotionless, broken me."

"I remember your laugh," Keahi speaks up fiercely. "I remember your giggle. The way you lit up when you saw me or Mama.

The way you'd throw your arms around my neck and hold on tight—"

"I don't remember any of that."

"You were the best of us—"

"I killed Orange Kitty. In New York. One day, I snapped her neck, just to see if I would cry. I didn't."

"You are strong. Good for you; in this world, women need to be tough. Look at what you just accomplished. Mac, his entire fortune, operation, business associates. All yours now. Fuck him. You win it all. As it should be."

"Do you think Brent is dead?"

A slight hesitation. "Probably."

"He was our escape plan."

"We'll make another one."

"How? We can't fly a plane."

"Then we'll wait for official rescue. You can tell them I did everything. I'll take the fall. For you, Leilani, I'll do anything. I will give you anything. All of these years... You were the one I saw. You were the one I missed. Pua lei... Roaming the streets of Honolulu, forced back to the shadows of our old home, locked up forever in a prison cell, I saw you everywhere. I will always see you everywhere."

Leilani brushes her hand against her cheek. Wiping away tears? I can't tell in the moonlight, and by her own admission, she doesn't cry, but I wonder. This exchange isn't anything I'd expected. I'd accused Leilani of doing all this out of teenage rebellion or financial ambition. But maybe this is their version of family therapy?

"There are a lot more people on this atoll we still have to kill."

"Let me bandage my ankle, and we'll get to it."

"I don't mind the violence. I honestly don't feel much one way or the other. But I'm tired, Keahi. Do you know what it's like, to look ahead and feel nothing but exhaustion?"

"Then we'll rest first. Even if Frankie has gotten away with one of the sat phones…It will be days before rescue arrives. Plenty of time. I'll take care of the rest."

"They still have a rifle. And now they're dispersed and on high alert. These aren't stupid rednecks you've lured home with the promise of sex. They're ready for you."

"I have some tricks up my sleeve."

"I'm tired."

"You are young. You will recover."

"And then? What happens next? They die. Maybe. Rescue comes and believes my story. Maybe. I return to Mac's old life and take over everything. Maybe. And then? I have hated you for so long. You and Daddy and Mac. The three of you did everything, took everything, were everything. Like the center of my entire world, except none of you cared about me. It was always about you. And I knew it. I couldn't change it. Not before. I could only hate and resent and plot and scheme…Rage is my only genuine emotion. Payback my one true mission. I'm not sure I know how to live without it. I'm not sure who I am without it."

"You have plenty of time to learn. You're still so young—"

"Then why do I feel so old?"

"Pua lei…"

"Do you remember when we were in Texas?" Leilani asks abruptly. "We shared a room. I can still picture it. Tiny and dark and so cramped the two single beds nearly touched one another."

"Yes."

"I hated the dark. But you would take my hand. While I was falling asleep. Every time I jerked awake. Your fingers, curling around mine. That first year in New York, I reached for you so many times." Leilani is moving, lowering herself to the ground. As I watch, she spreads herself out beside her sister's form. She extends her arm. Slowly, Keahi unfurls beside her. She also reaches out, her fingers finding her sister's, her daughter's.

And they lie there, just like that.

"Did you fear death awaiting your execution?"

"No."

"And now?"

"I'm with you, pua lei. I fear nothing." Keahi turns her head to the side, meets her daughter's eyes. "I still see you everywhere."

"I don't."

Leilani raises the pistol. She fires the first bullet into her mother's skull. The second into her own.

She slumps back to the sand, the sound of gunshots echoing away.

A moment later, the next wave rolls ashore, and the birds return to wheeling overhead.

CHAPTER 40

STUMBLE MY WAY BACK TO MacManus's lodge, sat phone in hand, babbling away to some poor person unfortunate enough to answer my 911 call.

"We need immediate medical assistance. Lots of people wounded. Gunshot victims, concussion victims, torture victims—"

"Ma'am—"

"He might be dead now. Not sure. Last time I saw him, he looked like a victim in a slasher film. The blood loss alone..."

"Ma'am, it's a crime to make a prank call to emergency services—"

"The Beautiful Butcher. She escaped from Texas a few days ago. She made it here, to Pomaikai. Had help. But she's dead now. Her sister shot her. Well, her daughter. Okay, a family member killed her. But not before plenty of carnage."

"I'm sorry, ma'am, but what is the nature of your emergency?"

"Escaped serial killer. Lots of casualties. In the middle of the Pacific."

"*Where* are you?"

"Pomaikai. Remote atoll. Near the equator. Send choppers, medical evac. Coast Guard, Navy, the Marines. Send everyone. We need help."

I finally crest the incline to the site of MacManus's lodge. All lights are still on, a fierce glow that's nearly blinding after so much time moving through the dark.

There, on the other side of the porch stairs, a lone shape collapsed on the ground.

"Send help!" I bark one last time into the sat phone. Then I drop it to the ground and lurch my way toward Vaughn.

HE MOANS THE first time I touch him. I take that as a positive sign. His side is wet with blood. It's too dark for me to tell how bad, but I'm already pretty sure it's not good. I shake him hard enough to rouse him and, with a bit of coaxing, get his arm around my shoulder. Together, we crawl our way up the stairs, into the lodge.

I get Vaughn collapsed into one of the overstuffed chairs. His T-shirt is plastered against his skin with blood.

He groans again. "Tried...to go...after you. Couldn't move."

"It's okay. They're dead. Leilani and Keahi both. You don't have to worry about them anymore."

I leave him long enough to check on MacManus, whose slumped form is still tied to a dining room chair.

There is so much blood, so many jagged wounds. I don't know where to touch. In the end, I drag the chair as close to the sofa as I can get. Then I saw through his bindings with kitchen shears before toppling him onto his side into the cushions.

He doesn't moan or make any sound at all. Mostly, I hear choking gasps, but those are coming from me.

Towels, first aid kits. I gather whatever I can find, piling it on the coffee table. My movements are short and jerky. My whole leg is on fire now, and my vision swims blearily. Shock, blood loss, both.

I keep moving, packing Vaughn's gunshot wound with gauze. Wrapping MacManus's bloody arms in towels. Bandaging a particularly large cut on his neck.

Then I'm swaying again, staggering toward the front door. I will myself to make it out, down the steps, and over to the UTV.

This is it. One last charge. Find the others. Summon them all to the lodge.

Tell them it's finally over.

Except, of course, it never really is.

IT DOESN'T TAKE three days for emergency medical evac. The first chopper sets down midmorning the next day, summoned by Charlie's much more succinct call to much bigger powers that be. Ronin does the honors of waving it down to the runway.

I don't know what he says. I'm running hot and cold, falling in and out of consciousness. My leg wound, infection, something. Trudy and Ann ply me with fluids while taking turns bathing my face with cold washcloths.

Captain Marilee and MacManus disappear into the first chopper. Soon there's another; then it feels like there's people in blue jumpsuits running around everywhere. I'm lifted up into a stretcher and then I'm in the sky, the sparkling ocean passing by underneath.

A brief break. Crashing waves against the hull of a ship. Then I'm up, up, up again, flying through the air.

Next time I come to, I register beeping machines, stark white corridors. Hospital sheets, hospital bed.

I close my eyes again, feeling the fever sear away my skin. But that's okay, I think. I can always grow it back again.

Voices I know.

Trudy and Ann. Tannis and Emi. A tirade in French.

"Vaughn?" I try to ask. But my lips don't move; the word is never formed.

"Rest," Ann orders me with a pat on the shoulder.

So I do.

WHEN I NEXT come to my senses, Charlie is sitting in a chair beside my bed. I stare at him for a long time, trying to figure out if this whole scene is real or if I've reached a new level of delirium.

He breaks into a huge grin and shakes his riot of salt-and-pepper curls. Certainly seems real enough.

"There you are, Sleeping Beauty. We were beginning to think you were using a teeny-weeny gunshot wound as an excuse to go on extended vacation."

I open my mouth, croak out a few sounds.

He takes the hint and fetches a plastic cup of water for me. A couple sips through the straw, and I feel better.

"Your head," I manage.

"Right as rain. Takes a lickin' as the saying goes."

"Captain . . . Marilee."

"Stable. Gonna need a bit more time before she tap dances out of here, but she's growing stronger each day."

I almost don't want to ask the next question: "Vaughn?"

"Took a bullet to his ribs. Did some damage, especially to his tattoo. Not gonna lie, that's definitely gonna need some touch-up. The rest of him is healing up nicely."

I manage a faint smile, consciously attempt to wiggle my toes, and am grateful when both feet respond.

"You're fine." Charlie pats the side of my bed. "Run-down, the doctors said, though I'm thinking that was before our little misadventure. You had a pellet wound to your calf, shouldn't have been that bad, but you spiked an infection. Apparently, one shouldn't drag open wounds along mucky beaches and through bird guano. Note for next time."

I grimace. Suck down more water.

"MacManus will live. Officially perky enough to be demanding his own plastic surgeon. But..."

"Leilani turned on him. All of this, it was her, trying to eliminate him. Apparently, before his business associates did away with them both."

"About that—he's agreed to turn federal witness. Testify against his crime boss cohorts about the money laundering in return for protective custody. He's not going back to his old life and he knows it."

"Your friend. The undercover agent whose remains we found?"

"We brought her home," Charlie supplies quietly. "Gave her the funeral she deserved and her family the closure they needed."

"Pomaikai? What will happen with the project? Aolani's design?"

"Given that the federal government has officially frozen all of MacManus's assets, nothing. Chances are he'll forfeit all profits from his illicit dealings as part of his plea bargain. At which time, the atoll will become property of the US. Maybe we can turn it into a getaway resort for overworked FBI agents. I'd volunteer to return as head engineer for that."

"Sorry I doubted you."

"Sorry I lied to you. Cost of being undercover. Now, since I'm back to being the real deal, I need to know exactly what happened with Leilani and Keahi at the end. Tell me everything."

I FIND VAUGHN'S room an hour later. It's not my first time roaming hospital corridors in a johnny, and I guess, given my life choices, it won't be my last. I'm still incredibly grateful to discover Vaughn appearing alive and semi-well, as he clicks through TV channels.

He lowers the remote immediately as I enter, then hits the off button. For a long moment, we simply look at each other, taking in all the new bumps and bruises on top of sights we know so well.

I walk closer to his bed. "Hey."

"Hey yourself."

"You're not dead."

"That's not how it feels when I first wake up in the morning." He gestures down to my bandaged limb. "How's the leg?"

"Not amputated. Does this mean you shot me?"

"Or you ran into a shotgun pellet."

"Fair enough." I grab a very uncomfortable-looking straight-backed chair and drag it closer. "So. I'm sorry your turtle tattoo didn't make it."

"Looks like a horror movie. But as casualties go, I'll take it."

"I hear Marilee is recovering."

"I assume from Charlie the fed who is fully vertical and making the rounds?"

"Yes. Plus Trudy and Ann have been by every day. Those two know everything."

"I hear a rumor they're going to open a restaurant with Chef Kiki."

"No!"

"Stranger things have happened," Vaughn observes. "I mean, once you've survived a serial killer, most anything seems possible."

"True." I fold my arms on the edge of his bed, rest my head on top of them. "Where do you go from here?"

"Most likely, my parents' place in Washington. Figure I'll take a month or two to get my bearings, then find the next project."

"Back to work?"

"I'm not one meant to idle. You?"

"I don't idle well either."

"Already got the next case in mind?"

"I did. I should. I could."

"But..."

"I don't like to stay in one place too long," I say abruptly, my gaze on his. There's something about him. It takes me a second, then I get it. I straighten back up, reach out an arm, and rake a hand through his hair till it stands on end. It feels soft against my fingertips. I fluff the strands a few extra times, more for my own sake than his, then sit back. "Better."

"Better?"

"Now you look like you."

His gaze goes up and down my johnny-clad form. "You look different, too. Still trying to put my finger on it."

"I'm not pissing you off," I supply. "Yet."

"Ahh, that's gotta be it. So, you were saying."

"Yeah, that. I'm not a permanent address kind of gal."

"Many people aren't."

"I always thought there was something wrong with me. I mean, you look around at everyone else living everyone else's lives and it's always one job, one house, one kind of day. It feels like some kind of secret society, where I've never known the magic password to get in."

"And now?"

"I liked meeting other people from nowhere. It gives me hope, knowing there's this entire group of vagabonds circling the globe, picking up jobs here, there, and everywhere, and the more they move around, the happier they are, especially in the company of other people from nowhere."

"Ah, the secret society within the secret society. You found us!"

"Nah, more like you found me." I stare at him intently. "I'm just me. And for me, I am enough. When I try to fit in, conform, twist myself into the person other people think I should be, doing what other people think I should do, wanting the things other people think I should want..."

"I'm just me," I repeat. "And for me, I am enough."

Vaughn nods sagely, as if I'm actually making some kind of sense. I think he's beautiful.

I take another deep breath, expel it slowly. "And I am tired," I state simply. "Deeply, profoundly, I-could-use-a-minute kind of exhausted. It won't last. Someday, I'll read an article and something about it will speak to something in me, and I'll need to go. That quick. I'll leave."

Another nod.

I take his silence as encouragement, giving up on the chair, climbing onto the side of his bed. His face flushes. A monitor beeps. We both ignore it as I curl up against him, rest my head lightly on his shoulder. His arm curls around me.

"Would you like to take maybe a week or two or three," I murmur at last, "and spend them doing nothing in particular with me?"

"You could come to Washington," he begins roughly.

"I've still never seen Hawaii."

"Or my friends have a place on the Big Island," he amends hastily.

I tilt my head up. His blue eyes are dark. I like them this color. The thrill of anticipation, the lull before the storm.

I run my fingers through his unshaven beard. The column of his throat, the line of his clavicle.

The hospital has robbed him of his tang of ocean air. But he is still him. I curl deeper in, absorbing the heat of his body, the comfort of his embrace. I take another deep, steadying breath and feel the tension of my body start to dissolve. I can rest here. I can heal here.

Someday, sometime, I will leave. But until then...

"My name is Frankie," I murmur up at him. "I'm a recovering alcoholic coming from a long line of alcoholics. I grow sad when it rains, and I'm obsessed with finding missing persons, though you should know I've sworn off working for serial killers."

"Hi, Frankie. I'm Vaughn. I'm also a recovering alcoholic. I'm a project manager, I prefer working off the grid, and in my time, I've made some big mistakes that have cost other people their lives. But every now and then, I also make a pretty amazing discovery, which keeps this business of life worth living."

"Promise to miss me a little. When this is all done. Promise you'll remember me now and then."

"Frankie, there are plenty of people who will remember you now and then. I'm just happy to be one of them."

I blink away the sting in my eyes. I place my hand back on his chest, feel the steady beating of his heart. It soothes me, draws me down deeper and deeper, till the next thing I know, my eyelids are drifting shut.

I hear a voice murmuring against my temple. "Rest now, honey. I got you."

And then I'm dreaming of white sandy beaches and a man laughing behind me. I give him a teasing smile, slip my hand from his, then take off down the beach.

I know as I run that soon I'll disappear. Vanish beyond his line of sight. And maybe the dark shadows I spy here and there will catch up with me, but maybe not. I puff out my chest. I pump my arms. And with the white sand flying from my bare feet, I pick a point on the far horizon and I *go*.

AUTHOR'S NOTE AND ACKNOWLEDGMENT

After thirty years of writing deadlines, I made the bold decision in the fall of 2021 to take a one-year sabbatical from my career. I would step away from my desk and explore the world. As you can imagine, my family and friends—not to mention agent and editor—instantly started placing bets that I'd end the year with a completed manuscript.

For the record, they were wrong. I managed to go the entire year without writing (who knew?). But they were right as well, as the extraordinary adventures I experienced working my way from the penguin-dotted ice shelves of Antarctica to a crab-covered atoll near the equator, to the polar bear–populated shores of the Arctic instantly inspired about thirty new novels in my head.

So first off to my amazing readers and loyal fans, thank you for your patience as you did not get a Lisa Gardner thriller in 2023. And now get ready, because I have so many stories to share with you!

In addition to seeing so many wonders of the world, I encountered so many wonderful people along the way. My deepest appreciation to The Nature Conservancy, who made it possible for me to visit their research station at Palmyra, a stunning atoll an hour's flight from Hawaii that may or may not bear a stunning resemblance to Pomaikai. ☺ Also, my eternal awe and dedication to the dedicated Palmyra staff, who are making phenomenal strides in the field of ecological restoration, especially regarding rehabilitating coral reefs. Their sense of humor, general camaraderie, and truly creative methods of entertainment given their off-the-grid lives was inspiring. I've never met such an impressive group of men and women working for the greater good. I also left promising never to whine about losing Wi-Fi again (though I've possibly already broken that pledge).

For more information on The Nature Conservancy and their work in Palmyra, check out: https://www.nature.org/en-us/get -involved/how-to-help/places-we-protect/palmyra-atoll/.

True to all my travel adventures, I made some fabulous new friends along the way: Andrea Burgess, Katie Franklin, Susie Hackler, Terry Huffington, Jennifer Morris, and Fran Ulmer, thank you for sharing a once-in-a-lifetime experience, and not laughing at me even when I continuously swore at the humidity, and the heat, and the humidity. And kudos to all of us for holding strong when we ended up stuck in paradise an extra three days because the plane couldn't land, and that was the same plane that had the new food provisions. Good times!

Pomaikai and the camp presented in this novel were definitely inspired by Palmyra and many of the folks I met along the way, but this remains a work of fiction. I took many liberties, not the least of which includes adding an escaped serial killer. The coconut crabs are entirely real, for the record. And yes, I got to share my cabin with Wolfie the spider and flower-loving Crabby. I still miss them.

Thank you, Chad Wiggins, (former) TNC Palmyra, who oversaw our trip, and in return for his hard work, got to spend another year answering my questions about the atoll, ecological developments, Hawaiian language, and any and all else I could throw at him. Thank you so much for your patience and generosity. Of course, all mistakes are mine and mine alone.

To Rick Gmirken, archaeologist. Thank you for walking me through the ecological and cultural research necessary for approving the possible development of a remote atoll. And also, for sharing with me the rich history of the Line Islands, which were known and enjoyed by the locals long before European sailors came along to "discover" them.

To Dr. Lee Jantz, my eternal gratitude to my absolute favorite forensic anthropologist from the Body Farm at the University of Tennessee, Knoxville, who has answered so many of my questions over the years. Congratulations on your retirement—I'm totally gonna miss you.

Let me repeat again, all mistakes in this novel are mine and mine alone, given the people above are really smart, while I mostly type for a living.

To my cousin, Chad LeDoux, thank you so much for your assistance with firearms of all kinds, and some truly interesting YouTube videos. I'm sorry I couldn't include all of your excellent details—Frankie's just not that knowledgeable about guns, and neither am I. But thanks to you, I'm getting smarter all the time.

Timothy Psaledakis, you are amazing! Thank you for letting me monopolize your gym time with random and often crazily in-depth questions regarding planes, ham radios, satellite phones, and all sorts of nonsense. You never failed to have the answers.

And to my favorite trainers, Maureen Egan and Mark Russo, who spend each week teaching me the nature of evil, um, thank you. And special shout-out to Maureen, who asked exactly the right question about Noodles the cat, even if she had no idea what I was prattling about at the time. Welcome to my world, where to know me is to be subject to constant streams of nonsense.

Once more, all mistakes are mine and mine alone. (It's so good to be a fiction novelist instead of someone who's actually supposed to know something.)

Now the fun part! Welcome to Lisa Gardner's genuine enjoyment of meeting really nice people and then throwing them into the grim world of a kill-or-be-killed thriller novel. What a kind thing to do, right?

To Ann Dickerson, Trudy Marsolini, Tannis Chefurka, Marilee Jensen, Brent Jones, Emi Estrada, and Kiki Roesch, my instant new best friends from Antarctica, and then the Arctic, and now soon, Patagonia. Thank you for being as travel crazy as I am, and may you enjoy your fictional counterparts' even crazier adventures on Pomaikai.

To Clara Gehweiler, longtime fan, for sharing your beautiful homemade cards, brownie recipes, and general good cheer. Given your Hawaiian address, I couldn't very well write a novel set in your home state and not include you.

To Sherry George. Happy birthday and, boy, does your sister, Dawn Brown, love you! Guess nothing says happy fiftieth birthday quite like being a corpse in a suspense novel. Hope it lives up to the hype! And the Three Square Food Bank in Las Vegas, Nevada, also sends their gratitude for your sister's thoughtful donation to make this all happen. Your family is amazing!

To the winner of the annual Kill a Friend, Maim a Buddy Sweepstakes at LisaGardner.com: Jennifer Komarnisky. Thank you for graciously nominating the very willing Victoria Twanow to die in this novel. For the record, Victoria recruited many, many friends to aid her quest for literary immortality. Hope you both enjoy! For those who didn't succeed this time around, no worries, literary death can still be yours as the contest is back up and running for 2025. Umm, good luck?

To my extraordinary support crew of proofreaders—Glenda Davis, Diana Chadwick, Gina Lorenz, and Michael Wertz, my eternal gratitude for helping me look good. To editors past, Mark Tavani, thank you for making me a better writer. And to editors future, Lyssa Keusch, thank you for welcoming Frankie and joining the ride. My new Team Hachette! Here's to a dazzling future!

While to my agent, Meg Ruley, and the entire Jane Rotrosen Agency—my continued devotion always.

It takes a village to create a novel. And it takes you, my dear readers, to make it all worthwhile.

ABOUT THE AUTHOR

Lisa Gardner, a number one *New York Times* bestselling thriller novelist, began her career in food service, but after catching her hair on fire numerous times, she took the hint and focused on writing instead. A self-described research junkie, she has transformed her interest in police procedure and criminal minds into a streak of internationally acclaimed novels, published across thirty countries. Her novel *The Neighbor* won Best Hardcover Novel from the International Thriller Writers. She has also been honored for her work with animal rescue and at-risk children. An avid hiker, gardener, and cribbage player, Lisa lives with her family in New England.